Hating Dr Fox

LAYLA PINE

CONTENT WARNING

This is an adult romance, containing multiple, explicit intimacy scenes. It is written for 18+ audience.

This book contains scenes / references to the following, which may be distressing for some readers:

- Abortion (off page, in the past)
- Cancer
- Death of a pet

For all of us who made stupid mistakes in our teens, and still wish we could take them back.

Contents

Now: The Boy Who Broke My Heart

GEORGIE

I *might be having a quarter-life crisis.*

I wasn't supposed to be enjoying this temporary foray into reality television. This wasn't my real job.

"No, Cara and Blaine need to switch. I want Cara walking the runway with Jai tonight. Blaine can pair with Mindi," I barked into my walkie-talkie, holding out my iPad and loosening my grip on it, knowing my assistant Jordyn would catch it. They were always there, always anticipating every need. I honestly couldn't live without Jordyn.

I rolled my eyes at the delay on the other end of the walkie-talkie. The team of assistant producers I was giving direction to were lucky to have two brain cells between them.

"Did I stutter?" I asked.

"Sorry Georgie, but … why do we want to split up Cara and Blaine? We just got that footage last night of them grinding in the hot tub!"

I snorted. "You just answered your own question! Separate them! Jai has been eye-fucking Cara since episode three. A love triangle will spice things up a bit."

I tossed the walkie-talkie to Jordyn, who caught it with their usual lightning reflexes. "What's on the agenda for tomorrow?" I asked. Jordyn didn't need another prompt—they were already talking a mile a minute.

"We're in head office all day tomorrow, G. Meetings with the board about expansion into the US market. Then we have a Zoom with manufacturing—they've shortlisted three new factories. All going well I'll book us flights to China for next week so you can tour them and make a call. And—"

The crackle of the walkie-talkie interrupted. "Georgie, they need you in makeup. Ilya's spitting the dummy again."

"Oh, for fuck's sake," I muttered, biting the inside of my cheek to stop myself from grinning. I was not a smiler. I hadn't gotten where I was in my career by smiling.

I really shouldn't find running a reality TV show enjoyable. I had what I'd always wanted. I had an MBA, I'd worked my way up the corporate ladder for Dudz, which under my time as head of Marketing had grown from a niche underwear range to Australia's number-one underwear, activewear and loungewear brand. I'd been promoted to General Manager only three months ago, and I wasn't even thirty yet. I hadn't fully taken over the reins from the previous GM because I'd pitched an idea for a reality slash fashion show, a collaboration between Reelflix and Dudz, before I'd been offered the promotion.

Reelflix had loved my idea so much they'd wanted to film it immediately, on the proviso that I was on-set for the majority of the filming. They wanted to ensure my vision came to life. It was a caveat I'd jumped at, because Dudz was my baby. And there was no way I was letting some crazy TV types do damage to my brand.

So that was how I'd come to be splitting my time between Sydney and the Gold Coast. *Dudz Bikini Cove* was like the best parts of *Project Runway* and *Australia's Next Top Model* rolled into one, with a splash of *Love Island,* to satisfy the voyeurs in the audience. Budding designers vied weekly to create pieces fit for a tropical holiday while models strutted it out to become the next faces of this new arm of the Dudz brand. The models lived together in a Gold Coast mansion, where in their 'down-time' (spoiler alert, there was no down-time, the cameras were rolling 24/7) they partied and screwed their way through the season.

We were one week away from the season finale. Three designers remained. Tonight, one would go home, as would two of the six models remaining. Next week, Dudz would have a new swimwear and resort-wear designer and two new brand ambassadors.

The uptick in sales across our entire range since the show began airing ten weeks ago had been astronomical. I should have been delighted about that. But my dirty little secret, the thing that I hadn't even told Jordyn, was that somewhere in the last ten weeks, the show had become my baby, too. She was a bitchy, angsty, tantrum-throwing baby. And I'd thrived on every second of the drama.

Honestly, the thought of flying back to Sydney, to the sterile offices of Dudz, and the never-ending meetings and red-eye flights and Excel spreadsheets and Zoom calls didn't give me the tingles the way it used to.

I sighed, as if the latest *Bikini Cove* drama was just a massive hassle, rather than the thing I'd secretly come to crave. I turned to my assistant. "Come on Jord. This whole show would fall apart if it weren't for us."

***

I'd been on autopilot all day. Red-eye flights did that to me every time, though you'd think I would have gotten used to them over the years. Luckily, I could do business in my sleep, and Jord was amazing at taking detailed minutes of all my meetings. One night at home, and back to the Gold Coast in the morning, ready for the final week of *Bikini Cove*. I ruthlessly stifled the disappointment I felt at that knowledge.

I unlocked my apartment door and bustled inside, flicking on lights as I headed for the laundry. I'd have time to put a load on before my virtual spin class started. Then I guessed I should probably let James know I was back in Sydney for one night only. Nothing like leaving it until the last minute.

Doing a load of washing was more enticing than spending the night with my boyfriend at this point. The time I'd been splitting between Sydney and Queensland had brought the issues in our relationship to a head.

He enjoyed sex. I didn't. Well, I didn't with him. Our sex life had gone from mediocre to downright awful in the time leading up to my diagnosis, and in the months since I'd been recovered enough from surgery to resume 'normal sexual activity', things hadn't improved. And then I'd left to spend most of my time in Queensland. James expected sex when I was in Sydney. I felt like I had to put out because, for the past ten weeks, I'd been virtually AWOL.

Talking to him about how crucial foreplay was to a woman's enjoyment of sex seemed like a complete waste of my time at this stage. We'd been together for two years now, and even before the surgery, he'd never bothered with it except to make sure I was lubricated enough to take him. And after my operation, when I was so in my head about the act, he just did his thing like nothing had changed. Which, I supposed, it hadn't. For him.

Separating whites from colours, I checked my watch. My class was about to start. I'd signed up for the virtual classes when I'd taken the Reelflix job. Spin was a non-negotiable for me, and I loved the instructor at my gym, so being able to log in and join from wherever I was worked perfectly for me.

I stripped out of my work clothes, tossing them into the machine. Wearing nothing but my Dudz g-string, I headed to my bedroom. I donned a pair of leggings, and a sports crop to cover my barely-more-than-a-bee-sting breasts, grabbing my trainers from my luggage. I clicked on the flatscreen in the corner and logged into the class, tying my long, dead-straight blonde hair up into a high ponytail before hopping onto my spin-bike.

Dillon waved at me through the screen. "Hey, babes! No beach views tonight?"

I grimaced. "Back in Sydney, just for tonight. I promise you'll still get the Surfer's Paradise views for our classes for another week, before you're back to my boring bedroom wall permanently."

"Well, with your pretty face to look at, the background doesn't matter so much." Dill was a total flirt, and he had the lean, cut body of an athlete—just the way I liked them. In my weaker moments, I sometimes wished I had a penis, just so he'd be into me.

I hopped onto my bike and began a slow warm-up pedal while we waited for others to join the class, chatting about nothing important with Dill and occasionally waving a greeting as more classmates came online.

My phone rang. With an apologetic smile, I muted myself and grabbed it. Kenneth's name flashed on the screen. I hopped off the bike, turning off my camera to take the call. Kenneth was the CEO of Reelflix. I needed to be on for this call.

"Evening, Kenneth," I said, thanking my stars that he hadn't called five minutes later when I'd already be puffed and sweaty from the class. "I hope everything's okay with *Bikini Cove?*"

"Everything is perfect with *Bikini Cove!* It's been one of our highest-rating shows to date. Which is why I'm calling you."

I paced my bedroom. "I know you're not begging me to reconsider on the second season, are you?" I warned. I'd been clear from the start—*Bikini Cove* was a one-and-done. Jumping the shark was, in my opinion, very real in reality TV. I'd watched so many shows do it to the point of being cringeworthy, and I wasn't prepared to risk Dudz being dragged down with subsequent *Bikini Cove* seasons that would never compare to the debut one.

"We've achieved our goal with one season," I reminded him firmly. "I'm not open to negotiations on this point."

"Oh, we heard you loud and clear, Georgie. I'm not stupid enough to push my luck with a woman like you in that respect. But I do have another proposal for you. I'd love to offer you a full-time showrunner position in our reality and documentary division."

I stopped my pacing to massage my forehead. "You … what?" I must not have heard him correctly.

"It's based in Sydney, so you wouldn't have to commute interstate. I'm prepared to make the package very worth your while."

I cleared my throat. "I'm taking on the GM position at Dudz when filming wraps on *Bikini Cove.*" I wished my stomach would stop fluttering. I couldn't abandon Dudz just like that … could I?

"Whatever they're paying you, I'll double it," Kenneth said. I sat down on the edge of my bed. "What you've done with *Bikini Cove* has been phenomenal. You're a born showrunner. You know how to manufacture drama so that it's still unscripted and realistic. You're a talent I can't let walk away from Reelflix."

My heart was pounding as fast as if he'd caught me halfway through my spin class. I wondered vaguely how many kilojoules I was burning just from my emotional state.

"I'd need to think about it."

Kenneth chuckled. "I'd expect nothing less from you. Email me tonight with what the GM position at Dudz is worth to you, and I'll put together a formal offer. That might help you to get your thoughts in order."

"Alright," I conceded. "I'll send it through to you before midnight." I hung up from the call, head spinning.

I couldn't take that position. I just couldn't. I had everything I'd ever wanted from life. I had a high-powered career with a business that continued to grow and expand, thanks to me. I had a perfect apartment right in the heart of the city. I had a good-looking boyfriend who didn't ask for much from me except to stick his medi-ocre member into me on a routine basis, and who encouraged my laser-focus on my career because he was the same with his.

But the thought of walking away when *Bikini Cove* wrapped, of going back to boardrooms and negotiations and never-ending busi-ness trips to spend yet more time in foreign boardrooms, negotiating via a translator …

And double the money? That would mean I could help Mim more …

What would James think about it though? He'd been derisive, verging on disgusted, when I'd told him about my idea for *Bikini Cove*. If I left a legitimate business in the lurch to head off and make more of what he deemed 'braindead television', how would he feel?

Did his opinion even matter?

I realised the class had started and my camera was still off, my sound muted. I climbed onto the bike and was about to join the class once more when my phone rang again.

James.

For a second, I contemplated letting him go to voicemail, calling back once the class was over, but he knew my schedule well enough that he would know that was what I'd done, and I'd never hear the end of it.

With a sigh, I answered.

"Hello?"

"I know you're home tonight, Gina," he accused. God, I hated it when he called me Gina. He insisted that it sounded more mature and professional than Georgie. We'd had the argument multiple times. Eventually I'd given up on trying to change him. Anyone else who called me Gina felt my wrath until they backed down, so I supposed my capitulation meant that I loved him.

It just didn't feel the way I'd expected love to feel … the way I'd thought it felt back when …

"I can't believe you didn't let me know earlier that you were home tonight!"

"It's been a hectic day, and a late night on-set last night," I explained, feeling weariness stealing into my bones as I made my excuses. "It honestly just slipped my mind."

An angry grunt came through the line. "Good to know I'm so fucking important to you that an opportunity to spend time with me just 'slipped your mind'."

"Did you want to come over tonight?" I asked, hoping that would nip his building rant in the bud. I glanced up at the TV screen. Spin was well and truly pumping. Everyone was out of their seats, sweating and gritting teeth and wiping at their foreheads. I just wanted to get James off the phone and join in.

"I don't!" he snapped. I rolled my eyes. I couldn't work out what this man wanted. I waited for him to continue. After a long pause, he sighed.

"I don't want to do this anymore, Gina," he muttered. Up until that point I had been pedalling at my usual warm-up pace on the bike, ready to jump back into the class as soon as I ended the call, but his words had my legs slowing, then stopping.

"Do what?" I asked, but I knew exactly what he was going to say. The weirdest part was, I didn't feel … anything.

"I can't keep pretending that I enjoy being with you," he continued. "Things weren't great before you left for Queensland, but I think that time and space has given me some perspective."

"Oh?" I asked, climbing off the bike. I was shocked at how even my voice was.

"Yes … um …" James stammered. Perhaps he'd been expecting me to start blubbering. "Well, I can't say sex has been anything but tedious with you for a long time."

That was the first thing he said that had my heartrate climbing, my skin heating. "Sex? Is that what this is about?"

"Sex is pretty fucking important in a strong relationship, Gina."

I bit the inside of my cheek to stop myself from screaming at him, taking a deep breath before I responded.

"Let me tell you a few home truths about our 'sex life', James," I began, my tone cold, my voice eerily monotonous. "Sex with you has never been enjoyable for me—"

"That's because—"

"No, you will listen, and you will not interrupt me. Never before you have I struggled to enjoy sex. Never. Every other partner I've had—with the exception of the inexperienced teenager who took my virginity—has been able to make me come. But you and your pathetic excuse for an erection have only managed to get me there once or twice. It might be your childish aversion to foreplay …" I paused to see if he would try to interrupt me to argue on that point. When all I heard was his heavy breathing, I continued.

"It might be the fact that you just aren't big enough to hit the right spot. Or that it usually takes you less than two minutes of thrusting to finish. But for you to say that sex has been unenjoyable for you for a long time, knowing that in the past year, I've battled cancer, shows how absolutely fucking selfish you are!"

I was really on a roll now, my indignant fury overwhelming my usual measured calm. "For months before my diagnosis, sex was uncomfortable for me. And then there were the weeks following the surgery where sex was off the table while I healed. And what did I do during that time? Gave you blow jobs every second day, like fucking clockwork!

"You say our sex has been unenjoyable for a long time. I say it's never been enjoyable. And, aside from the cancer, the only reason our sex has been crap is because *you* are terrible at it!"

For a long moment there was silence. Then his deep inhale of breath. "Well. I suppose this is a mutual break-up then?"

A chuckle burst out of my throat. "I think this is the only thing we've done together in a long time where we've both been on the same page."

"Yes … well … I hope you have a nice life, Gina," he said, and the thickness in his voice told me that he was the one who was struggling not to cry. Meanwhile all I felt was … relief. "I'll organize for a courier to return any of your belongings that remain at my place. If you could do the same, that would be most appreciated."

And there was the lawyer in him.

"Consider it done," I said pleasantly. "Goodbye James."

I hung up the phone, tossing it onto the bed. I glanced up. Spin was already twenty minutes into a forty-five-minute class, and I was nowhere near warm enough to join in now. I switched off the TV, headed to the kitchen and poured myself a very large glass of wine.

While I sipped, I stared at my phone. Was I in shock that my boyfriend of almost two years and I had just called it quits? I couldn't muster up any big feelings about it at all.

I took a deep swig of my wine and dialled Jordyn.

"What up, G?" Jordyn greeted me, cracking up at their ridiculous joke.

"So, James and I just broke up."

Jordyn gasped. "Really? Oh, no! I thought you two were, like, endgame!"

I almost spat my wine across the stone counter. "Don't be sarcastic. Although, sarcasm is better than an 'I told you so' lecture. But you'd know better than to give your boss one of those, wouldn't you?"

"Of course," they replied, their voice deceptively compliant.

Jordyn and I had an odd relationship. I was their boss, but they were my best friend, and for some reason, it worked.

"Anyway, we're already over the James thing," I continued. "But I do need to ask you a very important question."

"Which would be …?" Jordyn prompted, sounding intrigued. They were about to get the shock of their life.

"If I resign from Dudz, and take on a new role elsewhere, you'll come with me, won't you?" I tried not to couch it as a question, more as a polite order. There was no way in the world I was going anywhere without Jord. We were a package deal.

"Fuck right off, Georgie! We're going to work for Reelflix, aren't we?" Jordyn screeched. I winced, moving the phone away from my ear and taking another sip of wine.

"What makes you say that?" I deadpanned.

"Uh, just the way you actually look like life is worth living whenever you're on set."

I couldn't argue with that. In fact, I was speechless that they'd figured out my second-most closely held secret.

Masking my shock, I instructed Jordyn to put together an email to send to Kenneth, outlining my requirements, should I take on the new position, including a hefty salary for both me and Jord, and final sign-off on any show I would be producing.

"I know you love Dudz, G," Jord said quietly as they sent my demands to Kenneth from my email account. "But you should be excited about this new opportunity. New job, free of that dickhead James—this might be just the change you need to find your mojo again!"

"Thank you, Jordyn," I said, mock sternness in my tone. "I'll keep you posted about our new venture."

I hung up, pouring myself another glass of wine.

Less than an hour—and two more glasses of wine—later, Kenneth's reply came back. It was a yes to everything I'd asked for, plus a hefty bonus structure based on episode view stats. He'd even attached employment contracts for Jordyn and me, with a signing bonus if I got it back to him within twenty-four hours.

Feeling warm from the wine, I flipped open my laptop, pulled up the contract file, and without even thinking about it a second longer, I digitally signed and sent it right back to him. I also sent Jordyn a text telling them to get theirs signed ASAP.

And then, as the reality of what I'd just done hit me, my buzz started to fade, just slightly. I had to resign from Dudz. My whole career had been there. Eight years since finishing Uni, all working towards one goal.

But I'd achieved that goal. I mightn't have worked as the GM, but I'd been awarded the position. There was no challenge left for me there. Reelflix, and whatever shows they threw my way, would be a chaotic, crazy rollercoaster. And I was itching for it.

I showered, changed into cotton boy shorts and a crop top, and sat on my bed, brushing out my hair, staring at a blank Word document, as I tried to work out what my resignation letter should read like. My email pinged.

From: Kenneth Grace

To: Georgina Menzies

Subject: Your First Challenge

Georgie

I know you're a night owl like me, and you're probably still up.

Received your signed contract, and Jordyn's too. We're excited to have you both joining the Reelflix Team!

Your first show will be a doco/reality hybrid. The concept for the show is still up in the air at this stage, but we've secured talent already. He's definitely going to make for binge-worthy television.

I'd like you to take a look over the attached concept that the team has pitched, and also the profile of our contracted talent. I know your imagination will take this concept from bland to banging.

I look forward to hearing your thoughts, and to working with you to make *Beach Vet* a Reelflix hit to rival *Bikini Cove*.

Regards

Kenneth

With a snort at the working title for the show—*Beach Vet*, how droll—I clicked to open the concept pitch. I almost fell asleep before I finished reading it. What sort of unimaginative trolls did they have working in the creative department at Reelflix, to come up with this nonsense?

How could I make a reality show about a vet who lived beachside in Sydney? Where was the drama in that? The most exciting thing I could imagine a vet in a rich suburb dealing with was a celebrity client with a silly little yappy dog that had eaten too much caviar. Boring.

I had to turn their concept on its head to make anything worth watching. I wondered why Kenneth was so intent on pushing forward with this show. He must've locked down someone truly amazing to be his Beach Vet.

I flicked my hair over my shoulder and clicked to open the other file—the profile of the talent.

A photo appeared on my screen.

My throat closed over so fast I could barely gasp for breath.

Dr Xander Fox, twenty-nine years old, Bondi local, vet of five years.

What the profile didn't say was that this was the man who, as an eighteen-year-old boy, had broken my heart.

Then: Hot Xander

GEORGIE, 13 YEARS OLD

Dom's house was so much more fun than mine, so I always hung out there. Last year, 'always' had been every day after school and at least one day on weekends.

This year, Dom's parents had stupidly decided that he needed a private school education, so instead of attending Barrenjoey High School with me and all the other kids we went to primary school with, they'd kitted him out in the wankiest school uniform I'd ever seen and shipped him into the city to King Henry's College, where he boarded during the week so that he could make the most of their extra-curricular music program.

Starting high school without my best friend had been rough. We'd been such an inseparable pair all through primary school; we'd never tried to make friends with anyone else. So now, all the girls thought I was a tomboy, and all the boys thought I was just plain weird because I hung out with the guy with the funny accent who had always gotten solos in the primary school choir. Year seven had been pretty lonely, all in all. But at least Dom and I still got to hang out together on weekends.

"How are you, gorgeous girl?" Elena, Dom's mum, greeted me at the door in her melodic French accent. Dom had been born in

France, but his family moved to Australia when he was four. With all the time I spent at his house, by thirteen I was pretty much fluent in French.

"Tired. High school homework is hell, Elena," I complained, stepping into the house. "Is Dom upstairs in his room?"

Elena gave me an odd look, gesturing towards the back door. "He's out back. He's got a friend from school staying over tonight."

My stomach dropped. A friend? *I* was Dom's friend! His best friend! *I* was the one who got to have sleepovers, and pitch a tent out in his backyard, and terrify him with horror stories by torchlight.

Elena must have noticed how shaken I was by this news. She patted me on the arm kindly. "He'll be delighted to see you. All he did last night was hound me about whether you could join in the sleepover. But we … Louis and I … we thought that maybe two teenage boys might have been a bit much for you."

I snorted. "I can handle two teenage boys in my sleep," I reassured her. "Especially if this new one is anything like Dom."

Elena chuckled as I headed for the back door. "I should have known better than to underestimate you."

I raced out to the backyard. The small, flat expanse of lawn was covered with rumpled canvas and tent poles. Dom was leaning against the trampoline, two poles in one hand, scrubbing the other hand through his messy black hair.

"I swear, these two are supposed to join and form the central support," he muttered, confusion all over his face. I smirked, looking around the yard to see where this new 'friend' was hiding.

There was a rustling sound in the bushes, and a boy stepped out, waving a set of instructions triumphantly. "Found them!" he crowed in a deep voice.

My jaw dropped, and butterflies rioted in my belly. He was tall, taller than Dom, who wasn't short. His dark blonde hair was cut in a messy surfer style and his hazel eyes looked like they were dancing. Pouty lips that parted in a cheeky grin, revealing a set of colourful braces.

I must've gasped because both boys turned to look at me at the same time. My cheeks burned, and I tore my eyes away from Dom's gorgeous friend, throwing Dom a 'help me' look. He always had been able to read my mind. His eyes widened, but he quickly rallied.

"Oh, hey! It's lucky you're here—Xander and I have zero clue about how to set this stupid thing up."

I swallowed back my tumultuous emotions and took a few steps onto the lawn, forcing a smile onto my face as I glanced around at the mess they'd made.

"You gonna introduce me to Blondie?" Dom's friend Xander asked, flashing dimples as his grin widened. My breath caught in my throat, but something about his cocky demeanor triggered my inner bitch and I scowled, opening my mouth to give him a piece of my mind.

"This is our Georgina," Elena said from behind me, putting a hand on my shoulder. "She's an honorary Fournier … even though she's really a Menzies."

"I don't need an adult to introduce me," I grumbled under my breath, ignoring Elena's chuckle as I stuck out my hand, hoping it wasn't as clammy as the rest of me felt. "I'm Dom's best friend. And you are?" I looked him up and down as if I didn't think much of what I saw.

I thought lots of things about what I saw.

"Xander," he said, taking my hand and shaking it. His grip was warm, his fingers long. My stomach fluttered again. "Nice to meet you, Gina."

The silence that followed was broken by Dom's sucked-in breath while I glared at Xander, wishing he wasn't so hot, because he'd just stepped way out of line.

"Mate," Dom muttered. "You're in for it now."

Xander looked confused. "What'd I—" His words were cut short when I stepped closer, poking him solidly in the chest. I couldn't help but notice it was very firm beneath my finger.

"My name isn't Gina," I grated, meeting his gaze defiantly. He might have been the hottest boy I'd ever laid eyes on, but nobody called me Gina. "If you're lucky enough to become my friend, you get to call me Georgie. Otherwise, it's *Georgina*. Got it?"

He stepped back, hands raised above his head in surrender. "Okay, jeez. Sorry … Georgina."

I nodded in satisfaction. "That's better."

Hot Xander had the hide to laugh at that. "She's mean for such a pretty girl, isn't she?" he commented to Dom, who scowled back at him. I grinned wolfishly. Dom had my back. Hot Xander might be his new friend, but I was his *best* friend.

"Do you want me to pitch this tent for you, or not?" I demanded, crossing my arms over my virtually non-existent boobs. God, I wished I'd filled out over the school year like so many of the other girls in year seven. I barely even needed to wear a bra, except that Mum insisted that what I did have jiggled enough to be rude in public.

I hadn't worn a bra to Dom's house, though. Because it was just Dom.

Except it wasn't. It was Dom and Hot Xander.

"You keep glaring at me like that, and I'll be pitching a tent soon," Hot Xander murmured, his dimples even more defined. I blushed, guessing what he was talking about.

Dom's scowl deepened. "Georgie, can you sort out this mess, please—I'll owe you forever. Xander, come over here for a second." He grabbed his new friend by the elbow and practically dragged him to the other side of the trampoline. As if that was enough distance for me not to be able to hear what he was saying.

"Don't say shit like that to Georgie, got it?" Dom hissed. I pretended I was sorting through the tent poles, but really, I was listening on bated breath to hear how Hot Xander would respond.

"Sorry, Dom. I was just joking around. She's not really that pretty—if she didn't have all that hair, I'd have thought she was a guy."

Well, that stung. I decided I didn't really want to hear any more of their conversation. I'd set up their stupid tent, and then I'd leave them to their guy time.

Dom refused to let me leave.

"Oh, come on, Georgie," he begged, rummaging through a cupboard until he found the extra sleeping bag. "Xander's not as bad as he seems."

I twisted my lips, acting disgusted. "Well, he seems pretty bad. He made dirty comments about me!" I hissed, feeling my cheeks heat. There was no way I was going to tell Dom that those comments had made butterflies take flight in my belly.

"Yeah, well, I put him in his place. He won't be doing that again," Dom growled, and I had to stifle a giggle. Hot Xander was taller than Dom. He looked closer to fifteen than thirteen and had the deep voice to match. Dom, while tall, was all gangly limbs, and his voice had only just started to show signs of breaking in the last couple of weeks. The thought that Dom could boss Hot Xander around … kind of hilarious.

But Dom was my bestie, and I was loyal, so I pressed my lips together and pushed that giggle back down where it belonged.

"Okay, I'll give him another chance," I sighed. Like that would be a hardship. Just the thought of sleeping in a tent with Hot Xander was enough to set my heart racing.

I called Mum and told her I was staying over at Dom's. I very deliberately didn't mention Hot Xander. She was already suspicious enough of the amount of time Dom and I spent together, but she tolerated it because she'd known him since preschool. If she knew another boy was here too, guaranteed she'd think I was making out with him.

If anyone had asked me earlier in the day if I thought about making out with boys, I'd have gagged. But that was before I'd laid eyes on Hot Xander.

Louis set up the projector and the inflatable screen, and Elena brought us bowls of popcorn. Lounging on our sleeping bags, because it was far too hot to get into them, we watched a movie called *Black Sheep*. It was supposed to be a horror about a farmer who had been doing weird experiments on his sheep, and they'd turned fully evil and possessed, but I just couldn't stop laughing at how ridiculous it all was.

Dom, as usual, was horrified, shuffling closer to me every time something particularly gory happened. Hot Xander chowed down popcorn like it was going out of fashion. I wondered if he was doing it out of nerves … but he didn't seem to be paying a whole lot of attention to the movie. I felt the heat of his gaze on the side of my face more times than I could count. I tried to ignore it, but it made me squirm.

I might have been laughing at the absurdity of it all. He didn't think I was pretty—said I looked like a long-haired boy—but he was staring at me a hell of a lot. Maybe he liked long-haired boys?

"I'm not going to be able to sleep after that!" Dom muttered as we dragged our sleeping bags back inside the tent. I managed to ensure that mine was sandwiched between the boys. If I was the third wheel here, no way was I gonna let those boys have a chance to be whispering to each other about God knew what without including me!

In the end, I didn't need to worry about them trying to exclude me. Dom was all talk—he crashed out five minutes after we all scrambled into our sleeping bags, snoring like a minute later. The silence between each of his rumbling snores seemed to stretch, and I wondered whether Hot Xander had fallen asleep too.

"So …" Hot Xander whispered on my left. My breath hitched in my lungs, and I turned my head so I could face him, thankful for the dark. I could only make out the barest outline of his features, which meant he couldn't see whatever crazy expression I was wearing either.

"So …?" I repeated.

"Does Dom always snore this loud?"

Now: Tweaks to Beach Vet

GEORGIE

Filming had wrapped on *Bikini Cove*, and thankfully Ilya had been eliminated before the final. I would have felt so guilty foisting that diva onto my soon-to-be-ex-employer as the face of Dudz Femme.

My resignation from Dudz had come as a huge, and quite unwelcome, shock to the outgoing General Manager, who now had to stay in the role until they could hire a replacement.

"Honestly, Georgie, I have a yacht moored in the Greek Isles that I would like to enjoy before I die!" he'd berated me over the phone when I'd emailed my letter of resignation to him. "Is there anything I can offer you to reconsider?"

But I was unmoved. Even the knowledge that I'd be working with Dr Xander Fox on my first show didn't mar the thrill I felt at the new challenge.

Four weeks later, I left my farewell dinner with my old colleagues, most of whom were sadder to see Jordyn leave than me. It didn't bother me all that much; you didn't get to the top in business as a woman by being nice to people. I headed home, where I opened a bottle of wine and pulled up the *Beach Vet* pitch, and Dr Fox's profile, mulling over them as I poured myself a glass.

I spent far too long downing glass after glass of wine and staring at the grinning photo of Dr Fox, comparing the boy I'd known to the man in the picture. His chest and shoulders were broader, his hair was darker than it had been at eighteen, styled neater now with a short back and sides. It still curled just slightly on top.

He had some scruff on his cheeks that hadn't been there when he was eighteen, but it didn't mask those dimples. The ones I remembered tracing with my thumbs like it was yesterday.

I picked up my phone and dialled Mim. I had to vent to someone about the bombshell that was Xander Fox coming back into my life, and since she was the only one who knew the whole story—or at least the parts I hadn't hidden deep inside myself— Mim was it.

"I don't know if I can do this," I mumbled once I'd filled her in on everything.

Mim scoffed. "Georgina Menzies, I've never heard the words 'I can't' leave your mouth once in the past, and I'm not accepting them from you today," she said in her irascible tone. "You're a consummate professional, just do your job, and don't worry about that silly boy."

"That's the whole problem, Mim," I whined. "He's not a boy anymore. He's all man." A man I hated. A gorgeous, insanely well-built man I hated. A dimpled, grinning man with dancing hazel eyes I remembered like they were my own … who I hated.

"Inside every man is a silly boy who never left," Mim said. "Don't let the packaging fool you. Now, what's this show going to be about, anyway? Some wanky city vet giving pedicures to Cavoodles?"

I slurped more wine. "You've just hit on my other problem. The creative team quite frankly came up with a total stinker. From what I can gather, their idea was to film minimally in-clinic, and then spend most of the time taking slow motion shots of him swimming with his dog and walking out of the surf dripping with water and virtually naked." While the thought had my traitorous mouth salivating, the business-savvy part of my brain rebelled, and the slightly drunken cogs in my head spun in overtime.

"Hey, Mim, has Franklin Peters retired yet?" I asked, the barest bones of an idea coming to mind. An idea that had a slow, wicked grin tugging at the corners of my mouth. The Xander I knew would have absolutely hated me for what I was concocting.

"Retired? Good Lord, Georgie, he died last year! Heart attack while driving. Ran off the road into a ditch."

I choked on my wine. "Oh, God! That's awful! How's his wife doing?"

Mim snorted down the line. "Liz's coping mechanism has been to immerse herself in the dogs. She's raised two litters, and she's been entering Empress and Kingston in every dog show within a day's drive of here."

I grunted out a laugh. "That's on brand." Liz would give Dr Fox a run for his money. And the television we could make out of it would be delicious!

"Has anyone taken over his practice?" I asked, trying to sound innocent, but Mim saw right through it.

"I know where your mind is headed, my girl. No, we're currently having to rely on Dr Alex, who comes out once a fortnight from Millstone. You're an evil genius, Georgina Menzies. And I can't say that this old bat wouldn't be delighted to have you a bit closer, even if it's just for a couple of months."

I sighed. "I know I don't visit often enough. It's just …"

"You don't need to make bloody excuses, Georgie. It's a full day's drive, and you're a busy woman. But I miss you. The sheep miss you."

"The sheep?" I asked, wiping at a stray tear. "Really?"

"Alright, just Jumbo. He pines."

"Do you let him sleep in the laundry?" I asked.

"Yes, miss. And if whatever Machiavellian plot you're brewing in that clever brain of yours comes to fruition, and we see you soon, he will not be moving into your bedroom again. He's too smelly for that nowadays!"

"I'll call you again soon, Mim," I said with a laugh, ending the call and immediately opening my laptop to type up my pitch for a 'tweaked' version of *Beach Vet*.

Kenneth, who had clearly been iffy on the premise his creative team had pitched, but who was utterly enamoured with Dr Fox, called me first thing the next morning.

"Georgie, my girl, you're worth every cent of your crazy salary," he crowed over the phone. "I'll have to double check Xander's contract, but I'm almost certain that we included a clause allowing us to move him anywhere within New South Wales for the purposes of the show. It'll be an interesting conversation to have with him, though. I'm sure he's under the assumption that we'll be filming solely in Sydney."

"Well, if so, that's his problem for not reading his contract thoroughly," I replied. Secretly, though, there was a little tiny spark of delight at the thought of throwing Xander right in the deep end.

***

"Nothing looks right!" I snarled, tearing off the deep blue camisole and hurling it onto the bed. Jord watched me thoughtfully, their dark eyes assessing.

"You're overthinking this, G. To an insane degree."

I sighed. "I need to make the right impression," I argued, storming into my wardrobe and dragging off the cream cigarette pants I'd thought would be essential to the 'right impression' outfit last night.

Heart hammering for reasons I wasn't prepared to analyse, I rummaged through my racks of business attire, dragging out my failsafe 'Badass-Bitch-Who-Takes-Shit-From-Nobody' dress. I dragged it over my head, knocking my high pony loose in the process, and smoothed it down my body. Taking a deep breath, I returned to the bedroom.

"Well?" I demanded, placing my shaking hands on my hips and giving Jord a 'don't fuck with me' glare. They flinched dramatically.

"Well, you know that you look like a dominatrix in that dress, so I guess that gives off just the right vibe," they said. I turned to my mirror. The dress was black and sleeveless, sitting just above my knees with a moderate neckline. But it clung to every single one of my modest curves almost indecently. Paired with some black pumps and my retro glasses, dressing in this outfit was like donning armour. The tension in my body eased just a fraction.

I could do this. I could come face to face with Xander Fox today and not lose my cool.

Jord stood up and stretched. They were wearing their own signature look—the skinniest black jeans possible, a high-necked black blouse with a white lace collar. Their bright blue hair was styled in a fauxhawk, the shaved sides on display, and their titanium earlobe spacers drew all the attention. With their heavy eyeliner, septum piercing and scowling lips, they gave off such a 'stay away' vibe. But I knew better. Jord was a teddybear on the inside.

"He really did a number on you, didn't he?" Jord said. I swallowed thickly. I'd given Jord the CliffsNotes version of my history with Xander. There were things from my past with Xander that never needed to see the light of day again. Parts that not even Mim knew. Parts that swirled sickeningly in my gut if I ever let myself think about them. So I pushed them down, deep down.

"I was a silly teenager, I imagined myself in way too deep with him," I said, as if the whole thing didn't still make my lungs feel tight when I thought about it. I tugged my floppy ponytail out and dragged my hair back tightly once more. "It's ancient history now. It was a bit of a shock, that's all. I never thought I'd have to see him again, much less work with him."

"He's working *for* you—let's just frame it that way, right?" Jord reminded me. "You're the boss. And by the sounds of things, you're getting your own back on him, in your own, boss-bitch way."

My lips twisted in what was supposed to be a smile but felt more like a grimace. Oh, I was getting my own back, that was for sure.

"Well, regardless of his reaction to your changes to the show today, when he sees you wearing that, he's going to regret what he did to you in high school," Jord said.

I shrugged, as if it didn't matter to me either way. But I did smooth my dress down over my hips, hoping that when he saw me, he wished he hadn't ruined his chance to ever peel it off me.

He was running late.

"Not a great first impression this Dr Fox is making," I murmured to Kenneth as we sat around a boardroom table at the Reelflix head office. I wanted desperately to adjust my dress, which always rode up to mid-thigh when I sat down, but the table was glass, and I didn't want to draw attention to my legs by fiddling with it.

"He's still a working vet," Kenneth reminded me. "Maybe he's had an emergency he needed to deal with?"

I turned and caught Jord's eye. They didn't need me to speak to know that stress was getting to me. They hopped up, grabbing their phone.

"I'll make some calls, find out when we can expect him," they said, heading for the door, phone already to their ear.

As if on cue, a young girl scuttled through the door, looking harried when she almost collided with Jord. "Sorry, Mr Grace," she said to Kenneth in a rush. "Dr Fox called forty-five minutes ago. He said to apologise, and he asked if he could push the meeting back until midday—he had a patient with a stick lodged in its throat that he had to rush into emergency surgery."

Jord lowered their phone with an eyeroll in my direction.

"Why weren't we informed of this forty-five minutes ago?" Kenneth asked. Jord and I locked eyes again. If that was my assistant, I would've been tearing her a new one for the time I'd wasted, and Jord knew it. Because I'd torn them a new one a few times when they first started working for me.

"I'm so sorry, sir. I was in the middle of finalising the accommodation for the new show, and then Peter asked me to make him a coffee, and I just … I lost track of time."

I pressed my lips together. This was not my discussion to have.

"Well next time, a message regarding a time-sensitive meeting needs to be prioritised, Sacha. You understand, don't you?" Kenneth said, and Sacha nodded emphatically.

"I'm so sorry again for wasting everyone's time," Sacha apologised again. "I—"

"This room here?"

I would recognize that deep voice anywhere, despite the more-than-a-decade since I'd last heard it. My heart leapt into my throat, and I jumped to my feet, tugging frantically at the hem of my dress. Jord returned to their seat beside me, nudging me in the side.

"Calm your farm, G," they hissed out of the corner of their mouth.

I managed to school my expression into something I hoped said 'utter professional with no history with the talent worth mentioning to management', as I glanced towards the door just as he came into view.

The photo hadn't done him justice at all. Damn it. I struggled to breathe normally as his eyes swept the room until they fell on me.

Now: I Don't Think I Can Do This

XANDER

I lost my footing in the doorway when my frenzied scan of the room found her.

Not one of the dozen other people staring at me from around that table even registered in my brain.

Christ, twelve years had been kind to Georgie.

I'd promised myself, walking in here, that I wouldn't let myself drink her in as if I hadn't been thinking about her every single day for over a decade. This was just a job for both of us. We could be professional, film this damned show, and get on with our lives. Separately. I told myself I could ignore the heat from the years of pent-up anger over how she'd ghosted me, how she hadn't even let me explain.

I'd been a complete arse to imagine any of that would be possible.

She'd filled out a bit since high school, but she still had that lithe frame. Small, perky tits, narrow waist and a gentle hint of hips, toned legs, and that long mass of pale-blonde hair, currently pulled back tightly from her face.

I'd wrap my hand around that hair, tug her head back, grip her hip in my other hand, guide my dick between her legs …

Her lips parted as I eyed her, and it was like all the air was sucked out of the room. Then she cleared her throat, and that all too familiar spark of determination ignited in those icy eyes of hers behind the sexy librarian glasses she was wearing.

"Dr Fox, thank you for joining us," she said. Her tone left no room for doubt that she didn't think much of me. Clearly some things hadn't changed in the last twelve years. "Perhaps we could take a seat and get started."

Without waiting, she sat, and everyone else in the room watched expectantly until I took the last available seat at the table. Directly opposite her.

"We're meeting today to go over the details and filming schedule for *Beach Vet Goes Bush*," Georgie began. I didn't immediately absorb her words because I was caught up in the flood of memories hearing her voice unleashed. "As you know, we've—"

"I'm sorry," I interrupted as I realised what she'd just said, "but what the hell is *Beach Vet Goes Bush*? The previous brief said that—"

Georgie's eyes blazed as she stared me down. "That what, Dr Fox? Your contract clearly states that you belong to Reelflix for the duration of filming thirteen one-hour-long episodes of footage in a documentary slash reality format. It also states that filming can happen anywhere within New South Wales."

My fists clenched on the glass tabletop. *Don't get your back up, Xander. Just get to the bottom of this.*

"I'm aware, but all conversations I had prior to now had led me to believe that filming would happen within my own practice in Bondi," I grated. So much for not getting my back up.

"Yes, well, that was before I came on board to ensure that this show is a success."

"What exactly does 'goes bush' entail?" I asked, my nostrils flaring. Georgie's eyes widened slightly, her tongue darting out to wet her bottom lip.

"If you hadn't interrupted, I was about to explain that to you and our production team." Georgie's tight-lipped little smile had my blood boiling, but I forced what I hoped was an easy-going grin onto my face and leaned back in my chair, locking my fingers behind my neck so no one could see how tightly I was clenching them.

"Please, continue," I said. Georgie raised an eyebrow at me for a split second before she broke our stare, letting her eyes sweep the room.

"Week one will consist of filming in Dr Fox's practice in Bondi, focusing on his preparations for his outback move. Dr Fox will spend this week——"

"Did you say 'outback'?" I interrupted again. "This is nothing like the show that was originally pitched to me." My knuckles creaked behind my head. Georgie's tight-lipped smile had my muscles tensing.

"Perhaps I should spell this out for those of us who can't be bothered to read the production brief in front of them," she snarked. I glanced down at the bound booklet on the table but made no move to pick it up. I was too afraid I'd snatch the damned thing and hurl it across the table at her.

"*Beach Vet Goes Bush* is a reality-style documentary following a Sydney Eastern Suburbs veterinarian who has volunteered to spend three months as a resident vet for the small, remote township of Budgerigar in western New South Wales, a township that has been without a permanent vet for over a year now."

"Volunteered!" I snorted under my breath. Georgie glared daggers at me, which was the worst possible thing she could have done at that moment. Her indignance had always cranked my chain. An ache started in my dick, but I ignored it because I was fucking angry. She'd blindsided me with this shit, and I couldn't help but feel like it was deliberate. Like she was punishing me for something she thought I'd done to her twelve years ago. Something she'd never let me clear up or apologise for.

"Budgerigar has a population of just over fifteen hundred people, including those on farms in the surrounding area," Georgie continued as if I hadn't spoken. "The veterinarian for the town services both domestic pets and livestock."

"I've never treated——"

"Are you, or are you not, the holder of a veterinary science degree, Dr Fox?" she asked, eyes cold, lips pursed. Fury and lust warred in my blood as I returned her glare. Fuck, how could I have forgotten how much she affected me?

"I am the holder of a Doctor of Veterinary Medicine," I replied through gritted teeth. "That doesn't mean that I'm practiced in live-stock health management. In case you're unaware, there aren't many cattle farms in Bondi."

"It's mostly sheep around Budgerigar, Dr Fox." Georgie threw me a smirk, her eyes fiery. Christ, I needed to adjust myself. I was so fucking angry with her that all I could think about was bending her over this table, wrenching up her dress to her waist and leaving red handprints on that pert little arse of hers.

"Well, that makes everything just fine, doesn't it?" I snarled. I realised suddenly that the room was silent. Everyone else around the table was watching the action between Georgie and me like they were at a tennis match. With a monumental amount of effort, I blew out a breath and relaxed as much as I could manage.

Georgie's eyes scanned the room too, and I thought her mind had gone down the same path as mine because her lips relaxed just a fraction. "Jordyn, can you please take over briefing the production team? You know the schedule just as well as I do." The pierced, blue-haired person next to Georgie nodded before giving me some serious side-eye. "Dr Fox," Georgie continued, "I think you and I need to have a private conversation in my office."

She stood abruptly, tugging on the hem of her dress, covering her toned thighs. I attempted a subtle adjustment of my crotch before I stood too, following her to the door.

"Your briefing booklet, Dr Fox. You'll need it," she snipped. I huffed through my nostrils as I turned back, grabbing the booklet, ignoring the gaping stares of the production team, and headed out into the hallway. Georgie stood facing me, arms crossed over her chest, a belligerent expression on her face.

Just the way she'd looked the first day I'd met her, seventeen years ago. My chest lurched, and I cleared my throat, suddenly nervous to be alone with her.

"Follow me," she said before clicking off down the marble

hallway on her sky-high heels, her arse swaying in that tight black dress.

"I don't think I can do this," I muttered as I followed.

"Nothing that is in the brief you have in your hand is in breach of your contract," Georgie informed me matter-of-factly as she closed her office door behind me.

I whirled to face her. "Don't you dare try to pretend that blind-siding me with this drastic change in plans wasn't a calculated move on your part! How long have you been planning this?" I demanded, stalking towards her until the heat from her radiated against my body. I locked my arms to my sides, flexing my fingers to stop myself from grabbing her, turning her against the wall and grinding my hips against her backside, just to shock her the way she'd shocked me.

Shit, I couldn't think like that. My head was spinning.

The only indication that my nearness affected her was a slight widening in her eyes before she scowled, shouldering her way past me to take a seat behind her desk, gesturing for me to sit. I grunted but complied.

"Dr Fox, when I came on board with Reelflix, you'd already signed your contract. Kenneth brought me on because I've done very well for the business with another reality program, and he was concerned that the pitch for *Beach Vet* was falling a little flat. He needed some spark added to the concept. That's where the move to Budgerigar comes in."

"What do you mean, move?" I snarled, leaning forwards and pressing my fists into the black timber of her desk. Black like her goddamned heart. "I'm not moving to some bumfuck town in the middle of nowhere!"

Georgie rolled her eyes at me, folding her arms across her chest again, pushing those perky tits of hers even higher. I glanced away, biting on the inside of my cheek. Why did I still have to find her fucking irresistible?

"A temporary move. Twelve weeks in 'bumfuck middle of nowhere', as you so eloquently described it. It won't impact your practice here in Sydney. I'm sure your colleagues were made aware that your involvement in the show would mean them taking on the bulk of your workload during filming, so taking all of it on for three months won't be the end of the world. Think of it as an adventure."

"A fucking adventure!" I grated. "I have to leave everything behind for three bloody months, because you, of all people, have decided what I should do with my life? You get off on controlling me, don't you?"

Georgie's mouth fell open at my words. Finally, some indication from her that we had a history that had not ended well.

"Controlling, you, Dr Fox?" Her words sounded breathy, her crystalline eyes hooded by long lashes.

I leaned across the desk until my face was inches from hers. To her credit, she didn't back away, her jaw set determinedly.

"Are you really going to insist on calling me Dr Fox? I can still remember what your mouth tastes like. How your thighs feel when they're around my hips … what you look like when you come," I murmured.

The faintest tinge of pink spread across her face and a tiny huff of her breath fanned across my cheek. And God it felt good, knowing I could get under her skin the way she got under mine. Then she pushed back from her desk, turning towards her windows, looking out over Hyde Park.

"Filming starts in a fortnight. I'll come to your practice three days prior to plot out camera positioning and to go over the schedule for the first week of filming."

I sighed. I wanted to keep fighting with her, keep needling her until she cracked. I had no idea why I felt so strongly about it, considering I'd been determined to keep things professional. I'd broken my own rule right off the bloody bat.

"Is there really no vet in this town?" I asked. She turned back to her desk, eyeing me seriously.

"The town has been without a permanent vet since theirs died suddenly last year. There is another town about ninety minutes away that has a vet. He's been visiting one day a fortnight, but it's not enough. In an emergency, an hour-and-a-half drive is a lot."

She leaned her elbows on her desk. "This is not only going to make for very watchable television, but it's going to highlight the issue of the vet shortage in Australia, especially ones who are willing to live remotely."

I watched her face, hoping for some sign of the plotting bitch I'd assumed her to be minutes ago. But there was none. She genuinely believed in what she was doing here. Yeah, perhaps putting me out of my comfort zone was a bonus to her. But I didn't think it was her biggest motivator.

"Alright. I'll do it," I said quietly.

The tiniest smirk tipped the corners of her mouth. "You were doing it whether you wanted to or not. Now, I don't think there's much point in us returning to the planning meeting. You should take your briefing notes home, spend some time tonight reading over them. We can discuss any questions you might have over the phone or via email, Dr Fox."

"You're not going to back down on the Dr Fox thing, are you?" I asked her. She stood, strutted over to her door, and wrapped her fingers around the handle. I needed to bloody adjust myself again, imagining those fingers wrapped around me instead.

She lifted her gaze to mine, and with a tiny smile, shook her head. I ran my tongue over my teeth. Well, two could play this game. I walked up to her, but before she could open the door, I covered her hand with mine, gripping her fingers tight enough to stop her from turning the handle. I leaned in, my lips brushing the curve of her ear. Jesus, she smelled amazing, like peppermint and something herbal. No feminine perfumes for Georgina Menzies.

"I'm sure I'll have plenty of questions," I whispered, and when she shivered, I had to suppress a shudder of pleasure. "I'll be in touch … Gina."

Her sharp intake of breath was enough to have me grinning as I took a step back, pressed her hand down on the door handle, and let myself out before she had a chance to rip me a new one.

"It could have been worse," Dom said after I finished retelling in all the gory detail every moment of my afternoon with Georgie. He stared down into his scotch like the amber liquid held all the secrets of the universe.

I guffawed, carefully lifting my sleeping adolescent dog off my lap and onto the lounge beside me. I put my own glass down and flipped through the production brief booklet on the coffee table without really absorbing anything. "Oh, yeah, it could have been worse. I could have given in to my raging goddamned hormones, pushed her down on her desk and fucked her so hard she wouldn't walk straight for a week!"

I sighed, shoving the booklet away and grabbing the bottle of scotch to refill my glass. "I walked into that room, Dom, and my dick decided it was like the last twelve years hadn't happened. I took one look at her and I remembered her body under mine like it was yesterday. But in my head, I was still raging about the way she disappeared from my life. It was confusing as hell."

"Hmmm," Dom replied. I tilted the bottle in his direction, but he shook his head, covering the top of his glass with his hand as if I was planning to force more alcohol into him.

"There's something off about you, mate," I said, turning and looking at him properly. Dom was usually so put together, his hair perfectly styled, his clothes immaculate. But he looked rumpled. And there were dark circles under his eyes. "Are you sick? You look like you haven't slept a full night in weeks."

Dom scrubbed a hand over his neatly trimmed black beard, still staring down into his glass.

"I lost her too, you know," he muttered. "She was my best friend. I know you two had something … intense … going on. But she'd been mine for as long as I could remember. It was a big adjustment for me, doing life without her there. And her being back in your life, it's just dredging all the shit back up to the surface again."

I swallowed back the ridiculous, possessive growl that sat in my throat from hearing him refer to Georgie as 'his'. I wanted to snarl that unless he'd had her tongue in his mouth, unless he'd had his hips between her thighs, unless he'd thought, the night everything went to shit, that he was going to tell her he loved her, he had no right to use the word 'mine'.

"I get it," I managed to choke out instead. "It's dredging shit up for me, too. I'm just going to have to try and minimise my contact with her for the next three months. She's got an assistant she trusts. I'll use them as the go-between as much as possible."

Dom laughed darkly. "Good luck with that, mate. You never could stay away from her. And hearing everything you've just told me, I can safely say you've got a snowball's chance in hell this time around, too."

"Thanks Dom. I love our uplifting little chats." I nudged him with my shoulder to show him I was joking. Partly joking, anyway. I stood, stretching. It had been a much later night than I'd planned. I still had to work tomorrow.

"Fuck, I've got to tell Yumi and Patrick that not only do they have to shoulder the lion's share of my clients, but they have to take on all of them for three months! How the hell am I going to sell *that* to them?" I asked Dom, who was still staring off into space.

"Well … you could play up the 'shining a light on the vet shortage, an opportunity to help people to see how stressful being a vet is, how difficult it is to get vets in remote locations, etcetera. Pretend you're doing it to advocate and raise awareness."

I tugged on my bottom lip, thinking hard. "Yeah, that might work."

Dom sniffed but said nothing more. "I've got to go. I should've gone hours ago, really. Auditions for next year's intake start today." Dom was a vocal coach with the National Institute of Musical Theatre Arts. I didn't envy him. I'd rather spend an entire day expressing the anal glands of particularly vicious terriers than deal with the meltdowns of performing arts students with audition jitters.

I patted him on the back as he moved towards the door. "Do you … do you want me to say something to her? Tell her that maybe she should think about reaching out to you?" I hoped he said no, because I could picture how that conversation would go down, and it wasn't pretty.

Dom's shoulders slumped. "Don't bother. If she wanted to reach out to me, she's had twelve years of opportunity."

With that, he walked out the door, leaving me feeling sick in the guts, and not just because I'd had a few too many scotches.

I took Molly out for a wee, coming back in and plonking her on my bed before heading to the bathroom to shower. Returning in a pair of boxer briefs to a snoring Labrador, I dragged back the covers on my side of the bed, toppling in and snagging up the bloody production brief. I was supposed to read it overnight, but I'd barely glanced at it, and I was too drunk, and too tired, and too damn wired from seeing her again to be able to absorb any of it.

Tossing it to the floor, I turned off the light and fell into that deep sleep that alcohol brings.

"What the …?" I mumbled. I'd stumbled out of bed when my alarm when off, but I was standing on something … soggy. Squinting down, I realised with a wince that the soggy thing was the production brief. Chewed to shreds.

"Jesus, Molly, did you have to?" I demanded. Molly, who had been busy while I slept, lifted her head from the other side of the bed and eyed me innocently. I couldn't stay mad at her.

I'd have to email for another copy. Which meant I'd have to email Georgie. No chance of emailing her assistant—the list of contacts and emails had been on the first page of the destroyed booklet.

I grabbed my phone, navigating to the email app, managing a lopsided, hungover smirk as I began typing.

To: g.menzies@reelflix.com.au
From: dr_xander@thevetsbondi.com.au
Subject: The Dog Ate My Homework …
Hi Gina …

Then: Don't Ever, Ever Try To Date Her

XANDER, 13 YEARS OLD

"Does Dom always snore this loud?" I asked. It was the only thing that my stupid brain could come up with. Thank Christ she couldn't see me wincing in the dark.

"Oh … yeah, he's a shocker!" she whispered. "Sometimes I have to sneak inside in the middle of the night to climb into his bed, just so I can get some sleep."

Even her whisper sounded cute. Bloody hell, why did Dom have to have a cute girl for a best friend? A cute girl who could pitch a tent better than a boy scout, and who laughed at horror movies, and who had silvery hair that smelled like mint?

My stupid brain decided that would be a good time for me to vividly imagine Georgie and I both sneaking up to Dom's room and climbing into his single bed together.

God, I'd basically had a constant boner since she'd appeared in Dom's backyard that afternoon. It was worse than sitting through a double period of biology with Ms Maddox, known by King Henry's students as 'The Sexy Scientist'.

"You and Dom, you've been friends for a while?" I asked, trying to distract myself because my brain had decided I needed to think about Georgie and Ms Maddox climbing into the bed together ... naked.

My brain was filthy. And it was obviously my enemy.

"Since preschool. Poor Dom barely spoke five words of English. I don't remember much about it, but Elena and my mum love to remind us that we created our own weird little kid sign language to communicate. And that we bonded because all both of us wanted to do that first day was murder ants with magnifying glasses."

I snickered under my breath. "So, what you're telling me is I'm sleeping in a tent with two budding serial killers," I joked. She was silent, and I wondered if maybe I'd offended her. I'd never really tried to talk to girls before now. But Georgina didn't seem anything like the girls I'd known in primary school.

"Why d'you think I'm here? This way, only one of us needs to stay awake longer than you," she muttered. Her voice was dark, and for a second, my heart stuttered, because I honestly couldn't tell if she was joking, or if she was hiding a knife in her sleeping bag, just waiting for me to drift off.

Her giggle gave her away. "I wish it wasn't so dark in here—I bet the look on your face right now would be priceless!"

"You're a weird chick, Blondie," I muttered, but I was grinning. "Now I'm not going to be able to sleep tonight. You're worse than possessed sheep!"

"Wrong," she disagreed under her breath. "I'm better than possessed sheep."

I really couldn't argue with her there. I had no doubt she was better than a whole lot of things.

When I woke up, it was light enough that I could tell two things straight away. Dom was still asleep and still bloody snoring. And Georgie was nowhere to be seen. I checked my watch—five-thirty. Bloody hell.

Georgina and I had stayed up until after two just talking shit. I'd been mostly asleep towards the end. I remembered rambling and chuckling in my exhaustion a lot. I wondered where she was. I definitely remembered her drifting off next to me. I'd have to pay her out for her pathetic lack of stamina. No way she'd make it as a serial killer who murdered people in their sleep.

I got up and unzipped the tent flap, heading back towards the house to use the toilet. The bathroom was next to Dom's bedroom, and when I glanced through the door, my heart jolted in my chest. Georgina was sprawled on her back over Dom's bed, the sheet tangled around her slender legs. She was still wearing the tank top she'd had on yesterday, but the little running shorts she'd worn to bed last night were in a pile on the floor beside the bed. Which meant she was lying there in a tank top, and underpants. The undies were green, with a snake emblem and 'Slytherin' written on the front.

I snorted. I mean, yeah, she would totally get sorted into Slytherin. I could tell that from spending one night talking with her. But … come on … *Slytherin, Slither-In,* on the front of girl's undies?

My mind was so dirty.

I wrenched my eyes away from her underwear, but of course they zoomed in on her boobs. They were small, but her nipples were poking against the fabric. I couldn't stop staring at them.

She groaned in her sleep, rolling over onto her stomach. I jumped, forcing myself to stop perving on her like a total freak.

It's impossible to take a leak when you have a hard-on …

I couldn't stop looking at her at breakfast, even though I tried to pretend it wasn't obvious.

"How do I apply to get my own French chef?" I asked through a mouthful of the best-tasting pastries I'd ever eaten. Georgina grinned widely at me, dropping another of the flaky, chocolate-filled things onto my plate.

"Just stay on Dom's good side, and you too can eat like this every weekend," she whispered, shoving nearly an entire pastry into her mouth. I watched her, mouth agape, as she chewed.

"What?" she demanded through her mouthful. I closed my mouth, but I couldn't hold the question in for long.

"Where does it all go?" I asked.

Georgina's eyes narrowed. "What is that supposed to mean?"

I cleared my throat. "Uh, well, you're pretty thin, but you eat like a beast."

Dom guffawed around his own pastry, spluttering and grabbing some juice to wash it down.

Georgina glared at me the way she had yesterday, and my stomach jolted. Why did I like it so much when she looked angry with me?

"Like a beast, huh? Ever heard of metabolism? I have one, and it's fast! Plus, I do triathlon. It's kind of good for burning energy, you know?"

"Oh, well … wow, that's pretty cool," I said lamely. This girl was full of surprises.

Georgina stuffed the last of her food into her mouth as she stood up. "Speaking of which, I have a race this arvo, so I've gotta go get ready." She walked around to Dom, wrapping an arm around him and squeezing.

"You snored again last night, you know," she said. Dom gave her a disbelieving glare.

"I don't snore!" he said, looking to me for backup. I shrugged.

"Yeah, you do, mate. I almost came inside and climbed into your bed with Georgina to escape the noise."

Georgina's cheeks went bright pink, which only made my stomach clench more.

"Bye, Dom. I'll see you next weekend." Georgina turned to me. "Well, nice to meet you, Hot Xander. I guess you can call me Georgie now … if you want to."

My mouth started moving before my brain could kick in. "Hot Xander, huh?"

The pink turned to red. "Um, yeah. You were kind of lying half on top of me last night before I escaped to Dom's room. I was sweating up a storm!"

With that, she gave a stiff wave and headed for the door, calling out a goodbye to Dom's parents who were sitting in the front room drinking coffee.

For a moment, I basked in the knowledge that she was totally lying about why she called me Hot Xander. And then I grinned stupidly because she'd given me permission to call her Georgie. Which meant we were friends.

"Damn," I muttered, swiping my orange juice off the bench and slugging it down in one gulp. "I forgot to ask her if I could have a hug too."

"Don't," Dom said, a warning in his accented voice. I glanced up at him, and he looked bloody murderous.

"Don't what?" I asked as if I didn't know what he was talking about. Well, I kind of didn't.

"Don't flirt with her. Don't try to make out with her. And don't ever, ever try to date her."

I flinched. "Jesus, mate! Why're you so fired up?" An awful thought popped into my brain. "Do you have the hots for her or something?"

Dom's stare burned right inside of me, and it felt like he knew that I'd been perving on her while she slept that morning. I wanted to fidget, but that would just make me look guilty. So I just stood there, frozen like a complete moron.

"She's my best friend. You could be our best friend too. But if you ever did more with her, and things didn't work out? It would be more than awkward. So just … don't … alright?"

His slight French accent and the formal words he used made it sound like a threat. Which, I guessed, it probably was. Dom and I got along great. We shared a dorm room at school, and we would until we graduated. He was right; it would be super awkward if I tried to get with his girl best friend.

"Yeah, alright," I agreed, slumping back into my seat. He might be right, but I didn't have to like it.

And he couldn't stop me from thinking about her. Which I planned on doing a lot.

Now: Fodder For A Finger Bang

GEORGIE

"So, Liz is one hundred percent on board with everything?" I asked through my AirPods, taking a few breaths before I pretzelled my body into Yoganidrasana, thriving on the extreme stretch to my muscles.

Jordyn chuckled. "She's more than on board. I think she's planning to be nominated for an Oscar for her portrayal of the 'grumpy, horny, crazy old dog lady'. She spent most of yesterday afternoon following me around with suggestions on things she could say, and questions about how Xander might react."

I wanted to laugh, but the yoga pose was not conducive. I held it for a few more breaths before disentangling myself and moving into child's pose for some recovery.

"Okay, so you have everything else set up for Xander's big arrival?"

"Yes, G," Jord replied with the long-suffering tone of an extremely competent assistant who works for a micro-managing boss. I huffed out a chuckle.

"And the—"

"The truck will be delivered to your apartment before eight.

The cameras have already been installed. Dan's been sent to Dr Fox's clinic to get him mic'd up, the crew are already on site at the clinic so they can film his big farewell."

Jord took a deep breath. "Who've you got making the trip with him? I hope it's not Lou—she was drooling over him on the first day of filming like he was a total snack."

Well, he is a total snack, my traitorous brain offered up to me. I stood and rolled up my yoga mat.

"I didn't fail to notice," I replied in what I hoped was a dry, derisive tone. The way Lou's eyes had tracked Xander around the clinic as we'd filmed the footage in the lead-up to his big exodus to 'bumfuck middle of nowhere' had made my diaphragm feel like someone had lit a whole bunch of sparklers inside it. "Lou is off the project now. She's staying in Sydney to work with post-production."

Jord chuckled. "Good call, G. We wouldn't want anyone on crew lusting after our star, now, would we?" Their words were too pointy for my liking.

I took a long slug from my water bottle. Swallowing, I said snippily, "No, that would be less than ideal. And to answer your question, I'll be riding shotgun with Dr Fox today."

If I'd been able to bet on Jord's reaction to that, I would've won big. They sucked in a long, dramatic breath. "Are you sure that's the best idea, G? There was definitely … something going on between the two of you in that meeting."

There was. I still felt hot and bothered thinking about the way he'd been in my office. I'd gone home that night and gotten off with my own hand, replaying his words; *"I still remember what your mouth tastes like. How your thighs feel when they're around my hips … what you look like when you come."* God, I hated him! How dare he have so much power over my arousal after what he'd done.

Nothing wrong with releasing a bit of pressure. He'll never know you're thinking about him when you masturbate. It actually kind of gave me a sick sense of satisfaction, knowing I could use him that way without his permission.

"I feel like I'm uniquely positioned to really drill down to Dr

Fox's big emotions on his trip west," I said. "And after all, isn't getting the nitty gritty footage what we really want if we're aiming for maximum drama?"

"Just remember there's a camera, G," Jord warned, and my stomach fluttered. "While it's on, it will capture everything. And yes, you won't be mic'd up, but his mic will still pick up your voice."

I rolled my eyes as I headed for the shower. "What do you think I'm going to do? Talk dirty to him and give him a highway blow-job? Give me some credit! I might have a history with the man, but that is firmly in the past."

"Okay," Jordyn said dubiously. "I'm going to go now. I've got to brief the team, make sure we have everything ready for you to arrive this evening." We'd opted for a minimal crew to keep a raw, documentary feel to the production. I'd put Jordyn in charge of the team for day-to-day issues, and they were thriving in their new role.

"You've come such a long way from that timid little mouse who used to scuttle to me with even the most mundane questions," I said before Jord could hang up. "I'm really proud of you."

"Aw, G, you can't say stuff like that to me with no warning—I'm not wearing waterproof mascara today!"

"See you this evening, Jord."

I showered and dressed in my travel outfit. I'd spent a long time concocting my ensemble. It had to be a perfect balance of travelling comfort and professional boss lady. I opted for a grey bamboo wrap dress and white sneakers. I wanted to be comfy for the eight-hour drive while still maintaining that sense that I was in charge of Xander for the duration of filming.

The intercom buzzed, and the doorman informed me that there was a man here with a very large utility truck for me. I grinned, grabbing my suitcase and casting my eyes over my apartment. I wouldn't see it again for three months. And I couldn't be happier about that.

But are you happy because of the new job? Or the new colleague?

"Colleague," I snorted to myself as I signed for the truck and took the keys. "Subordinate more like it." If I was so inclined, I could make Xander Fox my bitch for the next three months. At times, that thought was very tempting. When he'd strolled out of my office after calling me Gina, I'd fantasized about all the ways I could make life miserable for him in Budgerigar.

A laugh burst out of me. Both Alan the doorman and the delivery guy threw me weird looks. I ignored them, striding confidently out and climbing into the driver's side of the vehicle. I plugged my phone into the dash before I pulled away from the curb.

The truck—a Goliath Stag—was insanely large for Sydney roads. It barely fit inside a single lane, and it towered over the other vehicles around it. Jordyn had managed to get the truck as part of a sponsorship deal. We'd feature the Goliath badge every time the vehicle was in use during filming.

The truck itself was the most obnoxious colour I'd ever seen—a shimmery, glittery cherry red. I'd specifically requested the colour because it would stand out like a sore thumb among the dusty monochromatic tray-back Utes of Budgerigar. Anything that would make Xander's 'outsider' status obvious was going to translate into ratings gold. It helped that I knew Xander would be disgusted by everything to do with the vehicle.

My phone rang about five minutes from Xander's clinic. I glanced at the monitor on the dash. It was my oncologist.

Heart thrumming, I answered the call.

"Hi, Dr Hartley," I greeted nervously. I hated when he called me. If it wasn't bad news, it was because he wanted to nag me about things I didn't want to make decisions on. And since my last screening had come back clear, I assumed it was the latter.

"Georgina, how are you?"

I sighed. "I'm fine. And you?"

Dr Hartley cleared his throat. "You know, I don't normally like to pester my patients."

"Are you sure about that?" I asked with a humph.

Dr Hartley chuckled. "I don't like to, but I do it anyway. Now, have you made a decision on the ovum retrieval we discussed at your last appointment?"

I should have known that was what he wanted to prod me

about. I let out a shaky breath. I honestly hadn't thought about it. I didn't want to think about it because it was just one step closer to the reality. That I was unlikely to conceive naturally, and by the time I turned thirty-five, it was more likely than not that it would be impossible.

I wasn't sure I wanted to have kids. But when faced with the possibility that I couldn't ...

"I've just been so busy with work—I started a new job a few weeks ago," I said in a rush, knowing Dr Hartley would see right through me. "I haven't had a chance to really think about it properly."

"Well, Georgina, I always recommend to my patients that they keep their options open. You never know how you're going to feel in a few years. Think of it as a failsafe. If you never use them, you can donate them, or have them destroyed."

Destroyed. That word gripped me by the throat and squeezed. I frantically sucked in air, willing my vision not to cloud with my panic.

"I ... I'm going away for work for three months, so I'm not in a position to have the procedure done at this stage," I blurted. "Can we reschedule this conversation for twelve weeks from now?"

I swallowed back bile as I waited for a response from Dr Hartley. Eventually he grunted, "Yes, that should be alright. In the meantime, you need to keep close tabs on your body, like I know you always do. If anything changes, you give me a call, okay?"

"Yes, Dr Hartley," I breathed. I hung up before he could lecture me any further.

"Just keep driving," I told myself as I wound through traffic on autopilot. "You don't have to think about this for another three months." I focused on taking deep, calming breaths in through my nose and out through my mouth. In for four. Hold for two. Out for six.

By the time I pulled up outside Xander's clinic, my professional mask was back in place. Luckily, because the curb outside the clinic was an utter circus. People with dogs on leads lined the street. There was an older man with a very large parrotty-looking thing on his shoulder.

Good luck Dr Fox! a giant banner stretching across the verandah of the practice read.

And in the middle of the chaos stood Xander, looking just as uncomfortable as I'd hoped in the clothing we'd had sent to him for today. I'd reached out to one of the designers we'd featured on *Bikini Cove*, who was more than happy to put together her 'take' on outback chic. A plaid shirt with short sleeves … and a few prominent buttons missing so that his tanned, muscular chest, dusted with dark gold hair, peeked out. Jeans in a stretch fabric that clung to the lines of his thighs … and other areas slightly north of there. A belt with a ridiculous pewter bull head and a pair of highly polished chocolate brown boots almost completed the ensemble.

I stifled a giggle as I climbed down from the truck and approached. Xander's eyes flashed angrily at me. I let my gaze trail slowly up his body from the boots.

Holy shit, he was packing in the crotch department. I pressed my lips together tightly to stop myself from licking them. *Fodder for a finger bang later*, I told myself.

"Where's your hat, Dr Fox?" I asked mildly, as if I hadn't just gotten caught ogling his impressive package. "More importantly, where's your dog? She should be in-shot for this." Xander scowled.

"They're around here somewhere. I think Levi's entertaining my niece with them."

My lips parted. "Niece? Levi's a father?" My stomach tensed the way it always did thinking about people from my past having kids now. Meanwhile I couldn't even make a decision about freezing my own eggs so that kids remained an option for me.

Xander shrugged. "Yeah, long story."

I wondered if eight hours in close quarters with one another could pry it out of him. Then I remembered that there would be a camera in the cab with us.

Professional topics only, Georgie. Needle him only about subjects that will translate well into usable footage.

"I see you've managed to summon up quite the farewell committee," I murmured, glancing around. Karl, one of the camera crew was approaching.

"Let's get this shot, so we can be on our way," I said to the pair of them, backing out of shot as Karl panned from the ridiculous red Ute through the crowds, now nattering excitedly and hamming it up for the camera, and finally to Xander, standing with his arms folded, an unreadable expression on his face.

I needed action. Scanning the crowd, my eyes fell on a gorgeous, tattooed man wearing an Akubra hat, a baby strapped to his chest. My heart lurched. Levi. Xander's little brother.

Memories assaulted me. I pushed them back, striding towards him.

"Levi, I need you to come farewell your brother," I said in a tone that was commanding rather than questioning. Levi turned, a slow grin pulling his lips up at the corners. It was a devastating smile.

Not as devastating as dimples over there, I thought.

"Georgina Menzies. You're a fucking blast from the past."

Why couldn't I have been working with this brother instead? We'd always had an easy relationship. Probably because I wasn't thinking about what he looked like naked every spare moment of my teenage years.

"No time now, Lev. Just get your butt over there, plonk that hat on your brother's head, and give us an adorable brotherly farewell."

With a smirk and a tilt of the hat, Levi did as he was bid.

"I can't believe he has a baby," I muttered to myself.

"Sometimes he can't believe it either," a sweet voice commented in my ear. I turned to find a pretty, curvy woman with wavy blonde hair and the loveliest smile, holding the lead of Xander's boisterous black Labrador.

"You know him?" I asked.

She nodded. "He's my partner."

"That's *your* baby?" I blurted. With a twitch of her lips, the woman shook her head.

"Step-daughter," she explained. "It's a long story. Do you know Levi?"

I shook my head, turning back to where Levi and Xander were

clasped in an awkward side hug, thumping each other on the shoulder as they both looked down with unmasked adulation at Levi's little baby.

Xander reached out, stroking the baby's downy head with feather-light fingertips, murmuring something as she lifted her tiny baby head in his direction. He leaned down, kissing her little forehead. The baby sneezed, and the dimpling grin that split Xander's face, crinkling his eyes at the corners, was too much.

I swallowed hard, turning away.

"I used to know him," I mumbled. The woman's eyes shot wide.

"Oh. Oooh, you must be Georgie!"

Great. No doubt I'd been the hot topic of conversation in the Fox family of late.

"I'll need to take the dog over to Dr Fox now," I said instead, keeping my face as neutral as possible. The woman handed the lead to me and crouched down, affectionately rubbing the dog's silky ears.

"See you in three months, Molly," she murmured. My heart jumped into my throat.

"Did you say Molly?" I asked, my chest constricting.

The woman eyed me curiously. "Yes, that's her name."

Without another word, I turned and started back towards the action. I needed this crowd to disperse. I needed space to breathe.

How could he? Was this some sort of nasty joke on his part? And how stupid had I been not to ask the name of the dog who had accompanied Xander to the clinic every day we'd filmed there the last week.

I hated the realization that dawned on me, that I'd been so caught up in trying to find the chinks in Xander's armour that I could manipulate into on-screen drama that I hadn't bothered much with the dog. That was a major oversight on my part.

Head in the game, Georgie. This is your career. Stop letting your personal feelings get in the way.

Breathing rhythmically and refusing to let the memories take hold, I was halfway through the crowd of farewellers when a dark-haired girl sprinted across the road and leapt into Xander's arms with a squeal.

He looked shocked for a split second, then his hands snaked out and gripped her backside as she wrapped her legs around his waist.

"I can't believe you didn't tell me that you're leaving!" she squawked. Xander held her close for a moment before setting her down on her feet.

"Dakota, I … uh … well I didn't think …"

Dakota, with the shiny brown hair and smattering of freckles, who looked maybe twenty-two and had a pair of gravity-defying boobs to show for it, smacked him playfully on the arm.

"Of course you didn't think, you big dork! Not much *thinking* went on between us, did it."

The innuendo in her tone had me grinding my molars as I pressed through the last of the crowd to get to Karl's side. Professional Georgie said, 'get as much footage of this encounter as possible'. Georgie the jilted teenager wanted to claw the bitch's eyes out.

Xander's hazel gaze met mine, and to my utter fury, his mouth curved up into that cheeky grin that still haunted my dreams, his dimples popping as he turned back to the girl, leaning close and murmuring something I couldn't hear into her ear. Whatever it was, she giggled and flushed, pressing her mouth to his. He kissed her briefly but firmly before setting her back on the ground and tweaking her cheek like she was a wayward toddler. She practically swooned as she gave his hand a last squeeze before backing away. Xander flicked his eyes back to mine, one eyebrow raised.

I pursed my lips, hating that I knew I'd be frantically reviewing the footage tonight to find out what he'd said to her. I spiralled my pointer finger in the air at him in the universal signal of 'let's get this moving'. Xander leered again, striding towards me.

His eyes sparkled, his fingers ghosting against my wrist as he took the lead off my arm. My blood was almost at boiling point from everything I'd already dealt with this morning.

"Molly? *Really?*" I hissed as he adjusted the lead in his hand. He stiffened for a second, his smirk dropping. But he said nothing as he walked back into frame, and in perfect pet timing, Molly the

Labrador's excitement in the crowd overwhelmed her, and she leapt towards Xander, her big front paws smacking him directly in the crotch.

With a garbled groan, he doubled over. Karl sucked in a sympathetic breath, but he knew better than to stop rolling. It was a cheap shot—I'd never stoop to the level of slapstick comedy in this show, but just being able to replay the moment his balls got smashed under those paws in the comfort of my own home was enough to take the sting out of my emotions.

He managed to rally fairly quickly, although his smile had been replaced with a pinched expression, his face pale. Karl followed Xander as he opened the back door of the Ute and encouraged the dog to jump in, fiddling with the harness and seatbelt attachment we'd installed for her. No riding in the tray for this pampered Sydney pooch. Just another thing Budgerigar locals would roll their eyes at.

Xander wasn't going to know what had hit him.

When Xander clambered into the driver's seat and drove away from the curb, Karl lowered his camera, flashing a thumbs-up at me. I turned to the crowd, clapping my hands for attention.

"Thank you for coming out to see Dr Fox off. Filming here has wrapped now, but for anyone who hasn't signed a release form, the Sydney crew will be in the clinic for the next hour or so and can sort you out with one. It's imperative if you want to be on TV that you sign one."

People began dispersing, and I snatched my phone from my bag, pulling up Xander's number.

"What?" he grouched.

I tried not to let my grin sound in my voice. "Turn around please, Dr Fox."

"Why? Do you need to catch another blooper reel moment where my dick gets pummelled by my dog? Maybe you'd like to have a go yourself? Get your knee in there?"

I had to take a few deep breaths so I didn't laugh down the phone at him. Oh God, but I wanted to.

"Not at all. I'll just wait to get you up close and personal with a disgruntled sheep once we arrive in Budgerigar. I promise, there will be ample opportunity."

Xander muttered something unintelligible. I chose to ignore it.

"You have to collect the producer who is riding with you."

There was a long silence. Then he let out a sigh. "Do I even need to ask which producer that is?"

I didn't bother to answer.

Now: A Clusterfuck Of Epic Proportions

XANDER

I pulled the giant, butt-ugly Ute up across the road from the clinic. There were still stragglers hanging around, and they all stared. Of course they bloody did. They'd just seen me cop a double whammy of dog paws to my goolies.

For some stupid reason, I wanted to punish Georgie for it. Not that she'd had any control over Molly leaping at my crotch, but the look of delight on her face when I'd glanced up through my pain made me want to …

I couldn't think about the things it made me want to do to her because my poor bruised dick did not need to get hard right now. Especially not in the spray-on jeans she'd insisted I wear.

Anger and lust warred in me with every breath. Another thing to punish her for. Just like this ridiculous sparkly magenta Ute.

The list of things I was sure Georgie had planned just to get back at me for what she thought happened twelve years ago was getting longer and longer. I was a complete fool for keeping tally. For all I knew, this was just what she'd been instructed to do in order to create the show Reelflix wanted, and it had nothing to do with me whatsoever.

Who was I kidding? This was one hundred percent personal for her. Because it felt personal to me, and I couldn't be feeling this alone, could I?

I glanced up to see her trotting across the road. Her tanned thigh kept peeking out of the split in her dress. Christ.

I'd thought watching her strut around my clinic in the figure-hugging dresses she'd worn every day for the last week while we filmed all the preliminary scenes—the dresses that cupped her arse like they were painted on—had been torture.

But that was nothing. I wasn't sure I was going to survive a whole day in the car with her in this dress. It might not have been as form-fitting, but her legs ... they'd only gotten sexier in the last twelve years.

Even the way she'd worn sneakers with it was such a Georgie thing to do—at least the Georgie I remembered. Who knew whether she was the same as that girl?

Her eyes met mine, and that spark in their silvery depths was so familiar to me my breath caught in my chest. And then she was opening the door and climbing in, the split on her dress parting to reveal more of that toned thigh.

I snapped my gaze back to the road as Georgie settled into her seat. The noises the brand-new leather made under her arse were utter torture.

"Time to leave, Dr Fox," she murmured, and with a clenched jaw, I pulled away from the curb.

I navigated the ridiculous Ute along narrow Sydney roads, until we crossed the Anzac Bridge and got onto the A4, where the traffic eased slightly.

"So ... Uncle Xander. How old is your niece?"

"Her name is Lily, and she's two months."

"Do you get to spend much time with her?"

I glanced sidelong at Georgie, but she was peering out the windscreen intently. "Levi brings her over once or twice a week. Molly is besotted with her. Must be that new baby smell."

Georgie huffed out a laugh, before lapsing into silence. Her lips were pulled into a tight line.

"*You* looked quite besotted with her," she eventually murmured.

I smiled. "I am."

"Is having a family in *your* life plan? You know, wife, two point five kids, cottage in the 'burbs?" she asked. I adjusted my grip on the steering wheel, flexing my wrists and stretching my arms around the sudden tension there. Discussing my future plans for a wife and kids was not something I wanted to do with this particular woman.

Oddly though, the urge to be honest with her overcame my discomfort.

"I do want kids. I'd love a whole soccer team of them. But I haven't … the right person hasn't …"

Georgie cleared her throat, giving me an out of my discomfort. She shifted in her seat, recrossing her legs, flashing more thigh. I clenched my jaw.

"So, Montana back there isn't quite ready to commit to marriage and babies?" she asked.

"Dakota," I corrected automatically, my ears warming up. "I wouldn't have a clue what her thoughts are on marriage and babies."

"Because not much thinking went on between the two of you when you were together?"

I fought a grin, my eyes flicking up to the camera once more. There was more than a touch of jealousy in her tone, which burned away some of the awkwardness of the wife and kids conversation.

"No. Thinking wasn't at the forefront of our minds," I replied. There was a grunting sound that for a second I thought had come from Molly, but a quick flick of my eyes in Georgie's direction showed me her pursed lips and furrowed brows. I chewed on the inside of my cheek to keep my smirk at bay.

She thought she'd be the one to make me feel uncomfortable for three months. Well, two could play at that game. And if my sex life was something that set her off, well, I had more than enough stories to keep her riled up.

"So, she's not the future Mrs Fox, wife and mother?" The question was asked between gritted teeth.

I shrugged, lips curling upwards despite my best efforts. "She's fun. But it's never going to be serious, if that's what you're asking.

She might be around when I get back, she might not. It's neither here nor there for me. Plenty more fish in the sea."

"Oh, and you're like a net scooping them all up, I imagine," Georgie remarked. I coughed to cover my laughter.

"I've never struggled romantically."

Georgie inhaled a sharp breath, and out of the corner of my eye I noticed that her cheeks paled.

Shit. That had been a low blow, considering the reason we hadn't spoken for the last twelve years. I was too busy thinking about how I could needle her, and I was acting like a callous arsehole as a result.

"G—"

"If you call me Gina, I'll twist your balls off with my bare hands. And I'd imagine they're already quite tender after Molly had her fun with them earlier." She turned her body so she was looking into the back seat, where I could see Molly in the mirror, sitting up, tongue lolling, delighted to be on a road trip.

"You're a clever girl, Molly," Georgie crooned. I ground my teeth together. Georgie had always been one to come out of an insult with all guns blazing.

"Camera," I reminded her coldly. Georgie turned to face forwards with a little shrug.

"I have final say on what gets included in each episode."

I snorted. "Of course you do. You have total control over my life for the next three months."

"How do you feel about spending Christmas away from your new niece?" Georgie asked, and the sudden change in topic had my head spinning.

"I … there will be plenty of Christmases. She's still so tiny, she's not going to remember this one anyway. I'll have to organize a gift to be delivered to her, though."

"Have you thought about inviting your parents out to spend Christmas Day with you? But I suppose they'll want to be with their granddaughter."

A harsh bark of laughter forced its way out of my throat. "Dad and Levi aren't on the best of terms—haven't been for years. I'm not sure whether things are improved enough for Levi to want to share Lily's first Christmas with him."

"What about your mum?" Georgie asked, and my heart stopped in my chest.

She didn't know. Of course she didn't know. She'd gone full radio silence on me two years before it happened.

"Mum …" I stopped and cleared my throat. "Mum died a decade ago. Breast cancer."

Georgie went utterly still. When the silence stretched long enough to feel alive again, she inhaled a ragged breath.

"I … I'm so sorry, Xander," she breathed. I looked over at her, watched her fists clench and unclench in her lap. Damn me, I wanted to reach over and grasp her hand, hook my pinkie around hers, stroke my thumb across the back of her knuckles. Anything to show her that it was okay that she hadn't known. It wasn't her fault.

She'd called me Xander. Not Dr Fox.

Instead, I remembered the camera filming everything, the microphone attached to my ridiculous shirt.

"It was a long time ago."

Georgie turned to look out her window, and the silence felt like a living beast between us. The only sound inside the cab was Molly panting in the back seat.

I couldn't handle the tension a second longer.

"You know, I ran through dozens of names for Molly in my head, but nothing else felt right." I blurted, staring ahead, slowing as we reached a red light. I flexed my fingers on the steering wheel. "You know, when she was smaller she used to try and sleep on my face, just like …"

It was as close to an apology as she was going to get. I didn't really owe her an explanation for why I'd chosen the name Molly. If she was as clever now as she had been twelve years ago, she'd figure it out anyway. And it probably wouldn't make any difference to how much she hated me.

"She sleeps in your bed?" Georgie asked, and I cracked a smile, glancing up at the camera mounted just below the rear-view mirror, remembering that I'd been told to engage with it when talking in the car.

"She sleeps in my bed every night. It was cute a few months ago when she was tiny. It's getting kind of annoying now, but she just whimpers all night if I lock her out of my bedroom, and honestly, that's worse."

Georgie let out a little huffing breath, and I glanced at her out of the corner of my eye, but she was looking down at her phone. She seemed somehow less fiery than she had in every other interaction we'd had recently.

"Something on your mind?" I asked before I could think about whether that was really a good idea or not. She cleared her throat and raised her eyes to the road ahead.

"We're here to discuss you, Dr Fox," she reminded me in a clipped tone. "What do you think it's going to be like, being a rural vet?"

I could tell she was reading from a list of questions she'd prepared earlier. I'd answered dozens of these over the last week of filming; what I was going to miss about the city most, what my friends and colleagues thought of my 'decision' to move.

"I think it's going to be a clusterfuck of epic proportions," I said. Georgie looked up at me sharply, her eyes calculating.

"In what way?"

I shifted my grip on the steering wheel.

"I'm a city boy through and through. Never even been camping once in my life. The 'outback' is a theoretical concept for me. I'm … the culture shock itself is going to … from what I've heard, rural vets work longer hours, with very little support, and deal with a wider variety of complex issues.

"And then there is having to treat livestock. It's daunting. It's a whole different ball game, not just in physical treatments, but in knowing the right medications and dosages, and farmers are very well versed in their livestock's needs. I'm probably going to make an utter fool of myself." It was raw honesty, a vulnerability I hadn't thought I wanted to give to Georgie.

It's for the show. You have to be honest for the show, I reminded myself. *That's all it is. Nothing to do with wanting to hear your name on her lips again.*

"You'll have Alex to help you—he's the vet from the nearest town who's been covering the clinic once a fortnight. We've prepared him to mentor you, he'll come out once a fortnight to do routine livestock appointments with you, and he has promised to be available for phone support if there are any emergencies."

Her tone was matter of fact, but the way her body turned towards me felt reassuring. She might want to capture drama, might want me to feel completely out of my comfort zone, but she didn't want me to outright fail at this crazy 'adventure' she was forcing me on.

"I'm not sure the people of Budgerigar are going to warm to me," I added, almost as an afterthought. Georgie chuckled, and when I looked over, she was eyeing me up and down, lips tilted in a smirk, the sparkle in those silver eyes sending my blood rushing south.

"Oh, I'm sure they'll warm to you just fine, Dr Fox," she murmured, a hint of pink spreading across her throat. I clenched the wheel, because if I didn't focus on driving, I was going to pull over, wrap my hand around that blushing throat of hers, and take her mouth with mine. Force her to feel what she did to me.

This is a game to her, I reminded myself harshly. *Making me feel this tense is her game plan.*

My need to take twelve years of pent-up anger out on her was so strong that I tasted blood as I bit the inside of my cheek to keep my feelings in check. I wanted to fuck the superior look off her face.

We were just over an hour into an eight-hour drive.

I really don't think I can do this.

Eight hours, four bathroom stops, several packets of Smith's salt and vinegar chips, and multiple really bloody awkward silences later, and the single-lane highway we'd been on for hours now declared that the town of Budgerigar was only another ten kilometres away.

The landscape for the last hour had been nothing more than dusty grassland, stands of straggly eucalyptus, and kangaroo and wombat roadkill. Georgie barely even raised an eyebrow at the sheer number of dead marsupials we passed.

"Have you been out here before?" I asked her. She stiffened, reaching into her bag and taking out her water bottle. I watched, mesmerized, at the way her throat bobbed as she swallowed before wrenching my gaze back to the road. I was going to be responsible for a mammalian hit-and-run if I didn't stop staring at her every chance I got.

"Why do you ask that?" she eventually replied, her voice carefully neutral. I was instantly suspicious.

"I thought you might've come out here to scout the place out before you decided to film here. Or did you get your blue-haired lackey to do all the grunt work?"

Her nostrils flared, and she turned those icy eyes on me. "I'm familiar with Budgerigar, and a number of the locals," she informed me. I bit back a sneer. Of course she was. Georgie had always been a girl who, if she was going to do something, she was going to do it to perfection.

"So, can we run through the plan for when we arrive?" I asked, as the first signs of a township started to come into view—weatherboard homesteads with dirt driveways set back from the road. Lawns around the houses but not much in the way of greenery anywhere else.

"How are the sheep farms going out here?" I asked. "Doesn't look like there's an abundance of fodder around."

Georgie turned to the window, her shoulders rising and falling with her breaths, her thigh slipping fully out of the slit in her dress. My knuckles went white on the wheel.

"Drought hasn't been kind to them, let's just put it that way. A lot of them are barely scraping by, having to purchase feed because there's just not enough. Some of the farmers are lucky to back onto the river, but even those ones are doing it tough with restrictions on drawing for irrigation."

"You've really done your homework, Blondie," I remarked. Georgie spun to face me, her ponytail flipping wildly.

"Blondie?" she repeated darkly. I chuckled.

"Take your pick. Gina, or Blondie. Or … here's a novel idea. You could drop the Dr Fox bullshit and I'll call you whatever you want me to."

"Or, you could be professional. Ms Menzies would be my preference." She grabbed at her ponytail as she said it, smoothing it over her shoulder. She'd always done that in the past when she was feeling uncomfortable. I chuckled under my breath. Good. Let her feel that way. Maybe then she'd feel a fraction the way I did, spending all day in a car with bruised junk, in too-tight jeans and a constant semi.

"Well, in high school I used to fantasise about you and Ms Maddox, our biology teacher. So, two Ms M's, that could work for me."

Georgie's mouth popped open, pink flooding her cheeks. "Camera!" she hissed. I laughed then.

"I thought you had final say on what ends up on air?"

She practically growled at me. "Yes, but I might not be the only one who'll have eyes on this footage, you Neanderthal!"

I grinned wide, feeling her eyes linger on my face. It was so intense it almost felt like the lightest touch of fingertips stroking me. I shivered. I might have been getting under her skin, but she was well and truly embedded deep in me, her essence running through my veins.

Being near her again was breaking me down. I had to fight it. I just had to get through the next three months.

I couldn't let her break me first.

Now: Damned Gratuitous Pants

GEORGIE

Daylight savings meant that even as we pulled into Main Street, Budgerigar after seven pm, the sun was still at that 'magic hour' position in the sky, reflecting reds and pinks and oranges and that hazy sheen of summer across the plains surrounding the town. I glanced at Xander's infuriatingly perfect face. That golden hair and the hint of stubble on his strong jaw would practically glow in this lighting. Damn him.

I'd gone eight full hours without taking a proper breath. Even when we'd stopped at dingy truck stops for bathroom breaks and I'd scuttled off to the ladies' room, I hadn't been able to relax knowing that he was out there, waiting for me.

Before things went downhill for us, I'd been more comfortable with him than with anyone else. But that was exactly the issue. That was before, this was now. After he'd ruined everything. But we'd both made mistakes back then. Mistakes neither of us could ever take back.

I wasn't sure there would be much salvageable from the in-car footage. It had mostly consisted of long, strained silences, interspersed with my attempts to get something juicy out of him, which had almost always descended into snarking. Or lewd comments about me and his high school science teacher.

I'd texted Jordyn when we were about half an hour out to make sure they had everything in place for Dr Fox's big arrival. Their response had been acidic, even over text.

> Jordyn: Am I an idiot? Everything is in place. You just need to get him to park where we agreed.

I had to chew on my lips to stop a Machiavellian grin from bursting onto my face. Xander was about to get an interesting introduction to Budgerigar.

"Do I really have to keep this butt-ugly outfit on?" Xander asked. "It's hot as hell out here, and whatever these jeans are made of, it's definitely not breathable." He reached down and adjusted his package. I watched, mesmerized, before swiftly turning back to stare at the road ahead a split second before Xander turned to me.

"It's only for tonight. You can wear whatever you brought with you starting tomorrow." My voice was strangled. His bulge was burned into my retinas.

Xander grunted but didn't complain again. I pointed up ahead, where our Budgerigar crew was waiting beside a lone scribbly bark gum tree that loomed at the side of the road.

"Okay, we're almost on now, Dr Fox," I told him. "You need to pull up and let me out of the vehicle, and then I need you to turn and head back three blocks, and when I text, you will drive in and park under that tree where the cameras are waiting and get yourself and Molly out of the car. Got it?"

Xander rolled his eyes. "I think I can manage." He pulled over and I slid out of the car. My wrap dress snagged on the seatbelt, and as I frantically tugged it free and readjusted myself, Xander's eyes felt like hot knives taking in the flash of my G-string and the bare skin surrounding it.

I smoothed my dress down, willing the heat in my cheeks to calm the hell down. Molly stood in the back seat, tail wagging and tongue lolling. I leaned in to give her a quick pat.

"Sorry, beautiful girl," I crooned to her through the still-open door. "Almost time for you to get out. You've been such a good girl today!"

My eyes caught on Xander as I backed away. He watched me with an expression that I couldn't decipher, but nevertheless sent tingles running up and down my spine.

Just another hour or so, and then you can get some privacy to work out this ridiculous tension, I told myself as I schooled my expression.

"Back three blocks, park under the tree," I reminded him. Xander gave a mocking salute.

"Yes sir, Ms Blondie," he muttered as I closed the door. Before I could wrench it open again to give him a piece of my mind, he turned and drove away as instructed. With a frustrated groan I trotted across the road to stand with Jordyn, who cocked an inquisitive, and maybe slightly accusatory, eyebrow at me.

"How was your day?" I asked, ignoring the fact that my head was spinning from too long near Xander.

I really don't know if I can do this for three months.

Jord pursed their lips. "We've done just fine. You, on the other hand, look like you've gone five rounds with Danny Green."

I glanced down, picking non-existent lint from my dress. Jord guffawed.

"Figuratively, G. I'm hoping that our good doctor is as frazzled as you, though. That'll translate perfectly with what Liz has in store for him."

"Should I be worried?" I asked out of the corner of my mouth as the cherry Ute approached. Jordyn grunted, which I interpreted as 'you'll love it, just let me get it done'.

The Ute pulled up smoothly to the curb, and Jord nodded to Jase the cameraman. He got into position as Xander opened the door and jumped out of the cab, landing far too gracefully. Even in the tightest denim I'd ever seen on a man, he managed to look …

"That's damned gratuitous, Georgie! I'm not sure whether to ream you out or hug you right now. Those pants alone are going to ensure we have an MA rating."

I followed her gaze and pinched the bridge of my nose, pressing my thighs together to try and stem the throbbing. It was impossible to miss the very prominent outline of what was definitely *not* a flaccid penis in his pants. It was pointing upwards and taking up a significant amount of real estate in fabric designed to leave nothing to the imagination.

I wondered, with a sickening mixture of satisfaction and humiliation, if his pants were even tighter than they had been minutes ago because of my wardrobe malfunction getting out of the truck.

The cameras followed Xander as he let Molly out of the back. He straightened, apparently either completely oblivious to the heat he was packing below his belt or not caring who saw it. He took a deep breath and his eyes fell on me for a split second, the golden flecks in them darkening minutely, enough to have my breath catching in my throat before he broke contact and let his eyes roam over the street.

Weatherboard shopfronts lined both sides of the narrow road. The little supermarket, which doubled as a chemist, was dark, already closed for the evening. The Chinese takeaway, with its red and gold painted dragon on the window was bustling as much as any business in a tiny township could bustle. As was the liquor store next door. The doctor and dentist shared a building. A hairdresser, the primary school, several other boutique-type stores, the library, and an old-school milk bar that sold greasy takeaway, lollies and chocolates, and of course, milkshakes and ice-creams, rounded out the rest.

At the far end of the street, next to the quaint sandstone church and cemetery, was the largest and busiest building in the town—the pub. The Budgie towered over the rest of the shops with its second-storey, large wraparound verandah, and red and white striped tin roof. That end of the street was crowded with dusty Utes, and the sounds of laughter and music wafted in our direction.

And then there was the vet clinic, visible over a small picket fence. On the outside, it looked like a little baby-blue weatherboard cottage with a stone path leading up to a verandah. The plaque on the gate was the only clue that it wasn't just a private home.

Xander's eyes fell on the sign, rubbing his lips together. I held my breath.

"Well, I guess there's no time like the present to check out my new practice." There was a slight shake in his voice. I wondered, as he and Molly approached the gate, cameras following, whether Xander was even more apprehensive about this move than he let on during the drive out here.

Molly stopped just inside the gate and squatted for a number two. I signalled to Jase to zoom in on the pooping dog, giving Jord a moment to hand the key to Xander out of shot. And then we were back on him again as he strode purposefully up the path, onto the verandah, and turned the key in the lock of the door.

I glanced back towards the Ute, a small smile pulling at my lips as I noticed a few white splatters on the windscreen and the bonnet. By the time we left the clinic for the evening, I could guarantee there would be a nice, thick coating of bird droppings on his car. After all, the town wasn't called Budgerigar for nothing—it was home to one of the largest wild populations of budgies in Australia.

And their favourite roosting tree was the same one we'd directed Xander to park under.

Now: They Breed 'Em Good In The Big Smoke

XANDER

The cottage exterior was where the similarities between this clinic, and the one I'd left behind in Bondi, ended.

The door opened with a sinister creak, and I stepped inside, mindful that the camera was right behind me, shining a spotlight into the otherwise dark space. The floors were cracked old linoleum, and the musty smell of disuse permeated the place.

"Where's the light switch?" I asked the crew behind me, but there was no answer as we all crowded into the waiting room. I glanced back, trying to catch Georgie's eye, but I couldn't see her with the camera light shining in my face.

A floorboard creaked deep within the practice, and I spun, my heart thumping erratically for God knew what reason—I wasn't bloody scared. I couldn't see a flipping thing as I blinked to try and clear the afterimage spots that the camera light had left in my vision.

"You punks got a good reason for breaking into my property?" a furious, high-pitched voice asked. Something cold, hard, and pointy poked me in the chest, the unmistakable click of a gun being cocked echoing in the silence.

"What the hell?" I blurted, cold sweat breaking out across my skin. "I'm the new vet. Isn't this the vet clinic?"

More silence from the crew as the gun was thumped against my sternum. My hands shot into the air. "I'm not breaking in; I have a key!"

There was another click, and my knees almost gave way under me. But it was just Georgie, flicking on the light switch. Her face was as pale as mine. I swallowed, looking down to the double barrel shotgun still pressed against my chest, and along its length, until my eyes locked on a tiny, ferocious woman, her steel grey hair in the tightest old-lady perm I'd ever seen, her eyes narrowed, her wrinkly lips pursed.

"It's considered polite, young man, to knock before you let your-self into someone else's home!" She didn't move the gun, but her eyes dragged over me from head to toe. I wasn't about to move even a centimetre. This crazy old bat was holding a rifle to my chest.

"Well, well, well, they breed 'em good in the big smoke!" Her fury turned into a leer that made me shudder, the gun barrel shaking against my chest. With a last, lingering look at my ridiculous jeans, the woman lifted the cold metal from my chest.

"What on God's green earth are you wearing, young man?" she asked, resting on the gun like it was nothing more than a walking stick and leaning in towards me. "I can see … everything," she whis-per-shouted, waving her hand in circles at my crotch.

Anger heated my blood. I glanced over at Georgie, who was whispering hurriedly with her assistant. Maybe she felt my glare, maybe it was just a coincidence, but she raised her eyes to mine, and immediately I knew.

She'd planned this. The ridiculous outfit, the twilight entry to the clinic. She'd set up this crazy old biddy to scare the living shit out of me. And it didn't feel like this was just for on-screen drama.

This felt personal.

Now: Bird Turd Tree

GEORGIE

"When I said to get Liz to make Xander feel uneasy, I didn't mean have her threaten to shoot him!" I hissed at Jordyn as Liz finally put her rifle down on the worn old reception desk. The kooky old thing had gone from murderous harpy to lecherous widow so fast I almost had whiplash.

She took Xander's arm, offering in her nasal voice to give him the 'full tour' of the clinic.

"The home I shared with my late husband, God rest his soul, is the back half of the cottage. Didn't anyone tell you that?" she prattled as she gripped his arm in her surprisingly strong knobbly old-lady fingers, drawing him away.

"No, that wasn't mentioned to me." The murderous glare Xander threw my way sent hot and cold chills racing along every nerve of my body. I dragged my eyes from him back to Jord, who looked as shocked as I felt about the whole thing.

"She went completely off script, G!" they muttered, gripping my arm and pulling me out of the way as the camera followed the pair into the bowels of the clinic. "We'd agreed that when she heard the door open, she'd come bustling through from the back, demanding to know what was going on. Nothing about pulling a gun on him!"

Liz's voice wafted through from the other room, prattling endlessly about the size of Xander's biceps, cooing over Molly and asking about her pedigree.

I sighed, pinching the bridge of my nose. "I should've known she'd go rogue. She's always been prone to melodrama."

Jord chuckled. "Listen, it'll translate to ratings. I wouldn't worry about it too much. Sure, it was unplanned, but we're making unscripted television. We have to expect the unexpected."

I sighed. "I kind of feel bad now that we made him park under Bird Turd Tree. I didn't want to traumatize him this much on his first night."

"*Sure* you didn't," Jord chortled. They looked up at me, no doubt noticing I was close to losing it. They grabbed my arm, tucking it around theirs as we followed at a distance behind the crew. "Don't you beat yourself up about this, G. It's going to make excellent viewing. Besides, thirty-year-old him needs to pay for what eighteen-year-old him did to you."

I looked away from their sneaky grin. Eighteen-year-old him had hurt me badly, but it wasn't as simple as the highly edited version I'd told Jord. I wondered with a vague sense of apprehension what thirty-year-old him might do in retaliation for all of this.

Should have accounted for that before *you set it all in motion.*

"You gave an old woman a fright, Dr Fox!" Liz said as she showed him around the surgery room and the hospital 'ward', where pets recovered from surgery or were kept under observation. "Here I was, just minding my own business, and in you waltz, with your chest hair poking out, and your todger sticking up, and *those dimples.*" She dragged him to a stop and reached up to squeeze his cheeks.

Xander looked like he was ready to commit murder. I didn't blame him. Liz was laying it on so thick we'd all be tasting it for weeks to come.

"But I wasn't expecting you until tomorrow morning. So of course I was a bit on edge when I heard people stomping around in my late husband's clinic."

Xander took a deep breath and flashed her the dimples she seemed to be obsessed with.

Oh God, those dimples …

"I'm really sorry the plans weren't communicated to you. From now on, come and see me, and I'll make sure that no one takes advantage of you. It must be difficult, having lost your husband, and now a stranger is coming into his space, with a camera crew in tow."

He sounded so genuinely contrite, so eager to make it up to Liz, that Jord turned to me and fanned their cheeks, mouthing, "He's adorable!"

I scowled. Too adorable. Oh well, he might be the king of the flirt, but we'd see how adorable he was when he saw the state of his Ute.

"You could make it up to me by having dinner with me at The Budgie tomorrow night," Liz suggested, stroking his forearm. "I assume you'll be spending the day here in the clinic to get everything in order, set up your things?"

Xander glanced in my direction, one eyebrow raised. I flashed him a thin-lipped smile and gave him a thumbs-up. For a split second, I was sure that I'd seen his eyes roll, but then he smiled that megawatt smile that made his eyes twinkle and those dimples pop. The one that made my heart lurch because it made him look eighteen again.

"A country pub meal with the most beautiful lady in Budgerigar —I couldn't ask for a better welcome to the town."

I rubbed my forehead as Liz beamed, her dentures glinting in the light. If I thought Liz had been laying it on thick before, Xander had just given her the green light to slather him up with her lecherous brand of flirtation.

"Oh, Xanny—can I call you Xanny? We're going to get along like a house on fire, my boy!" She ran her fingers over his bicep, giving a squeeze and letting out a high-pitched cackle. Jord pinched their lips closed with a finger and thumb, glancing at me with twinkling eyes as Liz dragged Xander away once more, prattling on about how she couldn't wait to introduce him to her Corgi 'babies' Empress and Kingston tomorrow.

"She'll steal the limelight if we're not careful," I warned Jord, motioning for Jase to wrap up filming inside, flicking my thumb over my shoulder to signal that his team should head out for Xander's next 'surprise'.

Jord shook their head, smirking. "If Xander keeps flashing us the outline of that monster peen, no one will even know Liz Peters exists. Entire social media accounts will be created solely to share thirst traps of Beach Vet's dick."

I dropped my head into my hands, taking a few shaky breaths. I'd gotten an inkling, twelve years ago, that he was packing down there. It was confirmed without a shadow of a doubt now, and I couldn't scrub the image from my brain.

It's your own stupid fault, Georgie. You had to go and put him in pants that left no room for imagination.

I stormed blindly out the front door, letting Jordyn deal with Xander and Lecherous Liz. The sun had finally set, leaving Main Street in darkness, interspersed with the clouds of thousands of moths dancing around the streetlights that lined the sidewalk. The air was the hot, thick late November air of western New South Wales. I couldn't breathe.

I can't do this. I can't be near him for three whole months. It'll kill him, or me. Or both of us. It's too ...

"What the fuck?" Xander groaned. I spun, having temporarily forgotten what was waiting for him outside the clinic. What I'd planned to be waiting for him.

"Oh, shit, I love unscripted television!" Jordyn hissed beside me as I gaped in utter shock. Xander's Ute was unrecognizable. It looked like it had reverse chickenpox. White splotches covered every inch of it, only letting the occasional glint of the cherry red peek through.

"Oh, Xanny! Didn't they tell you not to park under Bird Turd Tree?" Liz crowed in barely concealed delight from the verandah. Xander's head turned in slow motion to glare at me.

"No, they didn't," he grated through clenched teeth. I met his gaze with an expression that I hoped was unapologetic, but honestly, my face felt so tingly I had no idea what I looked like to him.

"Well, you've just had the official Budgerigar welcome, haven't you!" Liz continued as if Xander wasn't on the verge of a complete breakdown right there on the sidewalk. I couldn't move, couldn't take my eyes off him. His stare was dark, murderous, and intently focused on me. I forgot to breathe.

"Can I use your hose to clean this up?" Xander asked, finally breaking his stare-off with me and turning to Liz, a fake smile plastered on his face.

Liz shook her head, the sorrowful tilt of her mouth at complete odds with the mischievous sparkle in her eyes. "Sorry, Xanny, we're on water restrictions out here. Bucket washing only for vehicles. I can get you a bucket and sponge and show you where the tap is, though!"

"Thank you, Liz," Xander grunted. Somehow his muscles looked like they'd grown exponentially. I half expected him to start turning Hulk green at that point. I found myself gasping frantically for breath.

"G, calm down," Jord murmured. "This is absolute perfection! Dr Fox, getting all wet and frazzled as he scrubs budgie shit off his fancy car with nothing but a bucket of water and his own elbow grease. Oooh, do you think we can get him to take his shirt off?"

He hadn't met my eyes again, but I still felt like his attention was somehow zoomed in on me. My body burst into icy flames just thinking about how angry this would have made him.

"I don't know, Jord. But I do know this—you're riding in the Ute with him out to the accommodation. I can't … I can't be near him right now."

Now: Tell Me To Stop

XANDER

"Fuck!" I snarled, tumbling against the wall and clutching my throbbing foot, still cased in the stupid bloody pants that felt like they'd been glued to my skin all day. I'd attempted to kick them off, resulting in one mother of a stubbed toe. "I'm gonna tear these fucking shit cunting jeans to fucking shreds so she can never make me wear them again!"

"You're swearing worse than me, Xan." Levi's voice was amused through the phone speaker as I sat up, tugging at the bloody fabric until it finally popped off my foot. I'd expected my toe to be swollen, purple and possibly bleeding, based on my pain level. But it looked completely unharmed.

"Fucking stupid … shitting … piece of fucking …" I cursed.

"I fucking hope you're not still being filmed," Levi continued. "You're not exactly giving off 'wholesome country vet' vibes right now."

I fell back onto the bed, covering my eyes with my hand. "Since I woke up this morning, I've been forced into skin-tight jeans for a never-ending drive with a woman who hates me, then I had a gun shoved in my face the second I arrived, and now I have to take a lecherous old biddy out for dinner tomorrow night. Oh, and I am sweaty from scrubbing about thirty billion bird shits off that fucking ridiculous truck!" I grouched. "I think I have every right to not be feeling very wholesome right now!

"Besides, I think the 'wholesome vet' boat has well and truly sailed. Fucking Georgie. You saw what she was wearing today! I had to spend eight hours in a car with her dressed like that!"

"It just looked like a regular dress to me—nothing all that sexy about it," Levi commented after a pause. I grunted.

"The split in it kept falling open every time she moved. I swear, I've been gritting my teeth through a semi the entire day. And these fucking pants," I sat up and kicked them into the wall, "They let everyone see just how riled up I was."

Levi snorted out a laugh down the phone. "I think the dress had nothing to do with it. If it'd been any other woman in the car with you, wearing that same thing, you wouldn't have given a shit. But it was Georgie. You could get hard over her wearing a fucking clown suit."

I hated that he was right. I hated that I couldn't so much as glance at her without thinking about lifting up that dress and bending her over. And then she'd gotten out of the Ute and 'accidentally' flashed me her entire arse, bare except for that one taunting string tucked between her cheeks.

Fuck, I was getting hard again, and without a pair of insanely tight pants to somewhat stem the blood shooting to my dick.

"She's playing with me, Lev," I growled darkly. "She's set this up to make me look like the biggest idiot alive, because she has a personal vendetta against me."

"Jesus fuck, Xan, listen to yourself! Just because you're still obsessed with her after a fucking decade, doesn't mean *her* world revolves around *you*. Deflate that fucking ego of yours!"

I took a breath to swear at him some more when there was a knock on the door. I froze. It could only be one of two people. Georgie, or her sassy blue-haired assistant. The assistant who, on the drive out of town to this 'farm stay', had landed some stinging little barbs that had fired me up about my evening to the point that I'd just had a bloody meltdown over my pants as soon as I was alone. Honestly, I couldn't decide which one of them I'd hate to see on the other side of the door more at that moment.

"Gotta go, Lev. Someone's at the door."

"Call me tomorrow, after seven. I don't need my innocent daughter hearing you swearing like a fucking sailor."

I managed a huff of laughter as I hung up. His daughter heard just as bad from her own father's mouth.

The knock sounded again, louder this time.

"Give me a damn second!" I snapped, getting up and finding a pair of running shorts to tug on over my boxer briefs. At least my hard-on had waned enough that it wasn't too obvious in the shorts.

I tripped my way back down the loft ladder and wrenched the door open. My eyes fell on a blonde ponytail.

She was still in that fucking dress, looking up at me with eyes that gave absolutely nothing away. It was as if I'd imagined the little flashes of emotion I'd thought she'd let slip throughout the day. All those moments where her eyes had widened slightly, her lips parting, the silver of her eyes darkening. This was Georgie wearing a mask.

I fucking hated that mask more than anything else.

"What do you want?" I snapped, reaching up and leaning a hand on the door frame as I glared down at her. With a zing of satisfaction, I watched as her eyes slid down my body, her throat bobbing in a swallow as her gaze slid over my crotch. My dick twitched.

Anger. Lust. That was all I felt looking at her.

"How's your accommodation?" Georgie asked, leaning to one side to sneak a peek under my arm. Politeness told me to move aside, let her see it properly. But I didn't budge, just sneered down at her.

"Did you organize it?" I asked instead. She met my gaze for a split second and nodded before trying to look through me again.

"A local farmer started making tiny homes for a bit of extra income recently. I thought it would be nice to have you living in one of them, give his side business a bit of a kick—he's very grateful for the exposure."

I straightened, folded my arms across my chest and turned to take a proper look around the place—I'd been too angry to bother earlier.

The exterior was clad in timber. Georgie was standing on a small porch kitted out with a chair and table. The interior was cosy —there was a living nook with a TV and a built-in love seat and a dog bed that Molly had already claimed and was snoring quietly in.

The kitchen had a table for two, stainless steel benchtops and a small oven and a two-burner cooktop, a half dishwasher and a narrow fridge/freezer.

Through a door was a shower room. And then of course there was the ladder to the loft and the king bed I'd climbed up to and collapsed on earlier without even really absorbing my surroundings.

"It's … fine," I managed. It was more than fine. Whoever the guy was who made them had an eye for style as well as for function- ality. But I wasn't about to compliment it, not after the day Georgie had put me through.

"Well," she muttered, clearing her throat as I turned back to her. She tugged on the end of her ponytail, and my blood heated. She always used to do that as a teen when she was nervous. Perhaps I wasn't just imagining there were some actual emotions lurking beneath her mask.

"Let's talk schedule," Georgie continued, flipping the straight length of her hair over her shoulder. "Tomorrow, Jord or I will bring breakfast to you—the boys will come to film you eating and giving a tour of the tiny home. Then we're off to the clinic, so you can really get your hands dirty with settling in there."

"And then I have to wine and dine a pervy old woman. I'm guessing that was just another part of your plan?" I asked, taking a step down onto the porch. Georgie met my gaze, that spark of defi- ance I recalled so well from our youth lighting up her eyes, even as she took a step back to put some distance between us.

"We're making unscripted television, Dr Fox," she said primly, smoothing down her dress. The action made me think about those tanned legs underneath and that pert butt I'd gotten an eyeful of earlier.

"Unscripted, you say?" My voice was gravelly with suppressed fury … suppressed desire. I took another step towards her. She swallowed again, running her fingers through her ponytail, but she didn't back away. Her jaw twitched. My dick twitched. The rational part of my brain twitched—switched off.

I leaned closer, wrapping my fist around her hair, tugging her head to the side so I could tilt my lips against her ear. A tiny hiss of breath escaped her, and I felt it ghost across my skin like a zap of electricity right down to my soul.

"Because you told me to park under a tree that every fucking budgerigar in … well in fucking Budgerigar uses as their evening toilet. That didn't feel unscripted to me."

"It was—" Georgie started, but before she could get another word out, I gripped her shoulder and spun her until she was pressed against the siding of the tiny home. Her hands smacked against the timber with a satisfying slap. My palm slid down from her shoulder, grazing over the curve of her breast until I gripped her hip, digging my fingers into her flesh, pressing my front against her back. Crowding her.

What are you doing, Xander?

But I couldn't stop, even if I wanted to. Eight hours in the car with her and then all the shit she'd pulled all evening had addled my brain until all I could think about was my anger … and my lust.

It didn't help that Georgie let out a little mewl, arching her back, which rubbed her arse against my erection.

"And that old bat pulling a gun on me … are you going to tell me that was unscripted too?" I growled against her cheekbone.

"She went rogue," Georgie mumbled, her voice thick. "She was only supposed to ream you out, not hold you at gunpoint."

I grunted. She moaned. I shot harder, if that were even possible, as I tugged on her ponytail again until her head was tilted back, and I could look at her face.

Her lips were moist, parted. Her eyes shimmered silver in the moonlight. I'd expected her to be furious, to fight me. Instead, with a vindictive gleam in her eyes, she pressed the seam of her arse up against my dick, and rocked it very deliberately, a tiny smirk playing at the corners of her lips.

She knew I was closer to the edge than her.

Fury. Lust.

"And your 'accidental' arse flashing when you got out of the car?" I muttered against the soft skin of her cheek. "How unscripted was that?"

"That was completely unintended, you arsehole!" she snarled.

"So you didn't tuck your dress up inside your G-string and taunt me with that perky backside, just so I'd make a fool of myself getting out of the car sporting a very evident boner?" I replied, rubbing said boner against her backside. She melted against me, even as she smirked spitefully.

"It's not my fault you're incapable of controlling your penis, Dr Fox," she purred.

Red clouded my vision, and I tugged harder on her hair. She gasped, her pupils dilating and her cheeks pinking, but she stared up at me defiantly.

"Maybe not, but you've been getting off on the sudden power you have over me, haven't you, Blondie?"

"Feels like *you're* getting off on controlling *me*, right about now." Georgie's scoff turned to a gasp as I released her hip, snaking my hand around to her front.

"Tell me to stop, then," I muttered, my fingers inching up under her dress. I groaned against her cheekbone as she parted her legs wider, giving me better access. My fingers skated up the smooth, silky skin of her thigh. Her breaths got shorter, sharper.

"You're getting off on how on-edge you've got me, aren't you?" I mumbled, hooking my thumb around the teeny scrap of fabric covering her pussy. "Tell me to stop."

"Why would I do that?" she panted, licking her lips as I slipped a single finger along her folds.

She was bare, her skin soft and smooth, and so damned slippery with her arousal. I tugged on her ponytail again, my dick pulsing when she groaned softly. I ground myself against her arse, sliding my finger along the hot wetness, pressing until I was only slightly breaching her entrance.

"You're soaked, Blondie," I hissed, my dick jerking wildly

against her. "Is that because you love controlling me?" I pushed my finger into her, and her mouth fell open on a gasp, her eyes locked on mine, pupils overtaking those metallic irises. Her hips rocked again, taking my finger deeper, her walls squeezing me as she rubbed her backside against my cock.

I groaned, slipping my finger from her warm, tight pussy and finding her swollen clit, circling the slippery pad of my finger around it. "Or is it because you're enjoying your punishment?"

I tugged on her hair again. Her throat was so exposed to me like this. I could see it vibrate as she keened at my touch. A sheen of sweat coated her skin. I wanted to lick and nibble my way up the side of her neck like I'd never wanted anything in my life. My dick was painfully hard, and it would be a matter of a split second to pull it out of my shorts, tug that G-string aside and sink into her welcoming heat.

"This is a *punishment*?" she gasped, her fingers clawing against the wall, "So you're going to punish me with … with orgasms?" Her words broke off with a strangled moan, legs trembling and pussy fluttering as I thrust two fingers into her. "Is this supposed to be a disincentive?"

What the fuck are you doing, Xander? Where's your professionalism now?

With a stifled growl, I dragged my fingers out of her, released her ponytail, stepped back. I clenched my jaw so tightly my teeth creaked. Georgie dropped her head, rolling her neck. A pang of guilt fired through me—had I tugged her head back so far it hurt her? She remained facing the wall as she dragged her dress back down around her legs, smoothing it with hands that shook.

I looked down at my own shaking hands. Her arousal glistened on my fingers. I fisted them, trying to claw back my anger with her, but it was sinking under other, more visceral emotions. I swallowed hard.

"This never happened," I grunted as I made my way for the door, racing inside and closing it before she had a chance to speak again.

Now: Molly The Sheep Violator

GEORGIE

I barely dared to breathe for a good five minutes after I heard the shower turn on inside the tiny home. And when I did, it was to suck in lungful after trembling lungful of country oxygen.

He'd given me an out, told me to tell him to stop. I'd been stubborn, wanting to win … and enjoying what he was doing to me far too much. He'd come to his senses before I had. And I was left throbbing and unsatisfied, and reeling from how much I wanted to follow him inside and finish what we'd just started.

"I hate him," I reminded myself, turning on wobbly legs and teetering off the porch and into the darkness. Thankfully I could traverse this paddock drunk and with my eyes closed.

"I hate him," I muttered, my anger finally flaring over how he'd completely owned my body. How I'd actively encouraged him to do it. I might hate him, but right at that moment I was stupidly craving more of what he'd been doing to me. Hell, the way he'd tugged on my hair, stretching my neck and making me meet his dark, hungry eyes … I knew I'd be replaying that in bed while I tried to recreate the feeling of his long fingers inside me.

The part of me that remembered what he'd done to me that night, and everything that had come after because of it, that part of me hated him. The part that fired up at his controlling touch, the part that flooded my body with hormones … that was a complication I didn't need. I had a job to do. I was just here to make interesting television.

You're a little bit here to push his buttons, a sly voice in my head reminded me.

The kitchen light was still on in the mostly dark house. Mim had waited up for me. I glanced down at my watch to find with a rush of guilt that it was almost eleven—well past her bedtime when she woke at four. I should have gone to greet her rather than knocking on Xander's door. Everything I'd had to say to him could have been done over text. Or conveyed with Jordyn as my messenger.

I didn't want to admit that I'd needed to see him again. I could feel the same feelings I'd had as a teen bubbling up in me—that hit of adrenaline when my eyes met his. Only now it was tainted with what had happened twelve years ago—his callous cruelty towards me at a very vulnerable moment. And all of my subsequent mistakes—mistakes he never needed to find out about.

And now that adrenaline spike was mingled with an addictive hit of dopamine from his fingers, his dirty mouth.

Get all of that out of your system tonight, Georgie … alone, I told myself as I stepped up onto the creaky old wraparound verandah and reached for the kitchen doorknob. *Work that tension out and get back on your game tomorrow.*

"Mim," I called out softly. She might have fallen asleep waiting for me. Or she might have gone to bed and just left the light on for me.

"About bloody time!" My grandmother's voice was sharp. She appeared in the loungeroom doorway.

One look at her weathered, grinning face, those beady eyes taking me in, cataloguing everything about me, had my breath shuddering from my lungs, had my hands trembling.

"What's wrong, my Georgie?" she asked, concern lacing her tone as she strode across the room with the speed and agility of a woman much younger than her sixty-seven years.

"I can't do it," I mumbled, sinking into a chair at the little Formica kitchen table. "This was a huge mistake."

Mim plonked herself into the chair beside me and turned me so that I was facing her. "Is this about the boy? What's he done this time?" she asked. I shook my head, swallowing down as much of my emotions as I possibly could.

"It's not him," I whispered, although it absolutely was him. But it was me, too. "I just don't think we can work together, and not end up killing each other." Or making everything infinitely worse with more of what we'd just done. "I don't have the … control I need around him."

"You won't let this silly boy beat you, Georgina Menzies!" Mim snapped, gripping my chin and tilting my head until I was forced to meet her steely gaze. Her eyes sparked the way mine did when I was feeling particularly determined. "Now, what can I do to help you feel more in control?"

I toyed with the end of my ponytail as I tried to sort out my whirling thoughts. My neck was sore from how he'd tugged it back. But even as I remembered, my body heated, ached at the thought.

"Mim, have you still got your hairdressing kit?" I asked, hurrying the words out before I could lose my nerve.

Mim's eyes narrowed. "Yes. I'll need to sharpen the scissors— they haven't been used in a long time. Why?"

I took my phone out, and with shaking hands, I navigated through my Pinterest app and flipped the screen around to show her.

"I need it gone."

I stared in the mirror as Mim fiddled with the band around my ponytail.

"Are you sure about this, Georgie?" she asked, holding the length to the side so I could see just how much she was about to cut off. I nodded resolutely.

"Yes. Do it."

With a shrug, Mim took to my hair with her scissors. My breath spiked as she sawed through the thick length. I hadn't had more than the tiniest hair trim in as long as I could remember.

And then she snipped through the last of it, and my head was suddenly light. Quite literally.

"I had no idea how heavy that was to carry around!" I exclaimed as the shorter, jagged strands fell around my face. Mim watched me, expression inscrutable, in the mirror.

"Well. Let me tidy it all up for you. Are you sure about the fringe? It's a big step, you know."

I shrugged. "We've come this far, may as well go all out!" My voice sounded manic. My eyes were shining too brightly as I stared at my reflection, my hair barely scraping my shoulders as Mim sectioned it out and began styling it properly.

"Why the hair?" Mim asked. I chewed on my top lip. How much honesty to give her?

"It's been on my mind for months now," I replied. Not a lie—I had a whole folder of chin-length bob hairstyles that I'd been consistently adding to on Pinterest. "But he … touched it tonight. And I don't want him to be able to do that again."

I'd liked it far, far too much. And I couldn't like things he did to me. I hated him too much for that.

"Well. I'm glad it wasn't a knee-jerk reaction, then," Mim said with a roll of her eyes. "It will suit you like this, though. A big change."

A big change was what I needed. Something to remind myself—and Dr Fox—that I wasn't the same girl I'd been twelve years ago.

"Why was he touching your hair?"

I grimaced. That was not a question I wanted to give my grandmother an honest answer to. *'Oh, he just totally owned my body, had my throat exposed as he fingered me, while accusing me of all sorts of nefarious stuff, and I ground my butt against his very impressive erection, and it was the hottest sexual experience I've had since that threesome in university you know nothing about.'*

Nope. Mim knew a hell of a lot about me. But she didn't need to know that.

As Mim finished working her way around my head, tidying and trimming and giving me bangs for the first time in my life, I heard it.

The clip clop of cloven hooves in the hallway. My lips stretched into a grin as I glanced up at Mim.

"You didn't lock him in the laundry for the night?" I asked. She shook her head, her disapproving glare at odds with the way her mouth tweaked up at the corners.

"I figured you'd want to see him. He probably woke up and heard you. Now, sit still for a minute more, I'm almost done."

I could barely contain my jitters as Mim checked that everything was even, and I barely even glanced at the finished product in the mirror before leaping off the stool, giving Mim a quick hug, and sticking my head out around the door.

"Jumbo!" I called softly into the darkness. Twin spots of light appeared at the far end of the hallway, and then he was galloping, and I was kneeling and holding my arms out to him.

"He remembers my voice!" I mumbled against his fleece as Jumbo, my pet sheep, nuzzled into my neck. I sniffed, tears rolling down my face as my emotional day overwhelmed me.

"Of course he remembers your voice!" Mim chastised me. "You're the reason he's alive, for crying out loud!"

Jumbo sniffed around my dress, trying to find a non-existent pocket for the treat he always expected from me. I let out a watery giggle.

"Sorry mate, no treats tonight. In the morning, I promise. Oh God, it's been too long. He was still mostly a baby last time I saw him!"

"It was over a year ago," Mim reminded me. "Sheep grow fast, Georgie."

After a big cuddle with my now fully grown dwarf sheep, I walked him back to the laundry, where he settled down once more in his dog bed.

"Bloody pampered little twerp," Mim grouched, but her eyes were soft. "And now I really need to go to sleep. It's well past my bedtime." She eyed me up and down.

"You look beautiful with your hair like that, my Georgie. Softer."

She reached a tanned hand out to stroke my cheek before turning and heading for her bedroom.

I didn't know what to think about that. Soft had never been my aim. Soft wasn't someone I wanted to be.

But at the very least, it might throw Xander off whatever was going on in his head.

Yes, because changing yourself to unsettle Xander Fox is a really stable, sensible thing to do.

My body clock was set to wake me at five am, and being in Budgerigar was no exception.

After saying goodnight to Mim the night before, I'd showered, finally looking at my new reflection properly, marvelling at how the lines of the bob and the fringe did, in fact, soften my features.

And then I'd gone to bed and given myself an orgasm while tilting my head back as far as I could, trying to recreate the feel of what he'd done to me earlier. It had worked … sort of. It had been enough to help me to drift into a dreamless sleep.

I hopped out of bed and changed into some running clothes. *I can do this,* I decided. *I can work with him for three months.*

My gaze wandered out the window as I tucked what was left of my hair under a baseball cap and went off to do what I did every morning at five am. Go for a run.

In Sydney, running was done on my treadmill while listening to a podcast or having Siri read me my emails. My triathlon habits hadn't died, even though I hadn't competed since high school. Running, swimming, cycling. I still did all three on a regular basis.

The early morning sun tinted the sky that hazy, lemony colour that heralded a hot summer day. I pounded through the scraggly grass around the house, pausing only to open and close the gate that led to the fields.

I kicked up dust as I ran, and my breath caught in my chest— not from exertion, but from the realisation that the drought had gotten far, far worse than Mim had let on over the phone to me in the last year.

I hadn't transferred my signing bonus from Reelflix yet. I resolved to do that as soon as I got back to the house. Fodder and water were hugely expensive, and I wasn't going to try and have the chat with Mim again about it maybe being time to think about retiring.

'Your grandfather would roll over in his grave if I gave up this land, Georgina! I'll be carted off this farm in a box, and I'll haunt you until the end of your days if you even think about selling it when I'm gone!'

I knew a lost argument when I heard one.

The sheep looked curiously up at me as I jogged past them, and before long, I had a conga line of them following me, hopeful that I was bringing the food. Then the rumble of a tractor distracted them, and they all turned and galloped off towards Mim.

She drove into the paddock, her two working Border Collies, Tater and Pea, trailing behind. She left the tractor idling while she clambered onto the trailer to break up bales of fodder and throw them out into the paddock. The sheep fell on them with gusto. Poor hungry things.

I followed, wordlessly climbing up beside Mim and helping her to distribute the feed.

"You didn't tell me how bad it was," I accused quietly. Mim didn't respond immediately, but her tight lips spoke volumes.

"It's not your concern, Georgie. I've got it under control." She hopped down, motioning for me to follow. I did, and without a word, she climbed back into the tractor, turning it towards the shed.

She could say that all she liked, but it *was* my concern. My signing bonus would go a little way to helping. I knew she'd grouch, snarl, and try to make me take it back. What she always failed to recognise was that I got my stubbornness from her.

I followed at a walk, the sun already baking the ground. I glanced warily towards the tiny home, nestled against the backdrop of a stand of eucalyptus. The caravans that Jord and the crew were using were parked on the other side of the trees to give the illusion that Xander was out here alone.

Xander's abode was visible from my bedroom window in Mim's house. I knew this because I'd stared at it intently while dressing that morning.

Sweat was making my head itch, but there was no way I was taking off the cap. I would have some wicked hat hair, and I couldn't let Xander see my new hairstyle looking anything less than perfectly coiffed.

Why? Because I was an idiot. Plain and simple.

As if on cue, the door of the little timber house opened, and Xander stepped out, a black streak that was Molly zooming onto the grass and immediately squatting for a wee.

My footsteps faltered.

He was shirtless, in the running shorts he'd had on the night before. The ones that hadn't done anything but emphasise the dragon he was packing between his legs. His chest was broad—much wider than it had been as a teen—and the ripple of abs and pecs as he absently scratched at his stomach had my mouth dropping open.

In his other hand, he cradled a mug, taking a sip as he watched Molly cavorting on the lawn between the tiny home and Mim's heritage-listed homestead. Then, almost in slow motion, he turned, and his eyes locked with mine, a tiny smile twitching at the corners of his mouth.

I snapped my jaw shut with a clack and turned away from him, stalking back toward the house. Molly galloped up to me, and because she was adorable, and she didn't deserve to have me ignore her just because I hated her dad, I crouched down to give her a proper greeting.

"Hey lovely girl," I crooned, cupping her jaw and scratching behind her ears. She panted merrily at me until the sound of a screen door slamming had her turning and galumphing off again. I stood, a grin spreading across my face as Jumbo came trotting around the side of the house. Mim must've let him out when she got back.

Molly approached Jumbo with just the slightest hesitation, her tail dropping between her legs when Jumbo bleated at her. He was used to dogs. Molly clearly had never met a sheep in her life.

"She's intrigued."

I jumped at the deep, mellow sound of his voice in my ear. Instinctively I folded my arms across my chest, refusing to look in his direction.

'This never happened.'

I had to remember that. Last night hadn't happened. He hadn't left me dripping, and wanting, more aroused than I'd been in years, and a hairsbreadth away from bending over for him on the porch of his tiny home.

I cleared my throat, watching as Molly and Jumbo sniffed at one another. Molly's tail began a slow, tentative wag.

"She'll fit in just fine here," I said. Xander grunted, lifting the coffee mug to his lips. I was all too aware of the heat of his body, so very close, so very unclothed.

Was he as on edge as I felt right now?

"Should I prepare for worse than yesterday?" he asked, taking another sip of his coffee.

I chewed on my lips to stop them from quirking up at the corners, keeping my eyes fixed firmly on the odd dance that dog and sheep were doing with one another.

"Unscripted television, remember? There are no guarantees, Dr Fox. Has Jordyn dropped your breakfast off to you?"

"Mmm," he mumbled. "The guys are still inside getting some footage of the interior. I … needed a bit of space."

I glanced at him from the corner of my eye. The defined bulges of his upper arms and shoulders swam into view. "Did Jordyn ask you to remain shirtless for breakfast?"

The spread of his grin was visible even in profile.

"No. That was *all* me."

Hell.

I narrowed my eyes at him, suddenly certain that he was trying to turn the tables on me today.

Because he couldn't possibly be … flirting … with me. Could he?

"Can't believe you managed to tuck all of that hair into a little baseball cap, Blondie. I kind of want to take it off, just to see it tumble free."

No, I'd been right the first time. He was trying to throw me.

Well, two could play at that game. I almost felt like tearing the cap off myself, shocking him with the lack of the ponytail he thought he'd controlled me with last night.

I supposed, technically, he had controlled me with it. But I was conveniently discounting that particular fact.

Only the hat-hair situation stopped me from doing it. Perfection was power, and I could have that. Once I'd washed and dried and styled myself into that role.

A frantic bleat brought me out of my reverie, and I looked over to where Molly and Jumbo were playing.

Well, they weren't playing anymore.

"Get your dog off my sheep!" I screeched, stumbling forward in horror at the sight of Molly mounted on poor Jumbo's little body, her rear end rocking back and forth on him. Humping him.

Xander sighed, striding forwards a few steps. "Molly, no!" he said sternly, snapping his fingers. Molly looked at him, then back at Jumbo, so small beneath her, and kept going.

"Oh my God, is that the best you can do?" I shrieked. "You're supposed to be a vet for crying out loud! She's ... she's violating him!"

"She's just playing. It's a phase." Xander sounded so wholly unconcerned that I turned to him with a snarl.

"Oh, just a phase, is it? We're condoning inter-species sexual assault now, are we? She's assaulting my sheep!"

Xander smirked at me, crossing his arms over his chest. "She's a spayed female dog. She's not assaulting your sheep." Xander's brows furrowed. "Hold on ... *your* sheep? Why the hell do you have a sheep?"

I strode forward and grabbed Molly's collar, hauling her back. "Naughty, Molly! No humping!" I said in the sternest, deepest, most dominant voice I could manage.

She flopped free of my grip, rolling over onto her back and

sticking all four feet in the air. Jumbo sniffed at her belly, apparently completely unconcerned that he'd just been attacked by a delinquent teenage dog. Xander strolled up and rubbed at her exposed belly with one thong-clad foot.

My jaw ached from grinding it so hard, and I stood in a burst, glaring at him. "You're rewarding her for … for terrible behaviour!" I hissed, leaning down and scooping Jumbo into my arms. He bleated in protest, squirming. But I was going to win that battle of wills if it was the last thing I did. He was going to be comforted by me, whether he wanted it or not.

"For fuck's sake, Georgie, no harm was done!"

For a second, my voice caught in my throat. He'd said my name. Not Blondie, not … not Gina, or Ms Menzies, or any other insulting nickname.

I cleared my throat, locking my muscles against the struggling sheep in my arms. I must've looked ridiculous, but I couldn't even care. I met his dancing hazel eyes.

"Your horny dog attempted rape on my poor, innocent little lamb!"

Xander's head fell back as a burst of laughter bubbled out of him. "You can't be serious!"

I scowled, then grunted as Jumbo's hoof collided with my stomach. I doubled over, dropping Jumbo, who galloped off around the side of the house with Molly in hot pursuit. For a moment, I had that awful, I think I'm going to die sensation of not being able to draw in a breath.

"Shit, Blondie, are you alright?" Xander asked. His big, warm hands cupped my shoulders as I fought to drag air into my lungs. I couldn't even muster up enough breath to tell him I was fine, to let me go.

"Hey, Georgie. You're just winded, okay? Don't panic." The heat of his breath whispered across my ear, and I turned, managing to suck in the slightest hiss of breath when I found him crouching down beside me, his face so close to mine, hazel eyes wide and flicking between mine. A hint of dark gold stubble on his defined jaw, full lips parted.

How was I supposed to get my breath back with him so close to me, looking so concerned? As if he actually cared.

"What's going on here? Is she okay?" Mim demanded, her footsteps thumping on the hard-packed ground. And suddenly, I was able to breathe again, and I gasped shakily, dragging my gaze from Xander's warm eyes and very warm chest, turning to Mim.

"I'm okay," I panted.

"She just took a sheep hoof to the diaphragm," Xander explained, standing up. His hands left my shoulders, and despite the hot morning, the air felt cold on my skin. I got to my feet, turning to face Mim, who was eyeing Xander with tight lips and cold eyes.

"You're the vet?" she asked.

Xander, either not realising Mim was shooting daggers with her eyes at him, or choosing to ignore it, extended a hand, and flashed those godforsaken dimples at her.

"That's me. But you can call me Xander."

Mim sniffed, gripping his hand like she wished it was his throat.

"It's nice to meet you, Mrs …" Xander prompted. Mim eyed his naked chest with disdain. I hid a smirk behind my hand. She couldn't have reacted more differently to Liz last night.

"Mrs Menzies. Miriam," Mim replied just as the silence stretched past polite. I watched Xander from under my lashes as he did a double take at the surname, then turned to raise a questioning eyebrow at me.

I sighed. There was no point in trying to be coy now. He was living here for three months.

"Xander, this is my grandmother. She's very kindly allowed us to set up on her property for the duration of filming."

Xander's lips parted as he looked from me to Mim, and back again.

"Thank you, Mrs Menzies," he said softly. "I remember … I can see the family resemblance now."

Mim scoffed, but I watched Xander. I thought I still knew enough about his mannerisms to know when he was feeding someone a suave line and when he was being genuine. And this felt like the latter to me, which made my head spin.

What was his game here?

"Morning G!" Jord said merrily, and I turned to find them standing behind me, with Jase, the cameraman ... who was filming. "That little sheep got you good, didn't it?"

I glared at Jase until he grimaced and let the camera drop. "Sorry Georgie. But it was just such a fun interaction, I ..."

I raised my hand, and he fell silent immediately. I didn't fail to notice Xander chuckling behind me as I faced Jord.

"A word. Inside," I hissed, nodding towards the house and striding off without checking that they were following me.

"I'd better go get dressed. We've got a busy day ahead of us today," I heard Xander say behind us as I stepped onto the verandah.

"Yes, I'd highly recommend not putting yourself in Liz's crosshairs with that ... on display," Mim said.

I grinned, imagining Mim gesturing in distaste at Xander's rippling torso.

"Great advice. I definitely don't need to give her any more ammunition."

As I opened the screen door, I thought I heard Mim chuckle.

"We don't have to use the footage, G," Jord said as I rounded on them once we were both inside. "We just came out onto the deck and saw Molly playing with the little lamb, and it was adorable, and I told Jase to catch it. And then things escalated so quickly, and he just kept rolling."

I took my hat off, almost sighing in relief as I dragged my fingernails over my sweaty scalp. "Look. I get it. We film more than we need, catch everything we can, and pare it back from there. But I—"

"Your hair!"

I blinked. "Oh! Right, yes. Mim cut it for me last night."

"Why?" Jord wailed. "Your hair is ... was so beautiful! And it's all gone!"

I wrinkled my nose at them. "It's not all gone. I just needed a change, that's all." I hoped the flush that was creeping up my neck wasn't too obvious. But if it was, I could pass it off as being hot and having just run halfway around the property.

"I'm going to need a minute to come to terms with this," Jord muttered, and a bubble of laughter burst out of me.

"Well, you always wear black anyway, if you want to count it towards mourning for my lost ponytail. In fact, would you like me to go and get it? I kept it, but you could have it you know, if you wanted to snuggle up to it in bed tonight?"

Jord managed to rally with a sarcastic roll of their eyes. "Go get showered and dressed. I told Xander we'd leave at eight to head into the clinic. Am I riding with him again today?"

I thought about that for a moment. Would I unsettle him more climbing into the Ute with him, where he had no one around to filter his reaction to my new look? Or would it be better to catch him off guard, strut into the clinic while he was elbow-deep in getting the place sorted out?

I stopped, telling myself firmly that it didn't matter. That it wasn't about the little game I had planned for Xander.

Be professional, get through three months, go our separate ways.

The thought left a bad taste in my mouth, and I found myself telling Jord that I'd ride with Dr Fox into town. And then, before they could interrogate me further, I escaped to the shower.

Now: The Flipping Chemistry

XANDER

Nope. I wasn't going to react. Clearly that was what she was aiming for. Damn her, she was trying to kill me.

I bit the inside of my cheek—hard—as I opened the passenger door for her. I tried my bloody best not to stare intently at her backside as she climbed into the monster truck, wearing tiny cut-off denim shorts and a white tank top with skinny straps. So much tanned skin on display.

And her fucking hair.

Don't stare. Don't say anything. Pretend you haven't even noticed.

Of course she knows you've noticed, you moron. You told her you wanted to watch her hair tumble out of that cap just an hour ago.

And the whole time, she would've known there was no long hair to tumble out.

I tried valiantly not to think about last night, about tugging her head back with the now missing ponytail. And failed in the most miserable way.

But now all I could see was her neck, her throat, those exposed shoulders beneath the short hairstyle. All demanding my attention without the thick length of hair in the way.

And then, when I climbed behind the wheel and glanced over at her, I swallowed hard at the way the fringe softened her silvery eyes, made her cheeks look fuller, her lips more …

Nope. Not going to react.

I cleared my throat and started the ignition, reversing in an arc and heading back along the drive that I'd navigated in the dark last night, and out onto the dusty dirt road.

"So, just to clarify," I began, drumming my fingers on the wheel as Georgie fiddled with the camera mounted just below the rear-view mirror. She clicked it on, acknowledging me with a grunt before relaxing back into her seat.

"We're staying on your grandmother's farm. The same grandmother you used to write to back in high school. Your grandmother, who, I'm guessing, knows about us …"

"Mim was kind enough to offer her top paddock for accommodation. She won't be involved in the day to day of filming. Now that we've done the walk-through of the tiny home, I anticipate that most of the filming will happen elsewhere."

Well, that was a 'shut up and don't talk about our past' if I ever heard one. I tried not to let it rankle. The way her grandmother had glared at me, she absolutely knew what had gone down twelve years ago. If I'd thought yesterday that the next three months were going to be tense, things just got worse.

"Now you've had a night to sleep on it, what are your thoughts on the clinic, Dr Fox?" Georgie asked.

I glanced at her as she crossed one leg over the other, her sneaker-clad foot tapping at the centre console. Her thigh muscles contracted with each tap, and I had to white-knuckle the steering wheel to stop myself from reaching over and resting my palm on that taut skin.

I chewed on my lip as I tried to switch my brain onto her question and away from interpreting every little movement she made as something overtly sexual.

Last night never happened, I reminded myself.

I hadn't pressed her up against the wall and fingered her as I rocked my dick against her arse while she squirmed against me wantonly.

I hadn't gone into the bathroom after and immediately rubbed one out with her slippery arousal still coating my fingers. Christ, she'd been so wet.

I hadn't fallen into bed still hearing the breathy noises she'd made as I tilted her head back almost too far. Hadn't drifted off imagining sucking and biting at the skin on her neck until it was peppered with hickeys.

No, none of that had happened.

It couldn't have happened. Because we were both here to be professional and get this show made so we could get on with our separate lives once it was over.

"The clinic, Dr Fox?" Georgie said. "Thoughts? What's the next step, in your eyes?" I sniffed, ignoring the ache in my cock.

"It's clear the old fellow hadn't done much updating in years. If we're going to do this right, we need to give the place a facelift. Not just that, we need to get the records digitised—he was still keeping handwritten notes on his patients, and his inventory and invoices are a complete mess. None of that is my area of expertise."

Georgie was silent for a long moment as I navigated onto the sealed road that headed back into Budgerigar. It was probably not what she wanted to hear, but I wasn't about to lie. The place was barely usable as a clinic. It was dingy, outdated, and uninviting.

"I'm going to need someone who can get the back-of-house stuff in order, and we'll have to hire some contractors to revamp the waiting room and the treatment room, at the very least. New exam and operating tables … the cages in the holding area wouldn't meet code. And what little is left in consumables is out of date.

"And I'll need to hire a vet nurse, and a receptionist. I'm not sure how busy the clinic is, so we could probably get someone who can manage both jobs."

Georgie blew out a long breath. "So, to summarise. New flooring, new paint job, new fixtures and fittings, consumables, and staff. Anything else?"

"Nothing off the top of my head. But I don't know how we'll manage to have it finished and up and running within three months. I can't imagine tradies are thick on the ground out here."

"I'll get it done."

I eyed her, nostalgia like a bolt of lightning shuddering through me at the excited gleam in her eyes. How could I have forgotten how much Georgie loved a challenge?

She had her phone to her ear and was barking instructions to whoever was on the other end within ten seconds.

"Morning Lou, I've got a bunch of jobs for you ... yes, urgently required in Budgerigar ... a flooring contractor, a painter, I'd hazard a plumber and electrician as well ... a skip bin will be a priority ... yes ... and we'll need to get a delivery of furniture and fittings, and veterinary consumables ... computers ... yes, a reception desk ... I'll have Dr Fox compile a detailed list and send it through to you ... okay ... thanks Lou ... no, you need to stay in head office, I need you editing ... send one of the boys, if necessary ... you too, bye."

She hung up and turned to me. "We can have materials and labour arriving out here within forty-eight hours. You need to do a full inventory today, what we can keep, what we need to move on. What renovations are needed. What consumables and equipment you require. I'll need a list by midday, so we can have it delivered tomorrow evening. You can close your mouth, Dr Fox."

I lifted my jaw off the floor with an effort.

"Forty-eight hours?" I repeated. "And then what?"

She turned to me, and I lost my breath as that wicked grin I remembered like it was my own spread across her face.

"Then we make that clinic all yours."

"What about this space?" Jordyn prompted as I stepped into what Liz's late husband had been using as his filing room. Not that I thought much filing had been going on in there. Ever.

"We'll need to rip up the carpet in here," I said to the camera, wrinkling my nose at the smell. "Pretty sure that whichever dogs have had free range in the clinic have used this as their toilet at one time or another. Vinyl laminate flooring, same as the rest. It's easy to clean when you're in the business of pet bodily fluids. Even in the office spaces."

I navigated around a teetering pile of manila folders, Jase tracking my movements. I wasn't sure I'd ever get the hang of talking into the camera instead of to the person who was asking me questions, but Jordyn had reminded me enough in the last few hours, and in such a sharp tone, that I was afraid of what might happen to me the next time I got it wrong.

Jordyn, with those sharp, black eyes and that electric blue hair, looked like the type to pull out a cattle prod and use it on me.

"We'll have to hire someone to go through this … whatever this mess is," I explained, turning back to the camera and gesturing to the stack of files. "A temp to get the clinic records digitised at the very—"

My foot caught on something soft, and I went down, twisting my body at the last minute to take the brunt of the fall with my hands. The manila folder tower collapsed on top of me and whatever I'd half landed on.

"Oof!"

Whoever I'd half landed on. I pushed aside the mess of folders and yellowing papers to find a pair of wide, silvery eyes, framed by a white-blonde fringe. My groin was pressed into her abdomen, my hands had somehow hit the floor on either side of her face, her knees splayed on either side of my hips. Her body heat seeped into me. There was a strand of hair caught in the corner of her mouth, and before I could talk sense into myself, I'd reached out and smoothed it away, my thumb trailing her lip, her cheek. The smell of herbs and peppermint from her shampoo wafted into my nostrils as she trembled.

"Do you think you could let me up, Dr Fox?" Georgie asked breathlessly, cheeks rosy. Her tongue darted out to wet her bottom lip, and I closed my eyes, trying to unsee everything about this weirdly hot encounter. "I've already been winded by one animal today."

Clearing my throat—trying to clear my head—I jumped as

nimbly to my feet as the tight space and floor scattered with papers would allow.

"What are you doing down there?" I asked. She sat up, running a shaking hand through her hair. Christ, it looked so soft. My fingers twitched.

"I'm sorting through these files," she explained, trying to stand but slipping on a sheet of paper. I reached out and grabbed her hand before she fell. My thumb tucked into her palm, and I couldn't help but run it back and forth against her skin. She sucked in a tiny breath, eyes narrowed as she wrenched free of my grasp.

"Do you think we need to keep the invoices? I can scan them all with my phone and sort them into digital folders, but I'm not sure they'll be relevant. I do have quite a large pile of patient files …" She glanced at the mess strewn around us both. "Well, I did have quite a large pile."

"You … you didn't have to do this," I murmured as she bent to start gathering up the mess. I'd wondered why Jordyn was the one shadowing me this morning. I'd assumed Georgie was trying to put some distance between us after what 'didn't happen' last night.

Distance, and doing an absolute shitload of admin work that wasn't part of her job description.

I knelt, scooping a bunch of the files up from the floor and standing, trying to find a space on the desk that wasn't covered with yet more paperwork.

"Did old mate have anyone doing his admin for him? If he did, they were doing a piss-poor job," I grumbled as Georgie took the pile from me with a half-smile, her eyes flicking towards the door.

"Old mate's wife was in charge of the admin, you young upstart!" Liz's shrill voice blasted into the room. I flinched, turning slowly towards the scowling woman.

"Hello, Liz," I said, fighting against visibly cringing, clenching my fists so I wouldn't tug at the collar of my navy polo shirt. "I just meant that there seems to be a lot of filing that—"

"Oh Xanny," the old woman cooed, stepping into the room, flanked by two Corgis and my own Labrador. I narrowed my eyes at the little traitor as she followed Empress and Kingston into the room, tail wagging. "I can't stay mad at you. I mean, look at that chest!" She practically swooned, grabbing at Georgie's arm melodramatically. "Georgie, darling, have you taken a good gander at that chest?"

Georgie coughed, redness creeping up her neck. I fought a smirk.

"I'm not in the habit of ogling men in my place of work, Liz," she muttered.

Before I could filter, words burst out of my mouth. "Is that so? I reckon you were wishing for x-ray vision yesterday morning when you saw me in those jeans."

Georgie glared at me as if she was now wishing she could shoot fire out of her eyes before turning to Jase. "Cut!" she snarled.

Jordyn scowled in barely concealed mutiny as Jase lowered the camera. "G, if you don't want to interact on-camera, you can't get stuck elbow-deep into things that we need to film!"

Georgie stared Jordyn down. I'd been on the receiving end of that death stare more than once in my teen years. Just the memory of it sent cold chills running up and down my spine. But Jordyn gave it back and then some.

"If you need to film in a room I'm in, a simple heads-up will do the trick, and I'll be out of the way like that." Georgie snapped her fingers.

Jordyn's jaw twitched. "And then how do we explain when suddenly all the admin is up to date, as if by magic?"

Georgie tucked her short hair behind an ear. "I doubt the admin side of things will even make the final cut on this show. It hardly makes for interesting viewing."

"Of course it doesn't, but the flipping chemistry between you and Dr Fox is very, *very* interesting," Jordyn shot back.

Georgie went beet-red, her mouth falling open. Liz cackled and slapped at her leg. I wished the floor would just swallow me whole. Because shit, it wasn't just me feeling ... things. Jordyn could see it clear as day. So much for being professional.

Pretty sure you royally fucked up any chance of that when you felt up her dripping pussy last night.

"This is not a conversation for right now, Jord, and you know it," Georgie admonished. Jordyn had the sense to look away guiltily.

"Liz!" a melodic voice called out from the front of the clinic. "I can hear you laughing, I've just done the local rounds and wanted to see if you knew when the city-slicker and his entourage were arriving."

Footsteps approached the filing room. Georgie's brow furrowed, Jordyn's eyebrows shot up, and Liz practically guffawed.

"Oh, this'll be good," she said with relish.

"Jase, roll camera," Jord muttered. Confusion was written all over Georgie's face.

And then a woman appeared in the doorway. She was wearing sturdy grey work trousers, a pale blue button-up shirt, and steel-capped boots, her glossy brown hair hung in a braid over one shoulder. Her dark skin glowed, and her brown eyes shone as she stopped, her gaze sweeping over the lot of us.

"Pan to Xander," Jordyn whispered, and Jase moved the camera in my direction. I threw a wary glance at the camera, but my eyes were dragged back to the woman in the doorway.

"They're already here!" Liz announced, completely unnecessarily. "Xanny, this is Dr Alexandra Kingston. She's the vet in Millstone who's been doing home visits in Budgerigar once a fortnight since my husband passed." Liz stroked the woman's arm, a sly grin forming on her face. "She's an absolute angel. *And* she's single!"

Alexandra looked mildly horrified as she glanced between Liz and me. "Just call me Alex. It's nice to meet you, uh …"

I took two steps forward, holding my hand out to her. "Xander. I'm the city-slicker. No entourage, unfortunately, unless you count Jase and my two taskmasters here." I gestured to Georgie and Jordyn.

She shook my hand, flashing a brilliantly white, toothy smile. Her grip was firm, her hand warm. She was beautiful.

I felt nothing.

"I'm going to grab some lunch," Georgie muttered. "Jord, get as much footage as necessary of … this," she waved a hand between Alex and me. "I'll be back in a bit."

I pulled my hand from Alex's, my eyes flicking from the curvy brunette to the athletic blonde, who refused to even glance at me as she navigated her way to the door.

"Bit of competition never hurt, Georgie my girl," Liz said as Georgie passed the older woman and disappeared from sight.

"Excuse me for just a moment," I said to Alex. "My puppy hasn't been out for a wee in a while. I'll just …"

No one was fooled, so I stopped making excuses, called Molly to my side, and followed Georgie out.

She'd already disappeared. She must've sprinted out of there to get scarce so fast.

I tugged at my hair, blowing out a long breath as Molly snuffled around in the bushes by the fence before squatting to do her business.

I'd spent the last three hours on-camera, working room by room, talking about how I wanted everything to look, what we would need to get it done, all the while compiling a list on my phone to email to Georgie. I was bloody exhausted from being 'on' all morning. And I still had all afternoon, and dinner with that old hellcat Liz before I could take a break.

I collapsed onto the porch step, dragging my phone out and opening my notes, finishing off what I thought we needed for the office space—the last room in the clinic.

I was attaching it to an email to Georgie when someone sat beside me.

"Sorry about the city-slicker comment," Alex said.

I grunted, hitting send on the email and waiting for the swooshing sound to tell me it was gone before I looked up. "No harm done. I've been called worse in my life."

'You callous man-whore, you broke her fucking heart' … I flinched at the memory.

"Jordyn was telling me that you need to hire a nurse?" Alex leaned forwards, scooping up a budgie feather from the ground and twirling it between her fingers. "I've got two who job-share at the moment, but I reckon I could convince them both to move to full-time so I can lend you one of them. They're both front desk trained, too."

I turned to her then. Her eyes crinkled at the corners as she smiled. "That would … I was quietly freaking out about how to tempt a decent vet nurse out here. Thank you."

She smiled and handed me the feather. "It's a struggle, I'm not going to lie. I was born and bred on the Western Plains, and sometimes even I wonder why I stayed out here. Count yourself lucky that you can leave again once you've finished making your show."

I sighed, staring down the street, wondering where the hell Georgie escaped to. "Yeah. Well, I'm starting to realise that there isn't much waiting for me back in Sydney anyway."

"No girlfriend at home?" she asked quietly. I shook my head.

"Boyfriend?"

"Nope."

"Well, you never know, you might meet the love of your life right here in Budgerigar."

I huffed out a humourless laugh, getting to my feet. If only she bloody knew. Alex followed, dusting her backside and stepping back onto the porch.

"I've got nothing on for the rest of the day, and there's a few things I should clue you in on—there're a lot of very eccentric types in Budgerigar …"

"Of course there are," I grumbled but flashed her a small smile to make it seem like I wasn't too overwhelmed by it all.

Alex chuckled. "Speaking of eccentric types, I hear you're taking Liz out for dinner. Happy to volunteer as tribute to act as a buffer—I know she can be … a lot."

I snorted at that, grinning down at the mischievous gleam in her eyes.

"You really are an angel, aren't you?" I joked.

Of course, that was the exact damn moment the gate creaked, and there was Georgie striding up the path, her face that smooth, emotionless mask she was so bloody good at. She was holding a huge takeaway box. The smell wafting from it was insanely good, and my stomach growled.

"My treat," she said in a clipped tone, picking out a burger with an X on the bag and thrusting it at me unceremoniously. "Works, no beetroot."

She reached into the box and grabbed another out, handing it to Alex. "Hope you like burgers. I've got scallops and chips too, but you'll have to come inside to share those."

Before I could get my mouth to work to thank her, she'd stormed up the stairs. I turned to watch her go, only then realising that Jase and Jord were standing in the doorway, Jase with the camera on his shoulder.

Of course they were.

"Privacy? What the fuck is that?" I muttered to Alex as we followed Georgie. She snorted beside me.

"Alex, I'm Jordyn. We've been liaising via email and phone for a few weeks now. Can I have a quick word?" Jord murmured as we passed. Alex blinked, taking in the vibrant hair, the black clothes.

"Um … yes, of course," she mumbled, all the confidence and openness she'd shown me suddenly vanishing. "Xander, I'll … we'll chat more later."

I raised a curious eyebrow at the suddenly wide-eyed expression on her face, but I shrugged, nodded, and headed inside to eat my custom works burger … because Georgie hadn't forgotten.

I wondered what else she remembered. I wondered if she remembered everything … the way I did.

"Xanny!" Liz's horrified screech echoed from deep inside the clinic, shocking me out of my memories. "Come and discipline your wayward puppy! She's mounting my Kingston in the most pornographic way!"

I sighed. *Three months, Xander. Three months of this, and you can go back to Sydney and forget it ever happened.*

Then: Perky Enough On Your Own

GEORGIE, 14 YEARS OLD

"I can't believe you let Xander talk you into this!" I chortled. Dom scowled, following me out of the back seat of the car. Elena was already at the boot, dragging out camping chairs, an Esky, and a monstrous Thermos, which I was sure was full of coffee. Elena wasn't a morning person. Neither was Dom.

I was.

I grinned at both of them, rubbing my hands together and shouldering my backpack, practically dancing across the carpark towards the soccer field. Dom dragged his feet, eyeing the field with dread.

"Oh, come on, it won't be that bad!" I said, holding my hand out and waiting for him to catch up. He threw me a lopsided smile, linking his fingers with mine. I squeezed his hand reassuringly.

"You used to love soccer back in primary school," I reminded him, but I knew I sounded distracted. I was already looking around for someone tall, with dark blond hair and a smirk that did things to my insides.

"That was back when everyone got an encouragement award at the end of a season, and no one cared if you missed a goal, or tripped over your own feet," Dom muttered.

"Hmm," was all I could manage because there, in a sea of maroon and gold jerseys, was Xander.

Like I was watching in slow motion, he turned towards us. His smile spread so wide those dimples popped, and I coughed around my suddenly dry throat.

Then his eyes flicked down, to my hand in Dom's. With a hiss, I tugged my hand away, my eyes darting back to Xander. The dimples were gone.

Bugger!

"Uh, you'd better get over there with your team, number six," I croaked. Dom looked at me funny before he jogged away. I sighed, heading towards the fence where there was a gap in the gathering spectators wide enough for Elena and me to set up our chairs.

"That crush of yours is going swimmingly, I see," Elena said in my ear, and I jumped, almost colliding with the fence. She smirked at me knowingly. With a humph, I snatched one of the chair bags from her, tugging the chair out angrily.

"I have no idea how to talk to boys," I grumbled as I collapsed into it. Elena sat much more gracefully in hers, watching me thoughtfully.

"You've never had any problems talking to Dominic," she commented.

I sighed. "He's not a boy! Well … he *is* a boy, but … I don't see him like *that*. He's just … Dom."

Elena chuckled. "So, the prickly pear act you've been putting on for Xander every time you see him at our house … that is just you not having a clue how to talk to him? Finally, things make sense!"

I eyed her, caught between curiosity and frustration. "What finally makes sense?" I demanded.

"I thought you were attempting the 'treat him mean, keep him keen' tactic."

"I don't want to be mean to him. I just want to be able to talk to him without feeling like there's something squeezing my lungs closed. Honestly, it wasn't this bad a year ago! Why is it getting worse?"

Elena smiled fondly. "Because you're in deeper. A year ago, he was just a cute boy. Now …"

I sucked in a breath. "Now, what?"

"Well," Elena began, unscrewing the lid of the Thermos and pouring steaming, bitter coffee into a mug. I waited for her to explain, drumming my fingers on my knee impatiently.

"'Scuse me, are you Georgie?"

I turned, and horror crept up my spine when I saw the younger boy who was watching me intently from his own camping chair barely a metre from us.

"Um, yes, who are you?" I asked, even though I knew exactly who he was.

"I'm Levi. Xander's brother. I've heard a lot about you. Xan never shuts up about you!"

And there was the lung-squeezing feeling all over again.

"He … he doesn't?" I managed.

Levi grinned. "Nope!" He leaned closer, beckoning to me. Despite the fluttering in my stomach and the burning in my cheeks, I scooted to the edge of my chair, bending towards him.

"He wasn't shitting me when he said you were really pretty!" Levi said with feeling as an incredulous giggle burst out of me.

"Levi! Language!" the man sitting next to him admonished. Levi made a face at me, and I giggled again, more genuinely this time.

"Hey, do you wanna piss Xan right off?" Levi asked, grabbing a zinc stick and tossing it to me. "Write your mate Dom's number on your cheeks."

I uncapped the zinc stick, a sly grin spreading across my face. I swirled the number six onto each cheek as Levi chortled beside me.

I didn't stop laughing for the entire first half of the game. Levi was a cool kid, even though he was only eleven. He kept me entertained, commentating the game with the foulest mouth I'd ever heard on a tween.

His dad snapped at him on a constant loop, but for the most

part, Levi ignored it. His mum sat on the other side of his dad, crocheting away with muscle memory alone, from what I could tell, her eyes firmly on the game. She leapt up, screaming at the top of her lungs when Xander scored. Twice in the first half.

The whistle blew, signalling half-time. Our team was up by the two goals Xander had scored.

"Don't look now," Levi warned me, "but he's coming over. Act cool. Just talk to him the way you've talked to me for the last hour."

I huffed, trying to stifle the butterflies rioting in my stomach. "I can't believe I'm taking boy advice from an eleven-year-old."

"Hey, I'm a pro at this stuff! I've already got a girlfriend," Levi insisted. I snorted under my breath as Xander and Dom approached.

"Blondie!" Xander greeted me, and there they were—the dimples. I folded my arms over my chest because my lungs felt like they were about to burst. Levi nudged me with his elbow.

"Be cool, okay?" he hissed. I pursed my lips, glancing through my lashes at Xander, whose stare felt so intense. Dom appeared at his side, puffing and looking pissed off.

"I hate sport," he grouched.

Xander, who hadn't stopped staring at me, replied without turning, "You promised you'd do one season. Just one."

"That does *not* mean I have to like it." Dom tilted his head back, upending what looked like an entire bottle of water over his sweaty face. I couldn't help but grin—Dom might grouch, but he would do anything for his friends.

"If I had Georgie as my cheerleader, I'd perk up a bit," Xander said, quirking an eyebrow as he reached out to swipe at my cheek with his fingertip. It came away coated in fluorescent orange zinc. I wrinkled my nose, my heart hammering wildly. I'd forgotten I'd painted Dom's number six onto each cheek.

"Like *you* need a cheerleader," I retorted, knowing I was blushing. "You're the top goal scorer, I'm pretty sure you're perky enough on your own." I reached up to brush where my skin still tingled from his touch.

Xander leaned closer. "If you wipe one of these sixes off, and put my nine there, I reckon I can perk up enough to score three in the second half," he murmured, hazel eyes sparkling. I choked on a sudden inhale.

"You want me to write sixty-nine on my face?" I replied, chewing on my lip. Xander guffawed, leaning back and running a hand through his wavy blond hair.

"Or ninety-six. Here, let me do it for you." Before I could draw a breath to say anything, Xander was smearing away the zinc on my right cheek with his thumb. Levi bounced to his feet, shoving the zinc stick into Xander's hand. I closed my eyes, because his face was so near, and his fingers were warm on my chin, and it was just too weird … and too wonderful.

"We need to go, Xander," Dom said sharply, "the rest of the team is huddling."

I snapped my eyes open as Xander stepped away, his eyes wide, lips slightly parted. He rubbed absently at his fingers, smeared with orange zinc. Dom's dark eyes flicked from Xander, to me, and back again, as he gripped Xander's shoulder and steered him away. I watched them leave.

When had Dom gotten so tall? Xander barely had a couple of centimetres on him now.

"You two are weird as fuck," Levi grumbled. I narrowed my eyes at him.

"Why?" I demanded. Levi glanced around, checking that his parents weren't listening. His dad had gotten up to go to the canteen when Xander and Dom left. His mum was rummaging in her crocheting bag. He turned back to me with a grin.

"I mean, you've seriously got the hots for one another, it's almost gross to watch … but *you* go all silent and shit the second he comes near you, and *he* touches you and he's gaping like an idiot. Fucking hell, grow some balls the pair of you and just suck face already!"

My face was flaming as I wrinkled my nose at him. "One—disgusting! Who even says, 'suck face'? And two—you're eleven, what the hell would you know about any of this?"

Levi raised an eyebrow at me. "I have a girlfriend. And I got her by not being a complete dickhead around girls. So maybe if you two weren't complete dickheads around each other, things might be different."

"Levi! Language!" Mr Fox barked, plonking himself back into his chair and throwing a scowl at his son.

I glanced back at Elena, who was sipping her coffee with a knowing smirk. My cheeks burned. She'd heard everything.

"He's right, you know, Georgina. Just be yourself, and it will all work out." With that she stood and walked over to where Mrs Fox was sitting, crouching down and murmuring to her in low tones.

Elena was so different from my mum. She knew Mum's only rule about boys was that I was not to have contact with any of them, with the exception of Dom, until I finished school. But Elena didn't seem to feel the need to obey that rule.

I got why Mum was so psycho about it—she'd had me when she was barely sixteen. But I had zero intention of getting pregnant and ruining my life. Why couldn't Mum trust me to be sensible and safe instead of just assuming that if a boy so much as looked at me, I'd be knocked up?

She probably had nothing to worry about—if I kept up this streak of mortifying interactions with Xander, he'd be more than happy to have no contact with me.

God, why couldn't I just forget that I had a crush on him for five seconds? Just long enough to maybe seem like I wasn't a complete idiot in his presence.

Then: It's Not Sauce, It's Beetroot

XANDER, 14 YEARS OLD

"Why am I such a dickhead around her?" I muttered, mostly to myself, as we headed back towards the rest of the team.

Dom grunted. "Because you like her." He didn't sound happy about it, for all it was the bloody truth. "Stroking her face, taking any excuse to touch her. You couldn't be any more obvious if you tried."

"What about you?" I asked. "I saw you both holding hands this morning."

Dom huffed out a laugh. "I've been holding Georgie's hand for as long as I can remember, it doesn't mean anything."

A hot rush of jealousy flared through me, along with a sudden urge to punch Dom right in the face.

"So, if I decided to grab her hand after the game and walk her out to your car, that would be fine, because holding hands means nothing?"

Dom's face darkened. "It's not the same. I think she's terrified of you, by the way."

That shocked me. "Seriously? No, she just thinks I'm an idiot," I mumbled. Because I was an idiot.

Dom shrugged, which I guessed meant he agreed with me.

"Besides, I've said it over and over again, Xan. If you guys start something, and it goes badly … I don't want to have to be stuck in the middle of that. So just don't."

Dom loved to lecture me about this. I got the same speech every time I came over to his house, and every time Georgie texted him to say she was on her way to meet us. And then again when she left.

'Don't go there. Just be her friend. Don't ruin things for everyone.'

Jesus bloody Christ though, I wanted to kiss her like I hadn't wanted anything in my life before. But I wasn't about to confess that to Dom. He'd go off his tree at me.

Maybe I should just friendzone her. Maybe then she would go back to being that cool, chatty girl she'd been the first time I met her over a year ago. Not the awkward, silent girl she'd become.

Maybe, to convince her, and her overprotective best friend, that I was worth a shot, I had to play the long game.

"Well," I said with a clear of my throat. "I've got a hattrick to score this half. Don't want to let my mate's best friend down."

***

It was almost embarrassing, the way Dad fawned over me on the way out to lunch after the game.

"Six, Xander! Six goals! And you topped your class in mathematics and all your sciences in your half-yearlies." He eyed Levi in the rear-view mirror. "You see, Levi. It is possible to keep up good grades and enjoy a sport."

Levi slouched in his seat. "Let me give rowing a go and I'll study."

Dad shook his head. "You start at King Henry's next year. Show me solid results in your first year, and I'll consider the rowing team for year eight."

Mum flashed a quick look at Dad and reached back to give Levi's knee a squeeze. I chewed on the inside of my cheek. I hated when Dad said something nice to me, and immediately turned it around to ream Levi out. He'd never been great at school. Not that he was terrible, he just wasn't as good as me. Which apparently made Dad really pissed off.

"It'll be good to have lunch with your friends, Xander. I'm glad you've met some nice kids through school," Mum said.

"Yeah, Xander thinks Georgie is pretty fucking nice," Levi said, elbowing me in the ribs across the back seat of the car.

"Language, Levi!" Dad snapped, which just made Levi pull a face behind Dad's back. I was pretty sure Levi swore so much just to rile Dad up.

"Xander is allowed to have a crush on a girl," Mum continued as if Dad hadn't just barked at Levi. "Just like you have a crush on that girl Poppy in the other year six class."

Levi rolled his eyes. "It's not a crush, she's my girlfriend!" Levi insisted. "We sit together at recess and lunch, we hold hands, I even kissed her after school in the bus line last week! With tongue and everything!"

"Well, we know now why your school marks are abysmal. Maybe if you stopped mooning over girls, you'd put some effort into studying and homework." Dad's voice was basically a snarl.

"Calm down, George," Mum said in her always patient voice. "Let him be a boy."

"I don't remember being a boy involving kissing girls at the tender age of eleven!" Dad spluttered.

Mum chuckled. "It was a peck on the lips."

I glanced at Levi, who winked at me and mouthed, "With tongue!" I hid my laugh behind a cough, but there was a small stab of envy, too. I hadn't kissed a girl, and I was nearly fifteen.

Probably because the one girl I really wanted to kiss thought I was an idiot. And because her best friend was also my best friend, and he was horrified at the idea of me doing anything with her.

Dom and his mum—and Georgie—met us at a burger bar in Mosman. They'd already ordered and were sitting in a booth, leaving only one seat free, next to Georgie. If I sat there, Dom would freak out. But I didn't want to sit with Dad and listen to him grumble about Levi kissing girls, and burgers being terrible for the arteries, and whatever else he wanted to complain about.

So, I swallowed my nerves, and after ordering, and making double-sure the guy behind the counter was aware of the modification to my burger, I slid into the booth beside Georgie.

Just act friendly. Don't touch her, don't leer at her like a freak, okay?

"Six goals, Xander. Really?" Her voice was incredulous, and I couldn't work out of she was impressed with my skills or if she thought I was a total tosser.

"Well, I did promise you three in the second half. That fourth one was just for me." I could have kicked myself at how boastful I sounded. Why was I such a wanker when I spoke to her?

"Is soccer what you want to do when you finish school?" she asked, as a plate of chips and one of onion rings were placed on the table in front of us.

"Medicine!" Dad called from the next booth over, where he was obviously eavesdropping. I sighed.

"I love soccer, but it's not really a valid career option, is it? I mean, I'm not Beckham, or anything close to that."

"But, shouldn't you do what you love? Like, I love telling people what to do, so I'm going to manage a business one day."

I laughed, stopping when I saw the unimpressed expression on Georgie's face. "You're serious? Manage a business? That's a job, not a career!"

Georgie folded her arms across her chest, eyeing me angrily. "When I'm running a huge company, and all my employees are scared to step a toe out of line, I'll come and have this chat with you again."

"You can tell me what to do whenever you like, Blondie." The words came out before I could stop them. Georgie's eyes fluttered closed, and she turned away from me.

Yeah, she thought I was an idiot.

"I want to be a vet," I mumbled, twisting my napkin into a knot. Thankfully Dad didn't hear that truth bomb, he'd burst a blood vessel. Healing animals wasn't as prestigious as healing humans. He wouldn't tolerate it.

"Really?" Georgie gasped, and I glanced at her to find I had her full attention again. Those silvery eyes were wide and fixed on me. There was still a little smear of zinc high on her cheekbone. My hand itched to reach up and wipe it away, but I gripped my thighs under the table instead.

"Yeah, really."

"Don't you think it would be totally depressing though, to have to put animals down? I could never …" she looked mildly sick at the thought.

I shrugged. "The way I see it, they're in pain. They're so sick they'll never recover. Why would we want them to suffer? Seriously, we should let humans make that choice too if they have a terminal illness."

Georgie's eyebrows knitted together, and she looked so adorable that I wanted to wrap my hand around hers. I gripped my thighs harder. Our food arrived at just the right time, distracting me from Georgie's pretty, thoughtful face.

Georgie picked up her burger and took a monster bite. Juices trickled down her hands, and she chewed with relish. "Oh my God, this is sooo good!"

I grinned, picking my own up, too busy staring at the glob of barbecue sauce at the corner of her mouth to check my burger properly. I wasn't going to let Miss 'I have a fast metabolism and I compete in triathlons' outdo me in a burger-eating competition.

It wasn't until I'd chewed and swallowed that first enormous mouthful that I felt it. The tingling in my tongue that meant only one thing.

My face heated as I dropped the burger to my plate and lifted the top. And sure enough, there, right on top, was one huge slice of beetroot.

I closed the bun, heart hammering. *It's okay, one bite won't be too bad. At least you didn't eat the whole burger. It won't be much worse than a numb tongue.*

"I think you've got a bit of sauce on your mouth, Xan," Dom said from across the table, pointing to his lower lip. I mirrored his movement, but my fingers came away clean.

Shit. By this time Georgie was absolutely paying attention. She put her burger down, staring intently at my mouth. If I wasn't silently panicking, it would have been kind of hot, the way she was looking at me.

But I didn't bloody need her witnessing an allergic reaction. I especially didn't need Mum knowing about it and having a freakout. Or Dad grumbling about how much Mum babied us boys.

"You missed it," she muttered, and her hand stretched towards me. I flinched away, and she froze, eyes wide, cheeks going rosy.

"It's not sauce, okay?" I whispered back to her. "It's beetroot."

"Okay," Georgie said uncertainly, plucking an onion ring from the plate in the centre of the table and chewing it, her eyes still staring. My tongue felt fuzzy, and my lip stung. Definitely the beetroot.

"It's spreading," she whispered. I sighed.

"I get an allergic reaction to beetroot," I explained in a low voice, watching her eyes widen worriedly. I shook my head, giving a smile that felt off because of the swelling.

"It's not a bad one. Just a swollen mouth and my tongue goes numb. Sometimes a rash on my face and neck, if I eat enough."

Georgie looked from my burger to my face, and back again. "Then why didn't you ask for no beetroot? That's kind of a no-brainer, isn't it?"

My eyes flicked warily to the next booth. Thankfully Levi was telling some loud story, and neither of my parents had heard any of our conversation. But Dom was watching us both, chewing viciously on his burger.

"I did ask for no beetroot, I'm not an idiot," I hissed, gesturing to the obvious slice of beetroot on my open bun. "They must not have paid attention."

"Just take it back and ask for a new burger," Dom suggested, his voice snappy.

I grimaced. "And have Mum fussing over me like I'm about to die? No thanks!"

"*Are* you about to die?" Georgie asked, horrified. I glanced at Dom's mum, who was watching me with an eyebrow quirked. I loved her so much at that moment. I loved that she was waiting to hear from me before she raised an alarm to Mum.

"No, I only had one bite. I just need to take a Claratyne."

Elena rummaged in her purse, pulling out a sheet of pills and sliding them in my direction. With a grateful smile, I popped one out, downing it with my water.

"So, what are you going to eat, then?" Dom asked, gesturing to my open burger and the offending piece of beetroot. "The star striker needs to replenish."

I shrugged. "Some chips?"

"Oh, for crying out loud … boys!" Georgie grouched, snatching my plate out from in front of me and plonking hers down in its place. "My burger didn't come with beetroot."

I watched her, mouth agape, as she put the bun back on top of my burger and lifted it to her mouth, opening her jaw wide and taking a massive bite.

"Just promise me you're not lying about the beetroot thing," she said around her mouthful. "If you keel over in the onion rings, I'm gonna be so mad, because they're delicious."

I managed a small laugh, but I didn't pick the burger up right away. I reached for an onion ring instead, and practically moaned as I bit into it. Georgie was right. It was crunchy, and greasy, and sweet inside, and everything an onion ring should be.

"Thank you, Georgie," I managed once I'd swallowed every last bit of the onion ring. Georgie grinned at me through a mouthful of my burger, and I couldn't help myself. I reached under the table and gave her knee a little squeeze, leaving my hand there.

She froze mid-bite, put the burger down, and grabbed a napkin, wiping her hands on it. I smirked, picking up another onion ring in my free hand. But my smirk fell right off my face when she rested her hand on mine, winding her fingers around mine, before lifting my hand off her leg and placing it on my knee.

Then, without even so much as a glance in my direction, she picked up the burger and continued to eat.

And I had trouble chewing—not because of my fuzzy tongue, or my slightly puffy lip, but because I was suddenly sporting a stupid grin that I just couldn't wipe off my face.

Now: The Local Talent

GEORGIE

Xander laughed at something Dr Alex said, and she reached out and touched his hand where it rested next to his half-drunk schooner of beer. Jase and Karl hovered just out of shot of one another around the table, one camera trained on Xander, the other switching between Alex and Liz, seated side by side opposite him.

I flinched at the way she touched him, as if she really knew him, then scowled at my own stupidity and spun back towards the bar.

"Another merlot, Georgie?" Freddie, who'd owned and operated The Budgie for as long as I'd been alive, asked, smiling and tossing his towel over his shoulder. Against my better judgement, I nodded, massaging my temples as he set down a glass in front of me and poured. He was a handsome older man with curly silver hair and tanned skin that somehow kept him looking younger than his sixty years.

"They look cosy, don't they?" Jord remarked as they took the stool beside me. I grunted, flashing a wan smile at Freddie and taking a long glug of my wine.

"You know, I was kind of shocked that when Dr Fox opened his burger earlier, it wasn't stuffed entirely with beetroot," Jord continued, either ignoring or not noticing my foul mood. I tilted my head in their direction, eyeing them coldly.

"He's allergic, Jordyn. I'm not a complete monster."

"Well, I'm sure that the good Dr Alex would have been delighted to perform mouth-to-mouth on him."

My gaze flicked back to where Xander was smirking into his beer, hazel eyes sparkling as he watched Alex across the table. As if sensing my regard, his eyes flitted up to mine for a split second, his grin widening, dimples popping.

God, I hated him!

"You could have warned me that Dr Alex was a woman, you know," I hissed to Jordyn. They lifted their beer to their lips, taking a sip.

"I didn't know she was," Jordyn argued. I spun towards them with a roll of my eyes.

"You spoke to her on the phone, don't tell me you weren't aware."

Jordyn met my stare icily. "You should know better than anyone that I don't assume someone's gender purely from the sound of their voice."

I swallowed, my neck heating, blinking as I looked away guiltily. "Shit. You're right Jord. I'm so sorry."

Jordyn reached over and gave my shoulder a squeeze as Alex giggled and her hand brushed Xander's again.

"It's alright, G. No one's perfect. Slipping up doesn't stop you being one of the best allies I've met." They sipped another mouthful of beer. "But it looks like Alex being a woman is going to work out perfectly! There's definitely chemistry between them. Alex has offered to come weekly to spend time visiting livestock patients with Xander. We might be able to drag a bit of a romantic storyline out of this."

My stomach turned to stone, and I pressed my lips tightly together to stop myself from protesting.

Professional showrunner Georgie would be all over this, brainstorming ways to throw them together in intimate situations.

Heartbroken teenager Georgie was ready to curl up in a ball and sob, which was just ridiculous. I didn't want Xander Fox.

But I also didn't want to sit here and witness him turning that Fox charm on another woman while I stewed silently and forced myself to encourage it for the good of the show.

"You know, they might have chemistry, but what you and Xander have …" Jordyn fanned their face dramatically. "If only you'd agree to go on camera."

"My … history with Dr Fox is not something that needs to be aired on television," I retorted, draining the remainder of my wine. "Besides, can you imagine what Kenneth would have to say about it? Not the best way to start our careers with Reelflix, Jord."

They hmphed, and I turned my attention back to the table. Alex stood, and Xander followed. Liz looked from one of them to the other with a leer.

"I'd better be going. It's an hour and a half drive back to Millstone, and I'm due in my clinic at eight tomorrow," Alex said, a ridiculous little pout pushing her bottom lip out.

"I'll walk you out," Xander offered. I screwed up my nose as Alex turned, and Xander placed a hand on the small of her back to steer her through the busy pub. All eyes were on them as the cameras followed along behind, and conversation temporarily muted until they were out the door. Jord jumped off the bar stool and followed, and for that I was grateful.

Whatever sort of goodbye Xander gave Alex, it would be bad enough reviewing it in footage later. I couldn't cope with watching it live.

Get your act together! You are not seriously mooning over him, are you?

"Well, here's a sight for sore eyes!"

I turned, making a half-hearted attempt to wipe the frown from my face as I looked into a pair of blue-green eyes framed by dark lashes and a mop of black curls.

"Hi, Lachy," I managed to sound pleasant as he grinned his megawatt smile at me and settled into the stool Jord had just vacated. He reached out and flipped at my hair.

"I don't normally like shorter hair on women, but this suits you!" he said, and I tried not to roll my eyes. Lachlan Porter was unfortunately incredibly gorgeous, deeply tanned, with a wicked grin and a body that spoke of spending the last twenty years hauling hay bales around the farm.

It was unfortunate because he'd made no secret of the fact that he wouldn't mind taking me for a romp in his hay shed. I'd spent time in Budgerigar every year since I was eighteen, and every visit, he'd pursued me with single-minded intent, and very little in the way of interesting conversation.

"How's the tiny home going? Have you broken the bed in yet?" Lachy asked with a lopsided leer and a wink. I barely managed to contain my groan, pasting a smile on my face.

"It's stunning, thanks Lachy. This morning we filmed a full tour of it, we'll make sure to give you a big plug on the show. But … you know I'm not the one staying in it, right? That's Dr Fox—our Beach Vet. I'm just behind the scenes."

Lachy's brows furrowed. "You're not sleeping in it?"

I took a long, calming breath. "No, Lachy. I'm staying with Mim, like I always do when I'm out here. But Dr Fox is very impressed with it."

"Dr Fox is impressed with what?"

I almost fell off my stool at the sound of Xander's voice right next to my ear. Lachy jumped to his feet, eyeing Xander up and down. The expression on his face was almost comical.

"You're the Beach Vet?" he asked. Xander, who gave Lachy a much more disdainful once-over, eventually reached his hand out.

"You can call me Xander."

Lachy took his hand, gripping tighter than was needed. I could practically smell the testosterone as they sized one another up.

"Lachlan Porter. Owner of Porter-Bell Dwellings."

Xander's eyebrows twitched, his eyes sliding to mine and then back to Lachy. "You're the local farmer who builds tiny homes on the side? I'd imagined someone a bit …" Xander's words faded, his knuckles going white where his fingers wrapped around Lachy's until Lachy winced and tugged his hand free of their little dick-measuring competition.

"Yeah, well, farming's a tough gig, with the drought. We needed to try something different, and I'm good with my hands, so ..." Lachy smirked down at me, and I found myself blushing, knowing Xander was watching me too.

"Speaking of, Georgie, I heard you're gonna be doing some renos on the vet clinic. I thought I'd offer my ... expertise. You know, carpentry ... back rubs ... that sort of thing."

I fought to keep my expression neutral as Xander's face turned thunderous. "Your expertise? Yes, I'm sure you've been dying to help Georgie with some nailing." His voice was thick and furious, and for some reason, that sent a thrill through every nerve in my body.

Payback's a bitch, Dr Fox, I thought as I slid my hand onto Lachy's knee, rubbing up and down his thigh.

"That would be incredible, Lach! Local talent is what will make this show something spectacular. Why don't you pop by the clinic tomorrow, and you and Dr Fox can have a chat about how you can assist."

Lachy didn't respond immediately, his eyes following the movement of my hand on his denim-clad thigh. I was playing a dangerous game here—in all the past twelve years of Lachy and his blatant, often ridiculous to the point of nauseating come-ons, I'd never given him any reason to think I was interested.

But I knew how to handle myself, and I was sure I could handle a pretty-faced doofus like Lachlan Porter, too, if it came down to it.

"Uh, yeah, I'll do that." Lachy sounded flustered as he stood abruptly, adjusting the bulge in his jeans. I smirked, glancing up at his wide eyes and licking my lips.

"Looking forward to it," I purred. Lachy's mouth fell open.

"Well ... I'd better be going. You know, farmer life, and all that. Up at sparrow fart tomorrow, 'specially if I need to be in town again in the morning."

He paused for just a second longer, and then he leaned down so fast I barely knew what was happening and brushed his lips against my cheek.

"See you tomorrow?" he murmured. I swallowed down a sudden bubble of nausea and nodded.

"I'll be there!" I replied, far too brightly. A ghost of Lachy's goofy grin flitted across his face, and then he was off.

"Well, seems the last twelve years have taught *you* a thing or two about flirting," Xander growled.

I narrowed my eyes at him. "What the last twelve years has taught me is none of your business."

Xander grunted, looking everywhere but at me as he ran a hand through those blond waves, muttering something unintelligible. And there was that thrill again, zinging along every inch of my skin.

I was flustering him. And it felt divine.

"Dr Fox, I'll get you to take a seat, do a bit of a wrap-up of the day, and then we can all call it quits and head home for the night," Jord said, gesturing to the table he'd just vacated. Liz was nowhere to be seen.

"Thank fuck," Xander muttered, stalking off and collapsing into the chair. Jase set up camera opposite him, and Jord took the other seat, asking him open-ended questions.

"You're playing with fire, Georgina," Liz said in my ear. So that was where she'd gotten to.

"I have no idea what you're talking about," I replied, my eyes locked on Xander as he spoke into the camera. It annoyed me to admit, but he was a total natural at it. No wonder Kenneth had been so keen to cast him before he even had a fully fleshed concept to attach him to.

"Yes, you do, young lady," Freddie added from behind me. I turned, scowling at the pair of them.

"Look, I'm just here to do a job. How I get what I need on camera is *my* business."

Freddie eyed me with that look only an elderly person who has known you for far too long can muster. "And your job requires you to lead poor Lachy on? That boy's only had eyes for you for the last twelve years, and you've shut him down at every opportunity. But now there's a handsome city boy here with you, and all of a sudden, you're interested in Lachy?"

"It's mighty sus, Fred, that's what it is," Liz added, her sharp gaze taking me in. "Especially when the city boy is the same one who—"

"You don't know anything, Elizabeth Peters!" I whispered harshly. "So you keep your gossip to yourself!"

My heart thrummed as I took a nervous glance back to where Xander was talking into the camera. Jordyn was eyeing me thoughtfully. When they caught me staring, they quickly returned their attention to Xander.

"Just don't let Lachy think he's finally getting what he wants if you've no intention of following through, young lady," Liz grouched, but she gave my shoulder a quick, motherly pat before shuffling off the stool. With a wave and a wink in Xander's direction, she trotted out of The Budgie, leaving me pondering whether I'd just made things exponentially more complicated, solely on a whim to make Xander Fox jealous.

Damn him!

***

At nine the following morning, Lachy showed up on the front porch of the clinic wearing a wide grin, a wife beater singlet, navy shorts that were so short I was surprised a testicle wasn't hanging out, and a pair of worn work boots. A tool belt was slung low on his hips. He looked good—if you were into the Chippendale meets carpenter look. Which I wasn't.

"Morning Georgie!" he said as he swaggered inside the clinic. "The muscle is here."

"Oh great, the brawn has arrived to join the brains," I heard Xander mutter from the reception area, where he was already getting stuck in tearing up the stained, stinky old carpet.

I wanted to say something snarky to him about how he was at least as brawny as Lachy, but there were so many reasons why that was a terrible idea. Not least of which, there were two cameras trained on the action. The action I was trying not to be a part of. I let him inside, making sure to stay out of frame of the camera that was trained on him.

"Pulling up carpet, are we?" Lachy asked, stretching and revealing a tanned, rippling swathe of stomach and a dark happy trail in the process. I gestured for Jase to zoom in on that. If these two were going to have a pissing contest, we may as well utilise the opportunity for some thirst-trap footage.

Xander noticed, and the already dark look that had been brooding on his face since last night deepened. I stifled a grin.

"Bloody observant, aren't you?" Xander snapped, his biceps bulging as he tore up a length of carpet and rolled it, preparing to take it out to the skip bin that had just arrived.

"I'll grab that," Lachy insisted, snatching one end of the carpet. Xander's lips tightened, his grip tightening too. I covered my smile as they scowled at each other and tugged, neither of them willing to be the one to give in. Their faces got progressively redder and sweatier, even as their muscles bulged with the effort to be the one to come away victorious. Their prize apparently being a roll of pet-soiled carpet.

"For Pete's sake, boys!" Liz chastised as she appeared in the doorway, shadowed by her two Corgis and Molly, who'd humped and dumped poor Jumbo in favour of Kingston yesterday. "We know you both have big, juicy sausages. Stop trying to impress us ladies by outdoing one another, and get the bloody job done!"

I almost felt like kissing Liz as the pair of them, flushed and glistening and chastised, managed to work together to carry the long roll of carpet out the front door.

"Hear that, Georgie? Wanna come over for a barbecue tonight? I've got a big, juicy sausage with your name on it," Lachy said as he passed me. I swallowed back bile, stepping aside to give them some room.

"Sizzle down, Chipolata!" Xander grunted as he passed me. I glanced up, catching his eyes for a split second—just long enough to notice the cheeky gleam in them. It jolted my heart, stifling the giggle bubbling up my throat. I turned on my heel and fled.

I couldn't share little moments like that with Xander. It just felt

… wrong. Like I was falling backwards off a cliff. I knew that the fall itself would be a huge adrenaline rush, but the crash at the bottom … I wouldn't survive that crash.

Hating him was so much simpler.

I found Jordyn in the cluttered file room, phone on speaker, tinkling hold music playing. The laptop was open, and they were scrolling through a spreadsheet.

"Swap you," I said.

Jordyn looked up and raised one sharp eyebrow at me. "I'm fine here, thanks. You need to be out front. This is your show, G, not mine."

I pursed my lips. "It wasn't a request, Jordyn."

Jordyn sighed but stood, holding the phone out to me. "I'm on hold with Zovarta waiting to confirm that the pharmaceuticals won't arrive until after the new refrigerators. And the flooring is getting delivered separately, but the latest update shows no progress on the order. That's my next call. If I ever get off hold, that is."

I sighed. There was nothing I hated more than waiting on hold. Well, right now there was one thing I hated more.

Xander Fox's cheeky eye gleam.

"Alternatively," Jord continued, collapsing back into the chair, "you could just be the fucking boss you are, march back out there and produce the shit out of this show, and not let him get to you."

I clenched my jaw, wishing I could argue but knowing deep down that I had to do what Jord said. From the moment I'd seen his name on the talent profile, I'd been letting my feelings get in the way of doing my job—a job that I'd given up a career I'd been working towards since high school for. That wasn't the Georgina Menzies way.

"Fuck I hate it when you're right," I grumbled. Jord smirked at me, flicking a lock of electric blue hair out of their face and turning back to the laptop.

As I headed towards the door, Jord added, "If you can, get the pair of them shirtless before the end of the day. Ratings will skyrocket."

I managed a small titter of nervous laughter as I steeled myself to head back into the action.

———

The gladiatorial contest between Xander and Lachy continued all day. If they weren't arguing over who was carrying rubbish out past me, they were swinging mallets at a wall we'd decided to knock out in the waiting area, as if they wished they were swinging them at each other's heads instead.

It would have been amusing, if in the back of my mind I wasn't constantly thinking, *This has no context without a cut to me, sitting there watching them both trying to impress me.*

Although why Xander felt any need to impress me, I had no idea. Testosterone must be a weird hormone.

All day there had been a stream of curious Budgerigarians pausing by the gate, craning their necks to see if they could catch a glimpse inside.

The outside action got particularly enthusiastic in the half hour before school pick up, when the street suddenly seemed full of dawdling school mums who loitered by the fence, even though the school was at the far end of the street.

Coincidentally, around the same time, Lachy decided he was too hot in his singlet, and as he swaggered past me, he stripped it off. He paused in the open front door and used his singlet like a towel to wipe down his sweat-soaked abs.

He really did have a spectacular six-pack. I watched through hooded eyes as he tossed the singlet to the side, walking back over to where I was sitting behind the old reception desk and resting his elbows on it so his nipples were right in my line of sight, framed by a dusting of black hair.

"This is thirsty work, isn't it, Georgie?" he said, reaching over and grabbing a full bottle of water that I'd just gotten for myself and taking a long, deep slug of it. Jase came around my side of the desk to capture the view just as Xander appeared in the doorway. I dragged my eyes away from Lachy's chest just in time to see Xander scowling at me.

"Good thinking, Chippy, it's bloody hot in here."

I pressed my lips together as tightly as I could while Xander tugged his black t-shirt off over his head and dropped it on the reception desk next to me. I looked down at it in horror, then glanced back up at Xander.

Holy shit.

Sure, he'd been shirtless that first night—the night that didn't happen—but that had been in the dark, and for the most part, I'd had my back to him.

Today, the bright early afternoon sunlight gleamed off sweat-soaked pecs, glittering on the sprinkling of golden chest hair. Xander caught my eye for a split second, his lips quirking into a deeply self-satisfied smirk as he stretched.

His running shorts sat low on his narrow hips, showcasing a very prominent Adonis belt, golden hair running from his navel down into the waistband of his shorts.

How did I know this? Because I'd stood up so that I could see him properly over the top of the reception desk.

What on earth was I thinking? I clamped my gaping jaw shut, swallowed the saliva that was pooling in my mouth, and stormed out the back to the little, buzzing old refrigerator.

Cold water. It was the next best thing to a cold shower.

I grabbed the closest bottle and unscrewed the lid with shaking hands, tipping my head back and slugging desperately at the icy water.

"Bit thirsty there, Blondie?"

I gagged on the water, spitting out a mouthful in an indelicate spray. All over Xander's chest.

"Why are you following me?" I gasped, stopping as a hacking cough ripped out of my chest. Through watery eyes, Xander's expression morphed from gloating to concerned.

"Shit, Georgie! Are you …?" He stepped towards me, a warm hand resting between my shoulder blades, rubbing and patting.

"I'm … fine …" I managed, finally getting some air back into my lungs as I shrugged his hand off, stepping back to put some space between us. "Don't sneak up on me like that!"

"I just came to get a bottle of water," Xander murmured. "You know, since you were kind enough to get one for Chipolata out there, but not for me." He brushed against me as he leaned into the still-open fridge, plucking out a bottle. He didn't move back as he opened it, his body crowding mine against the fridge door, his damp, naked skin warm and slightly sticky against me. I watched in stunned silence as he brought the bottle to his lips, his head tilting back, his Adam's apple bobbing as he swallowed gulp after gulp.

I was panting by the time he finished the entire bottle and finally stepped back, grinning so wide his dimples popped. He reached out and closed my mouth with two fingers pressed under my chin, tilting his head down so his lips were close to my ear.

"Don't look at me like that, Blondie," he whispered, "Your rural Chippy out there might get a bit jealous." He turned to leave.

I found my voice. "For the record, Lachy isn't *my* anything."

Xander turned back, arching one dark gold eyebrow at me. "You sure about that? You seemed pretty cosy with him last night."

I swallowed, jutting my chin defiantly. "No cosier than you and Alex," I snapped. "But I suppose that's none of my business … a bit like my relationship with Lachy is none of yours. Grow up, Dr Fox!"

Xander smirked at me. "Oh, I've 'grown up' a lot in the last twelve years, Blondie." With a pointed glance down at his running shorts, he left the room, leaving me hot, and bothered, and so damned furious.

"Time to up the ante, G," Jord remarked coolly from the doorway, arms folded over their chest. "It's our job to get *him* all antsy. Not the other way around."

I couldn't contain myself for a second longer. Eyes blazing, I rounded on Jordyn.

"Yes, because that strategy worked so well the first night here! We got him so antsy that he pushed me up against a wall and fingered me," I hissed.

Jord flinched. "Shit, G. Are you okay?"

I leant against the fridge door, rubbing at my face. "I'm just trying to pretend it didn't happen. It's better that way, I think. We need to make this work for three months, that's all. I can't be … provoking him if that's the outcome."

"Was it … were you … did you consent?" Jord breathed, eyes roving my face. "He didn't assault you, did he?"

I shook my head, taking a step back. "No! He didn't … I … fuck, Jord, it was hotter than the hottest sex I've had in years."

Jord scoffed at that, although their eyes remained wary. "Well, considering you spent the last two years with James the ninety-second wonder, I'm not surprised."

I managed a weak laugh. "But can you see now why provoking him is not a good idea? I can't … we can't just infuriate one another to the point where he snaps and I grind against his erection while he fingerbangs me!"

Jord's eyebrow lifted until it disappeared under a flop of blue hair. "Oh, so there was grinding?"

"Jord," I mumbled, picking at a fingernail, "If he hadn't stopped himself when he did, I … I'm not sure where that encounter would have ended."

I spun on my heel and paced the small space, glancing out the window to where Liz was in the backyard, cavorting with the sprite-liness of a much younger woman with her two little fuzzballs and Molly. "I should never have agreed to this. Clearly I'm incapable of being professional around him."

"Do you really think some off-camera action between the two of you is going to ruin everything?"

I eyed them incredulously. "Yes! I do think that! Being involved with him again was never in my life plan."

Jord shrugged. "And yet here you are, eight hours from Sydney, in a tiny little town with a man who you loved for years." Their expression turned pleading. "G, life doesn't always work out according to plan. And you really, really need to get laid. Would Dr Fox be such a bad choice?"

I shook my head in horror. "Absolutely he would! I hate him!"

Jord snorted. "And what's wrong with a hot hate fuck? Look, I'm not going to lecture you on how to live your life. But seriously, is the only thing that's stopping you from going straight to bone town with the sexy vet not wanting to fraternise with the talent? If so, maybe go talk to Jase about how many of the crew were banging the models on *Bikini Cove*."

I sucked in a breath to reply that of course I knew about all the sordid goings on at *Bikini Cove*, and that it didn't change a thing because that wasn't why I couldn't go there with Xander. But before I could get a single word out, Jase came jogging down the hall, stopping all conversation in its tracks.

"Xan's got his first patient out front; I need one of you."

Jord glared at me and tilted their head towards the door. With a frown, I followed Jase.

Now: Squirting All Over The Place

GEORGIE

The scene that met me out front was bizarre.

A woman, probably late thirties with intensely red hair, was clutching the leash of a red cocker spaniel that huddled up against her legs. So far, the strangest thing was how similar the woman and her dog were.

But then … there was topless Xander, lying curled on his side on the ground, head tilted towards the cowering dog. And beside Xander, a small girl, probably about seven, lying on her stomach on the grass, feet kicked up behind her, watching Xander intently.

"Is he okay?" I mumbled to Jase as we approached. Karl was crouched down to one side, where he had a perfect angle to take in both Xander and the frightened dog.

"Yeah. He's … I can't even explain, just watch," Jase muttered back, shouldering his camera and training it on the woman's face.

Xander slowly reached out to the dog, crooning words softly enough that I couldn't make them out. His voice was deep, melodic and soothing, and my chest felt like it was turning inside out at the sound of him.

The dog allowed him to pet it, and then gently nuzzled into his palm as the little girl gasped quietly. Xander turned his head, saw me gaping, and smiled softly.

"Can you bring me the navy-blue bag I stashed under the reception desk, please?" he asked, still using that mesmerising voice. I snapped my mouth shut and ducked back inside, returning with the bag. By then, Xander had managed to sit up, and the dog was no longer cowering, instead timidly sniffing towards him. I placed the bag beside him and moved out of view of the camera.

Xander unzipped the bag, still talking quietly to the dog.

"I've got some treats for you in here. Would you like one, Gid?" he said, pulling out a small container and unclipping it, taking out a bite-sized treat and offering it on his flattened palm. The dog flinched, then sniffed towards the treat, stretched out, and plucked it from Xander's hand. He gently massaged the dog's ears as it chewed.

Keeping contact with the dog, he looked up at the woman, who was gaping at him, much the way you'd expect a middle-aged woman to gape at a semi-naked man sitting at her feet, crooning and wooing her pet.

"When was the last time he had them done?" Xander asked. I wrinkled my nose, confused.

The woman giggled nervously. "Uh, maybe three months ago? I'm so sorry, I'm usually all over it, but I'm pregnant, and the smell … I just can't. Even the thought of it—" The woman actually retched, covering her mouth and gagging.

"What are they talking about?" I whispered to Jase. He turned to me with a grin.

"Anal glands," Xander said loudly. Shit. I thought I'd been speaking too quietly for him to hear me.

Xander hand-fed the pup another treat. "This little dude, Gideon, is prone to blocked anal glands, which can cause infection if they're not manually drained. Sounds like he has a great mum, though, who usually does it for him. But she's right. It's a particularly pungent smell, and I don't blame a pregnant lady for not coping."

Xander dimpled up at the woman, who fluttered her eyelashes

at him. With a conscious effort, I unclenched my jaw, as topless, absolutely cut Xander lay on the grass feeding a cute dog and smiling at the camera as he explained what he'd need to do.

"He's just a bit nervous around new people, so I'm helping him to get comfortable with me." He turned back to the dog with another affectionate pat of his velvety ears. "After all, it's good manners to get to know each other before I start playing around with his bottom."

I swallowed down a laugh as Xander fed him another treat. He looked up at me with a wicked gleam in his eyes. A look that all but liquefied my insides.

"But I'll need a helper to hold him and comfort him while I express the glands. And since his mum can't …" His gaze sharpened on me. My head was shaking before I even knew what I was doing.

"Maybe Lachy could help?" I asked, desperation making my words breathy.

Jord appeared beside me and all but shoved me in Xander's direction. I stumbled, managing to right myself before I fell on top of the little girl. The dog didn't seem as concerned about me approaching, happily munching on his treat.

"Will he be frightened if I hold him?" I asked. The woman either didn't notice my pleading expression, or they were all in on some elaborate plot to get me on camera while Xander stuck his fingers up a dog's butthole.

"Oh, not at all," the woman assured me, holding out the lead for me to take. "He loves women, it's men he's afraid of. We got him as a rescue. He'd been mistreated by his previous owner. He was terrified of my husband for months when we first brought him home."

And yet here he was, eating out of Xander's hand five minutes after meeting him. I wanted to scowl, but deep down, I had to admit Xander's bedside manner—with the dog as well as with the owner —was too fricking adorable to be real.

"Okay," I said, taking the lead and squatting down beside the dog. He appraised me, decided I was okay, and let me scratch between his beautiful, floppy ears.

"You're a gorgeous boy, aren't you Gideon?" I murmured.

Xander sat slowly, reaching for his bag, taking out latex gloves, a tube of lube, a big wad of gauze squares and a packet of pet wipes. I froze.

"We're doing this here?" I squeaked. Xander smiled cheekily, nodding.

"Better here than inside. It's a mess in there at the moment. Besides, fresh air will help with the smell. Just give him a hug, keep his head and his front legs immobilised. Talk to him, reassure him."

Bile bubbled up in my throat. "I know how to keep a pet calm when they're in distress," I ground out. "I've done it before, you know."

Xander froze halfway through pulling on one of his gloves. "I know you have, Blondie," he murmured, but he wouldn't meet my eyes. I swallowed around the sudden lump in my throat, turning my wobbly smile back to Gideon, giving his shoulders a rub before wrapping my arms around his chest, tucking his front half onto my lap.

"You're such a good boy, Gid," I murmured. "Your butt's going to feel so much better after this."

The little girl giggled as her mum took her hand and moved her back to give us some space.

"Most dogs' anal glands are fairly easy to locate," Xander explained to the camera as he squeezed some lube onto his fingers. "Georgie, if you can just tuck one arm under Gideon's belly, hold him up so he's standing, that makes access a little easier."

Face heating, I followed his instructions. Gideon started to tremble just a little.

"You're okay, Gid," I promised him. "Plenty of treats for you when this is over."

I tuned out the explanation Xander was giving the camera, my eyes unfocused on the shiny, rusty colour of Gideon's head. I tried to tune out the fact that Xander was so close to me, so shirtless. So warm.

So competent, and calm, and …

"Oh, God! That's awful!" I gasped, heaving slightly at the cloying, fishy smell that seemed to cling to the insides of my nostrils.

Xander's smirk was pure evil. "It's a very strong odour, anal gland fluid. That's why we wear gloves, and we catch it on a gauze pad. You don't want this stuff squirting all over the place."

The cheeky way he looked at me while saying 'squirting' was too much. I ignored him as best I could, breathing through my mouth as best I could while Xander milked one, then the other of poor Gideon's clearly full to almost bursting anal glands.

"And they're all done!" Xander finally announced. "We just give him a clean with a pet wipe to get rid of any lingering fluid around his bottom, and he's good to go!"

I reached across, snagged a few more treats from the open tub, and fed them to poor, traumatised Gideon. "You earned these and then some, buddy," I muttered as Xander chuckled, scooping all the paraphernalia into a bag, taking off his gloves, and sealing the stench away.

Gideon guzzled down his treats as Xander leaned over and ruffled his ears, his fingers brushing against mine fleetingly, making my stomach jolt and my eyes flash up to meet his. Hazel, and gleaming, and full of wickedness.

I stood abruptly, Gideon tumbling from my lap, shaking himself before galloping off, probably feeling about three kilos lighter after his ordeal.

"I have to, uh, go wash up," I stammered, dusting my backside off and racing across the lawn without a single backwards glance at Xander or the woman and her daughter. Or the camera that had absolutely followed my every move.

"Oh, Molly, for crying out loud!" Xander growled behind me as I scuttled up the porch stairs. "I'm so sorry, she's just going through a phase. Molly, get off Gideon!"

I couldn't help the chuckle that burst out of me as I reached the relative safety of the front door. I turned to see Molly, arched over Gideon's back, staring Xander down defiantly as she humped away happily.

Something about him struggling to manage his wayward adolescent dog soothed the aching, hot feeling at the base of my ribcage from having a front-row seat to him working his magic on poor timid Gideon … while shirtless.

On a cheeky whim, I called out, "He doesn't seem all that upset by it," Xander paused and looked up at me, frustration and curiosity warring on his face. I smiled sweetly. "Seems as though Gideon has great taste—clearly *he* likes it when a woman takes control."

A bolt of satisfaction crashed through me as Xander's mouth dropped open. I didn't even care too much that Jase had his camera pointed squarely at me.

I was in control of final footage. I could cut myself out later.

"Well, that was quite a day!" Lachy said merrily as he traipsed into the reception area, now fully stripped of the dog pee carpet and the rickety old reception desk. "That wall was stubborn!"

I barely glanced at him, watching through the window as Jordyn headed out front with Xander to meet the truck of materials that had just arrived from Sydney.

"Let's go get this truck unloaded, and then we can call it a day," I muttered, pushing past him and heading outside.

"I'm going to need a sugar hit after this," he remarked as he followed. Xander approached us, pushing a trolley loaded with boxes and smirking in our direction.

"Sugar hit? I thought you were jonesing for a sausage sizzle tonight, Chippy," he said as he passed.

I rolled my eyes. It had been a very long day in so many ways, and none of us could leave until the truck was unloaded.

My phone pinged, and I tugged it from the pocket of my denim shorts.

> Mim: made spag bol for dinner serve in microwave for u. also why is there ten grand in my bank account that wasn't there yesterday georgina? I won't take your money we will talk about this further

I sighed as I tucked my phone away. I'd meant to have a chat with her about the money, to head her off before she tried to refuse it. My head was too busy with the show.

My head was too busy with Xander. I frowned, gesturing for Karl and Jase to wrap up whatever they were filming. "We've got enough footage for today. Let's just get this done so we can all go home."

Twenty minutes later, the clinic was full of building materials and vet supplies, the truck was empty, and the driver was at The Budgie having a counter meal, along with the tradies that Lou had sent. Freddie would be beside himself at the sudden influx of guests. Budgerigar never saw so many new people at once.

I collapsed on the front step to wait for Jordyn, psyching myself up to argue with them about who would travel home in the truck with Xander. Tonight I just had no energy for the tension between us.

I looked longingly over at the bottle shop across the street. A couple of glasses of wine would go down like a dream with dinner. I'd seen Xander duck in there a few minutes ago.

I palmed my phone, my fingers inched towards the messages app. Just one text asking him to pick me up a bottle of red wouldn't hurt, would it? Before I could make my mind up, he left the shop, a brown paper bag under one arm and a six-pack of Total Blonde dangling from his long, strong fingers. I tucked my phone away with a hand that shook.

That had been too close. I didn't need to let Xander think we could rekindle a friendship. I didn't need us getting any closer. He was already striding towards me like he wanted to talk.

I'd overdosed on Xander Fox today, and I needed to remind myself of all the reasons we were no longer friends … no longer anything. Even if some of those reasons made me sick to the stomach to think about.

But even forcing myself to relive that night, and all the heartbreak, and all the mistakes that were made, would be for nothing if he insisted on popping those goddamned dimples at me when I was too tired to put up my defences.

"Got my sugar hit!" Lachy crowed, launching himself athletically over the picket fence and plonking down beside me on the step. Xander stopped at the fence, resting his palms on the rails. I blinked away from his twitching forearm muscles, rippling under tanned skin and the dusting of golden hair.

"You earned it!" I said with more energy than I had to give. The heat of Xander's gaze scorched the side of my face. "Can I share?"

Lachy's leer was almost dirty. "You wanna lick?"

My eyes widened, face flushing as he produced a wrapped ice cream. "Oh, sorry Lach, I thought maybe you'd bought a bag of mixed lollies from the milk bar! I didn't—"

And then I saw what ice cream he was holding, and Xander's presence suddenly loomed on the other side of the fence. I tried so hard not to steal a glance at him, practically locking my neck muscles to stop myself.

"Blast from the past, eh, Georgie?" Lachy continued, completely oblivious to the palpable tension in the air. "These were my absolute fave when I was a kid."

"Mine, too," I managed to choke out as Lachy unwrapped the brightly coloured ice cream with its ridiculous cowboy hat and bubble gum ball nose.

"Ah, the humble Bubble-O-Bill," Xander commented, his voice thick, and even from across the yard, it was like his mouth was right at my ear. I let my eyes fall closed as the rest of his words descended on me. "I have … fond memories of Bill."

That memory rose viscerally to the front of my mind. I could almost feel his cold, sugary lips. The hint of his tongue … melted ice cream still lingering on the tip.

"I don't mind sharing, you know," Lachy persisted, holding the ice cream up to my mouth. Xander's eyes were a hot brand on my skin. Did I take a lick? It would drive him completely nuts. Tempting, but hadn't I decided I wasn't going to antagonise him?

I paused long enough that Lachy took matters into his own hands, jabbing the ice cream at me, smearing it across my lips.

"Oh, sorry Georgie!" Lachy said, but his grin and twinkling eyes told me he was not even slightly apologetic. With an eyeroll at his behaviour, I darted my tongue out to lick the sweet, sticky goo away. And then my eyes were rolling back in my head for a completely different reason.

"Oh God! I'd forgotten how good these taste," I moaned.

"I'll find Jordyn and head home," Xander announced, his voice flat. I turned to find him gripping the fence palings so tight the tendons in his knuckles stood out against his skin. His mouth was a thin slash. His obvious torment left my insides roiling.

"I'm guessing you're okay to catch a ride with Chippy here," he continued, "I don't think Molly will like sharing the back seat." He gestured to the cherry red Ute, where Molly's head poked out the back window, tongue lolling.

I pursed my lips and glared in his general direction. He'd just given me exactly what I wanted—an out of traveling with him—but I suddenly, stupidly felt like arguing.

"You want another lick, Georgie?" Lachy asked.

I shook my head. "Maybe next time, Lach." I turned back to Xander. "I'll hitch a ride with Jase. Lachy's heading out of town in the opposite direction—I don't want to put him out."

"Or … we could go in the same direction, and you could put me *in*, instead," Lachy suggested with a waggle of his eyebrows. "We're both already sweaty, why not make it worth our while?"

"Mate …" Xander's voice was full of warning.

"Ready to make tracks?" Jordyn asked from the porch behind us. I startled, leaping to my feet as they locked the clinic door, clocking what I was sure was a deer in the headlights expression on my face. "I'm guessing I'm riding with Dr Fox this evening?"

I managed a nod as Lachy slung an arm around me. "I wanna come home with you, Georgie," he murmured against my hair, and I could smell the ice cream on his breath. My eyes moved of their own accord, locking with Xander's.

I tried to act like Lachy being draped all over me didn't make me feel all kinds of uncomfortable. "While that sounds … fun, I have loads of work to do tonight. I'm not really …"

"She just got out of a serious relationship," Jordyn interjected coldly, their words emphasised by the creak of the front gate as they let themselves onto the footpath with Xander. "She's not looking for what you're offering."

I glared at Jord, caught between fury that they had aired my private business, and gratitude that the words had Lachy's arm dropping from my shoulders.

"Oh?" Lachy said in surprise. "How serious? Like, is that why you wouldn't … last year when we …?"

The tight, black look on Xander's face had my chest constricting. I blew out a breath, turned to Lachy and nodded. "James and I were together for two years."

Lachy scratched his head. "Well, that explains a lot." It explained exactly nothing—I'd turned Lachy down countless times before last year, but I supposed it didn't hurt to let him think James was the only reason I'd rebuffed him last time.

"So," I began after clearing my throat in a sad attempt to break the tension simmering in the air, "Jordyn will travel with Dr Fox, I'll hitch a lift with Jase and Karl, and Lachy, we'll see you in the morning … that is, if you're keen to continue working with us tomorrow?"

Lachy nodded, gazing at me with something akin to pity in his eyes. I would put money on it that tomorrow he would show up working a new angle. Out with the sleazy come-ons, in with, 'I'm your knight in shining armour, here to save you from your broken heart'.

"Bright and early tomorrow, Georgie. You can rely on me!" Yep, I'd just won my imaginary bet.

He launched himself over the fence, turning to grin briefly at me before jogging across the road to his beaten-up old Ute. I rubbed my temples. This whole show was starting to feel like more trouble than it was worth.

Xander watched me for just a moment too long, eyes startlingly intense, lips tilted in a tiny frown. Jordyn looked between the two of us, a matching frown on their face.

"Come on Dr Fox. We'd better get you home for a shower. A bird just crapped on your shoulder."

Xander's nose wrinkled in a way that made my insides hum as

he looked down at the white smear that had just appeared on his black t-shirt.

"For fuck's … fucking budgerigars!" he snarled, wrenching the keys from his pocket and storming towards the driver's door as the offending budgerigars chattered above us. I looked up to a cloud of them zooming through the purple-pink dusk towards Bird Turd Tree, ready to roost.

Despite my exhaustion, I couldn't help but smile about Xander's latest mishap as I trotted across the road to where Jase's van was parked.

Now: You Liked It A Little Too Much

XANDER

The brown paper bag taunted me.

Less than a week ago I'd walked out of the bottle-o after that bloody exhausting first day of clearing out the clinic with a six-pack of beer and a bottle of merlot—the one she'd been drinking in the pub the night before.

But then fucking Chipolata and his Bubble-O-Bill stopped me in my tracks … and *that* revelation about Georgie completely derailed my plans.

She'd just gotten out of a serious relationship.

Which meant she'd actually been able to *have* a serious relationship. Something I hadn't managed in twelve years.

I glowered at the paper bag. Wine wasn't going to make things any easier between Georgie and me. If anything, alcohol had the potential to make things far, far worse.

The car ride home after finding out about Georgie's 'serious' relationship had consisted of me grilling Jordyn over the details while trying not to grind my teeth too much.

Me: How long were they together?
Jordyn: Two years. She said that earlier.

Me: Did they live together?
Jordyn: No, but they split their time between each other's apartments.
Me: What was he like?
Jordyn: He was okay. Very career focussed, like Georgie.
Me: But was he … good-looking?
Jordyn: … Does that matter?
Me: Why did they split up?
Jordyn: Not my place to say.
Me: Has she been in any other serious relationships?
Jordyn: I wouldn't know, she started dating James not long after I met her. You seem to be overly interested in Georgie's private life. If you're that curious, why don't you just ask her yourself?

Why indeed?

I'd thought watching Chipolata draping himself all over her had been torture. Knowing she'd been with one guy—*James*—for two years felt like someone had poured acid directly into my chest cavity.

In twelve damned years, I hadn't managed to date a woman more than a few times. Screwing them? That was easy. It didn't require me to feel anything. But getting to know a woman … after a few dates, there had always been something that turned into a deal-breaker.

She was too giggly. She didn't have strong opinions on anything. Her voice was too squeaky. Her eyes weren't the right colour.

She wasn't Georgina Bloody Menzies.

She'd ruined me for everyone else, and after one stupid, selfish teenage boy mistake, she'd ghosted me. No one else would ever stack up to how she'd made me feel.

And I resented the hell out of her for it.

To add salt to the wound, I'd spent five days watching Lachy make repeated, ham-handed attempts to act chivalrous as we got stuck into the clinic renovations. I tried to tell myself that Georgie did nothing to encourage him. But she did nothing to dissuade him either. And she was much friendlier with him than she was with me. In fact, she'd been cold, verging on bloody Arctic with me.

I stared past the brown paper bag, out the window and across the lawn, to where a light glowed on the verandah of the old farmhouse that belonged to Georgie's grandmother. I watched that light every bloody night. I stayed up far too late, mesmerised by that light and the face it illuminated.

Georgie, reclined in a hammock strung between two of the verandah posts, her laptop balanced on her knees.

It had become our weird little game. We'd act distant during the day, and every evening, when filming was over, she would appear on the verandah across the lawn, and I'd stand by my kitchen sink and watch her through the window.

The miniature sheep she called Jumbo would come out and cavort on the lawn before retreating back to Georgie to be scratched on the head and fed treats from her pocket. I didn't let Molly out when the sheep was there—the last thing the strained tension between Georgie and I needed was non-consensual humping animals. But it was late tonight. Her sheep had long since been put to bed, and Molly was snoring.

I couldn't take it any longer. Snatching up the brown bag, I stormed out the door and down the porch steps.

"Ah, fuck!" I hissed, hopping back onto the porch and collapsing into the chair. "Bloody bindies!"

Muttering curses under my breath, my face hotter than the oppressive summer air, I plucked the spiky little suckers out of my feet and reached for my thongs, slipping them on and resuming my walk across the lawn to where Georgie was watching me, eyes full of withering amusement.

"You'll learn eventually," she muttered under her breath, clicking the touchpad on her laptop. "Footwear is a must in the country. Even for a twenty-metre walk."

"In three months' time I won't ever have to think about the country again," I grouched, stopping just short of stepping onto the verandah. Georgie's mouth twisted, but she didn't respond.

"What're you doing out here every night?" I asked, leaning one arm against the verandah post, setting the brown bag down out of her sight. Her eyes flicked up to me for a split second before blinking back to her screen.

"Reviewing footage, tagging segments to go to post-production," she replied in a monotone.

"Sounds riveting," I said. That made her look up at me, eyes narrowed, her top lip folded into that tiny sneer I knew so damned well. Had the air just gotten hotter?

"It's my job, Dr Fox. Not all of us get to swan around looking pretty in front of the camera, you know."

I grunted. "You *do* look pretty in front of the camera."

Even the cicadas stopped chirping as my comment seeped into the night. The silence stretched. Georgie stared at her screen without moving for so long I that actually started to hear my heartbeat pounding in my ears.

"Clinic's coming up well, and we're keeping to schedule," she eventually said. I winced. Things felt more awkward between us now than they had that first day in her office back in Sydney.

Because you went to third base with her and then told her to pretend it never happened. I was a bloody fool.

"Yeah," I agreed, clearing my throat. "I was actually thinking it might be good to do a grand opening type thing. I could do free tick and worm treatments. We could have a sausage sizzle—Chipolata would probably be keen to handle that."

Georgie finally looked up at me, one eyebrow raised, a tiny smile playing around her lips.

"I actually love that idea," she said before turning back to her computer. I stifled a sigh. For a second there, things had felt less strained. But then she started typing, beckoning me closer.

"We allocated a fortnight to the clinic renos. We're still on track to finish by Wednesday of next week." She pointed to the screen, and, heart hammering, I leaned closer, looking over her shoulder at the calendar she had pulled up.

"So, we could potentially do a soft open on Thursday, and have a grand opening lunch on Saturday. I can get some posters printed up to stick in the shop windows, create a Facebook event. Liz is on the Country Women's Association; she might even be able to wrangle the ladies to organise a cake stall."

Georgie turned to me suddenly, her eyes wide and gleaming.

"We could do a gold coin donation to drought relief in exchange for a flea and tick treatment! And we can donate the proceeds from the sausage sizzle and the cake stall too."

The excitement in her face came close to completely undoing me. I tugged at my hair, needing something to do with my free hand so I didn't reach for her.

"Yeah, that all sounds great," I managed.

Georgie turned back to her screen, adding an event to her calendar. "I'll get Jord onto organising it first thing tomorrow."

"Isn't Jordyn on the road with Alex and me tomorrow?" I asked.

Georgie bit her lip. "No … I'm on the road with you two. Jord's on clinic filming tomorrow."

"Oh. Right."

Georgie raised a brow at me. "Is that a problem?"

I scratched at the stubble on my jaw. "No … It's just that Jordyn's been riding with me most of the time, I assumed …"

"Here's a hot tip, Dr Fox. Don't assume. This is *my* show, and this is the first time you're visiting rural patients. I'm not delegating that to my assistant."

And there it was. The snark that boiled my blood and had me wanting to rage at her, tip her out of that hammock and wedge my hips between her thighs, wrap my fingers around her neck and suck bruises into her collarbone. I inhaled deeply, struggling against those urges.

"So, delegating every other moment this last week, totally normal, but the second I might be alone with Alex, I need your expert supervision?" My voice was rough, and before I could stop myself, I was looming over Georgie. She glared up at me, fire in her eyes.

My dick ached. I wanted to see that fire in her eyes while she took me between her lips. I pinched the bridge of my nose but didn't move away. I couldn't let her win this one.

"Were you *hoping* for alone time with Dr Alex?" she snapped back at me.

"Well, it'd be nice to have a scrap of positive female attention for once!"

"Oh, really?" Georgie scoffed, rolling her eyes in a way that made my balls tighten. "Because the procession of drooling school pick-up mums who flock at the gate, even though the school is at the other end of town, isn't positive enough for you?"

I snorted as she snapped her laptop shut, spinning towards me so fast that the hammock rocked wildly. Georgie's mouth popped open, her laptop slipping. She quickly pulled it to her chest, but the sudden movement only destabilised the hammock more, tilting her precariously backwards.

"Shit!" I hissed, lunging forward and snatching her up a second before she would have fallen backwards, plucking her laptop from her and setting it down on the verandah.

"Shit," Georgie repeated breathlessly as I clutched her closer. The minty scent of her hair hit me, and before I realised what I was doing, I had my hands tangled in it.

"I didn't tell you how much I like your hair like this," I murmured against the short strands, gripping fistfuls of it and inhaling deeply.

"I didn't cut it for you," she retorted, making me grin against the top of her head, suddenly positive she *had* cut it because of me.

"Didn't like me pulling your ponytail?" I asked, removing one hand from her hair and snaking it around her waist as she softened in my grip, caging her against me and my growing erection. Her hands went to my hips. Her breath was hot against my collarbone.

"Or … maybe you liked it a little *too* much," I suggested, rolling my groin against her stomach.

Those hands on my hips tightened. Christ, was that her lips on my neck?

But then she thrust me away, forcefully enough that I staggered two steps back from her.

"Not appropriate Dr Fox!" she gasped. My fingers found their way to my neck. There was a damp spot where her mouth had been. Air whooshed out of my lungs.

"Go … deal with that!" she snapped, gesticulating at my tented shorts.

"And be ready by six tomorrow—Dr Alex starts her rounds early."

She turned away, grabbing her laptop off the weathered old verandah.

"So, she gets Dr Alex, can I at least get Dr Xander?" I asked. Georgie stopped but didn't turn.

"Do you think you've earned that from me?" she asked quietly, and all of the adrenaline that had flooded my system a moment ago drained away. I didn't know how to answer that. Didn't know if there was a right answer.

Instead, I picked up the brown paper bag, stepped onto the verandah and pressed it to her stomach. Her slender fingers wrapped around it, gaze darting up to mine.

"What's this?"

I shrugged. "Bottle of merlot. I figured that was a safe bet, judging by how you were knocking them back the other night at the pub. Thought you might like it … to unwind."

Before she could respond, I hopped from the balcony and jogged back to the tiny home. Flicking off the kitchen light, I stood in the darkness like a bloody creeper and watched out the window. Georgie still stood where I'd left her, staring down at the brown paper bag in her hand.

It was ten minutes before she shook her head and stalked inside the house, and I felt like I could move again.

Straight into the shower to *take care of* my raging hard-on, thinking about her hands on my hips, and her hot breath on my collarbone, and her damp lips on my skin.

"I didn't realise how much of a toll the drought was taking on farmers," I muttered, climbing back into my butt-ugly Ute.

Alex grunted. "For the last eighteen months, the majority of my rural work has been trying to help farmers drought-manage their livestock. Analysing stock-feed diets, doing regular health checks, even lecturing some of them on paddock rotation and the need to reduce herd size. They can be stubborn buggers, some of them."

I started the car as Georgie climbed into the seat behind me, where she would be virtually invisible to the camera mounted on the windscreen.

"Yeah, an urban vet like me has zero experience with any of this. I'd be totally screwed without your help, Alex," I said. Alex reached over and squeezed my thigh, just above my knee. It was nothing more than friendly, but I glanced in the rear-view mirror, meeting Georgie's flashing silver eyes before they locked on my knee, her jaw twitching.

"How's Miriam coping with the drought?" I asked Georgie. She dragged her eyes away from where Alex's hand still sat on my leg.

"With her usual stubborn streak," Georgie retorted, folding her arms across her chest as Alex's thumb started drawing circles on the outside of my thigh. I shifted uncomfortably. A friendly pat was one thing. Caressing me was a bit more than friendly.

"Oh! Miriam Menzies?" Alex asked, swivelling in her seat to face Georgie, thankfully removing her questing hand. "She's a wily old goat, isn't she? How do you know her?"

"She's my grandmother," Georgie snarled back. "And if she ever heard you refer to her as an old goat, she'd string you up from the Hills Hoist by your intestines."

Alex let out a barking burst of laughter. "I don't doubt it for a second! She's one of the smarter farmers, she was the first in the area to adopt rotational grazing, even before the drought hit."

Georgie sniffed. "Yes, well, the drought's been going on too long now, even with best farming practice it's getting pretty dire. Feed and fresh water are expensive. She's already sold off thirty percent of her flock."

"They're all in the same boat, and it's heartbreaking," Alex sighed. She sank back into her seat, and suddenly her fingers interlocked with mine where they rested on the gear knob. I flinched but didn't knock her hand away. I was enjoying how riled it was getting Georgie too much to stop it.

Georgie made a disgusted sound in the back of her throat. "How many more house calls do you have today, Dr Kingston?"

I bit back a grin. So, Alex had been relegated to surname only, too. Georgie's growing iciness towards Alex stirred something hot and antagonistic in my chest, and I recklessly hooked my thumb around Alex's little finger, rubbing the knuckle. She sucked in a little gasp of air, her head snapping towards me.

"Just one more." Alex extricated her hand from mine, reaching over and tapping the address into the GPS. "A border collie that was hit by a car a few weeks ago. It's just a quick check to ensure healing is continuing. She was lucky—only broken bones, no head trauma, no internal bleeding. But she *is* a border collie, so keeping her still and quiet while she heals has been a struggle."

Alex stopped talking, and the silence in the car swelled until it was a living bloody thing. The silence pounded in my ears. It gripped me by the back of the neck. It squeezed my lungs until getting air into them was an effort. I chanced a glance in the mirror. Georgie's eyes were wide, her usually tanned face bleached of colour.

I opened my mouth. Closed it again. I had no words.

Georgie found some. "Looks like we have to head back through town on the way. You can drop me back at the clinic and take Jord for the last visit. I've got some urgent business, and I need to be in front of my computer."

I opened my mouth to ask what business she had, then snapped it shut when I caught the stricken expression on her face.

"Yep, can do," I mumbled instead, and we all sat in the most awkward bloody silence of my life for the twenty minutes back into Budgerigar.

"I think it's working!" Alex crowed with a satisfied smirk as Jord climbed into the seat Georgie had just vacated.

"What's working?" I asked through my scowl as I watched bloody Lachy come bounding out of the clinic like an overexcited

Dalmatian to grab Georgie's hand, exclaiming, "Come check out my surprise, babe!"

I wound up the window and pulled away from the kerb in disgust. Babe. Had there ever been a less inspired pet name?

"Alex," Jordyn hissed in warning, and I snapped my attention to inside the car.

"What's working?" I asked again.

"Oh, sugar, is he … are you not in on it?" Alex asked, an expression of horror that would usually have cracked me up morphing onto her face.

"In on what?"

Alex covered her face with her hands. "Oh my God, I never would have … if I'd known you didn't … Jordyn! This is not funny!"

Jordyn's villainous cackle echoed around the car. "It's a bit funny. But we're on camera here, don't forget."

I reached up and switched the camera off. "Not anymore, we're not. Now tell me what the hell you two are talking about!"

Jordyn sighed. "Look, Georgie wouldn't be keen on the idea, so she doesn't know the details. We need to inject some romance into the show. Renovating and running a rural vet clinic can only get us so far. Alex very kindly agreed to fake interest in you, to manufacture a romantic subplot for *Beach Vet Goes Bush*. So, if you could play along, that would be much appreciated."

I narrowed my eyes, but my retort was cut off by the GPS informing me I needed to turn off the highway. Once we were on the dusty dirt track that led to our last appointment for the day, I huffed out a breath.

"So, you touching my leg, and my hand … that was just you faking it for the show?" I asked, not taking my eyes from the road.

"I'm sorry, Xander. I thought Jordyn had told you everything." She turned to scowl into the back at Jordyn.

"How far are we expected to go for this 'romantic subplot'?" I demanded, my hands tightening on the steering wheel.

"Jordyn?" Alex prompted.

"You don't have to get physical if that's what you're worried about. But if, for instance, you happened to take Alex out to The Budgie for dinner tonight, maybe sling your arm around her. And if you happened to walk her back to her car at the end of the night, you might happen to lean down to whisper your goodbye in her ear. I'll keep the cameras back a bit, make it look like you think you're getting privacy."

"I didn't sign up for this," I grumbled. "I don't like keeping Georgie in the dark about it." I might have enjoyed seeing her get all riled in the car before, but this premeditated shit? Not my jam.

Jordyn snorted. "Why the fuck not? Look, the camera is off, I'm going to be straight with you. Georgie is not over whatever it is that happened between the two of you. She hasn't forgiven you, but she sure as shit needs to. It's impacting her work."

I grimaced as Jordyn continued, "So, this fake romance is a 'two birds, one stone' scenario—I get the romantic action for the show, and you poke the Georgie-bear into action."

"Let me get this straight," I grunted, dragging on the steering wheel to pull the car over to the side of the road. I turned to stare Jordyn down. "You think me embarking on a fake romance with Alex the gorgeous country vet is going to help Georgie to forgive me? Do you even know what I did to her?"

Jordyn shrugged. "She gave me the CliffsNotes."

An incredulous laugh burst from me. "If anything, this plan of yours is just going to prove to her how right she was to cut me out of her life in the first place!"

"I disagree," Jordyn said with a smug smile. "I've seen the way she looks at you. And I know what happened the first night you arrived in Budgerigar."

My eyes widened.

"Oooh, what happened the first night?" Alex asked.

"*Nothing* happened!" I snapped. "And *if* something *had* happened, how is me canoodling with another woman going to improve the situation?"

"She wants you, Xander. But she won't admit it to herself. So, we have to help her along. Jealousy is a fabulous motivator, don't you think?"

"You're Machiavellian!" Alex muttered, impressed, while I rubbed my forehead.

Jealousy *was* a fabulous motivator. I couldn't deny that jealousy over James, the poncy career-focused long-term ex-boyfriend who'd had a key to her apartment, had motivated me last night when I'd fisted her minty hair and rubbed my dick on her tight stomach. What might jealousy motivate Georgie to do to me?

Kiss me? Or kill me?

I growled and pulled the car back onto the road.

"Yes! Does this mean you agree?" Jordyn asked.

"No. Maybe. I'll play it by ear. But don't script out my romantic trysts for me," I locked eyes with Jordyn in the back before turning my glare on Alex. "Either of you. If I think it's warranted, I'll make a move, and it'll look a thousand times more bloody natural than anything you two come up with."

Now: In The Immortal Words Of Tay Tay

GEORGIE

Two can play this game, Xander Fox. In fact, two will *play this game.*

The Budgie was busy for a Thursday night. Alex and Xander sat across the table from me. Karl and Jase were set up on either side of them, capturing every moment of their flirtation. I pasted a smile on my face and sipped at my wine while Xander and Alex shared some joke that was apparently the funniest thing either of them had ever heard while downing matching schooners of beer.

I'd sent Jord off to scout the crowd in the hopes that we could film some local perspectives on the new 'city slicker' vet. The more colourful the character, the better.

Deidre, Freddie's wife, a ruddy-faced woman with smoker's mouth and sparkling green eyes, slapped a plate of garlic bread down in the centre of the table.

"Looks like you two are gonna need some carbs to soak up the schooners," she drawled. Alex giggled and Xander flashed the dimples at Deidre, who chuckled, completely immune to Xander's charm.

"Hey, Deidre, if you've got time, can you go see my assistant Jordyn, and sit down for a quick chat on camera?" I asked.

Deidre smirked. "Georgie, love, I've got a face for radio, and a voice for silent movies," she argued merrily. I grinned at her.

"But you've got your finger on the pulse of everything going on in Budgerigar. You're *almost* the town matriarch!" I pinched at my bottom lip, feigning thoughtfulness. "I suppose we could just give Liz more screen time."

Deidre's eyes narrowed. "That jumped up, randy old flirt? Where's this Jordyn person?"

I bit back my grin and gestured in Jord's direction, watching as Deidre stalked off before plucking a piece of garlic bread from the table.

"Do you know everyone in this bloody town?" Xander asked, watching me with inscrutable eyes. I shrugged.

"I've spent holidays here every year for the last twelve years. And it's a very small town."

Xander eyed me a moment longer before shrugging and turning back to Alex. They both reached for a piece of bread at the same time, their hands brushing. Cue more giggling from Alex and more dimpling from Xander.

Where the hell was Lachy? I couldn't beat Xander at this little game of his without my willing brawny local.

"How was your afternoon, Georgie?" Alex asked, her little finger stroking the back of Xander's palm. I stared at that movement for far too long, bitterness burbling up from my diaphragm. I swallowed it back down, but my smile felt tight.

"Lachy surprised me—he finished the waiting area today, brought in a bespoke reception desk that he's been working on every evening for the last week. It's …" I flicked my eyes to Xander, feeling my smile loosen into something wicked, "Impressive. I love a man who's good with his hands."

Xander's own hands curled into fists on the table, as Lachy, with perfect timing, slid into the chair beside me, slinging a casual arm around my shoulders.

"Who's good with his hands?" he asked. With the restraint of a saint, I didn't sneak a glance at Xander, instead fluttering my lashes up at Lachy.

"You, Lach!" I simpered, giving his thick, corded bicep a squeeze. "I was just telling these two about how amazing the new reception furniture is!"

Lachy grinned widely, his fingers walking up my neck, kneading the muscles there. "I'm good with my hands in other ways, too."

"Ever tried to repair a dog's torn ACL? Pretty sure it requires a little more finesse than nailing and screwing," Xander muttered. I took a sip of wine to hide my smirk.

"And banging!" Lachy added, his own smirk on full display. "There's a lot of banging involved in what I do."

"Another beer, Alex?" Xander asked, his chair scraping back with a sound reminiscent of nails on a chalkboard.

"I'll come with you," Alex said as she followed him to the bar. Jase tailed them while Jordyn beckoned Karl over to a small group of people headed by a determined-looking Deidre.

I was momentarily colleague free. I finally felt like I could take a breath. Until Lachy opened his mouth again.

"They look good together, don't they?"

I glanced over the top of my wine glass at the bar, where Xander and Alex were clinking their schooner glasses together, smiling at one another like they were sharing a secret. Jase was capturing every sickeningly cute moment of it.

And I'd have the rare, horrifying pleasure of reviewing all of this footage tomorrow night. Like a papercut with lemon juice poured into it, I already knew how much it was going to sting.

"Wouldn't it be completely nuts if they fell in love, and he moved here permanently?" Lachy said in my ear, his fingers tickling my shoulder. I locked my muscles so I wouldn't flinch.

"Completely nuts. There is no way in the world that Dr Fox isn't returning to Sydney at the end of all of this. He's counting down the days." How I managed to keep my voice so even I had no idea.

What if he wasn't counting down the days anymore? What if there was something real blooming between him and Alex? Alex, with her lustrous hair, and her beautiful dark skin, and her amazing round arse that looked like you could bounce a dollar coin off it in the tight jeans she was wearing.

Xander had been grinding his erection against me less than twenty-four hours ago, but past experience had shown that meant very little to him. And I'd convinced myself over twelve years that it also meant very little to me.

So why was hot, stabbing rage blooming under my ribcage. It wasn't jealousy. I *couldn't* be jealous. I didn't want him. I didn't. Because if I did, I could have had him last night. I could have done more than just press a single kiss to his neck. I could have nibbled my way up it and run my tongue along his jaw, and I could have hooked one leg around his hip and let him lift me until my core was right against that long, thick length I'd seen jutting from his shorts last night.

I'd kissed his neck. Before I'd pushed him away, I'd kissed his neck. And then I'd gone inside and masturbated while I fantasised about what could have happened if I hadn't pushed him away.

What the hell had I been thinking?

And now I was watching him drink and laugh and flirt with someone else.

History repeating. And it still hurt like a bitch.

"Georgie?"

I blinked, turning to Lachy, who looked down at me with worry in his eyes. He really was taking this protector role to the extreme. I blew out a breath, making my fringe flip.

"Sorry, Lach. I was somewhere else entirely. What were you saying?"

Warm fingers stroked up and down my arm. I shivered, looking anywhere but at Lachy. I should have been shrugging him off. I shouldn't be encouraging him, shouldn't be using him in this silent war I was waging with Xander—a war I wasn't even sure Xander knew he was engaged in.

But there he was, laughing and high-fiving Alex at the bar, winding his fingers through hers, showing her those dimples.

The searing urge to double down on this ridiculous flirt-off had me leaning into Lachy, resting my head on his muscular shoulder. Xander glanced over, his eyebrows shooting up, his jaw twitching before he turned back to Alex with an even bigger smile on his face.

"You thinking about him?" Lachy asked softly.

"Uh … no! Of course I'm not," I protested, struggling to keep my body from tensing. "Why would I be?"

Lachy leaned back to look at me like I was completely insane. "Because you were with him for two years, and you only broke up a few weeks ago, babe."

"Oh. James. Well—" The screech of microphone feedback cut me off.

"You all know Thursday is Karaoke night here at The Budgie!" Freddie boomed into the mic, and I sighed in profound relief that I was saved from having to attempt to make up something about the end of my relationship with James.

"Oh God, that's got to be my cue to leave," I muttered, shrugging from Lachy's grip and standing.

"Oh, come on, babe! I've seen you belting out Taylor Swift here before," Lachy said, gripping my hand to stop me from leaving.

I laughed lightly. "The last time I sang at The Budgie karaoke night, I was twenty-two, drunk as a skunk, and I got booed off the stage after singing *Love Story* in the key of tone deaf!"

"I've already signed you up. No backing out now. And you weren't *that* bad," Lachy tried to console me, but his tone told me that yes, I had indeed been that bad.

"Lach, I grew up with an opera singer. I can safely say I am well aware of how bad I am." Bringing up Dom filled my chest with a dull ache, one I'd grown all too accustomed to over the years. Were he and Xander still friends? It wasn't a topic I wanted to broach with Xander for so many reasons.

"Welcome to the stage to kick off our night, local legend Mr Lachlan Porter!" Freddie announced to a rousing round of cheers and jeers. With a wink, Lachy stood.

"Better get yourself over there to choose your song, babe. You're next." He strode confidently over to the stage.

"What am I doing?" I muttered as I followed a few steps behind him, veering off to where the jukebox was set up to one side of the little platform that passed as a stage. Navigating through the screens until I came to a list by artist, I went straight to the S's.

"Still haven't grown out of the Swiftie era, huh?"

I jumped, turning to glower at Xander. "Why are you here?"

Xander chuckled. "Well, I auditioned to be on this show, about a vet, and I guess they decided I was the best."

I rolled my eyes. "I meant why are you here at the jukebox?" I didn't look at him, instead scrolling through the long list of Taylor Swift songs. If I had to get up on stage, at the very least it would be to sing a song I knew like the back of my hand.

"Alex thought it'd be great for the show, me making a fool of myself in front of all the locals before I have a chance to show them that I'm actually more than competent as a vet. She put my name down. I'm on right after you."

I winced as Lachy started bellowing the opening lines of Bon Jovi's *Dead or Alive* into the microphone, with a great deal of enthusiasm and very little talent.

"What are you going to sing?" I asked Xander over Lachy's howling. The heat of his broad chest against my back was distracting—I'd scrolled past Taylor Swift and onto System of a Down. I quickly scrolled back up.

"Not Taylor Swift, that's for sure." His mouth was too close to my ear. I twitched my head to the side, making some space between us.

"Taylor Swift is one of the greatest musical storytellers of our generation!" I snarled under my breath. Xander chuckled. His arm came around and gripped the side of the jukebox, his elbow resting against my waist. I inhaled sharply, willing him not to notice how it affected me.

"And what story are you going to tell tonight, in the immortal words of Tay Tay?" he asked. I stared down at the screen. And then the answer jumped out at me. I tapped on my song to add it to the playlist and spun around with a grin that almost faltered at the intensity of his gaze.

"Don't look, it'll spoil the surprise," I told him before walking away, taking a spot on the other side of the stage next to Freddie and pretending to enjoy Lachy completely murdering Bon Jovi.

His song ended to a resounding echo of laughter and clapping, with a few boos interspersed. Lachy leapt off the stage and gave my hand a squeeze.

"No way you'll sound worse than that, babe," he whispered as Freddie took the mic from him.

"Our next singer has been an annual regular here in town for over a decade now, and we've adopted her as one of our own. Please welcome the great, great grand-daughter of one of the founding families of Budgerigar—Georgina Menzies!"

I drowned out the clapping and cheering as I took the stage. I let my eyes fall on Xander. He stood beside the jukebox, arms folded across his chest, a little smile playing at the corners of his lips. Any nerves I felt about getting back up on this stage melted away under his stare.

As the opening bars of the song began playing, and I started clicking my fingers along to the beat, Xander's brow furrowed. He didn't recognise the song. All the better.

"This one's for a boy who *used* to have a special place in my heart," I announced, watching Xander's eyes flash. And then the lyrics to *I Forgot That You Existed* started.

I might have been a little off-key at times, but I more than made up for it with my enthusiasm, as I strutted about the stage. More than once, I threw some side eye in Xander's direction, silently hoping he was picking up on the message I was sending.

The message was a raging lie, of course. There was no forgetting that Xander Fox existed. There was no indifference on my part. Just hate. Lots of hate. Yes, that was my line, I was sticking with it.

But he didn't need to know that.

I was belting my way through the bridge when I noticed he'd turned back to the jukebox and was frantically scrolling through songs, his jaw tight. I fought back a laugh, his sudden mood change buoying me enough to finish up the final chorus with hip shaking and a wink out at the crowd. As I stepped down to a significantly better reception from the crowd than the last time I'd sung on The Budgie's stage, I mentally high-fived myself for getting so under Xander's skin with my song choice that he'd felt the need to change whatever he was singing as a result.

"Well, that was a whole lot better than Georgie's last, infamous trip up onto this stage," Freddie remarked into the mic, to raucous laughter. I threw him a withering look, feeling too on top of the world to really be annoyed.

Beat that, Xander! I thought as I leaned against the wall where he'd been standing to watch me just a moment ago.

"Our newest import, all the way from the sunny sands of Bondi Beach, Sydney, make sure you say hello to him sometime tonight—you might get your mug on television! Dr Xander Fox!"

The applause was interspersed with shouts, whistles, and a lot of murmuring, particularly amongst the female patrons, about 'how bloody gorgeous' the town's new vet was.

For the first time, I felt a true pang of guilt about making this show. Because in three months' time, Xander Fox was going to waltz right back out of town again, leaving Budgerigar and all the surrounding farms in the lurch. All for the sake of a handful of episodes of reality television.

Unless he ended up falling for Alex Kingston. But I couldn't think about that in too much detail.

"Look, I know this song probably has some really deep meaning to it," Xander said, dragging a bar stool onto the stage and sitting. Guitar chords started playing over the speakers, and I froze.

No. He hadn't!

Except he had.

"But to me, this song will always be special because it was playing the first time I held a girl's hand. And not just any girl. One who became the world to me."

My throat closed over, and I swallowed frantically as Xander's hazel eyes bored into me. There was nothing playful about the way he was looking at me. Nothing teasing, or antagonistic, or even furious.

Those eyes were claiming me. I couldn't move. I wanted to run, but his gaze held me in place as he lifted the mic to his lips and sang the first line of Jeff Buckley's version of *Hallelujah*.

His voice was rough, husky, and for the entire six minutes of the song, his eyes never left mine. Even when his voice cracked over one verse, and as the words he'd just sung sank into me, I felt some of the protection I'd built around my heart twelve years ago start to crack too.

Applause roared in my ears, and I flinched. The song had ended, but it wasn't the applause of a country pub that I heard. It was the applause of a theatre full of people, with acoustics amplifying every clap, every cheer, to the point that it reverberated in every pore of my body.

Xander broke eye contact with me to hand the mic back to Freddie, and I turned, frantically weaving my way through the tables, bursting through the door and onto the verandah. The air was hot and dry as I gasped, sucking that burning air into my lungs. I leaned my hands on the verandah rail, arms trembling. There was no way my legs would hold me up on their own.

Warmth at my side. A little finger hooked through mine where it rested on the rail.

"Georgie, I ..." His voice was thick. I wrenched my finger away, storming back inside to get the keys to Jord's car. I couldn't look at him. I was terrified of what might happen if I did.

Then: I'm Here

GEORGIE, 15 YEARS OLD

Mum and Seth were fighting again. I froze just outside the kitchen to listen.

"This shouldn't be your call anymore, Grace," Seth said.

"Don't you dare lecture me on how to manage my own daughter!" Mum snarled back. Mum and Seth had been fighting on and off for the last year, but I'd never heard them fight about me. Usually it was money or how often Seth was away for work.

I checked my watch. I really needed them to finish up their argument so Mum could drive me into the city, or I was going to be late for Dom's performance.

But knowing why I was the subject of this latest whisper-shouting match was worth eavesdropping a few more minutes.

"I'm not lecturing you. I'm just saying—"

"'I'm just saying'," Mum mimicked, *"Definitely* not lecturing me!"

Seth sighed. "She's fifteen. She's old enough to decide for herself if she wants to meet—"

"No!" Mum hissed while my mind whirred. Meet who? Oh my God, were they talking about my biological father?

Seth was my dad, for all I called him by his first name. He and

Mum had been together since I was four, and he'd been all the dad I'd ever wanted and then some. I never even thought about the jerk who'd gotten Mum pregnant.

"Don't fight!" I called out, stepping into the kitchen. Mum and Seth froze guiltily, turning to me in unison. Mum's lips were white; she was pressing them so tightly together. Seth looked resigned. I wondered how many times they'd had this fight before, and I just hadn't noticed.

"Georgie, you—" Seth began.

"No, I don't want to meet him. Okay? I'm with Mum. If she doesn't think me meeting my birth father is a good idea, then I don't want it either."

Seth glared at Mum, who looked down at the floor. We all stood like that in silence for what felt like a thousand years. The longer the silence went on, the more confused I felt. But I didn't have time for whatever was happening.

"Dom's concert starts at three, so can we please leave?" I asked. Mum turned and stalked out of the kitchen.

"Seth can drop you," she said as she disappeared into her study. I turned back to Seth.

"Is that okay? It's right in the city. Mum said she'd do it."

Seth offered me a watery smile, grabbing the car keys off the bench. "No probs, G."

The forty-five-minute car ride into the city was kind of awkward. Seth seemed not to want to talk, which was unlike him. He liked to make sure I was all up to date on politics and current affairs. Usually I yawned and eye-rolled my way through it, but I was kind of craving anything to break the silence.

"You know you're the only dad I'll ever need, don't you Seth?" I said quietly as we approached the Harbour Bridge.

Seth sighed. "Georgie, I don't … I am so torn at the moment, because your mum really doesn't want you to know about this, but I feel like you're old enough that she should give you the choice."

"I don't want to meet him! He didn't want to meet me when I was born, so why should I give a crap about him now?" I snapped, pressing my hands between my knees to hide the shaking from Seth.

Another long silence. Seth navigated through the narrow, one-way streets of the CBD in the direction of King Henry's College. Traffic was hectic, and it was stop-and-start.

"It's not … G, it's not your father who wants to meet you."

I gaped. "But … I heard you both talking about …" I stopped, swallowed. What *had* they been talking about then? What was going on?

"It's your grandmother."

I flinched away from Seth. "No, my grandparents died when I was a toddler."

He shook his head. "They didn't. Your mother just didn't want to have anything to do with them. Look, it's not my story to tell. But your grandmother has been trying to get your mum to take you to visit for … for some time now, but your mum's stubborn."

I couldn't wrap my head around any of it.

"I wish you hadn't said anything," I muttered. Seth reached over and patted me on the knee.

"I'm sorry, G. I just … I feel like it's your right to know this stuff. You're old enough that you should get a say in whether you get to know your own flesh and blood."

"Why now? Why is she so keen to meet me now, if she never wanted to in the past?" The feeling of not being enough for my own grandmother for the first fifteen years of my life was burning a hole in my stomach.

"It's not like that. Your mum … look, you need to ask her about it. But … your grandmother reached out again in March, when your grandfather died."

Nope. I couldn't continue this conversation. My head was spinning, my stomach was churning, and my eyes were hot and aching, and I just couldn't think about a grandmother who wanted to meet me, and a dead grandfather who never would.

Seth pulled up at a traffic light. I could see the green of Hyde

Park up ahead, only a block away. King Henry's was just on the other side of the park.

"I'll text you when I'm done," I said, jumping out of the car. I didn't wait for a response from Seth. I slammed the door, sprinting off in the direction of the College.

I couldn't think about this mess. My best friend was about to perform his first solo at the King Henry's Gala. Today couldn't be about me and my family drama.

"Nice dress, Blondie."

I jumped, dropping my phone and turning to glare at Xander. He grinned back, and we both bent to retrieve it from the floor at the same time. Xander got there first, his long fingers wrapped around it and handed it to me. From my spot crouched on the floor, I looked at him properly for the first time since I'd last seen him a few weeks ago.

"Oh my God, you got your braces off!" I said. Xander flashed me a blinding white, metal-free, dimply grin. I stood up far too fast, my heart beating in my eardrums, and staggered to the side, stars floating in my vision.

"Are you swooning over my straight teeth?" Xander joked, gripping my elbow to steady me as I blinked and breathed through the light-headedness. Once I had myself under control, I looked at him properly again.

I probably was swooning. If I'd thought Hot Xander was hot when I first met him, *this* Xander, who was even taller than he'd been back then … and broader, and without braces, and with a deeper, huskier voice, and wearing a nice pair of khaki trousers and a navy-blue button up shirt … *so* much hotter.

I opened my mouth, then closed it again, turning to the ticket lady and unlocking my phone for her to scan my ticket.

Today had already been too much for me, with what Seth had just told me in the car. I didn't need Hotter Xander muddling my brain even more.

"It hasn't started yet, has it?" I asked as Xander led me up a very grand, red-carpeted staircase and along a corridor. He still held my elbow, and I wasn't going to shake him off.

"Nah, they always run late. It's not like the real theatre where if you don't arrive in time, they lock you out for the first ten minutes. The teachers always wait until everyone is in before they start. Wouldn't want some spoiled rich kid's mummy and daddy to miss his big opening number."

I stifled a giggle as the usher at the door shushed Xander with a scowl.

"You do know that you're a spoiled rich kid, right?" I whispered as he walked us through the dress circle, stopping at the second row from the front. Well-dressed adults sneered at me in my non-name brand floral dress over black tights and well-worn high-top sneakers, and barely moved their knees as we squeezed past them.

"Have you *seen* my school uniform?" Xander muttered. "I'm reminded of how much of a ponce I am every morning when I put it on."

I covered my mouth to stifle more giggles as we arrived at two empty seats. Elena and Louis grinned and waved at me. Xander took the first seat, leaving me to clamber over him so I was sandwiched between him and Elena. I blushed furiously as I caught my leg on his knee and teetered. His hands shot out and grabbed my hips, manoeuvring me into my seat.

"Thanks," I mumbled, not looking at him. "How are you so tall? Your legs take up too much space!"

Xander chuckled just as the lights went dark in King Henry's College Theatre.

"Welcome, families of King Henry's performing arts students! It's so lovely to see so many excited parents, grandparents ..."

The voice of the MC faded. Grandparents. Excited grandparents. I'd never had an excited grandparent to watch me in anything. Not in primary school choir (which I was dreadful at, but I'd joined because Dom wanted to). Not when I started competing in triathlons. Not when I started actually winning triathlons.

I'd been told they'd died. I'd been told there would never be a grandparent to show up to pick me up from school when Mum had to work late. I'd watched kids around me bringing their grandparents to school events, to end-of-year awards days, to drama nights.

How long had my grandmother been trying to get Mum to let me meet her? Did it even matter? Mum had told me she was dead. That they were both dead. And now my grandfather actually was dead, and I'd lost my chance to meet him. Because Mum had lied to me, my entire life.

What if I never got to meet my grandmother, either, because Mum was too stubborn to tell me the truth? Shouldn't I have a chance to decide if whatever they'd done to her was bad enough that I wanted to cut them out of my life the way she'd cut them out of hers?

Thank God it was so dark in the theatre—I could feel that horrible, hot, prickly sensation behind my eyeballs. I wished Seth hadn't said anything. I wished I could just go on in ignorance because that was easier than having this sticky, thick betrayal bubbling up in my stomach.

"You okay, Georgie?" Xander whispered, as applause rang out around me, cheers somewhere to our right from the family of whoever had just sung.

I swallowed back the lump in my throat and nodded briskly. "Yep."

"Dom's on next," he murmured, leaning close to my ear. I shivered as the heat of his breath fanned over my jaw.

Elena sat up straighter, holding her phone out, ready to record Dom's first solo performance at King Henry's. I blinked rapidly, a watery smile pulling at my lips as Dom walked out onto the stage, wearing black trousers and a white shirt, unbuttoned at the collar. His black hair was artfully styled, and his eyes seemed to scan the dress circle as if looking for us.

"Look at him, Louis! He looks so confident," Elena sighed proudly in French, pressing record on her phone. "His grand-mère and grand-père will love this!"

So much for blinking away my tears. Just the thought of Dom's grandparents, all the way in France, still being involved in his life through the wonders of technology. Where did my grandmother even live?

And then Dom started singing, and if I'd ever had a chance of keeping my tears in, it flew out the window.

Dom's voice was deep but mellow, and his song choice—Jeff Buckley's rendition of *Hallelujah*—showed off his vocal range with its soaring high notes and soulful lows.

It touched me. I wasn't sure what the words really meant, but something about the melody opened the floodgate of emotions I'd been holding in tightly all afternoon.

Thank goodness the room was so dark, and Elena was too busy recording to notice me shaking slightly. I gripped the arm rests, trying to just let the familiar, beautiful sound of Dom's voice wash over me, tried to imagine it plucking out the ache inside my chest and flying off with it.

I was forcefully reminded that Xander was right next to me, so very close, when the warm brush of a finger stroked the side of my hand where it clawed at the armrest between us.

"You're not okay," he murmured, which just made the tears flow faster. His little finger hooked over mine, and without thinking about it, I gripped it tight with my own.

"I'm here," he whispered. I hiccupped once, brushing at the tears with my free hand. Something about that little touch, that tiny connection between us, those two words he muttered to me. It gave me the strength to breathe, to find a little bit of calm.

When Dom's song ended to deafening applause and roaring cheers, Xander didn't unhook his pinkie finger from mine. He cheered along with everyone else, slapping his free hand on his thigh.

He didn't let go until the lights went on at intermission.

Then: The Greatest Ice Cream

XANDER, 15 YEARS OLD

"Are you gonna tell me what happened in there?" I asked. Georgie wouldn't look at me, instead peering at the price list for the concession stand like it would solve all the mysteries of the universe.

My pinkie finger still tingled where she'd held onto it like it was a lifeline. Like I was her lifeline. My chest felt like it would burst just thinking about sitting there in the dark, holding her hand and listening to our best friend sing about love. At least, I thought that's what the song was about. I actually had no bloody idea. It was now 'The Song That Georgie Held My Hand Through'.

"Have you ever tried a Bubble-O-Bill?" Georgie asked. Her voice was wavery, her cheeks tear-stained. I wanted to touch her there. Wanted to stroke away the stricken look on her face.

I wanted to kiss her there. And then on her mouth, and on her neck, and … everywhere else.

"Yeah, why? Haven't you?" I replied, like my brain wasn't full of a whole list of things I wanted to do with her … to her … that ranged from lovey-dovey to downright pornographic.

Georgie shrugged. I gaped.

"Are you seriously telling me you haven't tried one of the

greatest ice-creams Australia ever invented?" I gasped. Georgie threw me a withering look.

"I'm more of a Gaytime fan, but ... maybe it's time to step out of my comfort zone." She dragged her teeth across her lip, and her eyes went somewhere far away. I let my gaze rove over her. I'd never seen her wearing a dress before. She looked ... beautiful ... and her legs were bloody incredible, but it didn't suit her the way a t-shirt and shorts did, somehow.

"Next!" the bored attendant called, and I jumped. I'd been ogling Georgie, and she'd been staring off into space as the line dwindled in front of us.

"Uh, I'll have a Bubble-O-Bill, please," I said. The guy did the most over-the-top eye roll and slouched off to the freezer, returning with my ice cream.

"What d'you want?" he grouched at Georgie. Her gaze roved over the price list, then she eyed my ice-cream.

"Are they really that good?" she asked. I tugged it out of the wrapper with a grin.

"Want to try before you buy?" I held it out to her, expecting her to take it from me.

Instead, she leaned closer, her pink tongue darting out and taking one long, slow lick from the bottom to the top. I quickly stuffed my spare hand into my pocket, because damn it, I was about to embarrass myself in front of the first girl I'd ever held hands with. The only girl I'd ever wanted to hold hands with.

Her eyelids slid closed, and she licked a little milky spot off her top lip, and maybe it was my turn to swoon, because I suddenly felt like the room was tilting.

"Oh my God, that *is* good," she said breathily. I couldn't move, couldn't speak, couldn't do anything but stare at her.

"So, does that mean you want one?" the grumpy sales guy snapped. Georgie turned to him and nodded, and he thumped off to the freezer again, muttering under his breath.

I took a few deep breaths and cleared my throat a couple of times, but it was doing nothing to calm me down.

"You want the fresh one?" she asked, holding out the wrapped one the guy had slapped down on the counter. I snatched my hand back as she reached for the ice cream she'd licked.

"No, it's okay!" I blurted. Georgie gave me an odd look, then shrugged and unwrapped hers. I quickly leaned past her and tossed a tenner at the grumpy attendant.

"Hey!" Georgie complained. "I have money, you know, spoiled rich boy!"

I turned and wound my way out of the crowds around the snack stand, finally feeling the twitching in my pants settling down.

"You can pay me back by telling me what upset you so much in there," I said, finding an alcove that had a bench seat in it and sitting, patting the space beside me.

Georgie paused where she stood, focusing on her ice cream.

"I found out today that I have a grandmother who wants to meet me."

I took a bite, squinting through the brain freeze as I tried to work out what I was supposed to say to that.

"Isn't that good news?" I eventually asked. Georgie sighed, plonking herself down beside me.

"Well, considering my mum told me my grandparents died when I was little, it's a bit confronting."

"Oh," I replied, wincing at how stupid a response that was. "Why would she tell you that?"

Georgie shrugged. "Seth, my stepdad, said I need to ask her. He was the one who told me, because I overheard them fighting and I thought they were talking about my biological father wanting to meet me."

"He hasn't met you?"

She shook her head. "Nope. He told Mum to get an abortion, and if she didn't, he wasn't helping. Lucky me, I guess, that she didn't listen to that dickhead."

"Lucky all of us," I muttered. Georgie raised a questioning eyebrow at me. My face felt hot enough to melt the ice cream as I tried to explain.

"I mean, lucky for us she didn't listen. Because you're kind of … I'm just really glad you're around, that's all."

Silence. I cursed myself for acting like such a weirdo. But then Georgie nudged my shoulder with hers.

"Thanks, Xan," she murmured. "Race you to see who can finish Bill the fastest!"

I grinned, taking a huge bite and almost choking as the cold hit me between the eyes.

I should have known she'd beat me. Georgie was competitive. And she didn't seem to get brain freeze.

And also, I got caught up watching her lips wrap around the ice cream, and then I had other things to worry about.

"What are you going to do?" I asked, to distract myself from my tight pants.

"I don't know. I should probably talk to Mum." She fiddled with Bill's bubble-gum nose, her own nose wrinkling in the cutest way.

"Yeah, sounds like you and her have a lot to talk about," I agreed as I slurped up more ice cream.

"You look tired, Georgie!" Dom said after the show as he wrapped his arms around her. I stood to one side, shifting on my feet as Dom's parents smiled on, feeling like a creepy third wheel all of a sudden.

"It's nothing," Georgie said, her eyes flashing to me for a brief second. And suddenly, I didn't feel like the third wheel anymore. She'd told *me* her secret. Sure, she'd probably tell Dom too when we weren't milling around in the theatre foyer with hundreds of other people. But she'd told me first. She'd trusted me with it. She'd let me comfort her.

"How was it?" Dom asked, pulling away from Georgie and joining his parents and me.

"You were phenomenal, darling!" Elena cooed in her accented voice, Louis gruffly agreeing. Dom turned to Georgie, a question in his eyes.

"Well," Georgie said with a tiny smile and another sidelong

glance at me that had my stomach flipping. "It wasn't Taylor Swift or anything, but …"

Dom rolled his eyes, and Georgie giggled, poking him in the side.

"You really need to broaden your musical horizons," Dom said, pretending he was annoyed while grinning at her.

"I'll admit that song now holds a special place in my heart." Another flick of her eyes my way.

I held her gaze, lifting my pinkie finger and pressing it to my lips. Her lips parted, and she looked away, but not before I noticed a hint of pink spreading across her nose.

Then: Teen-Mum-Itis

GEORGIE, 15 YEARS OLD

Unknown Number: Did you talk to your mum yet?

Georgie: Who is this?

Unknown Number: Xander…

My stomach flipped and I flopped down onto my bed, staring at my screen, my hands shaking as I added him to my contacts.

Georgie: How did you get my number?

Hot Xander: I asked Dom

Hot Xander: Do you not want me to have your number?

Georgie: I can't believe Dom gave it to you!

Georgie: And why would I not want you to have my number?

Hot Xander: I dunno

Hot Xander: Because it's weird?

> Georgie: Why is it weird?

Hot Xander: I dunno don't mind me

Hot Xander: My brain feels kind of fuzzy
right now

> Georgie: Mine too

Hot Xander: Just FYI Dom was a bit weird
about it

Hot Xander: But then he said it was
'inevitable'

I giggled, totally picturing Dom's reaction to Xander's request. I'd seen his watchful expression flitting between Xander and me whenever the three of us were hanging out together. He never spoke about it when it was just the two of us. I wondered how many conversations he and Xander had about me.

> Georgie: Yeah that sounds like something
> Dom would say

Hot Xander: So did you?

> Georgie: Did I what?

Hot Xander: Did you talk to your mum about
your grandmother yet?

> Georgie: Nope

Hot Xander: Why not?

> Georgie: She doesn't even know I know
> about it. It's just awkward. I mean, how do I
> just casually tell her that I know she lied to
> me my entire life?

Hot Xander: Do you need me to come over
and hold your pinkie finger for courage?

I needed so much more than that from him. So much that it had me blushing furiously just from the tone of my thoughts. I drew my knees up to my stomach, attempting to stifle the madly fluttering butterflies in there, and tried to think of something flirty but not too obvious to say back to him.

> Georgie: Well, considering I'm not allowed to date until I'm 100, not sure having a boy holding my hand while I confront her would be helpful

> Hot Xander: WTF?!

> Hot Xander: You're not allowed to date?!

> Hot Xander: Why???!!!

> Georgie: My mother has teen-mum-itis. She's paranoid the first boy who so much as looks at me will knock me up

> Hot Xander: Well that sucks balls

> Hot Xander: I was hoping to ask you to year 10 formal next year

There was no chance I was stopping those butterflies from rioting now.

> Georgie: That's an entire year away! Why would you even be thinking about it already?

> Hot Xander: Dunno

> Hot Xander: I guess I was thinking I'd have to get in early before Dom snatched you out from under me

Oh God. My eyes slid closed. I bit my lip hard to stop the silly grin that was threatening to burst onto my face. I cursed my mother and her stupid obsession with keeping me away from any boy that wasn't Dom.

Hot Xander: At least if Dom brings you I can steal you for one dance

Georgie: You'll probably have a hot girlfriend by the end of next year

Hot Xander: Nah

Hot Xander: Not possible

Hot Xander: My hot girlfriend isn't allowed to date until she's 100

Had someone turned the air con up to forty degrees in my bedroom? Suddenly I was sweating under my jumper, despite the cool night.

Georgie: You can't say things like that!

Hot Xander: Like what??

Georgie: That I'm your hot girlfriend

Hot Xander: Why not? You're a girl, you're hot

Hot Xander: You ARE my friend, yes?

I giggled stupidly into my hand, rolling onto my stomach.

Georgie: Yeah, I'm your friend. But I am going now. Talk soon, OK?

Hot Xander: Text me as soon as you've talked to your mum. I really want to know what happens! It's like an episode of Spring Bay!

Georgie: *eyeroll*

Hot Xander: You'd look sexy in one of those tiny bikinis all the girls wear in that show

Georgie: Good night Xander!

Hot Xander: I expect an update tonight xxx

Georgie: If I promise to text you before I go to bed, will you let me go talk to my mum now?

Hot Xander: Text me once you're in bed, that sounds way more fun!

Georgie: If I listened to mum's rants, texting you in bed is a sure-fire way to fall pregnant

Hot Xander: You do know how babies are made, don't you Blondie?

Georgie: Please don't make me think about sex right now

Hot Xander: Right now? Do you not think about sex all the time?

Georgie: I'm not a boy, I can control myself

I wasn't feeling very controlled right at that moment. I was feeling overheated, and achy, and tingly all over.

A knock at my door had me sitting bolt upright on my bed. I tossed my phone into my bedside table, slamming the drawer. It was on silent, but that didn't stop it from vibrating noisily.

"Georgie, can I come in?" Mum asked tentatively through the door. My phone buzzed again. I willed Xander to stop messaging. Just until Mum left again.

"Yeah, come in," I said, my voice croaky. The door opened, and Mum stood there, not meeting my eyes. She looked like she'd been crying.

"What's wrong?" I asked, stretching my legs to climb off the bed. Mum held out a hand as if to stop me.

"Seth told me that you know … about your grandmother," she

muttered, and she reached up and wiped her eyes. "I'm sorry, G. I never should have lied to you about her."

"Mum, it's—"

"Please, just let me say what I need to say, okay?"

I snapped my mouth shut.

"It was wrong of me to keep her from you. She and I had a big fight, when I was pregnant with you. I left home and never went back. I haven't … we never reconciled. But I shouldn't have stopped you from having a relationship with her. Or her from having one with you."

She took a few steps into my room, dropping a piece of paper onto the bed, then stepped back.

"I'm not … I don't know if I'm ready to take that step back to her yet. But I thought, maybe you'd like to write to her?"

I opened the folded paper, reading the few lines of Mum's scrawl. Miriam Menzies, and an address.

"Budgerigar?" I asked, brow furrowed. "Where's that?"

Mum huffed out a small, watery laugh. "A very long way away."

"Are you okay with this, Mum?" I asked quietly. Mum's half smile wobbled.

"It's not about me. I made it about me for too long."

With that, she shuffled out of the room, closing the door behind her. I stared down at the address for a long time. What had my grandmother done to Mum to make her refuse contact for well over a decade? What could come between two people so fully that they just completely stopped communicating?

I didn't know what to do.

Chewing on my lip, I opened my drawer and pulled out my phone. There were a couple of messages there.

> Dom: I gave Xander your number. If he acts like a dick, put him in his place

I chuckled at that, typing 'lol' back and then clicking through to the other text thread.

Hot Xander: Control is overrated

Hot Xander: No cheeky reply? Losing your touch, Blondie

Hot Xander: I'm starting to feel a bit fragile here

Hot Xander: I'm going to assume you went to talk to your mum and you haven't read any of these

Hot Xander: Send pic in your pjs when you're done ;)

Hot Xander: Also details on the granny chat

Hot Xander: You know I'm just joking around, right? About the hot girlfriend stuff? Please don't ignore me

I didn't like that one bit. Maybe I needed to put a bit more effort into my text flirting. It was easier than trying to say flirty things to him face to face.

Georgie: Not ignoring you, I promise. Sorry mum just knocked on my door.

Georgie: She started the granny chat. Said she doesn't want to talk to her, but that I might like to write to her

Georgie: I have no idea what to do

Georgie: Help

Hot Xander: Write to her? Like a letter?

Georgie: Yep

Hot Xander: Do it

Georgie: That's your help?

Hot Xander: Nothing to lose here, Blondie. But a new family member to gain

Georgie: Wow

Georgie: That was shockingly deep

Georgie: And you're right

Hot Xander: I often am

Hot Xander: Right that is

Hot Xander: Not deep. Unless you want me to be

Georgie: Are you being dirty right now? It's hard to tell over text

Hot Xander: Do you want me to be?

Georgie: I don't know how to answer that …

Hot Xander: You just did! haha

Hot Xander: Deep and dirty Xander at your service

Georgie: You know …

Georgie: If I was allowed to be anybody's hot girlfriend, I'd want to be yours

Hot Xander: Blondie …

Georgie: But since I'm not, you'll just have to be satisfied that this hot girl is your friend

Georgie: I'm going to bed now. Night Xander

Now: Tan That Pert Arse

XANDER

> Xander: I think I might have fucked up with Georgie

I watched the screen, saw my message to Dom go from delivered to read. And then nothing.

Was he really going to bloody ignore me? I paced the length of the tiny home, dragging my hands through my hair until it was standing on end. Ten paces up. Ten back. Molly followed me curiously, her tail beating an occasional wag against the kitchen cupboards.

My phone pinged.

> Dom: What happened? Is she okay?

I sighed. It was like being transported back to our teens. Dom had always put Georgie first. Before himself even, at times.

> Xander: She's fine, just pissed off with me. I was hoping that I could make things better between us, try to remind her of our friendship, but I think I just made her angrier

Dom: What did you do?

Xander: I sang karaoke

Dom: Well, listening to you sing would make anyone angry

Xander: Fuck off

Dom: How is it? With Georgie? And also the show

Xander: It's awkward (Georgie), and its bloody exhausting (the show). There's the usual work of setting up a clinic, and then on top of that there's all the crap for filming. I had no idea what I was getting myself into

Dom: Sounds shit. I don't envy you

Dom: Has she asked about me?

I couldn't reply to that straight away. I didn't want to tell him that no, she hadn't said boo about him. I had no bloody idea how to break that news to him.

Pounding footsteps on the porch stopped my pacing in its tracks. I couldn't see anything in the dark outside.

Xander: Talk later, someone's at the door

I put my phone down and wrenched open the door. A furious pair of silver eyes glared back at me. Her face was pink, her hair damp, clinging to her cheeks in the oppressive December heat.

"I can't believe you!" she snarled. Molly pushed past me, knocking the back of my knee. I staggered onto the porch, bumping against Georgie, her hands instinctively coming up to my shoulders to steady me.

For a moment, the only sound was the scratch of Molly's nails on the porch as she galloped towards the grass.

"Hello, Blondie," I muttered. Her mouth twisted, and she

shoved me hard. I stumbled backwards, heat from whatever was brewing between us flooding me with adrenaline.

"That was a low blow tonight!" she snapped, eyes flashing. I folded my arms across my chest.

"You're one to talk!" I snapped back. Georgie's eyebrows shot up under her damp fringe.

"What's that supposed to mean? What the hell did I do to you?" she demanded, hands on hips. An ache started in my groin. Fighting with her was stupidly exhilarating.

My body couldn't seem to differentiate between fury and lust.

I scoffed. "Squeezing Chipolata's bicep like you were deciding which part of him to eat for dessert!"

A growl burst out of Georgie, and she lunged forward, poking my sternum hard. "Meanwhile, *I* was too busy trying not to throw up watching you and Alex holding hands and giggling like a pair of lovesick teens!"

I chuckled, reaching out to catch her finger as she went for another poke. "Wow, I really like you in green, Blondie," I murmured. She snatched her hand back from me, eyes narrowed.

"And then you sang *that* song. You *knew* what it would do to me!"

I frowned. "I *didn't* know! And you are *not* innocent here—if all you felt for me now was 'indifference', none of this would mean jack shit to you right now! I was trying to remind you that I haven't always been a complete arsehole to you!"

"You were when it really mattered!" she hissed, then clapped a hand over her mouth, her eyes so wide the whites showed all the way around the irises. Those words made me step back, pinching the bridge of my nose.

"We're going to do this now, are we?" I asked. I was in no way ready for this conversation, but if she was, I needed to grab the opportunity by the balls.

Georgie's throat bobbed twice as she swallowed. "I … I don't have the time or the energy for this bullshit right now." She blinked slowly, then started to turn away. Heart thumping against my ribs, I reached out and snagged her wrist.

"Running away again? That's your MO, isn't it? When things get too hard, you split!" I spat the last word out, my skin prickling with heat, my groin throbbing.

"What do you mean?" she asked, not looking at me.

"I mean, I made one stupid mistake, and you erased me from your life! You disappeared completely, with nothing more than a text to Elena! And I think it's past time you explain yourself. And it's *well* past time you let me fucking explain, too!"

Georgie wrenched her wrist out of my grip, but she didn't leave. "It's over a decade in the past. I don't see the point in dredging it all up again now." Her voice trembled, which somehow elevated my fury to eleven.

"It's twelve years in the past, and I'm still not over it!" I snarled. Georgie's head snapped around to stare incredulously at me. "What we had … what I fucked up … it's all still surface level for me, Georgie!"

Her mouth fell open. She gaped at me like that for a moment, then closed her mouth, sniffing once. "Well, that's too bad for you, isn't it?"

"Why the fuck can't we talk about it, Blondie?" I demanded. "Why the hell can't we just be truthful with one another?" Her eyes flickered, and she rounded on me.

"Stop calling me Blondie! You forfeited the right to have a nickname for me twelve years ago!" She stormed up until we were chest to chest. Her lips were so close I could feel her breath on my chin. My pulse thrummed in my veins as she continued.

"You don't get to force your explanation on me, Xander! Not after twelve years. You can take it and shove it up your arse!"

She'd used my name. In anger. The flames of my own fury licked through my veins and settled in my dick. I snatched the back of her neck, thumb pressing under her jaw until I forced her face up, until her lips were a breath away from mine. I felt her warm exhale against my skin, and it was … everything.

"It wouldn't have been twelve years if you'd just let me bloody explain back then!" I snarled. My lip grazed against hers, and she let out a tiny, shaky breath. I moved my face back just enough to look her in the eyes properly. The wariness in them made my throat go dry.

"It's not even about that, anymore," she muttered. My grip on her neck loosened just enough that she pulled away. "It's in the past—*we're* in the past."

No bloody way was I letting this go. I snatched her back to me, hauling her body against mine, pressing the small of her back until she was flush against me. My other hand snaked around behind her and slapped her thigh, just where her tiny cut-off denim shorts ended.

"You aren't walking away from me again," I growled as she bared her teeth at me.

"Did you seriously just spank me?" she hissed. I grinned ferally down at her, rubbing my hard-on against her hip. Her face was livid, but her body was softening, moulding to me. I wondered vaguely if she was even aware of it.

"I did," I said darkly, rocking my hips against her again. She sucked in a breath, her tongue darting out to wet her bottom lip. "And I bloody well want to do it again. Jesus, Georgie! I want to tan that pert arse until it's rosy red. I want to bend you over and watch my dick disappear inside your pussy while I leave my handprints on you."

I slid my hand up the warm, damp skin of her back until I found the nape of her neck, tangling my fingers into the short strands of hair there and holding her still. Her eyes glistened, her chest heaved. Her nipples were two tight peaks, rubbing against me through the fabrics of our clothes.

I leaned down to her ear. "I want to brand my name all over you, Georgina Menzies."

"God, you're even worse than I imagined," she panted, and I couldn't help myself. I nestled my lips into the juncture of her neck and shoulder, tongue darting out, tasting the salty tang of her sweat. My dick shot even harder at the taste as a tiny mewling sound fell from her lips.

"Fuck you, Xander," she breathed, but her hands found my hips, reached up under my shirt, her nails grazing up my sides. I groaned against her skin.

"Exactly, Blondie. Fuck me."

With a furious groan, her lips crashed into mine.

Now: More! Harder!

GEORGIE

Lips, and teeth, and tongue.

Digging my nails into the muscles of his back, his mouth devouring mine. My mouth devouring his. The tang of beer on his tongue.

My legs wrapped around his waist. His hands on the backs of my thighs, fingers splayed under the hem of my shorts. Another clash of our teeth, tongues fighting. A sharp pain as he nipped my bottom lip. My pussy throbbed in response.

"I really fucking hate you right now," I growled into his mouth, biting him back harder. His dick jerked against my core.

"I can hate fuck you and it'll feel so good, I promise," he snarled back, turning us, slamming my back against the door hard enough that I lost my breath for just a second. He used that second to slap me sharply on my thigh again, following it with a rough squeeze that had me moaning into his mouth, my tongue seeking his again.

"Inside," I mumbled into his mouth, dragging my nails down his back under his shirt hard enough that I was sure it would leave marks as he fumbled somewhere behind me for the door handle.

Seconds later I was deposited on the edge of the small timber dining table. He pressed my knees wide, wedging himself between them. I gazed down at the impressive bulge in his running shorts.

Twelve years, and I hadn't forgotten the sight of that bulge and what he'd done to me with it. Stupidly, I longed for it. My common sense had clearly flown the coop. I wasn't thinking with my head—my aching pussy had taken over.

"Need my mouth on your tits," he grunted, his big palms sliding along the tops of my thighs and finding the bottom of my singlet, gripping it and wrenching it off. My breasts bounced as he tugged it over them.

"No bra, Blondie," he said with a dirty smirk. I ignored him, dragging his shirt over his head, running my fingertips down his collarbone, over impressive pecs, until I found his nipples. I twisted them roughly. He hissed and nipped at my earlobe, sending shock-waves to my pussy.

"Enjoying yourself there?" he murmured. His hands skated up from my waist to stroke the undersides of my breasts.

"Isn't that the point?" I retorted, but my words lost their edge as he feathered his thumbs over my nipples. My head fell back, pressing my breasts into his hands. He groaned, even as he pushed me down until I was lying on the table with him looming over me.

"Look at your tits, begging for my touch," he said, palming the flesh and kneading, his thumbs taunting the tight peaks of my nipples as I writhed under him. "These pointy little nipples don't hate me."

His voice was rough, and before I could snarl at his cocky words, he leaned down and took one breast into his mouth, flicking his tongue teasingly around the bud as he pinched the other nipple just hard enough that it verged on painful.

My pussy pulsed at the sensation, my hands tangling in his dark blond hair, holding him against my breast.

"More, harder!" I grated. He laughed against my skin, then sucked my nipple forcefully into his mouth. My hips jerked, and his free hand reached down to grip my waist and pin me to the table.

"So demanding. You haven't changed all that much, have you, Blondie?" he muttered against my skin. I wished I had a mocking retort, but he was kissing and licking across my chest until he reached the other nipple, and I was mindless. He took it between his teeth and tugged. I writhed, held down to the table by his strong palm. His thumb teased a line back and forth across my abdomen, just under the waistband of my shorts, before he flicked the button open.

His mouth pulled at my nipple harder before releasing it with a pop, straightening just enough to undo my fly and drag my shorts and underwear off as one. I watched his face—eyes darkening, nostrils flaring as he took in my bare pussy.

"Jesus Christ," he muttered, eyes intent as he spread me wider. He reached under me and scooped me to the very edge of the table. And then his gaze lifted to meet mine, and the wicked gleam in his eyes stopped my breath as he went to his knees between my spread legs.

Now: Still Hate Me, Blondie?

One glimpse of her, naked and spread on a table, panting and pink and … Christ … absolutely soaked for me had me falling to my knees.

"You don't have to—" she gasped as I stroked my way up the inside of her toned thighs.

"I need to taste this slick little pussy," I ground out, pressing my thumbs to her pussy lips and spreading her. The moan that ripped from her throat had my dick throbbing insistently in my shorts. But I wasn't rushing through this. No bloody way.

If this was my only chance to have her, I was savouring every damned second of it.

I darted my tongue out for the swiftest flick against her swollen, rosy clit. She gasped, her body jerking. I grinned, nuzzling my lips deeper into her folds, pressing my tongue to her entrance.

I groaned at the sweet, salty, musky taste of her, my eyes falling shut as I thrust my tongue deeper into her. She widened her legs further, rubbing her pussy against my mouth. I lifted her knees over my shoulders and reached down, planting a light slap on her arse.

"Fuck!" she hissed as more of her delicious wetness gushed out to coat my tongue, snapping what semblance of control I was clinging to.

I gripped her arse cheeks, lifting her just slightly to get an angle where I could wrap my lips around her clit and suck it deep into my mouth. Her shriek turned me wilder, and I growled against her flesh, licking and sucking and nibbling on her clit, pressing my face deeper until I could feel her arousal dripping off my chin.

Georgie rocked against me, hands clawing at my hair, pulling me in. "Oh, God, oh, God," she panted hoarsely.

I grinned against her drenched flesh. "God works for me … it's miles better than Dr Fox," I muttered against her clit before sucking it into my mouth and flicking it with my tongue at the same time.

"Fuck you … oh my God!" she screamed, her body spasming, her pussy pulsing violently. But I wasn't done. Thrusting my tongue as deep as I could into her clenching pussy, I drank down every drop of her orgasm, licking her through the aftershocks. Her thighs quivered against my head as she slowly went boneless from her release.

"Still hate me, Blondie?" I asked, nibbling gently at her inner thighs.

"Uh-huh," she mumbled. I glanced up her body, past the toned stomach, past those beautiful, perky little tits, and there she was, propped up on her elbows, staring down at me, eyes semi-unfocused, a confused half-frown tickling the corners of her mouth.

I grinned at her expression, wiping her wetness from my chin and sucking it from my fingers, revelling in the way her eyes widened and her lips parted as she watched me.

"Yep, I can taste just how much you hate me," I murmured, standing to lean over her, licking my lips. Georgie rolled her eyes, but there wasn't the usual furious tension in her face. No, I'd just licked it right out of her.

"Do you want me to help you out in return?" she asked archly, rubbing her leg against my rock-hard erection. I grunted, thrusting my hips slightly, seeking that friction.

"Because if you do, you'd better stop acting like a cocky prick, just because you're insanely good at eating pussy," she warned, sitting up and reaching for the waistband of my shorts. I braced my arms on the table on either side of her, trying to keep my expression neutral.

"Insanely good, eh?" I managed, swallowing around my dry mouth as she pushed my shorts and boxer briefs down my legs. My cock sprang free, bobbing against my stomach, the head already damp with precum. With a little, breathy sigh, she wrapped her hand around me.

Watching her touch me like that was everything I'd dreamed about for so long I couldn't even bloody remember when it had started. I clenched my jaw, so I wouldn't whimper like a fool as she stroked the length of me. Her hand was warm, and soft, but she gripped me firmly, her thumb grazing the wet tip.

"Eating you out got me so damn close, Blondie," I grated. "So, unless you want me to come all over your hand, and not inside that delicious pussy, I'd stop now."

"Hmmm," she muttered, her fingers continuing their slow torture of my dick. "Make you unman yourself, or let you have me. Decisions, decisions."

I snorted, her challenging tone sending that fire through my veins again.

Gripping her hips, I lifted her, flipping her until she was face down on the table, legs on the floor, and bent at the waist so her arse and pussy were right there.

"Not your decision anymore, is it?" I growled.

The incensed gasp that fell out of her mouth had me so close to losing it and coming all over her arse cheeks. I gripped the tip of my cock tightly, forcing myself back from the brink as I spanked that tanned arse of hers just like I'd been dying to from that first sight of her in that boardroom. Her legs trembled, and she cried out.

"This is a good start," I said quietly, stroking soothing fingertips over the hand-shaped welt. With one knee, I knocked her legs further apart, then stroked down the crease of her arse until I found the dripping centre of her. I circled her entrance before sliding one finger inside, groaning when she pressed back against me so it slid all the way in. Her muscles pulsed around me, and we moaned in unison as I added a second finger. She squeezed me tightly. I slid those two fingers in and out a few times, parting them inside her, stretching her.

"I want your dick in me," Georgie muttered. I pulled my fingers out of her, rubbing the head of my cock against her swollen, slippery entrance.

"Birth control?" I asked hoarsely.

"Condoms?" she hissed back. "Do you have one?"

I snorted. "One! You think one's going to be enough for what I'm going to do to you?"

"Get the whole fucking packet then, Xander, just hurry!" Her hips rocked, and the tip of me slid inside her.

"Fuck," I grunted, pulling back and slapping her other arse cheek.

"Bastard!" she moaned, but the wetness dripping down her inner thighs told a totally different story. I smirked and bent to press a kiss to the new handprint on her backside.

"Don't you dare move a muscle, Blondie," I warned her as I practically raced to the bathroom, grabbing the packet of condoms I'd brought with me. I caught a glimpse of myself in the mirror— eyes shining, hair all over the place, face flushed. Barely in control.

I strode back out to her, trying not to think too hard about the fact that I'd packed this box of condoms in what I'd thought had been a vain hope that exactly this scenario would happen.

"You stayed put." I dragged a finger down her spine as I positioned myself behind her, rolling a condom over my length. "That's my good girl."

"Don't you fucking dare," she grumbled.

I chuckled as I stroked the head of my cock up and down her pussy lips. "The way your butt's wiggling for me right now, I think you like being praised."

"Oh, God, just fuck me already!" she demanded.

"Well, since you asked so nicely," I teased, my cock head breaching her entrance, slipping in a third of the way.

"Fuck, so tight," I muttered as she gloved me.

"So big," she hissed in response. "Go slow, Xander, okay? Let me … let me get used to your size."

"You know how to stroke a man's ego, don't you?" I grunted, gripping her arse cheeks and spreading them so I had an unimpeded view of my cock stretching her open as I inched my way inside that tight heat.

"Oh my God," she whimpered, her thighs quivering, her hips undulating against the table, taking more of me.

I clenched my jaw against my rising climax, forcing it back as I rocked myself deeper into her, and again, and again, until my cock was seated right to the root inside her. My head fell back, and I stilled, just letting myself savour the moment. I was balls-deep in Georgina Menzies. The only girl … woman … I'd ever wanted *more* from. The only woman I'd been sure I'd never get anything from.

I told myself that if sex was all I was going to get from her, it would be enough. It would have to be.

"Jesus, Xander, move, please!" she begged, wriggling, but I had her pinned between my hips and the table.

"The magic word gets you things, Georgie," I murmured, spanking her one more time for good measure, pulling out and thrusting back into her. Too slowly to send me over the edge, just enough to drive her crazy.

"Faster," she panted, her fingers finding the sides of the table and gripping on as she used those beautiful, strong legs of hers to push herself back onto me. "Fuck, Xander, faster, damn you! I need … Oh God!"

I gripped her hips as I found a rhythm that had her shaking under my hands, her moans almost guttural as she coiled tighter, her muscles gripping my cock.

"You going to come hard on me, Blondie?" I grated, digging my fingertips into the flesh of her arse, thrusting faster. "You like being fucked by me, don't you? Is that tight little pussy going to squeeze me until I see stars?"

She squirmed on my cock. "You cocky arseh—ooh! Don't stop, oh God, please, Xander!"

My hands slid from her hips to her waist as she keened and shuddered, and then her orgasm *was* squeezing me, and I *was* seeing stars as I roared, thrust into her two more times, and came harder than I ever bloody had before.

Now: Getting Your Rocks Off

GEORGIE

I floated, my pussy fluttering around Xander's softening cock.

He leaned down, pressing his chest to my back, and I stilled as his mouth descended on my shoulders, planting little kisses from one side to the other.

"Could've had that regularly for the last twelve years," he murmured against the shell of my ear. "Bet you're rethinking life decisions right about now." He followed those terrifying words with a shockingly tender kiss to my jaw, and I was slammed straight back into reality.

"Don't go anywhere," he warned as he straightened, slipping out of me. "I'm not done with you yet."

His footsteps retreated towards the bathroom, and I quickly stood, wincing at how sore I was. I'd known in the abstract that he was hung, back when we … but it was one thing to have a vague idea and another entirely to have that thing slamming into me from behind.

Not to mention I hadn't had anyone—or anything—that deep inside me since my surgery. I reached for my underwear and shorts with shaking hands, tugging them up my legs and buttoning them at my hips. Hopefully that soreness was just from being fucked properly and not because I'd done damage.

"Pretty sure I said, 'don't go anywhere', Blondie."

I turned, startled, to find him leaning against the bathroom door frame. Something in the tight set of his jaw told me he was disappointed.

But I couldn't let feelings—not his, not my own, whatever the hell *they* were—muddy the waters. I looked away, stooping to grab my singlet from the floor and tugging it over my head.

"This was ... nice. But it shouldn't have—"

"If you say it shouldn't have happened, I will spank you so hard you won't be able to sit down until the new year," he warned, but he didn't make a move towards me.

I shrugged, feigning nonchalance. "Alright, it happened. But it won't happen again."

Xander said nothing, just raised an eyebrow in my direction. I should have turned and left then, but more words came bubbling up my throat.

"It's not professional—I'm your boss!" I argued. Xander threw me a half-grin that didn't reach the darkness in his eyes as he started moving towards me. I was rooted to the spot, pinned by his eyes.

"You're not my boss. Kenneth is *our* boss," he argued. I sighed. He was technically correct.

"Well, I'm your producer, and you're my talent. Which still makes it unprofessional."

He moved close enough for his body to brush mine, and before I could take a step back to put some distance between us, his arm snaked around me, hooking me around the waist and hauling me against his ... Jesus Christ ... his erection.

"Oh, I'm talented, alright," he murmured into my ear, cupping my jaw with one hand, holding me still with the other as he rocked that hard length against my body.

My knees trembled, but I locked them in place. I couldn't let him sway my resolve, even as my body swayed towards him.

"It's done, Xander," I muttered, pressing my hands to his chest, pushing enough that he took the hint and stepped away. "We scratched an itch. End of story."

I allowed myself the briefest glance up at the muscle twitching in his jaw before I turned and scurried for the door, hoping he hadn't seen the tremor in my hands.

***

I staggered across the dusty lawn between the tiny home and Mim's homestead. The tremors had become a full body shake, like I was feverish.

Maybe I was. Maybe that would explain why my brain had just exploded. What the hell had I been thinking?

I hadn't been thinking. It was as simple as that.

God! Why did he have to be so good at sex? His cocky mouth, his long, thick dick … his talented tongue! I'd be feeling him inside me for days, I was sure. Not to mention the memories seared into my brain for all eternity.

Stupid, stupid Georgie!

"No, this is salvageable," I muttered to myself, stepping onto the verandah. "You've been clear it's never happening again, he can go right back to flirting with Alex, and you'll just …"

I rubbed at my temples, hating the thick feeling in my throat, the burn behind my eyes. I'd have to live with this awful feeling all over again. The same one I'd had twelve years ago. The one I'd promised myself I'd never let myself feel again—not for him, not for any man.

I crept in through the kitchen door, hoping it was late enough that Mim would be asleep.

"Good evening, Georgina."

I jumped, a yelp bursting from my throat as I fumbled for the light switch. There was Mim, sitting at the kitchen table, Jumbo in her lap, Molly curled up by her feet.

"Holy crap you scared me!" I gasped, collapsing into a chair, hand on my chest. Mim watched me with an unreadable expression, stroking Jumbo's downy head.

"You're giving off some very weird Dr Evil vibes right about now," I said with a nervous laugh. Molly's tail thumped against the floor.

"Don't sass me, Georgina Menzies," Mim replied primly. "And tell your Dr Fox that if he's going to be partaking in … adult activities of a night time, he needs to ensure his dog is secure beforehand."

My face was on fire. I glanced down at Molly so I wouldn't have to look at Mim. "He's not *my* Dr Fox," I mumbled.

Mim raised a snarky eyebrow at me. "So, you frequently partake in noisy sex with men who aren't yours?" she asked. My face was melting off. I garbled out some very unconvincing sounds of protest.

Mim chuckled. "My Georgie. I'm not judging you for getting your rocks off, alright?"

I surged to my feet. "Getting my rocks off!" I exclaimed, pacing towards the sink and grabbing a glass, filling it with shaking hands and guzzling the contents, hoping it would put out the fire coursing over every inch of my skin.

"Enjoying the company of a handsome man? Does that offend your sensibilities less?"

I scoffed. "At this point, nothing is going to make this conversation any less of a disaster."

Mim barked out a laugh, standing and plopping Jumbo to the floor. He trotted to me, nuzzled at my legs once, then headed off towards the laundry and his bed. Molly followed.

"I just need to know that you aren't getting yourself into a situation with the good doctor that's going to end up with you hurt again." Mim squeezed my shoulder.

I let out a long breath. "No chance of that," I muttered, praying that it wasn't a lie and I could hold onto the hate that had held me together the last twelve years. "It was a one-and-done, I made that abundantly clear to him."

Mim's expression was dubious. "Really." It wasn't even a question—she didn't believe me.

I nodded. "Really."

With a sniff, Mim moved back to the table, sitting and patting another chair. I complied, trying not to wince at how tender my sitting bits were.

Damn Xander Fox and his big hot dick.

"Well, now that you've well and truly shut that conversation down," Mim began, eyeing me with an expression that told me she knew I was full of it. "We need to talk about the ten grand."

I rolled my eyes, my stomach unknotting. *This* I could talk about.

"Mim, it's a gift. You don't get to return gifts," I told her firmly. Mim shook her head, resting her elbows on the table.

"It's already back in your bank account."

"Well, it'll be back in yours again first thing in the morning!" I retorted, folding my arms over my chest, wincing anew at how sensitive my nipples were. "It was a signing bonus—it was money I never needed or expected to have. I want you to have it. I know how much feeding and watering the flock is costing you."

Mim sighed, fixing me with her beady stare. "I will not accept any more money from you, Georgina. I will not allow you to throw good money after bad."

"But what about ..." I stammered, falling silent at the deathly serious expression on her face. My stomach knotted up again for a totally different reason.

"It's time, Georgie," Mim mumbled. "I'm getting too old to do this on my own. The drought is sending me backwards at an alarming rate. Despite my best efforts, the sheep are starting to become malnourished. If I sell the flock off now, I might have enough to live on for a while. If ..." Mim dropped her head into her hands. "If I sell the homestead, I'll be sorted for the rest of my life."

I blinked. Blinked again.

"Sell the homestead? You can't!" I whispered. "You'd never forgive yourself. You always said my grandfather would turn over in his grave if you even thought about it."

"Your grandfather also wouldn't want me breaking myself, and my granddaughter, to keep the farm afloat. He wouldn't want me to work myself into the grave."

I swallowed. "No. I'll stay. I'll … I'll leave my job, and I'll work the farm, and we'll see the drought through, and—"

"Don't be stupid, Georgie!" Mim snapped. "You'd be utterly miserable out here, and you know it! You love your work, you love city living. You need challenge."

I swallowed down the burning in my throat. "And what better challenge is there than keeping a farm afloat through a drought?" I argued, but Mim was already shaking her head.

"I'll be selling the flock in the coming weeks. The property itself I won't list until your show has wrapped."

"But—"

"No, Georgie. It's my decision, and I've made it." Her voice was so desolate that I started to cry. Too many emotions in the last few hours were taking their toll on me.

"Where will you live?" I asked, sniffling. Mim flashed me a sardonic grin.

"Liz has kindly offered to take me in. She has a spare room, and she's lonely. She'll appreciate the company."

What Mim didn't say, what I was just starting to realise, was that she was lonely, too. And it was selfish of me to try and argue with her. Even if this old house, and those dusty paddocks, felt more like home to me than anywhere ever had.

"I'm as stubborn as you are, Georgie," Mim said, standing and heading for the hallway. "I refused to see what was right in front of my face for too many years. But I can't ignore it any longer, so I need to act on it. And that's what I'm doing."

She smacked her palm against the door frame. "Might be something for you to consider, too."

With that, she thumped off up the hallway to her bedroom, leaving me wondering what on earth she was talking about.

I sighed. I needed another shower. I needed to wash the whole evening from my body.

I stuck my head in through the laundry door on my way to the bathroom, my lips tugging up at the sight of Jumbo and Molly curled up together in Jumbo's bed. Before I could talk myself out of it, I snapped a quick photo on my phone, opening my messages and sending it off.

> Georgie: Your dog has made an upgrade.

The reply came through almost instantly.

> Dr Fox: At least one of us is getting some spooning action tonight

> Georgie: Shall I send her home?

> Dr Fox: How about a swap? She stays with your weird little sheep, you come back here and climb into bed with me

I hated how much his cheeky flirting took me back a decade and a half. I hated how my stomach fluttered, how my core pulsed, reminding me exactly what he'd been doing to me not all that long ago.

> Georgie: He's not a weird little sheep, he's a Babydoll. They're bred to be small and adorable

No way was I going anywhere near the other part of his last text.

> Dr Fox: Just come back. I had plans for rounds two through six tonight

> Georgie: Not happening, Dr Fox

> Dr Fox: Oh, we're back to that, are we? I much preferred God

> Georgie: Don't flatter yourself

> Dr Fox: I'm not. I believe your exact words were 'insanely good at eating pussy'

> Dr Fox: My Godlike mouth is currently available

I couldn't help myself.

> Georgie: I'm sure Dr Kingston will very much appreciate it

I turned my phone off then and took myself into the bathroom, wishing that my last text to him felt like a big win and not a decisive loss.

My nightly footage review had just gotten interesting.

Very interesting.

I scrolled back through several minutes of black screen until the visual of the in-car footage we'd shot yesterday flashed on. Jord climbed into the back seat. Xander scowled at something through the windscreen. Probably me being accosted by Lachy. I smirked, taking a sip of wine. The merlot he'd bought for me was actually delicious.

And then Alex Kingston gleefully announced to the pair of them that 'it' was 'working'.

A weird little scuffle of a conversation followed, with Alex apologising, and Jord grinning, and Xander looking angry and mystified all at once, and then the screen went black.

But the microphone on Xander's shirt was still running, still connected via Bluetooth to the camera.

I swayed in the hammock, listening for the third time to the conversation. The 'fake dating' scenario that Jord had concocted, supposedly for ratings, with the added side benefit of making me jealous.

My big question: what to do with this new knowledge?

I could confront Jord immediately about it, chastise them for manipulating my past relationship with Xander, and for not looping me in on every production decision they made.

But something stopped me. The way Xander had been unwilling to go behind my back … until he'd suddenly seemed to reconsider his position at the thought of making me jealous. It made me want to see how far he would take this little ruse. How far he thought he could push me.

And part of me didn't want to come clean that I knew because then I'd have to face the fact that I'd let him bend me over a table because I *was* jealous.

I glanced across the yard to the tiny home. Xander was a shadow moving around the kitchen. I thought I caught a glimpse of a bare chest at the window, the bare chest I'd clawed at last night, and I hated how I ached to touch it again.

Would it really be so bad to just sleep with him again? a horny little part of me wondered. *It's just sex, doesn't need to mean anything.*

I shook myself, turning back to my screen, cropping the enlightening little conversation from the car footage, saving that to my own personal folder—the same one into which I filed away various clips of Xander and me. So much footage of us glaring at one another. The incident where he'd fallen on me in the file room, and several segments of that first drive to Budgerigar, all of which, for multiple reasons, could never make it to television. The only footage featuring me that I'd allowed through was the anal gland milking, purely because it was great viewing, and I was not the focus of that scene whatsoever. The close-ups of Xander's fingers up a dog's bum verged on gratuitous. Kenneth would love it.

No. I wouldn't be having sex with Xander again. And I wouldn't be letting on to any of the co-conspirators that I'd discovered their little plot. I'd flirt with Lachy shamelessly and see how much I could make Xander sweat.

If Xander on the edge of snapping didn't make for interesting television, I didn't know what would.

The days leading up to the clinic's soft opening were so hectic that I barely had time to scratch myself, let alone brood over Xander … or worry about Mim.

Even flirting with Lachy had taken a back seat to overseeing the multitude of deliveries that arrived throughout the day, every day, all the while trying to manage multiple trades buzzing around like a swarm of bees, painting and laying floors and tiling and assembling furniture. Juggling filming around all of them while ensuring that everything finished in time for Thursday was almost a nightmare. I didn't envy producers on renovation shows whatsoever.

Lachy had to finish up with us on Tuesday. He had a meeting on Wednesday with a business in Dubbo that was interested in selling portable versions of his tiny homes.

"Gonna miss working with you every day, Georgie," he murmured as he collected his tools, flashing me a white grin and a wink. "Drinks at The Budgie after the grand opening this weekend?"

I smiled genuinely back at him, reaching up and wrapping my arms around his neck to pull him in for a hug. "Sounds great. You've been so much help around here—we honestly couldn't have done it without you."

Lachy's strong arms curled around my waist, tugging me against his warm, slightly damp body. "You would've, you know. I just sped things up a bit. My shout on Saturday night."

I pulled back, giving his shoulders a quick squeeze, noticing movement out of the corner of my eye. Movement of the tall, dark blond variety. "You're on. Safe trip tomorrow."

Lachy's warm brown eyes bored into mine, his hand cupping my face, thumb brushing my cheek. I felt a stab of guilt that I wasn't shutting this down, but the weight of Xander's eyes was on me, and even without my plan to rile him up, I was intensely aware that pulling away now would give him ideas that he had something to do with it.

"Yeah, drive safe, Chippy," Xander boomed. Lachy's nostrils flared, but he pulled back, patting me on the cheek in a friendly gesture.

"Always do," he replied, flicking a salute in Xander's direction. I pursed my lips, gripping Lachy's arm to keep him from leaving and gesturing to Jase, who was hovering in the background with his camera.

"Can you and Dr Fox give us a bit more … oomph, right now? We've collected a lot of footage of you together this last fortnight. I think a fond farewell is warranted."

Xander's filthy look almost made me snort. "What exactly are you expecting here?"

I turned to Lachy, talking to him rather than to Xander. "Give us one of those bro hugs—you know, the ones where you try to back slap each other's organs to pulp? Think you can manage that?"

Lachy grinned. "Anything for you, Georgie." He stepped towards Xander, who couldn't have looked more disgusted if he tried.

I grinned into my hand as Lachy hammed it up for the camera, embracing Xander firmly, even managing some glistening in his eyes that we could easily pass off as tears. Although his eyes were probably madly watering from the violent way Xander pounded his spine.

"Thanks for your help, mate," Xander grated as they pulled away from one another. He even managed to make it sound semi-convincing. I flicked an impressed look in his direction as Lachy gave a wave and left, with Jase following to get footage of him driving off.

I turned back to the reception desk, picked up the packing list and continued to check off the most recent delivery of medications.

"So, Chipolata's rolled off the barbie, then?"

I jumped. I thought he'd left. I didn't turn, instead pretending to scan the list for an item. The words blurred in front of my face.

"He's back on Saturday," I replied, my voice ridiculously high. I cleared my throat. "Ironically, he's running the barbecue."

Xander snorted, his footsteps echoing across the space. Heat bloomed over my back as he stood far too close, his hands gripping the reception desk on either side of me, pinning me there. Fine specks of dust from the work he'd been doing still clung to the dark gold hairs on his arms. I fisted the packing slip in my hand, watching it crumple.

"Not appropriate, Dr Fox," I breathed.

"I'm not a fan of appropriate," he muttered against my ear. "Not when it comes to you."

My insides turned to flames at his words. Worse, my heart ached. Nope. I wasn't letting this happen. But Jesus, he tucked his leg between mine, pressed his hips up against my butt, and there was the bulge. The ache fled south, and all I could think was that I wanted him to bend me over again.

"I don't like you," I mumbled, sucking in a gasp when his lips brushed the top of my ear.

"Well, that's an improvement on hating me, isn't it, Blondie?" His tongue darted out and ran along the curve of my ear. "For the record, I never hated you. Not once in the last twelve years."

"Bullshit," I hissed. My body took over whatever was left of my common sense, and I ground my butt against him. His rough grunt had my pussy clenching. He took one hand from where it caged me against the desk, only to splay over my hip, holding me flush to him.

"Oh, don't get me wrong, I was furious with you every waking minute of it. I'm still bloody furious." His face tilted lower, nuzzling against my neck, heating my already scorching skin with his breath. "But I can think of more … productive ways to vent my fury on you now."

"Your fury feels a lot like foreplay to me," I whispered, the last thread of my self-control a hairsbreadth from snapping and making me turn to devour his mouth.

I flinched at a sharp slap against my butt.

"The two are very closely related for me." His voice was a low growl as he stroked light fingers over the spot where he'd just spanked me. Even through my cotton shorts, it smarted. And I hated how much I loved it.

"Ahem."

With a squawk, I leapt backwards from the reception desk,

sending Xander staggering. I lost my footing and teetered back-wards, arms pinwheeling.

Two warm hands gripped my waist, holding me steady until I could find my feet. Xander smirked down at me, hazel eyes sparkling. I stepped out of his reach, rubbing at my arms where he'd been.

"Karl's taking lunch now," Jordyn announced, standing in the doorway through to the back of house.

"Alright," I replied, narrowing my eyes at them. A crew member's mandated lunch break was not something I needed to be interrupted for.

Except when you're grinding against the talent right where everyone can see, the career-minded part of my brain reminded me.

Jordyn glanced between Xander and me, lips pressed together in a way that I knew meant they were trying not to laugh. "Alex has confirmed that she can do the livestock rounds with you tomorrow, Dr Fox, so you're free for the soft opening on Thursday."

"She's an angel," Xander replied with feeling.

"Well," I interrupted, my voice sharper than I intended. "If you're planning on galivanting around the countryside with Dr Kingston all day tomorrow, you'd better get cracking with the final touches around here. So, vamoose!" I punctuated my words with a glare at Xander.

Xander saluted me in much the same way Lachy had him earlier, except he added a cheeky wink.

"Actually," Jord interrupted. "It's school pick-up soon …"

"Fantastic," Xander muttered, running a hand through his hair until it stood on end. "Shirt on or off today?"

I stifled a grin. "It's hot out, and you *are* a bit sweaty. Off, I think." I shared a glance with Jord, who was also hiding a smirk, as Xander reached behind his head to drag his blue t-shirt off, turning to stride out the front door.

"Make sure Jase is rolling!" Jord called after him. I watched the muscles in his back ripple as he stiffened.

"Sure thing," he grated, and then he was gone. I turned back to Jord.

"Are you going out to supervise, or will I?" I asked, busying myself with smoothing the packing slip I'd scrunched when Xander started … whatever it was he'd been doing to me. "I've got plenty to get on with here, but someone needs to make sure the school mums don't get handsy with Dr Fox."

Jord snatched the paper from my hands and tossed it back into the box on the counter. "Georgina, you were letting him dry hump you!" they hissed. I bit my lip to stop myself from the verbal diarrhea that was threatening. Everything from him eating me out and then fucking me to, 'I know about your little plot with Alex to try and make me jealous!'

"What's going on?" Jord pressed.

I shook my head. "Nothing. He's just …" I really had no words to get myself out of this.

"He's just infatuated with you, the same way he was back in high school," Liz said.

We both looked up to see her leering at us with Empress and Kingston the Corgis, and Molly winding around her denim-clad legs. Even in the blistering summer heat, she was always wearing jeans, the crazy old goose.

"No one asked for your opinion, Liz," I mumbled.

Liz cackled. "I don't need anyone to ask for it, dear!" She eyed me defiantly as she scratched Empress on the head. "And if I were you, I'd be channelling my inner koala and climbing that beefy specimen like a gum tree!"

Jord made a gagging face, which I usually would have found hilarious, but since we were talking about me climbing Xander like a tree, it lost its humour.

"What *are* you going to do about him?" Jord asked. "I mean, are you going to encourage this behaviour? He seems to be getting along so well with Alex." If I hadn't known they'd brewed up that entire scenario, I might almost have believed the worried expression on Jord's face.

"I'm going out to produce my television show," I announced. "Quite frankly, I'd rather watch shirtless Dr Fox schmooze the middle-aged mothers into coming to the grand opening on Saturday than stay here and be *interrogated* by you—" I pointed an accusing finger at Jord— "and listen to unsolicited, and frankly far too horny advice from *you*!" I swung around to glare at Liz.

I left the building to the echoes of Liz's laughter.

Now: She Found A Sausage, Alright!

GEORGIE

Alex's bubbly smile churned my stomach. And when she turned to Xander, and it brightened considerably, I itched to slap her.

It's all pretence, I reminded myself. *You're onto them.*

But what if it wasn't? What if it had started that way, but feelings were developing? I tried to reassure myself that it didn't matter because there was nothing between Xander and me.

What a raging lie that was. I was still tender from our 'adult activities'. Not to mention my head was a complete mess. But I wasn't dwelling on that. No. *Get the job done, Georgina Menzies.*

"I've brought along Calli—she's the vet nurse I promised you, to work under Xander," Alex said, and from behind her popped a short, stunning woman. She had honey-coloured hair, bright green eyes, and a smattering of freckles across her nose. But I barely glanced at her pretty face because my eyes were immediately drawn downwards. Her boobs were truly something else. I was surprised her petite frame could hold up melons like that.

Apparently it wasn't enough to have the stunning Alex Kingston with her dark looks, blinding smile and round butt. Now we had perky Calli with the monster knockers and the cute-as-a-button freckles. Who'd be working *under* Xander.

"Nice to meet you, Calli," Xander said, holding a hand out for her to shake as Jase zoomed in on her cleavage. Fantastic. At least for his part, Xander kept his eyes firmly above collar level. Probably because he was dimpling at Alex instead. "You coming for a ride-along to the livestock appointments today?"

Calli nodded. "I'd love to!"

Oh God, even her voice was perky. I closed my eyes rather than rolling them, opening them again to find Xander smirking at me from across the room.

"Well, why don't I give you the grand tour of the clinic, Calli, and then we can be on our way?" he said, but his eyes never left mine. I turned and stalked out.

"You're on the road with Dr Fox today," I snapped at Jordyn when I found them in the kitchen, downing a bacon and egg roll from the milk bar up the street. They chewed their monstrous bite, watching me with those dark, thoughtful eyes.

"Alex brought Calli, didn't she?" Jord said. I sighed. Normally I'd open up to Jord about how confused I was feeling … how on edge, and how … damned horny I was. How I wished that I could separate my feelings about Xander from my absolute craving for more of what we'd done the other night.

"Yep," was all I said instead. Jord narrowed their eyes.

"G, I'm gonna be straight with you, okay?" they said, gripping my shoulders and forcing me to look them in the eyes. "You say you hate him, but is it really *hate*? Or is it just *hurt*?"

"Does it really matter?" I muttered.

Jord shook me. "Hate, there's no coming back from. Hurt … well, hurt you can heal. But it would mean talking to him about what happened back then."

I was shaking my head before Jord even finished speaking. "That's a *hell no* from me."

Jord released me with a sigh and a shrug. "Well, it's your decision, G. But for the record, I think it's the wrong one."

They walked out before I could find words to argue. And even after they'd all left for the day, and I sat to use the downtime to get ahead on my footage reviews, I still couldn't think of an argument. Not one that didn't mean me coming clean that there was more to that night twelve years ago. Things that no one—not even Mim— knew the whole truth about.

I stared at the laptop screen for a long time, and when my finger moved, it wasn't to the raw footage folder. It was to the folder holding all the snippets of Xander and me.

If I was going to feel miserable, may as well make a proper go of it.

Saturday morning—grand opening day—dawned the way every morning had since we'd arrived in Budgerigar, with a clear sky and bone-scorching heat.

My morning run down to what was left of the river had become a chore rather than a pleasure the last couple of days. What was left of the flock had been collected by a buyer, a farmer in Victoria who was lucky enough to own land in an area that had continued to get steady rainfall the past few years.

It was a bitter pill to swallow, taking that run through empty fields, desolate without the bleating and movement of hundreds and hundreds of sheep. I'd taken to letting Jumbo follow me on my run to keep me company—it wasn't as if there was any reason to shut the gates behind me anymore. But he generally got about two hundred metres or so from the house before his little legs got tired and he headed back.

I forced myself to run until my fit watch showed a good five k's before I turned and headed back through the paddocks. Sweat dripped down my spine and between my breasts. I pushed wet strands of hair off my face as I glanced over to the tiny home, almost swallowing my tongue when I saw Xander, shirtless, doing push-ups on the timber porch. He was sweaty too, but his sweat was the sexy, glistening beads that clung to taut muscles and drizzled their way down the hills and valleys of defined abs.

His biceps bulged as he grunted through his set, and suddenly it wasn't just sweat that was making me damp. Those grunting sounds took me back … to a few nights ago … to twelve years ago.

He finished his set and stood, grabbing a water bottle from the chair and taking a long slug. His throat bobbed as he swallowed. My heart pounded as if I were still running.

"Welcome to join in, Blondie," he called out, and I flinched. I'd been so focused on his body that I hadn't realised I was standing in full view of him, drinking him in. "Hip thrusters are a fun exercise to do with a friend."

I threw him what I hoped was a disgusted look, but judging by his smirk, he'd seen right through it. He set himself up, using the edge of the porch to brace his back, planting his feet and thrusting skywards. His grey shorts left nothing to the imagination as he held at the top of his thrust before lowering, his eyes never leaving mine.

I could have sworn that on the next thrust, the bulge in those shorts was … more.

"And there's the peen silhouette again," Jord said, approaching with Jase, who was frantically fumbling to get his camera up to capture the action. "Dr Fox is packing, G."

I huffed out a shaky breath and turned for Mim's, as Jumbo and Molly came galloping around the corner together.

"Those two have really made friends, haven't they?" Jord continued, following behind me. "Shame about their owners."

I rounded on them. "Why are you harping about this? Why do you care if I hate Dr Fox, or hump him?"

Jord stopped, watching me with wide eyes. "*Have* you humped him? As in, not the dry variety?"

I threw my hands up in the air, grunting in frustration. "We are not discussing this! Go and handle Mr Thirst Trap over there, then get ready to head to the clinic. I'm taking a shower."

I stormed into the house, past a smirking Mim, who I hadn't noticed had been watching the entire debacle from the verandah of the homestead.

I ran the shower cold, but all that did was bud my nipples until they ached. I soaped myself swiftly, trying not to graze the sensitive peaks, trying to swipe the soap between my legs with businesslike briskness. Water was a commodity. I couldn't let myself get carried away, couldn't give my body the release I so desperately craved. Even if it would probably only take about thirty seconds, given how worked up I was. I closed my eyes and stuck my head under the spray, and pecs with sweat beads pearling on them swam into my vision.

I growled and reached for the shampoo. No time for masturbating when I had to wash my hair.

You can work that tension out tonight, just get through today, that's all you have to do.

I checked my email on the ride into the clinic—with Karl and Jase because I was already on edge enough about Xander today. And the email that had come through from Kenneth at two in the morning threatened to tip me over that edge.

From: Kenneth Grace

To: Georgina Menzies

Subject: Beach Vet Goes Bush

Georgie

I'm loving where you've taken this concept! I've reviewed your vetted footage (forgive me, I'm chuckling at my own pun here), and the town, crazy old Liz and her dogs, The Budgie Pub, THE BIRD POO! To borrow a phrase from today's youth, I'm dead. Xander is charming, and the hot-weather shirtless renovation is perfect. Can we get more of this Lachy fellow, please? There's some weird, dick measuring energy going on between him and Xander and I can't put my finger on it, but I'm loving it.

The only other feedback I have relates to Alex. Adoring the genuine, flirty vibe you've fostered between her and Xander. Is that real or manufactured? Actually, don't tell me, preserve the magic! But if there is any opportunity to catch them getting a bit steamy, it would only improve on the foundation. A kiss? Perhaps

her sneaking out of the adorable tiny home early one morning?
Something saucy please!
Good luck with your grand opening today.
Ken

Fantastic. No way in the world could I handle his request. Considering Jordyn was the mastermind behind the whole Alex and Xander thing, it was only fair they put their money where their mouth was. I flicked the email on to them, with a snippy 'You're in charge of this'.

And then I tried my hardest to put the thought of him kissing Alex … of Alex spending the night with him … out of my mind.

***

"Can I slip a juicy sausage in your buns?" Lachy asked me with a leer, waving a cooked-to-perfection sausage in my direction. I huffed out a laugh, handing him a slice of bread on a napkin. Karl got all of that on camera, of course. Just more for me to cut out.

I'd put myself on Lachy duty today, seeing as Kenneth was keen on more of him. It was a perfect excuse to keep my distance from Xander and Alex and perky Calli, who were all administering complimentary flea treatments and dog treats up on the front porch of the clinic while the rest of us were set up in the yard to the side.

Lachy turned back to the woman he was serving. "Sauce for the saucy lady?"

She giggled, gesturing to the tomato sauce bottle. While Lachy flirted shamelessly with her, I served about seven other people who were waiting, not so patiently, behind her.

"He can cook a mean snag, but his customer service leaves a bit to be desired," Liz chortled.

I turned to find Mim and Liz standing to one side. Mim was halfway through an angel cupcake, a dot of icing sugar that looked like cocaine on her nose. I reached out to wipe it away.

"The yard is jam-packed, Georgie girl!" Liz commented,

shoving a tray of the cakes in my face. How did you get all of these stalls on such short notice?"

"Dr Dimples," Lachy replied. I hadn't realised he was paying attention to us, as he took the gold coin donation from a customer, dropping it into our bucket.

"Dr Dimples?" Mim asked, glancing at me with a hint of a smile playing about her mouth. I rolled my eyes, but the blush gave me away.

"He's been working hard schmoozing all the school mums every afternoon. He's been turning his dimples on them, mentioning that we're having a fundraiser for drought relief, and asking if they'd like to come along. And suddenly they're all showing up this morning, setting up gazebos and tables full of random craft things their kids have made—all proceeds to drought relief."

Liz raised her eyebrows, leering at me. "Well, Dr Dimples is already pulling his weight in the community!" she said. "What'll it take to lure him here for good, d'you think Georgie girl?"

I opened my mouth but couldn't think of anything to say. Lachy piped up again, saving me from my confusion.

"Short of him falling head over heels for Alex, I doubt you'll manage it, even with all your skills, Liz."

I let my eyes wander over the crowds, milling around stalls selling crocheted tea cosies, homemade slime, and wonky clay earrings. I tried to ignore the heat of Mim's regard, burning a hole in the back of my neck.

"Well, if it's not Alex, maybe Calli'll have more luck wooing Dr Dimples," Liz said, and I could practically hear the cogs whirring in her brain, trying to work out how to make it happen.

That pang of guilt flooded me again. Budgerigar needed a permanent vet. Not a celebrity one here for a good time, not a long time. I resolved to speak with Kenneth. Maybe we could make more seasons of the show, entice a different vet each season to leave the city for a three-month stint. At least then the town would have *a* someone they could rely on in an emergency, even if it wasn't the *same* someone.

Which would mean me staying out here to produce it. Which

might mean that Mim wouldn't need to sell the homestead—I could support her with my salary.

"Who's Calli?" Lachy asked, and something in his tone snapped me from my own whirring cogs. His face was suddenly mask-like, which for someone as expressive as Lachy, seemed very off.

"Don't tell me you've forgotten Calli," Mim said. "In any case, she's a vet nurse now, she's moving over from Millstone to help Dr Xander out," Mim replied before I could switch my brain on again. I flashed a sharp look at her.

"How do you know all of this?" I demanded.

Mim chuckled. "Country gossip, my Georgie. News travels fast in Budgerigar."

"Of course it does," I muttered, glancing up to see the object of our discussion bouncing perkily in our direction, her ponytail swinging shinily from side to side.

"Calli?" Lachy choked out beside me. The mask had dropped, and on his face was a look of utter shock and … longing.

Calli stopped in her tracks, her pretty mouth falling open. "Lach?" she squeaked, her hand flying to her ample cleavage.

"This'll be good watching," Liz whispered, handing me a cupcake. I took it in numb fingers.

"What's going on?" I whispered back.

Liz chuckled. "Just watch."

Lachy dropped the tongs on the barbecue, wrenching the apron over his head.

"What're you doing back here?" he demanded, his voice hoarse as he launched himself out from under the gazebo, taking three strides towards where Calli was frozen, stopping just short of colliding with her.

"I moved back to Millstone last year," she mumbled, rubbing at her chest. I found myself doing the same thing, trying to ease the confused ache that had settled there.

"You've been back for over a year, and you never once tried to see me?" Lachy asked. The pain in his voice stabbed through me.

"I … I figured you would have moved on, Lach."

His hand shot out, cupping the side of her face. "Never. Kitten, I never moved on."

"Seriously, what is going on here?" I hissed to Liz, my heart thudding painfully. I glanced at Jase, filming every moment of this … whatever it was.

"They were high school sweethearts. But when they graduated, he wanted to stay here, learn the land, take over his family's farm. She wanted to move to the coast, wanted to try the big city life. They didn't part on the best terms. Haven't spoken in … oh it'd be a good decade and a bit now, wouldn't it, Mim?"

"Twelve years." Mim's piercing stare sucked the breath from my lungs.

"Can we … can I take you to lunch?" Lachy asked her, his thumb tickling at the corner of her mouth. Those green eyes of hers were wide as she nodded up at him, then blinked, clearing her throat, raising a hand to wrap her fingers around his wrist.

"I'll have to check with Dr Xander, but … well, I was supposed to be taking a break anyway. I was heading here for a sausage."

"Oh, she found a sausage alright!" Liz chortled under her breath. I found a tiny bit of spark and elbowed her in the ribs.

"Dimples'll let you go with me, we're good mates," Lachy assured her. I stifled a snort at that, but even the ridiculous lie didn't shake the lurching sensation in the pit of my stomach. "I want to take you out properly," he continued. "Counter lunch at The Budgie."

City Career-Woman Georgie would have had a chuckle at the thought of a counter lunch at the only pub in town being the definition of 'taken out properly'.

But the Georgie who was standing in the yard of Budgerigar Vet, watching two people who hadn't spoken since high school very obviously pining for one another, secretly wished that Xander Fox would come charging into the yard, cup my face in his big, warm palm, and promise me all the proper things he could wrangle.

"Well."

I stiffened at the sound of his voice in my ear. I didn't turn, but his presence was so overwhelming that I could feel every inch of my skin tingling, and he wasn't even touching me.

"Well what?" I asked, eyes on Lachy as he trailed his hand down Calli's arm and wound his fingers through hers, and off they walked together.

"Well, it seems I've temporarily lost my practice nurse … but you've permanently lost your rebound guy."

I spun to him, heat pulsing through my veins, my fingers itching to slap the cheeky, dimpled, infuriatingly adorable look off his face.

"My *rebound* guy?" I snarled under my breath. Xander had the gall to chuckle at that.

I slapped him.

And then I stormed off to the bathroom inside the clinic to douse myself in cold water and hope I could soothe the raging fire inside me.

Now: Pinch It

XANDER

I cupped my cheek where she'd just packed one hell of a slap on me. I'd definitely taken the teasing too far this time. Liz and Miriam both chortled away to one side, stuffing their faces with angel cakes like they were front row at a live improv theatre.

"Follow her, you fucking idiot!" Jordyn snapped at me, appearing by my side. How had I totally forgotten there was a camera trained on me all the bloody time?

"I'm not going in there unless you promise me that the cameras stay outside," I said, eyeing Jord darkly. The shrug I got in response didn't fill me with confidence. But the fire was raging again. She'd slapped me. Getting any sort of real emotion from her was a bloody aphrodisiac.

I strode off, weaving through the crowds of people packed into the yard and up the back stairs of the clinic. The air inside was barely cooler than outside. I peered into the kitchen—empty. The office and surgery areas were, too.

But then I heard water running in the bathroom. The door was shut.

I turned the handle, expecting it to be locked. It wasn't.

Georgie was bent over the basin, splashing her face with water. She hadn't heard me come in.

"Bit hot and bothered?" I asked, grinning when she jumped, spinning towards me and flicking water across my shirt from the sodden strands of her hair.

"What the hell are you doing in here? Get out!" she snarled. I closed the door behind me, making sure to flick the lock as she watched, hands on hips, face flushed, water trickling down her chest and beneath the blue sundress she was wearing.

'I was out of line out there," I muttered. The fiery glare she threw at me had my insides jumping the way they had when I was a teenager.

"Damn right you were!" she retorted, turning back to the sink, gripping the edges of the counter like she wished she could slap me again. Oh, I knew that feeling well, with her presenting her perky butt in that little dress to me, like she was begging me to slide that fabric up to her waist and spank that …

I swallowed, ignoring the urge, running a hand through my hair. "But seriously, Blondie, everyone could see from a mile away that what you had going on with Chippy was just an act."

Her furious eyes met mine in the mirror. "Don't you *dare* talk to me about acting!" She spun around to face me. "Here's an insider tip for you, Dr Fox! If you want to come up with sordid little plots in your car with Dr Kingston and Jord, you might want to switch off your mic next time, not just the camera."

My mouth fell open. Shit. I hadn't thought about the microphone. I very deliberately reached up and switched the one I was wearing off. Whatever was about to happen didn't need to be on record anywhere.

"How long have you known about that conversation?" I asked, rubbing at the back of my neck as she turned back towards the mirror. I wracked my brain, trying to remember exactly what I'd said and how pissed off she would be with me because of it.

"About a week now," she replied, her reflection glaring at me with slitted eyes. "So, you don't get to accuse me of acting. You're a thousand times worse, Xander! And for the record, you failed miserably at making me jealous."

"Sure I did," I murmured, taking a step towards her. "Say it again."

Her nose wrinkled in incomprehension. "Say what again?"

I took another step. One more and my hips would be touching her arse. I met her eyes in the mirror. Her lips were pressed tight together, but her eyes were silver fire.

"Say my name. I bloody love hearing you say it."

"Fuck off, *Xander*," she murmured. I took that last step, brushing my groin against her backside. She let out a tiny hiss that had all my blood roaring south.

"Christ, Georgie. Even when your voice is full of hate, seeing those lips of yours shape my name …" I grazed my rock-hard erection across her arse again to finish my sentence. "How wet did it make you?" I asked.

"What are you …?" Her words cut off with a gasp when I snaked a hand around her, palming her tight belly and pulling her back flush against my front.

"Slapping me. How turned on did it make you? Because for some bloody reason it, riled me right up." I thrust my dick against her, the length of it pressing between her butt cheeks. Georgie's eyes slid closed, her throat bobbing as she swallowed.

"Why don't you check for yourself?" she murmured, her head falling back against my shoulder. "Wouldn't be the first time you helped yourself inside my pants."

With a growl, I fisted the hem of her dress and dragged it up, bunching it at her waist. Gripping the back of one thigh, I lifted her leg, bending it until her knee rested on the countertop. She let out a tiny breath as I slid my hand up her raised thigh and between her legs.

"Christ," I muttered. "You've soaked through your underwear."

"Guess I'm not the only one who confuses fury and foreplay," she purred back, turning her head to nip at my jaw. My dick jerked, and my brain went to complete mush.

I fisted the flimsy fabric of her panties and tore them off her.

Her body jerked, and she squeaked, her eyes flying open again, meeting mine in the mirror.

"They were ruined anyway," I said, sliding my finger along her slippery pussy lips. She caught her bottom lip between her teeth, wriggling her hips to get my finger where she wanted it.

"Completely unsalvageable," I murmured, circling her clit as she mumbled little sounds against my neck, nipping and licking me there. "Now, fuck my fingers, Blondie. Seems like the best way for us to work our fury out is on each other."

I slid one, then two fingers into the tight, wet heat of her, and she stifled a moan, rocking her hips to grind her clit against my palm as I thrust into her. Every movement stroked her bare arse against my dick, aching to be free of my shorts.

"Fuck," I muttered, curling my fingers inside her, enjoying the guttural moan that told me I was hitting the right spot.

"Fuck," she agreed breathily, and suddenly one of her hands was reaching behind her, between us, fumbling with the button on my shorts.

"I'm *really* furious with you right now," she said. "Take out your dick, Xander."

Her fumbling finally succeeded, the button popping open. I frantically reached between us and tugged the fly down, pushing my shorts and underwear down my legs.

"I don't have a condom," I whispered against the side of her face. Georgie smirked up at me, eyes twinkling.

"You're not getting inside me," she replied. "I'm fucking your fingers; you're going to fuck my hand."

With that, she gripped me, her arm twisted behind her but still able to get an angle that had my eyes rolling back with each pull.

"My clit," she demanded, rolling her hips again, thumbing my tip, and then stroking back down again. "Pinch it."

"Jesus," I hissed, slipping my fingers out of her pussy and rolling her swollen clit between a finger and thumb.

"Harder," she breathed, stroking me faster. I squeezed it, and her legs shook. "Again!"

"Bossy," I grated, using my free hand to tug on her hair,

exposing the side of her neck and sucking the skin into my mouth as I pinched her again, growling against her skin as her clit throbbed between my fingers.

"God, that's good," she whimpered, stroking me faster. "Leave a mark on my neck."

I sucked harder on her skin, flicking teasingly at her clit, then pinching again. Flick, then pinch, in a rhythm that had her mewling into the crook of my neck.

"Fuck," she hissed. "Finger me, quick, I'm about to … oh … oh God!"

I pressed two fingers inside her just as her pussy started squeezing around them, as her panting became breathy moans. Her hand on my dick stilled, and her stomach contracted violently with her orgasm.

Heat raced down my spine, but I gritted my teeth against it. I wanted to feel every second of her climax. I could sort myself out later.

I'd never wanted a woman's pleasure so much more than my own before. Well, once before. Twelve years ago.

"Feeling less furious now?" I whispered against the hot, damp skin of her neck, helping her to bring her bent leg back down off the counter. Her eyes, pupils huge, gazed back at me in the mirror's reflection, full of pleasure.

That look … that was the thing that almost did me in. My dick throbbed, and I pressed my eyes closed, bending down to retrieve my shorts.

"That still looks pretty angry, though," Georgie said slyly, and I cracked my eyes open to see her staring at my engorged dick. Just her eyes on me had me leaking precum all over the place.

"Yeah, well—" My words were cut off with a low groan as Georgie went to her knees in front of me, her hands on my hips, and with the hottest, dirtiest grin I'd ever seen, she licked her lips, wetting them, opened her mouth and swallowed me whole. She pulled back, then took me deep again. And again.

"Jesus … fuck, Georgie, I've fantasised about that mouth of yours on my dick for years, but this … this is wild." I grunted, feeling the back of her throat as I bottomed out. She gagged around me, pulling back and sucking my head as she pumped the base in her fist, giving herself a quick breather before she sucked me deep again, and again.

"Christ, look at you, taking all of me ..." My words came out stuttered. "I'm already so close." Tension was building in the base of my spine, coiling in my abdomen. She moaned around me, the sound vibrating up into my chest.

"That's my girl. Eyes on me when I come down your throat, Blondie," I groaned, and she brought her hand up to work me again as she licked and sucked. Her mouth might have been busy, but those eyes, they were smiling up at me like the cat that got the cream.

That look of satisfaction was enough to tip me from teetering on the brink to freefalling right over it. My back bowed, my dick swelled, and I caught her cheeks in my hands, stroking her soft skin as I thrust into her hand, her mouth, moaning as wave after wave of ecstasy shot through me, pumping cum into her. I watched her throat working to swallow it down.

And not once had her eyes left mine. Not even as she released my dick with a little pop and licked her lips.

"Taste better than Bubble-O-Bill?" I murmured, my chest expanding as the beginnings of a proper smile worked at the corners of her mouth.

"Xander, you in there?" Jord called from the other side of the door. The words were followed by a light tap.

"Fuck," I hissed, reaching down and scooping a suddenly serious, wide-eyed Georgie up off the floor. Fuck indeed.

After that performance, all I wanted to do was kiss her stupid and taste myself on her tongue. Smooth that dress back over her pretty arse. Hold on to her for longer than was sensible. Longer than she would let me.

Longer than I wanted to admit to myself.

"Answer!" Georgie whispered, handing my shorts and underwear to me. "I'll hide in the shower."

"Yeah," I called out to Jord, wincing at how sus my voice

sounded. "Give me a second. Just … finishing up." Georgie threw me a withering look as she stepped into the shower cubicle, tugging the curtain closed. I sorted out my still half-mast dick, tucking it away inside my boxer briefs and buttoning my shorts before reaching over and flushing the toilet, as if that's what had kept me in the bathroom for so long. I noisily washed my hands, then turned and opened the door, stepping out and closing it immediately behind me.

"I … wouldn't go in there for a while, if I were you," I said, hoping the flush on my face would be interpreted as bowel-related embarrassment and not post-orgasmic glow.

Jord's eyes narrowed. "Did you find Georgie?"

I shook my head, trying to keep my expression neutral. "Uh, no. Maybe she took a walk?"

Jordyn didn't believe a word I was saying.

"You've got a patient. It looks like an emergency."

Now: I Fucking Hate It

GEORGIE

I'd officially gone completely insane.

There was no other explanation for what had just happened. I'd been so angry with him. And damn him, he'd been right. Slapping him had rekindled that fire inside me, the same one that had ended up with me bent over his dining table last week.

But there was a big difference between hot, horny sex in the heat of the moment, and kneeling in front of him, deep-throating him in a way that I'd never even attempted with other, less well-endowed guys. The act had been so erotic, but it hadn't felt angry to me. It had felt … giving … worshiping even.

I'd thought oral had become a chore for me. Probably because I'd spent the last two years giving it to someone who expected an orgasm out of it. But on the rare occasions he returned the favour, it was never with my climax in mind. It was just a box to tick quickly before he got to the main course—*licked her a little, she's wet, time to bone.*

It hadn't been that way with Xander last week. He'd fully committed to my pleasure. And returning that favour today had felt … perfect.

Too damn perfect.

I was still reeling from the force of my own orgasm, still stuck in the moment with him. Cursing that he'd been called away so suddenly, and not because we'd almost been caught … because we'd been interrupted.

I climbed back out of the shower as silently as I could, staring at myself in the mirror. My hair was a complete bird's nest. My cheeks were pink, my lips swollen from taking his cock. And the giant, reddish-purple hickey on my neck …

I was certifiably insane for letting him do that to me. For demanding he do it to me. For having imagined that after I'd swallowed his cum, he would have lifted me into his arms, would have tasted himself on my tongue as he smoothed my dress back down my thighs, and finger-combed my hair back into something resembling a presentable hairstyle. And for imagining that I would have nuzzled my nose against the little bit of chest hair popping out of the V of his t-shirt, inhaling the warm, masculine scent of him, and I would have wrapped my arms around his waist and just held on.

What on earth had gotten into me?

Compartmentalise, Georgie, I told myself firmly, running my own fingers through my hair to tidy it, splashing yet more water on my face. There was nothing to be done about the love bite. I didn't have makeup in this tiny bathroom. I'd just have to brazen it out, stare down anyone who so much as glanced twice until they knew not to mention it.

If there really was an emergency out there, I needed to be doing my job and producing it. And I needed to stop wallowing in my tangled feelings about Xander Fox.

I stepped out of the bathroom, coming up short when I spotted Jordyn leaning against the wall outside, arms folded across their chest. I swallowed, took a deep breath, and chose the high road.

"Fill me in on the emergency," I commanded, heading down the hallway in the direction of the consult room. "And why aren't you in there producing it?"

"I'm not the showrunner here, G. Sometimes I think you forget that."

I snorted, rounding the corner and coming into the empty

reception area. "You could have fooled me, with the amount of plotting you and Alex and Dr Fox have been doing behind my back!"

Jord stopped, lips twitching in defiance. "Well, someone had to sort out a romantic storyline. We can only go so far with thirst traps. We need emotion, and Alex was amenable. I did my job, G. I did *your* job."

I clenched my jaw, because damn it, despite the whole 'let's make Georgie jealous' angle, Jord was right. I was far too emotionally invested in totally the wrong ways.

"Emergency?" I repeated, not wanting to have the conversation Jord was clearly angling for.

"Young guy, his border collie is very lethargic, off his food, it all happened very suddenly over the last forty-eight hours. Xander's been asking all the medical history questions. He's happy to be filmed, for now. Jase is in there with them."

Jord nodded towards the consult room, where the door was ajar.

"I'll take over here, you're back outside with Karl." I strode over to the consult room, leaning in the doorway out of frame to listen.

"There's definitely a mass here in the abdomen," Xander said quietly. He was squatting down on the floor, feeling around the dog's belly. The dog lay prone, eyes glassy, panting erratically. My heart lurched, and I half turned away. This was hard to watch.

"It's very likely that Boots has abdominal cancer. Unfortunately, it's particularly nasty, and it progresses swiftly. By the time a dog shows signs of being unwell, nine times out of ten it's too late to treat." Xander's tone was empathetic and somehow also matter of fact. I couldn't see his face, but the set of his shoulders told me he was bracing himself for the rest of the conversation.

"Are you saying that … that he's dying?" the man sitting in the chair facing the door asked, his voice cracking on the last word. His elbows dropped to his knees, his head into his hands.

"I'm so sorry, mate," Xander replied, his own voice thick. "I know it's not what you want to hear. Generally, when they're suddenly off their food, not wanting to move, it means the cancer has ruptured. There's internal bleeding."

"Oh God," the young man sobbed, scrubbing at his face. "Are you sure? I mean, you've just poked around his belly a bit, are you positive that's what it is?"

Xander sat back on his heels, giving the man a pat on the knee and standing. "I'd like to do an ultrasound to be absolutely sure. I'll go get the machine and bring it in." He stood and turned for the door, noticing me there. His jaw ticked. His eyes were bleak.

He didn't need the ultrasound to know that dog wasn't going home again.

"Dr Fox?" the man called out. Xander turned back. "If you're right ... if it is cancer ...?"

The side of Xander's face that I could see lifted in a sad half-smile. "Then the kindest thing to do is euthanise. But let's get this ultrasound done first, then we can talk more."

Xander walked from the room as the man dropped to the floor beside the panting dog, wrapping his arms around his neck and crying quietly into his fur. Boots lifted his head and licked feebly at the man's cheek.

Swallowing around the lump in my throat, brushing away a tear, I tapped Jase on the shoulder, beckoning him out.

"Follow Xander, we'll get some footage of him talking about the diagnosis, and how he feels about it. Leave the poor guy in there to hold his pet in peace."

Jase nodded, his own jaw tight, and he trailed Xander out to the surgery. I stopped at the reception desk, leaning against it and taking a few shaky breaths. Memories of Molly—my Molly—swam before my eyes. As if I didn't have enough emotional turmoil with Xander, and Mim and the property, it seemed that life was intent on making me dredge up more and more of the past I didn't want to remember.

The ultrasound was done, the diagnosis remained the same. Boots was bleeding internally from abdominal cancer. There was no treatment, no cure at this late stage. Boots could go home and slowly bleed to death, or the man, Jackson, could give the go-ahead and let him leave peacefully here and now.

I hated this. I hated everything about it. I hated that this poor guy had come in with a sick dog, and within minutes he was facing having him die horribly and painfully at home or choosing to end his life.

I'd never had to make that choice with my Molly, which was the only light in that whole bleak experience.

Jackson, tears streaming down his face, opted to euthanise. Xander nodded and gave him a squeeze on the shoulder.

"I'll head out and get everything prepped. You take as long as you need in here. Call me in when you're … when it's time." He squeezed Jackson on the shoulder again. "You're doing the right thing, mate. It's one of the toughest parts of loving a pet—making that call when we're the ones left behind to grieve. What you're doing is kind, and it's brave, and it's selfless."

Xander left the room again, and I gestured for Jase to follow once more.

"You won't go back in there again, now, okay?" I told him as once again, we headed into the surgery. "You film Xander out back, but once he returns to the clinic, you stay out. Jackson and Boots need their privacy now." I looked over to where Xander was standing with his back to us, gripping the operating table with white knuckles.

"Maybe give us five minutes in here, too, Jase," I said quietly. Jase nodded solemnly and lowered his camera, retreating to the reception area.

I moved until I was standing beside Xander, not looking at him, just listening to his shaky breaths.

"I fucking hate it," he confessed. I nodded but said nothing.

"I hate having to be the bearer of bad news. I hate seeing an animal in pain and knowing what the best—the only—outcome is for them, and still I hate the feeling in here," he tapped at his chest with the heel of his hand, "that I get, knowing I'm about to break people every time I have to tell them there's no hope."

I let out my own shaky breath. "You did it with such calm and compassion, Xander," I murmured. He sucked in air, his face turning to me. I kept my eyes trained on the table. "You gave him the information, and the permission, to make that choice without guilt. And you gave him words of peace. It was … it was …"

I didn't know how to finish that sentence, so instead I slid my hand along the table edge, until it bumped up against his, and I hooked my pinkie over his, squeezing. He squeezed back, his breaths ragged.

"I'm here," I whispered.

And we stood like that until Xander sniffed, scrubbed at his face with his free hand, and gruffly told me that he needed to prep his materials. I unlinked my pinkie and turned, finding Jase and sending him back in to film Xander getting ready to do something that I could never do. Something that I was in absolute awe of him for being able to do.

And then I went back to the bathroom and ugly cried about Boots, and my Molly … and the fact that I hated that I didn't really hate Dr Xander Fox at all.

"So …" Jord began as we finished packing up for the day. Xander had been quiet ever since Jackson and Boots, and he'd let Alex and Calli (once she returned from her counter lunch, smiling very brightly and glancing up at Lachy, who wouldn't stop beaming down at her) take over the free treatment stall.

He spent the afternoon wandering the yard, chatting to the primary school girls selling loom band bracelets and homemade bath bombs, eating more than his fair share of jam thumbprint biscuits, and just showing his face in the community.

They already loved him. And by March, he'd be gone again.

"So …" I prompted, watching Xander strolling around the now empty lawn, Molly cavorting at his heels. She leapt up, he let her rest her paws on his hip as he scratched her ears.

"Alex said she's up for a sleepover with Dr Fox," Jord finished. My muscles tightened, but I breathed through the rolling nausea in my stomach, schooled my expression into 'neutral professional' and turned to her.

"How would this play out?" I asked flatly. Jord watched me too long for their thoughts to be innocent.

"For the cameras only," Jord explained, eyeing me. "Because we all know behind closed doors there's a whole other story going on."

I couldn't help the flush that rose, or the way my hand flew to the hickey on my neck. Jord smirked, which only got my back up further.

"Technical details only. I want your take on how we play this," I said, my eyes on Xander as Alex approached him. The smile he gave her was like a punch to the chest. I couldn't even pretend it wasn't jealousy anymore. His smile quickly faltered as she spoke, and his gaze flicked to me.

"Are you even listening to me?"

I blinked, turning back to Jord. "I'm guessing Dr Kingston is informing Dr Fox of the plans?" I asked.

"Do you even know what the plans are?" Jord retorted. "Because if you were listening to me instead of mooning over him, you would've heard them for yourself."

"You've made your point, Jord. Now summarise for me, please."

Jord sighed. "We'll film them going in together—from a distance, as if they think they're flying under the radar. There will be a kiss, in the kitchen window." Jord stopped, watching me. I set my jaw, kept my expression as bland as possible.

"It won't just be a peck. It'll have to be convincing, as if it's heading for the bedroom."

I waved a hand in a dismissive gesture, ignoring the way my fingers shook. "And will she actually spend the night?"

Jord shook their head. "We'll film what we need. Alex will stay in the trailer with me—your bed hasn't been slept in once, so it makes sense." Jord's cheeks pinked, and I pressed my lips together, wondering if I'd missed something else going on in my distraction.

They cleared their throat and continued. "We'll do an early wake-up, Alex'll get back over there, and we'll 'catch' them having a loving farewell on the porch just before sunrise."

I shrugged, because this all sounded totally fine … if the

thought of having to watch Xander kissing Alex passionately in his kitchen didn't turn my insides to ash.

"Sounds like you and Alex have it all planned out," I deadpanned, and Jord's sheepish expression eased some of the charred feelings inside me.

"Looks like I'm not the only one mooning around here," I murmured with a sidelong glance at Jord. They rolled their eyes, but the small smile that slipped across their mouth for the briefest second warmed me.

"You know, I've sent Kenneth an email asking if maybe we could run multiple seasons of *Beach Vet Goes Bush*. Chuck a new city vet in the deep end every three months. But it would mean us being out here for the medium term. If he approves it, that is. Something to think about … if there's something keeping you in Budgerigar, anyway."

I turned and walked in Xander's direction, feeling a little high that I'd managed to get the last word in on Jord for the first time in what felt like forever.

Now, I just had to act like Xander's tongue in Alex's mouth was totally fine by me. Which it should be. Because he wasn't mine, and I didn't want him to be.

I definitely didn't.

But by the time I got to Xander's truck, I was struck with a whole other dilemma. And it wasn't Alex pressed against Xander's side, his arm slung around her shoulders, fingers caressing her.

It was the people getting out of a car parked right in front of Xander's. Levi straightened from the back door of the car, his sleepy baby in his arms. His pretty blonde girlfriend was already standing on the kerb, looking around with interest at Main Street as she stretched.

And then the driver's door opened, and a long, muscular leg appeared. And then another.

My hand clapped to my chest of its own accord as the rest of him unfolded from the car. Tall, broader than I remembered, and with a neatly trimmed beard to match his neatly trimmed (although somewhat travel-mussed) hair.

I would know that hair anywhere. I'd mussed that hair myself on many an occasion just because I loved how much it riled him up. He'd always been so particular about his hair.

"Dom." His name escaped me without my permission, and he glanced past Xander and Alex to where I was standing a few paces behind. My eyes darted to Xander. He watched me, a tiny furrow forming on his brow.

I had absolutely no idea what my face was giving away, but if it was anything like the frantic thrumming in my chest, it wasn't good.

And then Dom, in three long-legged strides, was in front of me, and his arms were around me, and he was hauling me against his body.

"Georgie," he murmured into my hair.

I froze.

Now: I've Got You All Over Me

XANDER

Alex hissed, flinching away from me.

"Shit, sorry!" I muttered as she rubbed at her shoulder. I flexed the fingers that I'd been digging into her.

"Christ, Xander, you're strong," she replied, but my attention had already strayed back to the oddest reunion in history. I vaguely registered Alex moving away from me to introduce herself properly to Amanda.

Dom swept Georgie up off the pavement, inhaling her hair as he rocked her back and forth like every moment they'd spent apart had been utter torture for him.

Georgie, on the other hand, was stiff as a board in his arms, that pale, wide-eyed, fish out of water expression frozen on her face.

I had a sudden, utterly insane urge to storm over there, drag him off her, and wrap her up in my arms, stroke her cheeks and brush my lips over her forehead until that awful expression melted away.

This was a pair of friends who had held hands, and hugged, and kissed each other's cheeks with the casual affection of people who knew everything about one another. Their history was so much weightier than Georgie's and mine. And she had a much greater reason to hate me than she did Dom.

I'd always wondered why she'd ghosted him as completely as she had me. I'd assumed he was tainted by his association with me.

Now, I wasn't so sure, and the feeling sat wrong in the pit of my stomach.

"You look like someone took a shit in your Weetbix," Levi murmured, and I turned to where he stood, Lily in her carrier, his hands covering her ears.

"Still in denial that your daughter's first word will be swearing, Levi?" I managed to snort, but my eyes had already wandered back to Georgie. Dom had put her down now. They were talking. It looked … awkward.

Even before Georgie and I gave in to whatever this venting of frustration was we were doing, things had never been as uncomfortable as this.

"Do they seem awkward to you?" I asked my brother.

"Hi Levi, so great to see you! This is a huge surprise, what the fudge are you doing out here? And you brought my favourite niece with you, too!" Levi mocked, bumping my shoulder with his.

"Yeah, shock and awe, all of that. But *do* they seem awkward to you?"

"He's been weird as fuck the entire drive here, Xan. Barely spoke, but when he did, it was something about her," he added quietly. I managed to tear my eyes off her, raising my brows at Levi.

"What was he saying?" I asked.

"He kept randomly blurting out stories from when they were kids. And then he'd go silent again for half an hour. It was fucking bizarre."

Georgie flashed a strained smile at Dom and turned towards me, pressing her lips together and heading in our direction. I didn't miss how she knotted her hands in the floaty material of her dress.

"Okay, Dr Fox, remember when we spoke about unscripted television being … unscripted?" she began. To most people, her tone would sound short. But I could hear the quaver at the ends of her words, and how she cut them off sharply to try and hide it.

I stifled a snort at the mention of unscripted, given I'd just been told by Alex that she was having a 'sleepover' with me tonight.

"Uh, yeah," I said.

"Well, this is obviously unscripted," she muttered, sucking both her lips into her mouth before releasing them with an audible pop. "So, we're just going to roll with it."

She turned to Levi. "You came out here to surprise your brother with an early Christmas, okay?"

"You're the boss, Georgie!" Levi replied with a cheeky salute. Georgie rolled her eyes at him, but a little of the tension in her seemed to dissipate. Levi had that effect on people.

"I'm going to send Jordyn over to the grocery store. We'll just do cold meats and salads, I think. Not much time for anything fancier."

"I'll go grab some wine, if you like," Amanda offered, reaching out a hand for Georgie to shake. "Sorry, there wasn't much time back in Sydney the day you both left for me to properly introduce myself. I'm Amanda."

Georgie took her hand, her eyes warming. "Georgie. Thank you, that would be fantastic." She turned back to me.

"Now, Jase said he caught your candid reaction to seeing Levi, but I just need to get … uh … I need you and Dom to greet each other on camera, please Dr Fox." Her face tightened once more. What was going on in her head? Did seeing Dom do this to her?

I sighed, knowing she probably wouldn't open up to me about it. "Sure, no worries, I mean, I don't think he came out here to see me, but I've gotten really good at pretending in front of the cameras lately."

A spark of fire kindled in Georgie's eyes. "Oscar-worthy performances all around." She said, full of sass. She turned to Alex, grabbed her arm, and dragged her towards me. "While we're on the subject, you can introduce your best mate to your new girlfriend. Since she's *sleeping over* tonight."

Without another word, she snapped her fingers at Jase, gesturing towards us, and went to lean against the clinic fence, arms folded across her chest, daring me to argue with her.

Damn her, I wanted to argue so badly. I wanted to pin her

between that fence and my hips and tell her I was sick and bloody tired of pretending that things were real between Alex and me, pretending that things between Georgie and me weren't the most real thing I'd felt in twelve years.

But the camera was rolling, so I pasted on a smile, grabbed Alex's hand, and strode towards Dom, reaching out and giving him a one-armed bro-hug. With extra back beating, because someone had to take the brunt of my frustration.

———

Levi snickered under his breath, serving himself another cold chicken leg and biting into it.

"What's so bloody funny?" I muttered, stabbing at a cherry tomato with my fork.

"Still acting like total dickheads around each other, I see?" he replied with a smirk.

I looked over at Georgie, who was knocking back her fourth glass of wine since this impromptu dinner had started. Yes, I'd been counting. I'd also been counting the number of times Dom's eyes got dark and worried when he looked at her.

Well, I *had* been counting that. But it happened so often that I'd given up on keeping track.

"This whole scenario isn't exactly conducive to anything *but* dickheadery," I muttered into the neck of my beer bottle, taking a sip. I was pacing myself. Even though Georgie had shooed Jord and the camera guys away once they'd gotten some footage of the start of the meal, I didn't want to get wasted.

I tried to tell myself it had nothing to do with how messy she was getting, giggling over there with Alex and Amanda like they were all lifelong besties. That I wasn't thinking, somewhere deep in my lizard brain, that she needed me to look out for her tonight.

Dom was watching me. I turned to him, raising my beer and my eyebrow, taking another sip. I stood abruptly, the chair tilting and almost falling, if Levi hadn't been so swift to grab it mid-fall.

"I need some air," I said. Levi tilted his head, eyes gleaming in the dark.

"We're outside. There's air fucking everywhere."

"Don't be so damn literal. You know what I mean." I didn't wait for a response, turning and stepping down off my porch, heading around towards the stand of trees that separated the crew caravans from us.

I stopped, tugging at my hair and wondering why I felt so bloody on edge.

"What's going on between you two?" Dom asked.

"Jesus Christ! You scared the shit out of me!" I rubbed at my chest, willing my heart to stop racing.

"Have you two … are you trying to start something with her again?" he persisted, stuffing his hands into the pockets of his shorts and fixing me with that piercing stare of his. I tugged at my hair again. I didn't want to lie to my best friend. But I also felt like telling him even the bones of what had been going on between Georgie and me felt like betraying her. Would she want him to know? Was what we were doing even something she'd think worth mentioning to him?

"It's not like that," I hedged, staring into the trees. "Being near her has … it's made me realise how little I'd gotten over what happened. I mean, deep down I always knew that I hadn't, but I made a bloody good show of pretending."

Dom chuckled with zero humour. "She did say earlier you were Oscar-worthy." He was suddenly by my side. "Have you … has she spoken to you about what happened back then?"

I shook my head, my shoulders dropping. "She says it's in the past. She doesn't want to dredge it up. And I get that. But …" I couldn't keep it in. Dom was the one person who had been there for me in the weeks after, when I'd been an utter mess. He'd helped me through, even though he'd lost his best friend out of it. Because of me.

"We've … we've been messing around. A bit. Not on purpose."

Dom huffed out a sharp breath. "Accidentally messing around. Really?" His tone was derisive. A hot gust of wind surged past us, rustling the eucalypts, and doing nothing to help cool the raging feelings that were building in me. Dom couldn't understand. He'd never been out of control with a woman before.

"You never could stay away from one another," he said quietly.

I snorted. "Well, she did a bloody great job of it, for twelve years!"

Dom was quiet for a long moment as I gritted my teeth and stared up into the sparse foliage above us. I tried to imagine what it would be like to not have to feel angry at her for disappearing. To not have to feel furious with myself for being the reason she'd done it.

To not still want her the way I did. To not want more, the way I did.

To not want it all, with her.

"She's … changed," he mused. I turned to look at him then, and the stricken expression on his face made my heart jolt.

"Do you think she thinks we've changed?" I asked him. "Do you think she wonders what it would have been like, being with us through uni, and starting careers, and buying houses, and …"

I trailed off, my throat suddenly thick. Because if she'd been there, if she hadn't left … if I hadn't fucked my chances with her, then Dom would have become the third wheel. Because I would have worshiped her, and it would have been us buying a house together, and us hanging out on Friday nights with a couple of drinks in our lounge room.

And maybe it would have been us smiling down at our baby the way Levi and Amanda smiled down at Lily.

"What the hell is in this beer?" I grouched after clearing my throat. "My thoughts are bloody maudlin all of a sudden."

Dom chuckled dryly. "They have been for over a decade now. You were just really good at pretending they weren't."

He knew me far too well. So why did I have a sudden, sickening feeling that I didn't know him the same way?

"I'd better get back," I mumbled. I didn't want to continue this conversation. It was going to lead to things I didn't want to talk about.

"Just … don't break her heart again," Dom said.

I stopped, my shoulders tightening, but I didn't turn.

"If you knew how bloody much I wished I hadn't in the first place," I grated.

I kept walking, leaving him behind, but I was sure that I heard him mutter, "I do know, Xan."

I returned to find Georgie strutting up and down the porch, singing into an empty beer bottle. Alex and Amanda were cheering and clapping her. Levi watched with a smirk, cradling Lily, who drowsily suckled on a bottle.

"She's still a Swiftie, I see," he chuckled, tilting his head in Georgie's direction. I couldn't answer—couldn't take my eyes off the sway of her hips. The unconsciously sexy way she grabbed a fistful of her dress as she spun tipsily on the spot.

The way her mouth moved as she shaped the words of the song. That mouth had been wrapped around my cock just a few short hours ago. Those hips had rocked against me as I made her come on my fingers.

That pinkie that was sticking up in the air as she grasped her fake microphone had linked with mine when I was feeling like shit.

Don't break her heart again, Dom had warned me. But maybe I should start worrying that it might be her doing the breaking this time around.

"Come dance, Xander!" she called out. 'Xander' sounded more like 'Schander'.

"How many drinks has she had since I left?" I asked Levi.

"Two. Go dance with her, because when she sobers up, she'll probably slap you in the face instead."

I winced, rubbing at the place she'd done just that earlier. "That's hitting too close to home right now, Lev." But I did what I was told and approached her. She grinned up at me, swaying slightly, a fine sheen of sweat on her chest. I wanted to run my tongue over it.

"You going to serenade us while we dance, are you, Blondie?" I asked, injecting as much humour into my tone as I could possibly muster. As if they'd plotted this, another Taylor Swift song burst into the air, this time from Alex's phone. She and Amanda shared a knowing look.

"I'm just gonna dance with you the way we never got to at your year ten formal," she breathed against my jaw, wrapping one hand around my neck, taking my hand in the other, and leaning into me, rocking from side to side.

How was I supposed to respond to that? We both knew why we had never danced that night. We both knew how two years later that same reason would come back to haunt us.

"This is a sad song," I eventually mumbled against her hair, inhaling the minty scent and closing my eyes because it all just felt like too much for me.

"Yeah," she sighed against my neck. "It's about struggling to get over someone."

I stilled. She didn't seem to notice, continuing her drunken shuffle as I suddenly paid extra attention to the lyrics.

"Do you … are you trying to clean yourself of me … to get free?" I asked. She shook her head, rubbing her nose against my chest just above the V-neck of my t-shirt.

"Mmmm, wanted to do this earlier. You know, in the bathroom at the clinic, after I sucked you off."

Alex and Amanda burst into giggles. I ignored them.

"You wanted to do what, Blondie? Dance with me?" I couldn't get enough air.

"Wanted to hold you, and nuzzle you right here—" she ran her nose across my skin again— "and cling to you for so long … too long … forever really."

She looked up at me then, her eyes slightly unfocused. "I've got you all over me, Xander Fox. And I'm not sure I even want to get clean anymore."

I was so stunned by her words, I didn't realise we'd shuffled too close to the edge of the deck until she was stumbling sideways. I snatched her against me, stepping back from the edge as she suddenly went from melancholy to uncontrollable giggles.

"Might be time for you to call it a night," I mumbled as she cackled in my arms. Instead, she ground her hips against mine.

"God, girls, his bulge! Did I tell you about the bulge in the jeans I put him in the first day?" She hiccupped through her giggles.

"I was there," Amanda said with a rueful laugh. "I haven't forgotten."

"Ooh, I need to hear this story," Alex said with relish, just as Georgie's head lolled against my chest.

"Maybe another time," I muttered, clasping Georgie tighter to me and looking towards the homestead. Was Miriam asleep? Could I sneak Georgie into her room?

"It's bulging against me right now!" she whisper-shouted, her hand sliding down my stomach. I grabbed her wrist and tucked her arm around my neck. She pouted up at me.

"Another time," I repeated, more firmly than I'd spoken to Alex. The girls giggled. How much wine had they all consumed?

Jord appeared from around the corner of the tiny home, Jase following with the camera already on his shoulder. He looked shifty. Jord's face was conspicuously bland.

"It's time for us to get our sleepover footage," Jord said, eyeing Georgie in my arms. Georgie turned and glared at Jord.

"Another time!" I said, clapping a hand over Georgie's mouth before she could say anything to inflame the situation. "Clearly I've got my hands full right now."

Georgie ranted against my hand, but the words were muffled. Thankfully. Whatever drunken ramblings she had cued up did not need to be heard by this audience.

Jord watched this with a calculating look in their eyes. "Fine, another time," they conceded eventually, folding their arms across their chest. "It's a good thing we don't film on Sundays, G."

Georgie struggled in my arms, but I pulled her to my chest, leaning down until my lips were at her ear.

"You want to sleep over with me, Blondie?" I asked. "I'll take the couch, you can have the bed. If you can make it up the ladder to the loft, that is."

She leaned back, her eyes narrowed. Gripping the hand I still had over her mouth, she peeled my fingers back.

"Challenge accepted," she muttered. I grinned, and without another glance at our audience, I steered her to the door.

"Merry Christmas!" I called out to them as I shut the door, locked it, and tore off my mic, tossing it across the room. I suddenly felt like I couldn't trust anyone who was in on this farce we were concocting.

I really, really wanted to trust her, though.

"Xander, this ladder is a menace!" Georgie slurred, kicking off her sandals while simultaneously failing to get her foot onto the bottom rung. When her toes slipped off, she giggled, falling back against the wall.

A small smile slid over my lips as I approached. "Do you need the bathroom, Blondie? Because once you're up there, you're there for the night."

Georgie's unfocused eyes found mine, and she shook her head, her hair swinging around her face. "Oh, wow, that made me dizzy."

I chuckled, wrapped an arm around her waist, and lifted her against my side. "Legs around me."

Georgie complied too easily, the warmth of her thighs as they surrounded me making me clench my jaw against arousal. She didn't need me being horny tonight. She needed water, and she needed sleep. She needed to be taken care of.

And I really wanted to take care of her.

I climbed the ladder carefully, holding her like precious cargo so I didn't accidentally bang her head against the wall. At the top I set her on her feet, steadying her with my palms on her hips as she swayed.

"Oh … God, sorry, I do need to pee. Like, really, *really* need to pee," Georgie moaned, looking so adorably mortified that it took everything in me not to take those rosy cheeks between my palms and kiss her.

"Alright then, back down we go."

Downstairs, I deposited her in the bathroom and turned to leave. She grabbed my wrist.

"Stay," she said, already lifting her dress and struggling to tug down her underwear with one hand.

"I'll just wait outside the—"

"Stay, Xander. I mean, you've had your face down there. Watching me pee is nothing," she said, sitting with her dress held up around her waist, her knickers around her ankles.

I closed my eyes, leaning against the wall. This was so intimate, and the swell of emotion in my chest was reaching unbearable levels.

"You look so handsome, all gruff and embarrassed over there." Georgie giggled to the sound of far too much toilet paper being pulled from the roll. "Whoops! I definitely don't need that much for one little wee."

My lips curled, but I kept my eyes firmly closed until the toilet flushed and the tap was running. I opened them to find Georgie messily applying toothpaste to my brush.

"I'll just be a sec. No one likes furry teeth," she remarked, brushing sloppily, white foam dripping down her chin and into the basin.

God, I'd thought eating her pussy was my biggest fantasy. I clearly hadn't considered watching her use my toothbrush.

Pushing away my sappy thoughts, I carried her up the ladder once more. At the top, I busied myself with turning the sheet back, plumping the pillows, and thanking God that I'd actually bothered to make my bed that morning. Not that Georgie was in any state to really notice what my bed looked like.

"Xander," she purred, and I straightened, turning to find her sliding her hands up her legs, grasping the hem of her dress and tugging it up, up that toned body.

"Georgie," I replied warily.

She grinned lopsidedly. "You know what would be fun?"

I chewed on the inside of my cheek as her dress reached up past her navel. "What?"

"If you stayed up here, and slept with your dick inside me. What do they call that—there's a word for it …"

"Swaddling," I grated, willing my dick to ignore what I was seeing, what I was hearing. I reached towards the shelf where I kept my t-shirts and brought one out for her. "But we aren't doing that tonight, Blondie. You're going to get into bed, have some water, and go to sleep."

"Can we at least do the sleeping naked?" she asked, her dress fully off. No bra, her perky little tits pointing right at me, nipples peaked and pink and beautiful. "Both of us?"

"No, Georgie. I'm sleeping on the couch, remember?" I needed to be canonised—I was an utter saint for being so restrained.

She pouted, and I took the opportunity to slide my t-shirt over her head. It fell just below her arse, and was loose enough to hide her athletic curves, for which I was abundantly grateful.

"In," I said, pointing to the bed. "I'm going to get you some water."

I escaped down the ladder, taking myself to the bathroom. I doused my face with water and grabbed the toothbrush she'd just used. It was still damp from her, and my chest tightened again as I used it.

"Good girl," I murmured when I returned with an empty glass and a full water jug to find her already in bed, the sheet at her hips.

She smirked lopsidedly at me. "It makes me tingle between my legs when you call me that." She took the glass I passed her, draining the water and handing it back to me as I blew a calming breath out between my lips.

"Does it?" I asked, trying to act casual when my body felt anything but. I filled the glass again and pressed it into her hand.

She watched me over the rim. "Yeah, but earlier, when you said, 'that's my girl' … you know, when I was sucking you off … that really did something to me."

She returned the glass, slipping down in the bed, her eyes falling closed.

"Did it?" I asked, my voice hoarse.

"Yeah, Xander. It did. All I ever wanted was to be your girl," she mumbled. Her words were slurred, but more from sleep than drunkenness I thought. I hoped.

"Christ, Blondie," I whispered, pinching the bridge of my nose because my eyes burned. I stood, needing to take myself away from her, to retreat to the couch and sort through the tangle of emotions that was knotted in my chest.

"Don't go," she mumbled, flinging an arm out to pat the space beside her.

"Just … cuddle me until I fall asleep."

"I don't know if that's such—"

"It's just spooning."

I sighed, looking down at her rumpled hair, in a t-shirt several sizes too big for her, long lashes curling on her cheekbone.

Damn it. I couldn't say no to spooning. Just until she fell asleep, though.

I tugged off my shorts and shirt and climbed into the bed. Within seconds she'd scooted her backside over, nestling it against me, pressing her warm back against my chest.

"This is … so nice," she murmured, tugging my arm over her until she was completely ensconced. "I'd take this, right now, a thousand times over dancing at your formal." I barely dared to breathe as her body relaxed against mine, her breathing slowing in sleep.

I could have extricated myself then. I could have gotten up. I could have taken myself downstairs and tried to be angry that the only time she could be soft with me was when she was drunk. But what I really wanted to feel was exactly how I felt right at that moment—needed, and wanted, and content.

So I closed my eyes and inhaled the mint of her shampoo, and the warmth of her skin, until sleep took me too.

Then: Something For The Spank Bank

GEORGIE, 16 YEARS OLD

> Hot Xander: Did you get another letter from Granny yet?

> Hot Xander: I'm on the edge of my seat

> Hot Xander: I'm gonna send an email to the producers of Spring Bay. Guarantee there'll be a granny who returns from the dead next season

> Hot Xander: They're going to eat that shit right up! It's television gold

> Hot Xander: What are you wearing to the formal? I don't want to clash with you

It was times like this I really wished I had some close girlfriends to squeal with. But while I was friendly with a group of girls, and occasionally we did something together on weekends, they didn't get my friendship with Dom. And they knew nothing about Xander.

He felt too precious to share with anyone except Dom.

I wasn't sure how Xander managed to sneakily text me at school

—my high school had a zero-tolerance policy for mobile phones during school hours—but every day when I dragged it out of my bag as I walked to the bus line, there was always a string of texts from him. Some of them about random weird things that happened in his school day. Sometimes they relayed an entire conversation he and Dom had the night before when they were deliriously tired and talking shit.

Often it was asking me about what was happening in my life, how my exams had gone, when I was racing next—sometimes he and Dom would come and watch from the finish line to high-five me as I passed them.

He loved joking about my old-school correspondence with my grandmother.

Miriam—who asked me to call her Mim, since it sounded more grandmotherly without putting that label on things—was forthright to the point of bluntness in her letters, with everything except the reason she and Mum didn't talk. Which was fine with me—we got on like a house on fire in all other ways, and I didn't want to rock the boat by prying further.

I smiled as I typed up a response.

> Georgie: I only sent my latest letter yesterday—Australia Post is nowhere near that efficient!

> Georgie: I'm wearing a gold dress. I hope that's not too flashy for you, not that it really matters if I match you, since we aren't going together

> Hot Xander: Are we talking like, glittery gold? Shimmery gold? Matte gold? I honestly have NFI what I'm talking about here. I just want to match my tie to your dress

> Hot Xander: I don't care if we're not going together. I just want one photo of us matching

> Hot Xander: I need something for the spank bank

I giggled, biting my lip when the senior boy in line ahead of me turned to eye me with curiosity.

Georgie: Most normal boys ask for a topless selfie. You want us fully clothed with your tie matching my dress. You're so weird

Hot Xander: Don't diss my kinks, Blondie!

Hot Xander: But is a topless selfie on the table here? Asking for a friend

Hot Xander: No, I'm asking for me, I would NEVER share naked pics of you with anyone!!!

Hot Xander: Actually, forget I just sent that, ok? I am a gentleman (who occasionally jerks off thinking about you) that's all

Georgie: I'm going to pretend you didn't say any of that. And also, I'm pretty sure Dom is wearing a gold bow tie. So are we gonna have a matchy-matchy threesome photo?

Hot Xander: Not sure if Dom scowling at us would really help me get off, but okay, as long as we can have one photo of just you and me. When I'm wanking I like to pretend you're all mine, and I don't have to share you with him

Georgie: If my mum ever saw our text conversations I would be grounded for life! She wouldn't even care that you're joking around

Hot Xander: Am I though?

I had to put my phone down then. He liked to flirt. That was just Xander. Sure, I liked him in a more than friendly way. And I thought he felt that way about me, too, but was he serious when he said stuff like that?

Did he really touch himself, thinking about me? I mean, I

thought about him … but I would never tell him that, not in a million years. Too embarrassing. Was Xander more honest with me than I'd given him credit for?

And great, now I was sitting on a packed school bus, my head full of images of Xander, naked, touching himself.

I stuffed my phone in my bag and pulled out my laptop, finding my maths homework. Nothing got my mind out of the gutter like index laws in algebraic expressions.

"Happy Christmas!" Mum and Seth called out from the kitchen as I unlocked the front door.

"Why are you both home so early?" I shouted back, dropping my school bag in the entry and slouching along the hall. "And what are you talking about? Christmas isn't until next month."

I turned into the kitchen to see Mum and Seth, with matching, giant, fake-looking smiles plastered across their faces, holding out a bundle of black puppy with a tartan ribbon tied around its neck. I stopped dead in the doorway.

"What's going on?" I breathed, but my hands were already reaching for the puppy. "Who is this?"

Seth plopped the adorable thing into my arms.

"This is your early Christmas present. Mum and I picked her up from the foster carer earlier today. She's twelve weeks old. They think she's a Labrador German Shepherd mix."

I rubbed my nose against the soft puppy hair, inhaling the smell of her. "She's the cutest wuffy ever, that's what she is," I crooned against her as she licked at my face, breathing puppy breath into my nostrils. I giggled.

"Why?" I asked, looking back up at Mum and Seth. "I've begged for a dog for years, why are you suddenly caving?"

Seth's smile slipped into something slightly sheepish. Mum's dropped off her face entirely.

"Well, you remember how we had that incident a few weeks

back when Seth was away," Mum began, her voice clipped, her eyes narrowed at Seth.

"You mean, when the wind banged the front door shut and you were sure a murderer was breaking in?" I asked. Mum's frown deepened.

"You know I feel unsafe when Seth's not home. And … well, you've always wanted a dog. So Seth, in his wisdom, started looking into rescue pups that would be a good pet, but also have a big bark, to deter potential intruders."

Clearly this was yet another of their passive-aggressive arguments. The ones they'd started having in front of me more and more, ever since Seth told me the truth about Mim.

I wasn't going to get stuck in the middle of it. No way.

"This is the best Christmas present ever!" I said, tucking my puppy under one arm and wrapping the other around Mum before doing the same with Seth.

"I'm going to take her out back, see if she needs to wee."

And I escaped, taking a quick detour to grab my phone out of my backpack. Once I was safely out of earshot of whatever argument they decided to reignite over this, I held my phone up and snapped a selfie. I put her down on the grass and sat while she sniffed me, then the grass, then the garden bed, then squatted to do her business.

> Georgie: Check out my early Christmas present! Help me pick a name?

> Hot Xander: aww, so beautiful! And the dog is pretty cute too. Boy or girl?

> Georgie: Girl. She's probably a labrador german shepherd cross. She's a rescue dog

> Hot Xander: Well, my mum always used to say that if I'd been a girl, she would have called me Molly …

I looked over at the cavorting little black bundle. Her paws and her ears were too big for her body.

> Georgie: You would have made a very cute Molly

> Georgie: I kind of love it. Well, that was easy!

> Hot Xander: Things are always easy with you and me

I tugged on my bottom lip, wondering if I wanted to rekindle the conversation we'd been having earlier. He hadn't texted again about it, but did that mean he was over it? Or that he was waiting for me to respond, overthinking everything he thought was happening between us?

I was projecting. Xander wasn't like that, was he? He wasn't analysing every word we ever said to one another, wondering if he was missing some undercurrent, wondering if the flirting was real, or if it was just for fun.

No, that was just me. Surely it was just me.

Then: I'm Not Dating You

XANDER, 16 YEARS OLD

"Did you tell her yet?" Dom asked, sitting on his bed and crossing his ankle over his knee, staring intently at me. I looked up from my phone, wishing I could just keep flirt-texting with Georgie without getting the third degree from her best friend.

I sighed. "No."

"Come on, Xander, how do you think this is going to go down? She arrives to the formal with me, and gets utterly blindsided by Rhiannon the curvy little brunette clinging to you?"

I flopped back on my bed, rubbing my hands down my face. "Shit."

Dom snorted. "Shit is putting it mildly. Why didn't you just stand up to your father?"

I grabbed my pillow and threw it at him. "You have no bloody idea! Keeping the peace with him is a full-time job. You've seen what he's like with Levi. Honestly, it's just easier to do what he wants and avoid the explosion."

Dom sighed. "Yeah, alright, I understand. But you need to set Georgie straight on this, before the formal. It's going to hurt her enough hearing it from you first."

I rolled onto my stomach, pummelling the mattress with my fists.

"Is it though? I can't bloody work her out, Dom. Sometimes she texts me something, and I swear I'm not imagining this … this feeling I have about her. But then she'll go radio silence on me other times, and I never know if I've taken it too far, if she's not into me the way I'm into her. It's driving me crazy!"

My mattress moved as Dom sat beside me. "She's into you. She's so very into you, she doesn't know how to act. She's scared that you're just a flirty guy, that it's not just her you're a complete lunatic around."

"How do you know all this?" I grouched. "Don't you both have a rule where you don't discuss me?"

"We do. I don't need to talk about you to know how she feels. It's written all over her face. Xander, tell her. Tonight."

I knew he was right. I knew that it was the right thing to do. I knew telling her myself gave me the chance to reassure her that me taking Rhiannon, the daughter of my dad's biggest client, to my formal meant absolutely nothing to me. I was doing a favour for my dad, that was all. I'd met the girl a total of twice before now. She was not my type.

She wasn't Georgina Menzies.

"Okay. Get the hell out. I need peace and quiet for this conversation."

Dom sucked in a breath. "You're going to call her?"

I laughed. "No, you idiot! Who calls anyone? I just need to focus on writing a really good text, and I don't need you breathing down my neck, trying to tell me what I'm doing wrong."

Dom raised his hands over his head, backing towards the door. "Good luck—you're going to need it."

If I hadn't already thrown my pillow at him, I would have done it then.

> Xander: I have something else I need to tell you about the formal

> Blondie: You want to know where I bought my stilettos so you can match them too?

I groaned, falling back on the bed. Georgie in stilettos. New fantasy unlocked.

Get your head in the game, Xander. This is bloody important.

> Xander: I have to bring a family friend along as my plus one. I promised dad. I'm not into her or anything, I barely know her. I've told you what dad can be like, so it was easier just to tell him yes than argue. It doesn't change anything for you and me. She probably won't even hang around me once she's in the door, I think she just wants a chance to mingle with King Henry's boys. I'm still wearing a gold tie, and I'm still expecting my dance with you

I hit send before I could second guess any of it, falling back onto my pillow and cursing when I hit the bedhead where my pillow would have been, if I hadn't lobbed it at Dom.

It felt like a decade before the text went from delivered to read. And then a century before the little dots started jumping around. And then a millennium before they stopped, and a message came through.

> Blondie: That was the longest text you've ever sent me. All good. See you there

Was that it? How the hell was I supposed to know how she felt from that?

> Xander: Is that all you're going to say?

> Blondie: Yep

> Xander: Are you ok with this?

> Blondie: I don't get to have an opinion. I'm not dating you

> Xander: That's bullshit Blondie

Blondie: It's the truth

Blondie: I'll see you on Saturday night

263

Then: Putting Out Won't Get Him To Stay

GEORGIE, 16 YEARS OLD

"Am I crazy?" I asked Elena as she picked up another section of my hair and rolled it around her curling iron.

"Not at all, Georgie darling," she replied in her lilting accent. "You have every right to feel upset right now. But …" she trailed off, grabbing a hairpin and fiddling with the curl she'd just made.

"But what?" I demanded. I was clammy from the heat of the curling iron, and from my own nerves about seeing Xander and this girl together. I was probably going to have sweat stains all over my beautiful dress before I even made it to King Henry's Great Hall.

"But you're going with a friend, and he had no choice but to accept that. So … maybe it's okay to feel upset, but perhaps not to feel angry with Xander."

"Ugh, I know you're right!" I grouched. "But I did tell him that if I could date, I would absolutely have gone with him."

"But does that mean he should be dateless, because you turned him down?" Elena asked.

"I didn't turn him down. I wouldn't have been allowed to go with him!" I argued, but I knew I sounded stupid. It didn't matter what my reason was. I'd said no when he asked me.

I hated how everything Elena said made complete sense. All I wanted was someone to tell me that it was okay to feel like slapping him for taking this girl, then slapping her for being there with him when I wasn't allowed to be.

It was my own fault. I'd assumed that going with Dom was a chance to spend the evening with the pair of them, the way we always did when we hung out at Dom's on weekends.

"Sometimes I wish I was better at sneaking around behind Mum's back," I muttered. "Then I could have just told her I was going with Dom, and gone with Xander anyway."

Elena's throaty chuckle echoed around the bathroom. "You've always been too honest for your own good, Georgie. It is one of the things I love best about you. And … all done!"

I looked into the mirror and gaped at the elaborate style of curls pinned around my head and spilling down my back.

"I look beautiful!" I gasped.

"You're always beautiful, Georgie. You're just fancy now, too. Shall I do your makeup? And then you can slip into your gown. I promised your mother I would take photos, and the limousine will be here in about forty-five minutes."

The look on Dom's face when I appeared downstairs was enough to make that clammy feeling erupt all over my body again.

"He's going to regret Rhiannon all night," Dom breathed, his eyes raking from my bare shoulders, across my collarbone and to the modest cleavage I'd been able to manufacture with the help of a very padded push-up bra, then down the sleek lines of the shimmering gold fabric to where my thigh peeked out from the split that started just below my hip, and then to the heels that were already making my feet ache.

"Don't talk about it, please, I'm nervous enough as it is," I hissed, swatting at his arm. The wistful smile that flitted across his face made my heart thrum violently.

"I would happily place a bet that when we get there, I'll have her foisted onto me, and he'll whisk you away for the entire evening," he murmured, and there was a flash of sadness in his dark eyes that had mine prickling.

"Don't be stupid, I would never abandon you like that!" I argued, but a tiny part of my heart rebelled at the lie. I might very well do just that if it meant having Xander all to myself all night.

"She's really … something else, isn't she?" Dom said to Xander about half an hour into the evening. I snagged a mini quiche from a roving waiter and bit into it violently.

"She's borderline stalkerish, that's what she is," Xander muttered, his eyes grazing over my body for what felt like the billionth time since I'd arrived. "Thank Christ she needed to pee!"

"I'm shocked she didn't ask you to go with her!" I said, trying and failing to keep the snappy tone out of my voice. "You'll have indents on your arm from where she's been holding on to you all night."

"I'm so sorry, Blondie," Xander mumbled, running a hand through his hair. "I feel like this is ruining our night. And you look so …" He looked me up and down again, slowly, his eyes lingering on my boobs and the split in my dress. Heat flooded every inch of my skin.

"So what?" Rhiannon asked, panting slightly as she skidded to a halt beside Xander, her fingers wrapping around his forearm once more. Xander winced.

"Did you sprint to the bathroom or something?" I asked, feeling a flash of envy that she could run in heels that were twice as high as mine. And she was still a head shorter than me.

She was a tiny, petite thing with glowing olive skin, glossy dark hair that fell in a silky waterfall down her back. Big, brown eyes, a teeny nose and full lips smothered in cherry red lipstick to match her cherry red gown, with cleavage that definitely didn't require inches of padding to achieve.

I felt like a giraffe beside her, all legs and neck, no curves to speak of.

"You have something green stuck in your teeth," she said with a smirk. I hated her even more than I had just a moment ago. I turned, running my tongue along my teeth and hoping that it was gone.

Thankfully a bell rang out around the huge hall, signalling that it was time to take our seats for dinner. Rhiannon clawed at Xander's arm, dragging him across the floor. He glanced back at us with a miserable expression on his face.

Well, at least he wasn't enjoying her stage-five clinging. If he had been, I would have just walked straight out. I was one more of Rhiannon's snarky comments away from doing just that anyway.

"Is it gone?" I hissed to Dom, baring my teeth. He winced, reaching into my mouth to dig it out.

"She's a handful," he muttered, his hand on the small of my back as he steered me towards the large round tables set up beside the dance floor. The school had forked out for a live band, and the guitarist was playing some classical piece on his acoustic guitar as we took our seats. My eyes widened slightly to see that I was sand-wiched between Xander and Dom, with Rhiannon on Xander's other side.

I plonked my clutch down on the table in front of me and took my seat. My dress slid open, exposing my left thigh as Dom tucked my chair under the table. I felt Xander's gaze on the bare skin like he was branding me, and when I glanced at him, his jaw was tight, his hand flexing where it rested on the table between us.

I wanted to wrap my pinkie around his. I wondered what Rhiannon would think of that as I tapped my own fingers in agita-tion on the tablecloth while our entrées were served.

"So, how long have you and Dom been dating?" Rhiannon asked me, her eyes skating over my face with an expression of distaste. I'd just put a forkful of cherry tomato into my mouth, so I couldn't answer her.

"They're not dating, they're just friends," Xander grated beside me.

"We've known one another since we were four. She's like a sister to me," Dom added in a much more pleasant tone.

Rhiannon's expression instantly soured, and she turned to her own plate, pushing food around but not eating anything. Meanwhile, I attacked my food with vigour—it gave me something to focus on that wasn't the icy atmosphere between all of us.

Rhiannon filled the silence with prattle about herself. *She was a dancer, which apparently made her extremely flexible. Maybe one weekend, Xander could come over to her house and she'd show him a few of her 'dance' moves?*

Red was her favourite colour, did Xander think it suited her? Not everyone could pull off red (said with a snide glance in my direction). *It really needed a rich complexion. She got her olive skin from her Spanish mother, who still looked in her twenties, despite being in her forties.*

By the end of dessert, I knew everything about her except her bra size, although I'm sure she was working up to that.

When the band started up their first dancing number, and the music drowned her out, My shoulders dropped. I hadn't realised how tense listening to her had made me. The rest of the couples at our table moved out onto the dancefloor.

"Dance, Xander!" she demanded, tugging at his sleeve, already standing. Xander sighed, throwing a desperate glance in my direction as he started to get out of his chair.

Dom shot up. "Actually, Xander promised the first dance of the night to Georgie," he said. "I'd love to dance with you, though."

My eyebrows shot up. How was he so good at lying?

Xander reached down and wrapped his fingers around my hand. I looked up into his blazing eyes just as he was jerked away from me.

"You're here with me, Xander!" she hissed loudly in his ear. "You don't dance with anyone but *me*."

"I did promise Georgie a dance tonight," he insisted, his voice strained. I wondered how much of him just wanted to tell her where to shove it. I hoped a big part.

"Can I have you to myself?" she asked. "Or do you share everything with Dom and his dorky non-girlfriend?"

I saw red. I started from my seat, Dom's hand coming down to rest on my shoulder, pushing me back down into it and holding me there despite my struggles.

"Don't you dare speak about her that way," Xander growled, shocking me enough that I stopped fighting Dom. I gaped up at Xander, watching his jaw tick and his fist clench by his side.

"You don't get to demand I bring you along tonight, even though I barely bloody know you, and then spend all night acting like a bitch to my best friends!" he continued. "Why the hell did you even want to come tonight, anyway?"

Rhiannon's mouth fell open. "I … I didn't *demand* anything!" she insisted. "My dad told me that your dad said you needed a date, and would I like to volunteer! I felt *sorry* for you, Xander!"

She turned to me with a sneer. "Should've known as soon as I saw your stupid gold tie that you and Dom are sharing more than just a dorm room."

She pushed past Xander, leaning down into my face until I could see every single one of the fake eyelashes she was wearing as she glared at me.

"Which end does Xander get? Your mouth? Or your vag? Or do you let them take turns?"

I swallowed, too shocked by her words to think straight. But she wasn't finished, digging her red nails into my arm.

"Sluts from public schools don't keep hold of guys like Xander Fox. Just warning you. Putting out won't get him to stay." She leaned closer, her voice softer so Xander and Dom wouldn't be able to hear. "And all I have to do is be patient until he gets sick of you."

She stood, smirking down at my burning face. Xander stepped between her and me as I tried to pull air into my lungs.

"Get out," he growled. Rhiannon patted him on the cheek, for all the world as if she hadn't just said the most disgusting things to me.

"Can't wait to tell Dad all about how you treat a girl who does a favour for you," she said, and the false pleasantness in her tone hid something that made me feel cold all over.

"Out," Xander repeated. "Don't make me make a scene and haul you out of here."

With that she flounced off, her hips swaying in her tight dress as she headed for the exit, plucking her phone out of her pocket and texting vigorously.

"That was ..." Dom muttered, his hand still gripping my shoulder.

"Shit. That's what it was." Xander dropped into the chair beside me, turning mine and dragging it closer until my knees were nestled between his spread legs. The warmth of his thighs seeped into me.

"You okay?" he asked softly, his hands resting on my knees. One of which was bare, the split in the dress exposing it.

"I need some air," I mumbled, standing abruptly and heading for a door on the opposite side of the hall to where Rhiannon had just disappeared.

Then: The View Out Here Is Much Better

XANDER, 16 YEARS OLD

I stood, watching Georgie fleeing across the floor, weaving her way between the dancing couples as the band blasted their way through Lady Gaga's *Bad Romance*. I had to laugh at the irony, even if it came out kind of choked.

"Go after her, you idiot," Dom grunted, shoving my shoulder. "Go and fix this."

"Bloody hell," I muttered under my breath as my feet took me after her. How was I supposed to do that? How could I possibly make right what Rhiannon had just totally screwed up?

Well, I couldn't entirely blame Rhiannon. I hadn't been able to keep my eyes off Georgie from the moment she walked in, hand in hand with Dom. They looked like a couple. And she looked …

She looked like my every single fantasy, wrapped up in shimmery gold paper. The way her athletic body moved in that slinky dress. The way her toned thigh kept peeking out from the split in her dress, taunting me. The creamy tops of her breasts. Christ, I'd been adjusting myself every thirty seconds.

Rhiannon clearly hadn't missed my fixation, and it had been like a red flag to a bull. She was out to stake a claim on me. But why? Why had she wanted to come with me tonight?

Or had that been a lie on Dad's part? Had he told me I was doing her a favour, while also telling her dad that she'd be doing me one? Either she was lying, or Dad was. And I couldn't work out why Dad would lie to me about this. Why would he conspire to have me take out some random girl I barely knew?

I stepped outside, and every thought fled my brain. The night was breathtaking on her, turning her hair into silver curls, her skin shimmering like pearls. She leaned against a column, looking out at the manicured lawns of my school. I tugged at the gold tie around my neck, loosening it and unfastening the top two buttons, trying to find space to breathe when she took my bloody breath away.

She turned to me, her lips pressed tight, her eyes lit with angry fire. Arms crossed, pushing her breasts together. I stared at them for longer than was polite. I could happily have stared at them forever.

"My school might be public, but it's an affluent school. I go to school with the kids of lawyers and doctors too, you know. They're just ones who value having a quality public education system."

I took a step towards her. "You know I don't believe any of that shit she said," I murmured, stepping closer again, until I was leaning against the pillar too, facing her. Close enough that I could easily wrap an arm around her slender waist and tug her against me. My fingers twitched with wanting, but I kept my arms folded, mirroring her.

"And the things she said about us … and Dom." Georgie actually shuddered as she said it. "What the hell is wrong with her, to even think those things?"

"She was jealous. She wanted to justify why I … why I couldn't stop staring at you all night."

Georgie's eyes flashed up to mine, unblinking as her lips parted. I sucked in a breath and continued. "If she thought you were putting out like that, for both of us, in her mind it probably explained me preferring you over her."

"*Do* you prefer me over her?" Georgie whispered. Had she moved closer? Or had I? All I knew was I could feel the heat of her breath on my jaw, and it made me shiver.

"Blondie," I grated, raking my eyes over her face, and lower, drinking in the view of her mesmerising tits before dragging my eyes back up to hers. "I prefer you over every girl." I had to adjust myself, leaving my hands hanging by my sides.

She unfolded her arms, reaching out and hooking both her pinkies around mine, dropping her head to stare down at our hands, joined in such a small way as my heart tried to beat its way out of my chest.

"I never know what to think when you say things like that," she mumbled. I unhooked one finger from hers, reaching up to lift her chin.

"Look at me, Georgie," I said. Her eyes flicked up to mine, and the uncertainty in them shattered me. "You know that we're more than just friends."

She blinked, her tongue darting out to wet her bottom lip. Damn it, I wanted it to be my tongue licking her there. Parting her lips until she was licking me back.

"I think it all the time, but I never feel sure … about you. I don't want you waiting around for me, if this isn't what you want. I can't date until after high school. Mum would disown me. And I can't sneak around behind her back either—I'm just not built that way."

I caved then, grabbing her and pulling her against me, touching my lips to the top of her head, pressing a hand into the small of her back to keep her there.

I wanted to do so much more. I wanted her lips, and her tongue. I wanted her breath in my mouth and her body against mine. I wanted to play out all the filthy fantasies I had about her on a nightly basis. But I wanted all the silly, lovesick daydreams too.

Her free hand slipped around my waist, clutching the back of my shirt, fingers digging into my skin, making me hiss as my pants were suddenly uncomfortably tight. Her nose rubbed against my collarbone.

"I have never once considered not waiting for you. I haven't even kissed another girl, Georgie. I don't want my first kiss to be with anyone but you."

I felt her suck in a breath against my chest. I felt the shift of her hips as she tucked herself in closer to me. Felt her little squeak when she realised I was hard.

Felt all the bloody things when she rubbed herself against me.

"Don't," I groaned. "Let's not start this until we can finish it."

With a tiny, hot sigh that steamed against my skin, she shifted back, just enough to put a little space between her hips and my aching dick.

"I'd wait, too. For you," she murmured, her lips tracing the words on my neck. I groaned low in my throat at how bloody incredible that felt as my mind whirred at all the other places her mouth would feel good on my body.

Then her mouth found the corner of mine, and I froze, closing my eyes because this moment felt like perfect bloody torture. Her lips brushed mine for a fraction of a second, and then she stepped back, a little gleam in her eyes, colour staining across her nose and cheekbones.

"Until we can have our first real kiss," she whispered, touching her own lips, rubbing those fingers back and forth across them, like she couldn't believe she'd just done that.

"When we have our first real kiss, Blondie," I said roughly, reaching out to tug at a stray curl on her cheek, "you'd better be ready for so much more."

"Oh, I'll be ready."

I cleared my throat. "Want to have that dance now?"

Georgie watched me carefully, her eyes darting between mine. "Actually, I kind of like it better out here. But you go back inside, have fun. Dance with Dom and give them all something to gossip about."

A laugh barked out of me at that. "I'm pretty sure I've already given them plenty of that tonight. Besides, I think the view out here is much better anyway." I tucked her hair behind her ear, letting my knuckles graze her cheek.

Georgie sighed but said nothing. So I leaned back against that pillar, and she leaned beside me. With my pinkie finger still entwined with hers, she stared out at the night, and I drank her in.

Now: It Happened, Blondie

GEORGIE

God, I was so warm. Too warm.

I cracked an eye, wincing at the light spilling in, reflecting off white sheets. Slowly my situation came into focus.

Of course I was warm. There was a man wrapped around me like a blanket. I blinked, trying to see said man properly, but he had me caged by his body, one arm draped over my waist, the other cradling my neck. One of his muscular legs was between mine, one of my legs hooked over his hip. The tangle of sheets was all that separated his crotch from mine.

And oh God, that bulge.

I groaned. Memories of some of the things I'd said about the bulge the night before trickled back into my consciousness.

"Bit dusty this morning, Blondie?" he asked, his voice rough from sleep. His stubble grazed the side of my face, and I shivered. Then groaned again as I registered the throbbing in my head, the parched feeling in my mouth.

"Dust storm might be more apt," I muttered. Xander chuckled, and I felt it everywhere our bodies touched. Which was a lot of places. "Is there water up here?"

I sighed with … relief? … disappointment? … as he extricated

275

his body from mine, rolling over and passing me a glass. I sat up with a wince, taking it from him with a grimace. He handed me two Panadol as well.

"Not sure this will be strong enough, but it's all I had," he explained. I downed the pills with a long slug from the glass.

"Don't I remember you saying you'd sleep on the couch?" I asked. Xander chuckled again.

"Yes, well, lots of things happened after that conversation," he explained, his hazel eyes twinkling.

"Like what?"

"Like, you needed to be carried up here. And then you told me you needed to pee, less than half a minute later, so I carried you back down to the bathroom. Which, by the way, you wouldn't let me leave while you were using the toilet."

"Oh my God," I groaned into my hand, nausea rising up into my chest that I didn't think had anything to do with my hangover.

"And then, when I carried you back up, you still wouldn't let me leave," Xander continued, leaning back against his pillow, his body turned towards me, one arm propping up his head, watching me with wary amusement. "You … said a lot of things last night."

I rubbed at my temples, the effort of trying to remember making my already throbbing head ready to explode. "Things like …?"

"Things like how you wanted to fall asleep with me inside you." His voice was suddenly deep. And it was then I registered that I wasn't wearing my dress, but one of his t-shirts.

"Oh God, we didn't …"

Xander's eyes darkened. "Do you really think I'd take advantage of you when you were that drunk?" he asked, slipping the sheet from his hips to show he was wearing a pair of boxer briefs. They did nothing to hide his morning erection from me.

"No," I muttered, blinking away from that mesmerising bulge. "So, I told you to stick your dick in me and fall asleep like that … then what?"

Xander sighed. "Then you stripped out of your dress and told me to get naked." He pinched the bridge of his nose. "And I put a t-shirt on you and made you drink two glasses of water. And then you asked me to hold you, just until you fell asleep … so I did. But I must've fallen asleep too."

"Well …" I began, staring down at the sheet, twisting it in my hands. "Thank you for being a gentleman about it."

Xander snorted, and I looked up at him. His eyes were burning holes through me. "Georgie, you have no bloody idea."

I swallowed, glancing away. His expression was too intense for me. "What's that supposed to mean?"

Xander sat up against the headboard, staring up at the ceiling, running his hand through his hair. "Sleeping with you in my arms … Georgie, that was … a fantasy come true. Even if you did snore like a lawn mower."

I glared at him as the pensive expression on his face morphed into a smirk. "See, this jokiness—this is why I never could work out if you meant the things you said to me, back then!" I grouched before I really thought about the words coming out of my mouth.

That gorgeous, cheeky smile slipped off his face as quickly as it had appeared. "I meant every single word. Except the ones in that text. Those words were the stupidest mistake of my life."

I turned to climb off the bed, my skin blazing, my heart hammering in a way that wasn't just from a hangover. "I shouldn't have … I don't want to have this conversation," I muttered, glancing around for my dress, finding it folded up neatly at the foot of the bed, and snagging it up. "Can we just … forget last night ever happened?"

"Not a chance in hell of that," he rasped. "All of it happened. Even the snoring. And it was bloody incredible … but … a couple of things would have made it better."

I shouldn't have asked. Should have just climbed down from the loft and left. Things between us were … changing. And I wasn't in a frame of mind to deal with it. But curiosity got the better of me.

"Like what?"

"Like you being sober when we danced and you said you wanted to hold onto me forever. And us falling asleep with my cock still inside you after I gave you half a dozen orgasms."

The way my knees gave way for a split second had everything to do with the hangover. Nothing at all to do with what he said.

"This never happened," I repeated, my voice shaking.

"It happened, Blondie."

———

My walk of shame across the lawn somehow felt so much more shameful knowing I hadn't been up all night getting the half-dozen orgasms he'd just put in my head. Everything was upside down in my fuzzy brain.

Had he really just cuddled me all night? Why did that make me feel queasy with nerves? Or was that just the far too many glasses of wine still sloshing around in my stomach.

Molly and Jumbo were cavorting on the grass, and when they spotted me, they came galloping over, almost knocking me down in their enthusiasm.

"Not now, kids," I mumbled, giving them both a brief scratch on the head. "I need a shower, a greasy bacon and egg roll and a litre of Powerade. And some bleach for my brain."

Mim's dry chuckle wafted from the shade on the verandah. "Did some regrettable things last night, Georgie girl?"

I squinted, the December sun blinding me as I tried to make her out in the shadows. "Some, but probably not the ones you're accusing me of."

"I was thinking about the off-key country music."

I grimaced. "Taylor Swift is so much more than just country music, thank you. But it got worse." I stepped up onto the verandah and collapsed into a chair beside Mim, who was sipping at her black tea and watching the pets.

"Looks like Jumbo's figured out how to escape Molly's amorous advances," I commented, watching Jumbo do a commando roll to break free of the Labrador's determined humping.

"No chance you're getting out of this chat lightly, my girl," Mim said sharply. "Now, before you go and take a shower, what has you looking like you might throw up … aside from the alcohol that is?"

My head throbbed. I rubbed at it. "I think I might have said some things … while drunk … that Xander might misconstrue."

Mim sipped her tea in silence for a moment. When she placed it down with a clink on the table between us, she spoke.

"I don't want, or need, details, Georgie. But I need you to hear this. He hurt you, back then. He made a stupid mistake, and I think he knows that. And maybe you should have told him the truth back then, and heard him out."

I opened my mouth, but Mim shook her head. "I'm not finished. But then maybe you needed the space of years. I don't know. You've never really let anyone in about how it affected you. But it's clear to anyone who sees the pair of you that whatever was between you is still unresolved. You need to resolve it, one way or another. No more denying your feelings—whatever they are. You've never really moved on from what happened back then. And I think you need to stop hiding from how you feel, and either forgive him, or forget him."

"It's not that simple," I argued weakly, staring across the lawn to where Xander strode towards his ridiculous Ute, climbing in and heading off down the dusty drive towards the road. Probably going to have breakfast at The Budgie with his brother and his best friend. And his gorgeous little niece.

I wondered if they were leaving again today or if they were staying a bit longer. I hoped they'd leave, because the thought of having to see Dom again, without the buffer of alcohol … there was a reason I'd drunk so much last night, and it had very little to do with Xander.

"Georgie, are you listening to me?" Mim demanded, and I blinked.

"Sorry, stuck in my head," I muttered.

Mim slapped her thigh. "This is exactly what I'm talking about! Something life-changing happened to you twelve years ago, and it's been stuck in your head ever since—and you've been stuck in there with it! The only way out is to talk to him about it. Does he even know the whole story?"

Nausea rolled up my throat. "I'm going to be sick," I gasped, leaping from the chair and racing into the dark house, down the hallway and into the bathroom just in time to vomit into the toilet.

After I was done, I wiped my face, panting, flushing the toilet and running the shower cold. Stepping under the spray, I rinsed my mouth and drank deeply, letting the cool water course over my skin.

Xander didn't know the whole story. No one, not even Mim, knew the whole story. And I intended to keep it that way.

But a tiny flame was sparking deep inside me. A flame that knew the drunken things I'd told Xander were more than just silly ramblings. They were my deepest wishes, breaking free from the place inside me that I'd hidden them.

Those wishes were not possible. Not with the awful truth that lurked in me, casting a shadow over any future either of us might be starting to fantasise about. If Xander knew the whole story … I didn't even want to think about it.

I could have stood under the cool water for hours, trying to douse that little flame. But water was precious, so I emerged from the shower after a few minutes, towelled my hair, brushed my furry teeth, and threw on my slouchiest pair of running shorts and an oversized tank top.

I lay on my bed, staring at the ceiling. The paint was yellowing and bubbled in places. The whole house needed a lot of TLC. Sadness stabbed at me under my ribcage. It would be some other family's labour of love to bring this place back to its former glory.

I groaned, rolling onto my side, knowing I'd have to make the ten-minute drive into Budgerigar to get myself some greasy breakfast and electrolytes, and dreading it.

"Georgie!" Mim called out. I sighed, dragging myself off the bed and heading down the hall. Immediately the smell of bacon accosted me.

"Are you making me breakfast? It smells del—" My words and my feet stopped dead in the doorway when I saw Xander standing in Mim's kitchen, a white paper bag in one hand and a two-litre bottle of red Powerade—my favourite—in the other.

"You have a delivery," Mim chuckled, pushing past me and

stomping off down the hallway. "I'd be leaving a handsome tip, if I were you."

I didn't move, just stood there gaping at him.

"I decided against the bleach. I like your brain the way it is," he said with a wink. He set the bag and the bottle down on the bench, leaning against it with a satisfied smirk on his face that instantly got my back up.

"What're you so pleased about?" I asked, crossing my arms over my chest.

He straightened, heading towards me with intent in his eyes. "Just wanted to look after my girl."

"Your girl?" I blurted, hoping I sounded indignant. He rested a hand against the door frame above me, looming over me with a wicked gleam in his eyes.

"Clearly you haven't remembered everything you said last night," he murmured, his other hand reaching for mine, hooking our pinkies together.

"I was very drunk," I protested, stomach fluttering. There was more?

With a grin, he leaned right in until his mouth was against my ear. "Just before you fell asleep, you told me that when I called you my girl, when your mouth was around my cock, it did things to you. You said all you ever wanted was to be my girl."

My eyes slid closed as his lips brushed over my earlobe, down my jaw, across my cheek until they touched the corner of my mouth. My body went boneless, melting against the door frame he had me pinned to.

"Will you be my girl, Georgie?" he breathed against my lips.

Fear flooded my veins.

"I ... I don't think ..." I stammered.

The silence was so long that I chanced a peek at Xander. His expression, a moment ago playful, had turned flat.

"Well ... will you be mine just until the show wraps? I want this —I want you—whatever little piece you'll give me."

I squeezed my eyes firmly shut. I knew if I so much as caught a glimpse of his eyes, I'd be blathering things like, *I'm not sure that two more months with you will be enough,' or, 'whatever we're doing is only going to fuck us both up so much more when it ends,' or, 'can I be your girl forever?'*

I managed a tiny shake of my head. "I can't … I can't give you an answer."

With a tiny sigh, he pressed a kiss to the corner of my mouth before pulling back, until the only part of us still joined was our pinkie fingers.

"Well, you know where to find me if that answer ever sneaks up on you," he murmured, and then he was stepping away, that last tenuous connection between us broken as he pulled his hand from mine. I opened my eyes to see him retreating across the kitchen.

"Enjoy your breakfast," he said as he opened the door, giving me one last lingering look before he strode back to his Ute.

Only my desperation for whatever delicious thing he'd collected from town stopped me from collapsing to the floor in a miserable heap. I tore into the bacon and egg roll with gusto, drinking the Powerade straight from the giant bottle as I lamented my position. The teenage charm he'd had in spades was now the masculine allure of a man. And he knew exactly how to press my buttons. Even after twelve years apart.

But I couldn't let that happen. It would be ruinous for both of us.

———

I spent the next couple of hours sitting on the verandah, Mim's little handheld fan pointed right at my face, sipping at the last of the Powerade. I couldn't even lie to myself that I wasn't waiting for Xander's truck to reappear.

Where had he gone? Back into town to Levi and Dom? Had he had an emergency call that he needed to attend to? That was the life of a rural vet—always on call, no matter what time or day it was.

"Take the truck, go find him," Mim grouched behind me, and I jumped, spinning to face her and wincing at the dull ache in my temples.

"How long have you been standing there?" I asked.

Mim rolled her eyes, hands on her hips. "Long enough to know you keep looking to the end of the driveway and sighing. He'll be in town, no doubt. Take the truck and go find him. All this dancing around one another, it's starting to drive me crazy."

"Heaven forbid *you* feel crazy about it," I said.

Mim chuckled. "I can only imagine what's going through your head right now, Georgie girl. But the only way you're going to resolve all of this is by talking to *him* about it. Not sitting here moping and trying to pretend there isn't anything wrong with you."

I flinched. "There *isn't* anything wrong with me!"

Mim just raised a steel-coloured eyebrow at me and stared me down until I stood with a huff.

"Alright," I sighed. "I'll take the truck."

Now: Holding A Stone Penis

GEORGIE

For a sleepy little town, Main Street was bustling. The church service had probably just finished. I pulled Mim's ten-year-old extra-cab Ute into a parking spot outside Emporium of Intuition—the boutique store that sold candles and tarot cards and crystals and all of that new-age nonsense.

I was shocked that a place like it could survive in a township of a couple of thousand people. Then again, I was totally not their target market, and they had been trading for at least the last twelve years, so they must've found a customer base.

As I climbed out of the Ute, a woman's voice called my name. I looked up, thankful that I was wearing a pair of oversized sunglasses hiding the hangover bags under my eyes, to see Amanda opening the door of the shop and beckoning me inside. She was wearing the little bub in a carrier on her chest, looking every inch the doting mother … or stepmother, I remembered.

"Come in here and bask in the air-conditioning!" she said, holding the door open for me. I hesitated for only a second before I traipsed up the stairs, hoping that she was alone and that Levi and Dom were somewhere else, occupied with Xander.

The overwhelming scent of sandalwood incense assaulted me as soon as I crossed the doorway, and it took my eyes a second to adjust to the dimness after the blinding sun outside. I blinked, Amanda's face coming into focus.

"It's easier to see in here without sunglasses on, I think," she said with a little smile. I pushed them up onto my head, managing a sheepish grin.

"They're probably more to protect others from me today, than the other way around," I explained.

Amanda assessed me, looking confused. "You look gorgeous … maybe a little tired, though." Her smile widened. "Did you keep Xander up all night? He looked pretty wiped out this morning, too."

"Where is he?" I asked, pressing my lips together when I realised how sharp my tone was.

Amanda shrugged. "I left them outside a while ago. Lily got grizzly in the heat, so I came looking for somewhere cool, and here I am!"

She turned and picked something up off the shelf. "What on earth is this?" she whispered, holding it up for me to see. I choked on a giggle, staring with wide eyes down at the overtly phallic rose-quartz … thing she was holding.

"I think it's a …" I began, but the giggles stopped me from finishing.

"It's a dildo, isn't it?" Amanda gasped, shaking with mirth. "I'm holding a stone penis, aren't I?" Lily burbled in the carrier as if she was sharing in our joke.

"It's called a Yoni Wand," a deep, rich voice said behind us, and we froze. Amanda's face flushed crimson as we slowly turned towards the owner of the voice.

I'd gotten to know many of the locals over the last twelve years of summer breaks I'd taken out here, but this guy was a complete stranger to me. His hair, light brown and greying at the temples, was swept up into a messy topknot. His eyes were dark grey and piercing as he looked both of us over.

Amanda, still holding the wand thing, gaped at him. I pressed my lips together to try and hold in the hysterical giggle threatening to bubble out as the man plucked it from her hand.

"A Yoni Wand is much more than a dildo," he said, as if this was something he explained to female customers all the time. "They're designed not just for pleasure, but to infuse a woman with serenity upon climax."

He turned it over in his hands, stroking the stone as both Amanda and I stood in frozen mortification. "Rose-quartz Yoni Wands are particularly powerful at calming and cleansing your aura, bringing you feelings of love, peace and trust. Thus, they are of particular value when used with a partner."

He eyed us both up and down. "In addition, this curve is ergonomically designed to help women achieve squirt."

"Uh, what?" I blurted before snapping my teeth shut. Amanda stared at me with wide, horrified eyes as the man gestured to the curved shape of the stone.

"When inserted correctly, this design stimulates the female G-spot, and is designed to enhance wetness and help women to ejaculate."

"Oh my God," Amanda muttered under her breath. I pressed two fingers to my lips, trying not to scream in embarrassment.

The man ignored her, turning directly to me, his eyes boring holes through me. "Your sacral chakra is blocked."

"My sacral chakra?" I repeated, mystified. Amanda hyperventilated behind her hand.

"You have issues with sexual pleasure. With the ability to form and maintain intimate relationships. With your fertility and your child-bearing organs."

My mouth dropped open, all the blood draining from my face. Amanda's fingers wrapped around my arm.

"Come on, Georgie, you don't need to listen to this woo."

I shook her off, not taking my eyes off the man. "I … I recently had a cervical cancer removed," I whispered.

Amanda sucked in a breath. The man nodded sagely, as if it made total sense.

"You would benefit from some yoga poses, to help you unblock. I have a set of cards for this specific chakra. I also have a sacral chakra crystal pack; I think that would be worth looking into for you. And affirmations. The sacral chakra is closely related to your mood and your sense of self-worth, so working on these things can have a positive impact."

Amanda stared at me with wide eyes as I soundlessly followed the man back to the counter, numbly holding out my credit card for him as he rang up a bunch of stuff that I had no idea about.

As he handed me a paper bag with my items, he leaned closer. "You might benefit from one of the Yoni Wands, you know," he whispered. "Finding ways to bring yourself pleasure would be beneficial for you."

I swallowed, my face flaming. "I think I'll just give these things a try, first," I mumbled, throwing what I hoped was a grateful smile in his direction and walking on shaky legs for the door.

"Does Xander know?" Amanda asked as we stepped out into the blinding summer sunlight.

I turned to her, thankful I could put my glasses back on to hide what I was sure was my haunted expression. The sun hit the baby's face and she squirmed, grizzling until Amanda shaded her eyes with a hand.

"It's not something he needs to know," I said, my voice trembling. Amanda pursed her lips as if she wanted to say more, but I grabbed her arm before she could speak.

"Please, don't tell him. Or Levi for that matter. I …"

Amanda smiled softly, her hand coming over mine and giving me a reassuring squeeze. "I wouldn't dream of sharing something so personal with either of them. But Georgie, if you ever need someone to talk to about this … I mean, cervical cancer is something that can impact a woman in so many ways, and …"

She chewed on her bottom lip, looking away before taking a breath and turning back to me. "Well, I don't know you very well, but you seem like the kind of woman who maybe doesn't have many people she can trust with the big, important stuff in her life."

"Wow," I mumbled, flashing a wobbly smile at her. "It seems like everyone I talk to today has x-ray vision into the inner workings of my brain!"

Amanda gave a gentle laugh, and I sighed.

"Thanks. For the offer. I might never take you up on it, but it's nice to know it's there anyway."

She smiled at me again. "It's an open-ended offer. Also … you know that crystals and yoga poses aren't a cure for cancer, right?"

I laugh-coughed into my hand. "Oh, I know. I was just blind-sided by how he guessed I had reproductive issues. And also, I really just wanted to get out of there before he started giving us a grand tour of his entire stone dick collection. I figured buying something else from him was a good escape."

Amanda snickered into her hand. "That's good to know. That you're not sucked into that new-age bull crap … and that you were prepared to take the fall so we didn't end up becoming unwilling experts in crystal penises."

"I already know far more than I ever wanted to know about them," I added emphatically as Amanda turned to walk along the street towards the school and the sports field. Cheering echoed up ahead.

"What's going on?" I asked. "It's out of season for weekend sports."

Amanda laughed. She laughed a lot, and it was such a happy sound that some of the lingering cold from the reminder of my cancer melted away.

"It sounds like they've gotten a bit of an audience since the church service finished. There were some young boys kicking a soccer ball around on the field beside the school earlier, and Xander's eyes lit up like a kid at Christmas."

A chuckle burst out of me. "He hasn't changed much since high school," I replied. Amanda gave me a long look out of the corner of her eye.

"Hasn't he?" she asked quietly as we reached the fence where a bunch of parents were leaning, in their church clothes, fanning their faces in the scorching heat.

I shrugged. "In some ways, he's very different. In others … I think most men don't fully outgrow their teenage selves."

"It must be strange, seeing both of them again after so many years," Amanda remarked. I pretended I was too focused on weaving my way through the crowd to answer. But when we reached the fence and I looked up at the scene before me, I found words pushing their way up from my chest.

"It's very strange," I admitted, watching Xander. Eyes fixed on the ball, he dribbled as well as he had when he played high school soccer—better, even—towards the goal at one end before grinning at one of the boys, pointing to him as he passed the ball to him to score.

"His smile is still the same—the dimples," I mumbled as cheers erupted around us. Xander beamed at the boy, high-fiving him before heading back down the field to get into position. I scanned the field, finding Dom defending goal, looking overheated and bored.

I chuckled. "Dom looks like he hates sport just as much as he used to."

Someone called, "Time!" The players converged on one another, laughing and clapping each other on the back. Xander was accosted by a bunch of twelve-year-old boys, all talking at him at once. He listened for a minute, the smile on his face turning from jubilant to strained. He said a few words, patting one of the boys on the shoulder, and then he glanced up.

Our eyes met.

And his grin morphed again into something … possessive, and delighted, all at once.

"My God, I need to fan myself just from witnessing the heat of that eye contact!" Amanda said beside me. But I couldn't take my eyes off Xander as he wiped sweat from his face with his forearm, accepting a bottle of water from one of the church mums, and guzzling half of it, dousing himself in the rest.

The white t-shirt he was wearing went transparent, clinging to pecs and abs that I wanted to touch, and kiss, and lick, with a force that almost overwhelmed me.

"That's not the body of a teenager," Amanda murmured beside me.

"Uhnffh," was all I could manage as Xander turned and began to make his way towards me, eyes still intent on mine.

"Hey, Blondie," he panted, coming to a stop on the other side of the fence. His hand came down to cover mine. I trembled, but I didn't stop him. His grin widened, his thumb drawing circles on my wrist. I felt that like a livewire straight between my legs.

Yoni Wand be damned. I just needed Xander's wand.

"Georgie."

I startled, turning to see Dom standing beside Xander. He'd stripped out of his sweaty t-shirt, standing there in nothing but a pair of grey gym shorts and joggers. I was shocked by how muscular his body was. He'd never been skinny, but he'd always leaned towards slender, whereas Xander had been broad.

Not anymore.

"Have you discovered a love of steroids in the last decade?" I blurted. Xander's fingers tensed on mine, punctuated by a shocked giggle from Amanda.

Levi sauntered up between his brother and Dom, slinging a tattooed arm around them both.

"Dom got ripped, hey Georgie!" he said. "He keeps telling me that the arts are better than sport, but he's been a solid gym junkie for years now."

Dom rolled his eyes, and just like that, the tension in the air dissipated. Levi had always been good at that.

"Keeping fit and healthy is not the same as getting paid to run around a football field … or row around a river," Dom argued, raising a black eyebrow at Levi, who guffawed. Clearly this was a conversation they'd hashed out many times before.

"I get paid sweet fuck all to row around a river," Levi said, stretching and revealing a prominent Adonis belt. A titter arose from the church mums still loitering around. "It's the looking pensive in front of a fucking camera while wearing some shit that I would never buy myself that pays the bills. And that, I believe, would come under the umbrella of the fucking arts."

"Modelling is not art, Levi," Dom retorted, his voice dry.

"It's fucking art when I do it," Levi chuckled, winking at Dom as if he knew he was taking the piss.

I realised that I missed Dom's friendship, just as he turned to me and said, "Can we talk for a few minutes?"

"Uh, yeah, okay," I stammered. Xander's hand pumped mine, and I glanced up at him.

"You okay?" he mouthed. I gave a tiny nod, pulling my hand from under his and following Dom.

When we were far enough to be out of earshot of the others, Dom turned to me, his dark eyes flickering over me before returning to my face.

"I know things can't be the way they were … before," he began, and suddenly he was looking everywhere but at me. "But I … damn it, I've missed you so much, Georgie. When Xander said you were working together, I … I felt miserable, knowing that he would get to reconcile with you, and I couldn't."

I swallowed once, looking down at the brown grass of the field. "That's not what this is about. It's just work. Last night was … anomalous."

Dom sighed. "I know you and he are … that there is something being rekindled between you. Even if he hadn't told me last night, it's as clear as day to me." He scratched at his neck, and then his gaze fixed back on my face. "You two were never going to be able to stay away from each other."

I shook my head, not wanting to hear this. Not from him. "Dom, I hated him for twelve years. I held onto that hatred like a lifeline. It's not something I can just dismantle at the drop of a hat."

Dom laughed humourlessly. "And yet you are. You let him take care of you last night. You said things to him on that deck last night that I know, deep down, are real. I saw you just then, holding his hand, him checking in with you that you are okay to be alone with me. You never hated him, Georgie. You were hurt by him, but you loved him. I think, deep down, you still do."

'Thank God for the sunglasses' was officially my mantra for the day. I blinked furiously behind them, willing the burning sensation away, willing the tears to stay in.

"I'm terrified, though," he continued, his voice thick. "I'm so scared that you really do hate *me*. I … Georgie, that morning, when I realised you were gone, and my messages weren't delivering, and I had no idea what had happened to you, I was terrified! I told Mum … everything. And she just looked at me and said, 'She's fine, but you need to leave her alone, she doesn't want to talk to you or Xander' … and I was so relieved to know you were okay, but I felt sick too, knowing you'd rather leave a message with my mother than talk to *me*."

"I … oh God, Dom, I never hated you! I could never hate you. I just … I couldn't …" Even now I couldn't find the words to explain how that night had changed me. "I just want to put the past behind me."

Dom cleared his throat, scrubbing at his eyes with the heels of his hands. "I get that. I want the same. But … does putting the past behind you mean putting me behind you too? Forever? Or am I going to get another chance the way Xander does?"

I shook my head. "This is too much right now. I … I can't give you a definite answer, my head is … but … it's not a no. Can that be enough for now?"

Dom watched me for what felt like an eternity, then gave a small nod, and some of the tension I'd been carrying fell away from me.

"Just know that I'm here, waiting. I just want my friend back," Dom murmured, and I pressed a hand over my mouth to stifle the sob that wanted to burst out.

"Okay," I managed. Dom reached out and squeezed my arm, as if he knew I couldn't cope with anything more than that at this point.

"And if you and Xander … if things get serious between you— no, don't shake your head, I know you, Georgie. Even after twelve years apart, I know you."

I clenched my jaw against the protests that clamoured. Dom was right.

"If they do, are you going to tell him about what happened that night?" he asked. I was shaking my head before he finished asking.

"No … no," I muttered, watching as Dom's eyes fell shut. He knew how much that night had broken me, broken us. And he didn't even know all of it.

"I'm not sure if you're making the right choice, but I'm … I hope that it works out."

I managed a watery snort. "I don't know if there will be anything *to* work out."

"He never got over you, Georgie," Dom said, giving my arm another squeeze. "He spent twelve years trying to forget, and all he managed was to make himself feel worse. Don't … just be careful with him, okay? He fucked up. But he knows it. And he'll never hurt you again."

With those shocking words, Dom leaned in and planted a tiny kiss on my cheek before letting me go and walking away, leaving me feeling like breathing was never going to work right for me again.

"That didn't seem like you're okay, Blondie," Xander said behind me. I gasped, pulling air into lungs that a second ago had felt frozen.

"What am I missing here? Why are things between us … the way they are, and things with you and Dom are awkward as hell?" Xander mused. Anxiety bloomed in my chest, and with it, anger.

"Do you want me to go and work through my feelings about Dom by sucking his dick, too?" I hissed. Xander chuckled, but as I glared up at him, his eyes were wary.

"What feelings are we talking about here?" he asked, his voice low. Fear trickled into my stomach. This conversation was getting too close to that night.

"For the record, Dr Fox, I owe you no explanations about … about anything!" I snarled.

Xander's lips twisted. "Oh, we're back to Dr Fox, are we, Gina?" he muttered. I turned until we were face to face, fury boiling in my veins, thankfully burning away the worry as the conversation steered into a much safer argument.

"Don't call me Gina, you know I hate it!"

"I know, that's why I said it," he explained with a smirk that didn't meet those cautious eyes.

"Urgh!" I growled. "Just stop talking." I smacked a hand against his chest. He caught it, holding my palm to his sternum. His heart pounded against it.

Xander's other hand snaked up around my back, his fingers stroking up and down my spine so gently, in complete contrast to the argument we were having.

"I can think of other, more productive things I could be doing with my mouth right now," he murmured against my hair. When had he pulled me against him? And why hadn't I fought him off? And why was I softening into him as he pressed a light kiss to my forehead?

"Oh, really," I breathed against his collarbone, letting my lips rest there. Under my palm, now trapped between our bodies, his heartbeat thundered. "And are these things appropriate PDA material?"

"Some of them are," he growled against my temple. "But I'm not sure how you feel about PDA with me," he broke away, moving to put space between our bodies. He flashed me a sad smile as he strode over to where his brother was watching us with a sly grin on his face.

It was wrong how much I hated him putting that distance between us. I should have been relieved that he had the self-control not to maul me in public when that would be disastrous for both of us. He had a television persona to maintain, one that was supposed to be dating the gorgeous Dr Kingston. No filming today meant nothing in a town like Budgerigar. We didn't need the town thinking he was a player, wooing two women at once.

And my disaster? I'd told Dom I couldn't just dismantle my hatred of Xander that easily. But that ten-foot wall I'd been protecting myself with was already just a pile of rubble at my feet.

Xander plucked baby Lily out of Levi's arms, peppering kisses on her little downy head, cradling her gently as he smiled sweetly down at her. She stared up at him with wide, blue eyes, and his sad expression melted away. His face lit up when that little baby reached up and gripped his pinkie finger, and I knew.

I knew this would never last between Xander and me, even without the mistakes of our past.

It would never last because he'd make such a good father—one glance at his interaction with his niece told me that. I recalled his words that had given me a brief pang, on our trip out here. *"I want kids. I'd love a whole soccer team of them."* That pang was a throb now. A giant, gaping, aching throb in my chest.

Parenthood was something that me and my defective reproductive system may well never be able to offer him. It wouldn't be fair, to be greedy and want more, to take that choice away from him.

We had so much history, that had ended abruptly when he'd hurt me all those years ago. But I'd taken that hurt and had turned it into one of the biggest mistakes of my life.

I couldn't give him the future he wanted. I couldn't get over our past, and if he knew the truth, I was sure he couldn't either. Anything between us was doomed.

It didn't stop that silly part of me wanting the impossible with him.

Now: Something Fragile

XANDER

"You got home safe?" I asked, cradling my phone with my shoulder as I collapsed onto a chair on my porch and took a long swig of my beer.

"Yeah, home safe," Levi replied. "Lily was a fucking champ for such a long drive. Gives me confidence that she'll cope on the plane to Paris next year."

I almost spat beer out on the deck. Molly watched me, tongue lolling as I coughed and spluttered, "You're taking Lily to Paris?"

"Yeah. Emilee and Mateo are heading to Spain, to visit his family. They arrive towards the end of the Olympics, so Amanda and I are taking Lil over with us, and after, we'll travel to Spain, and she can spend another two weeks there with her mum and stepdad. Works fucking great for me, I get both my girls there with me when I win gold."

I rubbed my knuckles vigorously against my sternum, hating the pang of jealousy there that Levi seemed to have everything he'd ever wanted. A woman he worshipped, a baby they both doted on, making enough money with his modelling to tell Dad where to stick it, and his Olympic Gold dream so close he could smell it.

And here I was, pining over a woman I'd broken over a decade ago … and who was halfway to breaking me this time around.

"I can't do this …" I muttered.

"Do what?" Levi asked.

I pinched the bridge of my nose. "I thought working with her was going to be hard. But it's worse. I want her, Lev. I want her so bloody badly."

Levi chuckled. "And you've only just figured this out? The pair of you are fucking dickheads."

"Not helpful," I grumbled. "And it's not like I didn't know all along that I'd want her. I just thought I'd have enough anger over … everything … that it'd cancel everything else out."

I took another long gulp of beer. "But even that's not the real issue. It's that she's giving me bloody signals. And not just the hot sex, or the best bloody blowjob of my life. It feels like she wants this to be more. But I can't work it out for sure. I've never been able to work her out."

"Do you want it to be more? Maybe that's the better fucking question here," Levi said.

"Shit." I put my beer and my phone down and lifted Molly up off the porch and onto my lap. She was far too big for it these days, but I just needed her warm, doggy affection. She licked my face once, curling her body up to almost fit on my thighs.

"I want everything," I confessed. "But I have no idea how to get that from her."

Levi sighed. "You want my advice?"

"Well, you managed to get Amanda to put up with your sorry arse, I kind of feel like you might have some useful insight here."

"Okay. This is what you have to do. Don't. Be. A. Dickhead."

I rolled my eyes. "Well, that was in no way useful. Thanks!"

Levi snorted. "It's very fucking useful. She can't say what she means unless she's falling down drunk, and you … well I don't even know what your fucking problem is, but you need to get over it."

"My problem is that every time I even mention the idea of more with her, she turns cold and avoids me for days afterwards. I even straight up asked her if she'd be my girl, just yesterday morning when I took her breakfast, and her face, Lev. Jesus, I backtracked so fast, offered her a get-out clause when filming wraps, and she still wasn't giving me anything."

Levi scoffed. "You asked her to be your girl? What the fuck? Are you trying to love her or buy her for fuck's sake?"

I winced. "Saying it like that seemed less intimidating than using the L word."

"Try making yourself a bit fucking vulnerable, Xan. She's not going to take you seriously otherwise. Put it all out there!"

I shook my head. "If I put my heart on the line, tell her I'm in this one-hundred-percent, that I want a real future, I'm terrified that I'll lose her altogether. I don't know if she's ever going to get past what I did. I can't put myself out there like that, not unless I can talk to her about what happened back then, be sure that she's really able to move past it together."

"And she doesn't want to talk about it?"

"Nope," I grunted, reaching for my beer.

"Right. So, you have two choices, Xan. Option one, you grow a fucking pair, tell her you're all in—no backing down—and cop it on the chin if she's not interested. Option two, you keep doing the dick-head thing you're doing now, and when you finish making this show, you lose her. Only one option gives you the chance of getting what you want with her."

"High risk, high reward," I muttered, draining my beer. "Well, this has been enlightening. No bloody idea what I'm going to do with this information, but … yeah."

"Just don't be a dickhead. Simple. Now, I've got to go, Amanda is waiting in the bedroom with her vibrator, and I have a very big night planned for them both."

I winced. "Jesus Christ, I did not need to know that."

Levi guffawed. "These are the things you have to look forward to, if you finally get yourself a proper girlfriend. Oh, and speaking of—"

"Speaking of what? Girlfriends, or sex toys?" I interrupted.

"Funnily enough, sex toys. Amanda said she and Georgie had a crazy encounter in the crystal shop in town yesterday. Apparently, they learned a lot about something called a Yoni Wand, a kind of crystal dildo … and how it helps women squirt."

"Why are you telling me this?" I asked, pinching the bridge of my nose because all of a sudden, all I could think about was making Georgie squirt.

"Because you're going to go pick one of them up and post it to me. I'd go online, but I figured you should be supporting small businesses out there."

"Sure, why not?" I muttered, sarcasm lacing my tone. "I love going sex toy shopping for my brother in a small town where everyone knows everyone else's business."

"Of course you do. You have nothing else important going on in your life—you know, no love of your life suddenly reappearing and making you come in her mouth but not wanting to talk about the fact that you two are fucking obsessed with one another."

"Bye, Levi," I grouched, hanging up the phone before he could say anything else.

The next week started with a bang. People who had been putting off routine visits for vaccinations and health checks because driving to Millstone was a big ask suddenly wanted to make appointments.

Calli and I were inundated with patients. Between a hectic schedule and the complications of filming—needing to have release forms signed before we could film, trying to do my job around cameras and clients who were either too nervous around the cameras or too giggly around the cameras—I was tired.

To top it all off, Georgie was avoiding me again. It was so bloody obvious. Jordyn had been given all the producing work for the week, and while Georgie was present at the clinic, she was reviewing footage, or answering emails, cloistered away in the back office.

Between appointments, I peeked my head into the office and found her entering existing patients into the new software I'd had installed. I was trying to get all the paper files left behind by Liz's husband updated to the twenty-first century. It was the least I could do, given I'd be leaving this town in the lurch come March.

Guilt swam in my stomach at the thought. While the town knew the show had an expiry date, it seemed no one was acknowledging it. To them, I was their new vet and would be for the foreseeable future.

Those kids on the soccer field … even thinking about the hope shining in their eyes when they asked if I'd coach their soccer team next season, made me want to bash my head against a wall. I hadn't had the heart to tell them I'd be long gone back to Sydney before registration even kicked off properly.

I forced myself not to think about how shitty it was that we were doing all this work here just to abandon the town again so soon. Instead, I focused on Georgie, and my heart lurched painfully for a whole new reason. I watched the way her tongue just slightly poked out of the corner of her mouth while she typed. Her sexy librarian glasses slipped down her nose, and she pushed them back up with one knuckle, not taking her eyes from the paperwork.

I backed away before I did something stupid, like charged in, locked the door behind me, ripped off the bloody microphone and worshipped her from head to toe the way I was truly dying to, while confessing how I wanted to be able to do things to her body for the rest of my life.

I went straight to the kitchen, grabbed a bottle of water from the fridge and chugged the entire thing down, trying to cool the needy fire raging inside me. She was avoiding me for a reason. What that reason was—embarrassment over things she'd said to me while drunk, or me coming on too strong … or something to do with Dom and their uncomfortable interactions … I had no bloody idea. But I needed to calm the hell down and stop fantasising about things she clearly had no interest in.

"So, Alex tomorrow night," Jordyn said from the doorway. I almost choked on the last mouthful of water, spraying it onto the floor.

"Why creep up on me like that?" I demanded, grabbing a tea

towel out of the drawer and dropping it, using my foot to mop up the spill. Jordyn watched me, lips pursed.

"Alex is here again for the livestock patient visits tomorrow. I figured it'd be as good a time as any to do the sleepover footage. You know, since the showrunner got drunk last time and ruined an otherwise perfect set-up."

I narrowed my eyes. "I'm sure I didn't just hear you badmouth Georgie, did I?" I leaned against the fridge and stared Jordyn down. "Because that would be highly unprofessional."

Jordyn raised an eyebrow at me. "She got wasted on a work night! Tell me that's the height of professionalism, I dare you."

Anger rolled up in my chest, and before I knew it, I was across the kitchen, staring Jordyn down. "She was off the clock! She was with people she hadn't spent time with in over a decade, people she has conflicting feelings about. She had every right to drink as much as she liked!"

Jordyn glared right back up at me. "She knew we had a late scene to film, and because she was incapacitated, we put Alex out!"

A disbelieving laugh jumped up my throat. "That's bloody rich, Jordyn! I wasn't born yesterday. You and I both know that Alex was in no way put out by hanging around that night. I saw her car still parked outside your caravan when I drove into town Sunday morning."

Jordyn's face flushed crimson. "She'd had a few drinks—she wasn't safe to drive."

I smirked. "Look, what you do with Alex when you're off the clock is your business, and no one else's. Maybe you should extend Georgie that same courtesy." I smacked a hand against the door frame as I pushed past them. "I'm sure Alex doesn't mind having a do-over tomorrow, if it means spending the night with you again."

I didn't bother to wait for Jordyn's response. I headed straight back to the front of house, where Jase was waiting with my next patient.

Georgie didn't come to supervise the filming of the 'sleepover'. I knew she was home, though. I'd figured out that her bedroom window faced my tiny home, and I could see the light on in there and a person-shaped shadow moving around. I wondered if she'd just gotten out of the shower and then cursed myself for thinking things with the potential for getting me semi-hard when I was about to fake-kiss another woman.

"Right, so Jase will be set up over there," Jord explained, gesturing into the distance. "With the porch light and the kitchen light on, we'll be able to see enough from that distance without the two of you having to get too …"

"We get it," I snapped. Alex flinched, looking up at me with trepidation. I sighed. "Sorry, I'm just … you know I've never been a fan of this."

Alex managed a wan smile. "Yeah, I get it. This is a bad deal for you now, seeing as you and Georgie are official."

I gaped at her. "I'm sorry, what?"

Alex's brow furrowed. "I heard that you two had a very intimate moment at the soccer field last Sunday. Cuddles and kisses all 'round."

I shook my head. "It wasn't what it looked like," I managed, hating the sticky feeling in the back of my throat at the lie. To me, it was exactly that. To Georgie, on the other hand … "I was just offering reassurance to an old friend."

"Right," Alex said, completely unconvinced.

"Can we just get this scene filmed so I can go to bed?" I grated. Alex saluted me cheekily and headed off with Jord to where her car was parked further along the driveway, so Jase could 'catch' her driving in and parking beside my car. Their heads were bent together, and they were whispering furiously.

I couldn't even care anymore. I just wanted to get this over, and I hoped to hell that the higher-ups were satisfied with one steamy scene for this bloody show.

I pottered around at the kitchen sink just like I'd been instructed while waiting for the knock. When it came, I dried off my hands, took the three steps to the door, and pulled it open. Alex looked up at me, all big brown eyes, glowing brown skin, and glossy brown hair.

Objectively she was beautiful.

She just wasn't Georgina Menzies.

"Let's make this good," I murmured, grabbing her hand and dragging her against me, burying my nose in her hair. She smelled like flowers, not mint. I wasn't a fan.

She was stiff for just a second, then softened against me, her arms wrapping around my waist.

"Thank God they said no mics for this' I muttered against her hair, backing us inside and slamming the door. Alex huffed out a sound of agreement as I lifted her until she was sitting on the kitchen bench, her back to the window. Just like we'd discussed.

"So, you and Jordyn, huh?" I said against her ear, my hands splayed on her back. From Jase's vantage, it would look like I was nibbling her earlobe.

Alex flinched. "What about me and Jordyn?"

I chuckled, taking her cheeks in my hands and tilting her head so it would look like I was going in for a deep kiss. "Don't play coy. It was clear as day to me the first time we met. You were all nervous and shy around them. You've never been like that with me."

Alex let out a breathy laugh. Her eyelashes brushed my cheek as she closed her eyes. "I've never been very brave around people I find attractive."

I chuckled, running my fingers through her hair, tangling in it. "Pleased to know I'm ugly to you."

"You're … objectively handsome, Xander," she said, which only made me laugh harder. "You're just not my type."

"Clearly. I don't have electric blue hair and a snarky attitude."

Alex let her head fall against my chest, shaking with laughter. I stroked up and down her back.

"It's funny. I was just thinking earlier that you're objectively beautiful, but not my type either."

Alex lifted her head, eyeing me with understanding. "Because I'm not a bossy blonde Amazon?"

I shrugged, tilting her chin and leaning close, pretending to take her mouth again. "Got me in one."

"So, why'd you say you're just friends?" she asked against my jaw.

I sighed. "It's really bloody complicated."

"Because you screwed up back in high school, and she won't forgive you?"

I flinched. "Jordyn's been dealing in secrets during pillow talk, huh?"

Alex shrugged. "Or maybe Georgie told Amanda and me her side of the story last weekend."

Possible. But even if Georgie had spilled to them, didn't mean I had to. There was only one person I wanted to dredge up the past with, and that person had no interest.

The walkie-talkie that Jordyn had left with me crackled to life. "Okay, that's more than enough canoodling. Lift Alex down off the bench and head towards the loft."

With simultaneous sighs of relief, I helped Alex to her feet, wrapping an arm around her and moving away from the window and Jase's line of sight.

"This feels so bloody disingenuous," I grumbled, standing at the foot of the loft ladder and rubbing at my stubble. "I thought this show was going to be hell for me because of Georgie, but the lying is even worse. And not just this farce, either. Half the bloody town is delighted they've finally got a vet back. What the hell is going to happen to them come March when we wrap, and I disappear?"

Alex sighed, collecting her long hair in her hands and rapidly plaiting it with deft fingers. "I guess at least now I have a very fancy clinic to work out of once a fortnight when I help out here."

I shook my head. "It's not good enough."

Alex glanced at me, then away. "Georgie told Jordyn that she's asked the higher-ups if there is a chance of multiple seasons, bringing a new vet out for a three-month stint each time."

I froze. "So … she's planning on staying out here indefinitely?"

Alex shrugged. "No idea. Jord said that Georgie doesn't think the boss will okay it until he sees how season one is received."

Dread licked at my veins. I tried to tell myself it wouldn't matter, that regardless of whether Georgie and I both returned to Sydney at the end of this, we weren't together. But the irrational, lovesick part of my brain refused to believe it.

The walkie-talkie static broke me out of my shock. "Got it! That was very … convincing, guys." Jordyn's voice was strained, and I grinned tightly down at Alex.

"You'd better go and reassure Jord that blue hair and penis-free is still your thing," I said. Alex's lips twitched as she headed for the door.

"Why don't *you* go talk to Georgie tonight?" she suggested as she turned the handle. "Why don't you just tell her you're in this for real, and see what happens? Honestly, after the things she said to us on Sunday night, I'd be shocked if she wasn't feeling the same way."

I rubbed at my temples. "It's …"

"Complicated, I know," Alex said. "I'll see you in the morning for part two of the sham sleepover." Smiling, she waltzed out the door.

I blew out a long breath, heading straight for the fridge and a beer. I found myself gravitating to the porch, where I had a good view of Georgie's bedroom across the lawn. Molly followed me out, heading straight for the grass to sniff around.

Sipping my beer, I pondered the warm light spilling from that window. Was Georgie in there? She usually came out to the hammock at night, where there was a chance of a slightly cool breeze, to work on her laptop. But there was no sign of her tonight.

I wondered how much of that had to do with the thought of me kissing Alex. When I'd been trying to prod her with jealousy, it had felt invigorating. But now … there was something unspoken between us, something fragile, and I was terrified that I'd just royally screwed it up.

"Take a drive down to the river with me?"

I almost leapt out of my chair at the sound of her voice.

"Holy … how the hell did you sneak up on me, Blondie?" I asked, rubbing at my frantically beating heart. Georgie's lips tilted upwards. She stood on the grass, holding a small Esky, with a picnic blanket draped over the other arm. She was wearing a pair of battered old brown leather boots with the blue sundress she'd had on the day of the grand opening.

"I came from the shed. I went into town, I … I needed some space." Her eyes fell to the ground, and she scuffed one boot into the dirt. I didn't need three guesses to know that my worries about the faux sleepover weren't far off the mark.

I stood, abandoning my beer and hopping down from the porch until I was right in front of her, taking the blanket from her and reaching out to hook her pinkie with mine.

"A drive sounds perfect."

Then: Our First Real Kiss

GEORGIE, 17 YEARS OLD

I raced into my bedroom, slamming the door, hands shaking, fingers fumbling as I typed.

> Georgie: Where are you?

> Hot Xander: Home feeling bored and lonely. Why? You bored and lonely too?

> Georgie: Pick me up and take a drive with me?

> Hot Xander: Driving? or … 'DRIVING' ;)

> Georgie: lol but seriously I need to get out of here NOW

> Hot Xander: You ok Blondie?

> Georgie: No

> Hot Xander: What's wrong?

> Georgie: Tell you on the drive. Please hurry

Hot Xander: Leaving now. I'll be there in 30.
Want me to call you from the car?

Georgie: It's not that dire! Just hurry, ok? But
not law-breaking levels of hurrying

"Where are you going?" Mum asked as I brushed past her to get my sunglasses. I didn't want to talk to her, not after what I'd just seen.

"Out." I picked my sunglasses up and popped them on my head, taking Molly over to her bowl and scooping her dinner into it.

"With who? Dom's in France," Mum asked, eyes narrowing.

"With another friend," I replied, just as a horn sounded out the front. "He's here now."

"He?" Mum started around the bench, striding towards the hallway and the front door, but I stepped in her way, blocking her path.

"Yes, he," I replied, turning and heading for the door. Her footsteps hurried after me.

"You're not allowed to—"

I rounded on her, the expression of loathing on my face shutting her up mid-rant. "After what I just saw, you don't get to lecture me about boys ever again. I'm not stupid enough to get knocked up like you."

Her mouth fell open in shock, but I had no more fucks to give.

I turned and strode to the door.

"Are you going to tell Seth?"

I ignored her, slamming the door behind me, sprinting down the path to where Xander was waiting in his Mazda.

I flung myself into the passenger seat.

"Hey, Blondie," Xander said, his usually sunny grin looking tight. "Where's the fire?"

"Please, just drive," I mumbled, glancing towards the house. Mum was standing on the front verandah, arms crossed, eyes narrowed.

"She looks—"

"Just go, Xan!" I interrupted. With a wry salute, he pulled away from the curb.

"Where?"

"Anywhere away from here."

We drove in silence for a while, Xander navigating the streets of Avalon like a local. I supposed he kind of was, since he spent most of his weekends here with Dom and me.

I watched him, the casual way he rested one hand on the steering wheel, the other on the gear knob. Impulsively I reached out, hooking my pinkie through his.

He sucked in a tiny breath. "You going to tell me what's going on, Blondie?" he asked.

I sighed. "Let's park at the beach."

Xander's lips tightened for a second, then he flicked the indicator on and turned into the beach carpark. It was getting close to sundown. A few surfers still in the waves, some fitness junkies jogging along the beach. Most of the families had already packed up for the day, but the small kiosk was still open.

"Get the blanket out of the boot," Xander suggested as he pulled up. "It's too nice to sit in the car this evening. I'll meet you down on the beach, just need to do something first."

I nodded, heading around the back of the car and lifting the boot. I giggled when I saw the rainbow, patchwork monstrosity folded up in there. I looked up to make a cheeky remark to Xander about it, but he was halfway to the kiosk. With a shrug, I grabbed it out, slamming the boot shut.

On the sand, I found a fairly secluded spot and spread out the giant, colourful rug. No way Xander wouldn't be able to find me with this thing acting like a beacon. I stared out over the water, letting the rumble of the waves wash over me, trying to focus my brain on the soothing crash and hiss, and let go of the image impaled in there.

"Thought this might be a Bubble-O conversation," Xander said above me. I looked up, my heart racing. He grinned down at me, one dark blond curl falling over his forehead as he held the ice cream out to me. My eyes started to prickle, my lip trembled, and all of a sudden I was sobbing.

"Hey, Georgie, talk to me. I'm here." Those words reached into my chest and wrapped around my heart as his arm came around my shoulders, and he pulled me against his side, the warmth of his skin seeping through his t-shirt and mine. I turned my face into him, inhaling the fresh scent of his deodorant and the mouth-watering maleness underneath it.

"I …" I hiccupped. "I got sent home from work early today …"

Xander sucked air through his teeth. "They didn't fire you, did they? Fuckers!" His hand tightened on my shoulder, and through my tears I managed a watery laugh at how adorable it was that he got so angry on my behalf.

"No, it was just quiet, so they cut my shift short. And please don't interrupt me, this is … God it's so hard to say out loud."

"Sorry," he mumbled against my hair, his fingers trailing circles on my shoulder. "Get it all out."

I took a deep breath. "So, Seth's overseas for work at the moment. But when I got home, I could hear a man's voice in the living room. And …" I buried my face harder against his chest. "I stupidly, stupidly got curious, and went in to see who it was, and …"

"Who was there?" Xander demanded, his voice suddenly an octave deeper. "Did he … did someone hurt you?" He pulled me back from his chest, tilting my chin until I was looking into his face. His thumb swiped the tears from my cheek. I forgot to breathe for a moment.

"Georgie. Are you hurt?" he asked again, his eyes searching mine.

I shook my head. "No, nothing like that. I just … I walked in, and Mum was there, with some guy, and he was … they were fucking. Like, he had her bent over the armrest of the sofa, and he was really … he was grunting, and she was moaning into the cushion I always cuddle when I'm up late watching a movie."

I swallowed back bile, reaching for the Bubble-O, trying to tear it open with fingers that shook. I needed something, anything to take the sour taste out of my mouth. Warm, strong hands encased mine, taking the treat from me and returning it without the wrapper. I looked up into concerned hazel eyes.

"That's ... that's bloody awful, Georgie," he murmured, opening his own Bubble-O and taking a bite. My eyes locked on his lips, at the way they wrapped around the ice cream, how he gently sucked, pulling back and licking up a drip as it headed towards his hand. Warmth pooled low in my belly.

My God, how was it possible to be completely disgusted by what I'd seen Mum doing, and at the same time, wondering what it would be like if Xander was doing those things to me ...

"What did you do?" Xander's question startled me out of my daydream. I took a huge bite of Bill to mask the fact that I'd basically been drooling over him. I pinched my forehead through the brain freeze.

"I screamed." I winced at his horrified expression. "I know, alright? I was shocked, I couldn't help it. I wish I hadn't, because they both jumped up, turned to look at me ... the guy, his dick ... And Mum was trying to cover herself with *my* cushion ..."

I sucked in a breath. "And then I just ran for my room and texted you."

Xander took another suck of his ice cream. "What are you going to do?"

I shrugged, picking at Bill's bubblegum nose. "Mum tried to talk to me. She asked me if I was going to tell Seth."

"Are you?"

I shook my head. "I have a feeling he already knows. Or suspects. Seriously, they argue more than anything else when he's home. I've heard her accusing him of cheating when he travels for work. Maybe he does ... I don't know."

"And how do you feel about it?" he asked.

"No idea," I sighed. "I think I'm still in shock. It was disgusting, seeing my mum like that. But I feel angry, too. Like, Seth has been so good to both of us. He's my dad, even if he's not my father. I hate Mum for doing this to him, and I hate that she tells me I can't be trusted with boys, when she's out being such a dirty hypocrite.

But I wish I didn't have to think about any of this, to be honest. I'd rather it be going on behind my back."

Xander nodded. "It's shitty timing for you, too, with the HSC starting next week."

I snorted. "Look, if anything, a bunch of life-changing exams might be good for me, give me something to focus on that's not … this." I paused, slurping at my rapidly melting ice cream. "You know what really sucks? That my birthday is right in the middle of exams—no going out and getting drunk on my eighteenth for me."

Xander nudged me with his shoulder. "Hey, my birthday's not until November, so I wouldn't be able to party with you anyway."

"Poor Dom, he must be stressed out of his mind, with his grandfather dying, and having to go to France now, with exams right around the corner."

Xander nodded. "He gets special consideration for grief, so that's something at least." Xander's pinkie finger found mine, tangling them together. "I know you probably would have preferred him to be here for you today, with all of this, but I'm glad you trust me enough to ask for my help."

My eyes drew up to meet his. "I didn't even think of him, to be honest. I … the first person I think of lately, when I want to talk to anyone, is you."

His eyes glistened intently, meeting mine, then dropping to my lips. I brought the ice cream to my mouth, and he mirrored the movement, wrapping his lips around it and sucking, the way I did.

The air between us felt charged with electricity. Together we matched each other, licking and sucking until I was pulling the empty stick out of my mouth, the Bubble-O-Bill all gone.

"Georgie," Xander rasped, dropping his stick on the sand beside us and turning his body towards mine.

"Hmm?" I asked, my heart thrumming, heat flashing across every inch of my skin.

"Do you think you're ready for our first real kiss?"

I sucked in a nervous breath to tell him that I was more than ready, that I'd been ready for years, that I didn't care about sneaking around behind Mum's back anymore.

But none of those words came out because Xander's mouth pressed against mine, and every single thought that I had completely disintegrated.

His mouth was cold, and sweet. He licked the seam of my lips, and I gasped, and then his tongue was in my mouth, cool from the ice cream, but warming rapidly as he stroked it against mine. I reached out, clutching his shoulders as I tentatively moved my tongue against his.

"Unngh," he groaned into my mouth, and suddenly I was falling, my back against the crazy patchwork picnic blanket, Xander's body over mine, propped up on his elbows as our tongues tangled.

"This okay?" he murmured against my lips, shifting his body so that we were chest to chest.

"Yeah," I breathed, parting my legs, letting him sink down between them. I moaned when I felt how hard he was through his shorts, and how it pressed against my centre.

"Georgie, I … this is too fast," he mumbled, but his mouth moved against mine, his tongue darting and retreating, circling, making all that heat that had been flashing over me earlier converge between my legs.

"No, it's not," I protested, my hands finding his hair and clawing into it. "I want this. I want more."

Xander stilled, his mouth brushing mine as he panted. "You don't want … everything, though, do you?"

I grinned against his lips, pulling him back to me and kissing him fiercely, my heart thundering at the meaning of his question.

"Not everything … yet," I whispered. "But this …" I rocked my hips, hissing at the friction of my core rubbing against him. "… this is perfect."

"Christ," Xander mumbled, and then his mouth was working mine again, teeth clacking as he kissed me frantically, one hand slipping between our bodies to squeeze at my breast, his thumb running over my nipple.

I jerked under him, the sensation like electricity running straight between my legs. He muttered a curse under his breath, and I grinned against his mouth.

"Feel good?" I asked, then sucked in a breath as his fingers rolled my nipple through my shirt.

"Too good. You have no idea how good," he panted. "You … you're everything, Georgie."

His words had my heart soaring, and I opened my mouth to tell him he was everything to me, too, when he rolled his hips, rubbing himself against me, and all that came out was, "Oooooh!"

"Does that feel nice?" he murmured breathlessly, his mouth moving from mine to kiss along my cheek, until his lips were at my ear. "Can I keep doing it?"

"Please," I gasped.

Xander's "Thank God," was like a prayer as he moved against me again, and I parted my legs further.

"Yes," he whispered against my skin, his fingers still working my nipple through my shirt, a fine sheen of sweat breaking out on his face and chest. "This is … so … good."

His mouth found mine again, his tongue moving in time with the thrusts of his hips. A tingling ache started building inside me from the feel of him grinding his hardness against my centre.

"God, this is better than when I do it myself," I mumbled into his mouth. His groan vibrated all the way through me, his movements speeding up.

"Can you … will you … like this?" he asked, his hips rocking faster, rubbing right where I needed it. "Because … fuck, Georgie … I will."

Just the thought of that had more heat, more aching, more tingling erupting between my legs.

"I want to," I answered. I moved my hips against him, pressing us closer together. Sweat dripped from his forehead onto mine, and he leaned down to kiss me again, running his tongue along my lips, licking into my mouth, wet and hot and so delicious. All the while his length stroked against me, his stomach against mine, the feel of his muscles working over me.

I was overwhelmed with sensation, and when I closed my eyes, sucking his bottom lip into my mouth, it was like I was floating, flying … soaring.

"Oh, God, Georgie, please … I'm so close," Xander breathed against my mouth, his hips snapping faster and more erratically against me. The ache was so intense, so incredible, but maybe not quite enough to send me over the edge.

"It's okay if you do, Xan," I whispered against his neck, my fingers clutching at him there, slipping a bit in his sweat. "This is great for me."

"No," he hissed. "I won't until you do."

Rolling us until we were side by side, his hand found its way down my body, between my legs, fingers circling through my clothes. I gasped against his shoulder, trembling as I wrapped my fingers around his wrist, moving his hand, sliding it under my shorts and underpants.

"Fuck," he grunted, his fingers slipping against my slickness. "Tell me what to … how to …" His finger stroked me in just the right spot, and a moan ripped out of me.

"There?" he asked, doing it again. I nodded, panting, against his shoulder as he found a new rhythm with his finger this time, and the ache built, faster and stronger than when I touched myself. I pulled Xander's mouth down to mine, kissing and sucking and licking wildly as the sensation I was seeking multiplied.

Xander's hips rocked, rubbing himself against my thigh as he circled and stroked. Just when I felt like this much pleasure couldn't possibly be normal, he grunted into my mouth, his hips snapping one last time, and as he shuddered beside me, he pressed his finger firmly against my bud, and I cried out as stars burst behind my eyelids and I shuddered against him, too.

Then: It Stretches On Forever

XANDER, 17 YEARS OLD

The feel of Georgie throbbing against my finger as she panted hoarsely into my shoulder was enough for me not to give a crap that my underwear was a hot, sticky mess now.

Breathing hard, I ran my finger through her wetness, grinning at the way she spasmed against me. My chest ached with pride that I managed to get her there, too.

"Stop now," she begged breathlessly, tugging at my wrist. "I'm … it's really sensitive, after …"

I grinned down at her as I pulled my hand out from her underwear, running the thumb of my other hand over the blush on her cheeks, surreptitiously wiping her arousal on the picnic blanket.

"I can't believe we just … on the beach, where anyone could have seen!" she muttered, scandalised. But her eyes were shimmering silver, and her lips were swollen from our kissing, a sly little smile tugging at them. She looked so beautiful, with her hair splayed out like a halo under her.

The words were on the tip of my tongue, my heart battering against my ribs, insisting that I say them. But I swallowed back the *"I love you"* and kissed her again gently instead.

I didn't want her to think I was saying it because we made each other come. I wanted the first time I said those words to her to be about everything that had grown between us over six years, and not just about the last twenty minutes.

So instead, I lay down, pulling her into my arms. She rested her head against my chest, and I peppered little kisses over her forehead. I wondered if she knew every heartbeat against her ear was for her.

"Why did we wait so long to do that?" she mumbled, her voice scratchy from how she'd cried out as she came.

I chuckled. "Pretty sure that was all you, Blondie."

She turned and tucked her chin against me, looking up at me with a sparkle in her eyes. "Well, maybe the wait made it better."

"It was pretty epic," I agreed. "Although my dick may permanently be glued to the inside of my boxers if I don't clean myself up soon." I waggled my eyebrows as Georgie's laughter vibrated against me.

As I leaned in to kiss her forehead she said, "Well, we wouldn't want that—I have lots of future plans for it."

I groaned against her hairline. "How far in the future, exactly, are these plans?"

She wriggled up my body, pressing her lips to mine. "Let's just get the HSC out of the way, and then we can talk. I mean, we do need to focus on our exams, not on getting each other off."

"I can multitask," I grumbled, which had Georgie's mouth grinning against mine.

"It's only a month. Just a month, and then …" She pressed another kiss to my lips.

"And then," I agreed, knowing exactly what that 'and then' meant to me.

And then I can tell you that this future you're talking about, it stretches on forever.

Now: Did I Just Make You Squirt?

A drive. What the hell had I been thinking? I didn't need to be out alone at night with Xander Fox! I needed to keep doing exactly what I'd been doing all week—avoid, avoid, avoid.

But something about watching Jordyn setting up Xander's big, steamy night with Alex made me snap. I'd grabbed the keys to Mim's Ute, driven hell for leather into Budgerigar, and bought a couple of items. And now those items were in an Esky in my hand, except for the one in my pocket, and I was about to do something that clearly indicated I'd lost my mind.

I waited, nerves jangling, as Xander popped Molly back inside, and tied on a pair of joggers and scooped up the picnic blanket. He bumped my shoulder with his as we headed towards his monster truck. Clambering in, I set the Esky down between my feet. Xander lobbed the blanket into the back seat before getting behind the wheel.

I pointed the way towards the open gate that would take us into the now-empty paddocks.

If he was wondering why I had an Esky, or why I'd brought a picnic blanket, he didn't show it. Meanwhile I was having a tiny meltdown inside my own brain.

You can do this. You deserve this. Just until he goes back to Sydney. No commitment, no sharing secrets. Just enjoying each other, with a wrap date. Take what he's offered, and nothing more.

I'd done casual relationships in the past. I'd enjoyed casual relationships in the past. No expectations outside of mutual pleasure. No jealousy if they found someone else and moved on. No vulnerability.

I knew deep down that Xander and I could never be like that. But I was trying to ignore the part of me that was whispering what a bad idea this was. That I was going to be broken worse the second time around, and this time it would be all my fault. Not just mostly mine, like last time.

"The stars out here are something else." Xander's voice was thick as he peered through the windscreen at the wide-open sky.

"They really are," I murmured, not even remotely interested in the stars. His strong jaw was dusted with blond stubble that glimmered in the moonlight. I wanted to graze my teeth along that jaw, feel his scruff scratch at my lips.

I wanted to taste his tongue, cold and sweet with the contents of the Esky, and try to claw back that feeling from twelve years ago. The one where everything felt overwhelming, and exciting, and … hopeful.

"How far to the river?" he asked, snapping me back into the present.

"See that tree," I pointed out his window. "Pull over there. Just … not under the tree itself, okay?"

Xander snorted, turning the wheel. I wondered if he'd heard how much my voice shook.

Pull yourself together, Georgie! Be a boss, take what you want! And you want Xander's body all over you.

Xander cut the engine, but before he could say or do anything, I opened the Esky and thrust half the contents at him.

"Let's sit in the back and eat," I blurted. Xander looked down, his lips curving into a toe-curling grin.

"Taking a stroll down memory lane tonight, Blondie?" he asked roughly, his hand wrapping around the Bubble-O-Bill, his eyebrow cocked.

I shrugged, feeling my own smile pulling at my mouth. *"Some* memories are worth revisiting."

"I bloody hope you let me take my pants off this time around."

I opened my door, sliding from the seat. "Play your cards right, and anything's on the table."

I slammed the door before he had a chance to answer, walking around to the back of the Ute, pulling down the tailgate. Xander was barely a second behind me, his hand slipping up my thigh, cupping me between the legs. I bit back a moan at the contact.

"Just giving you a boost up," he murmured, lifting me into the tray with that one hand. I shook as I stood, breaking that filthy hot contact and holding out a hand to take the blanket from him, busying myself with spreading it out.

Even once I was settled on the blanket, the heat of his palm lingered, liquid between my legs. I peeled the wrapper from my ice cream and wrapped my lips around the chocolate hat.

"Tastes like teen spirit," Xander said, climbing up and settling down beside me. I licked my lips, rolling my eyes at his obvious misquote. He chuckled, his eyes dark, intent on my mouth.

"So," he began, and now I was the one who couldn't take my eyes off the way his tongue lapped over the already softening ice cream. He gestured up at the nearby tree. "You're helping me avoid getting bird shit all over this ridiculous truck now. This is progress!"

I stifled a nervous giggle by taking a huge bite of the cowboy hat, wincing at the brain freeze.

"Shut up and eat Bill," I mumbled through the mouthful.

Xander's hand found my leg, sliding up and under the hem of my short dress. "I'd rather eat Blondie," he murmured, his gaze lingering on my face, his fingers stroking light, tantalising circles on the inside of my thigh.

I couldn't look at him. I couldn't *not* look at him. My eyes roved from where his touch stoked my libido to a hot, achy mess, up his muscular arm, across that scruffy jaw, and up to meet burning hazel eyes.

"Why not both?" I breathed. His pupils dilated, his Adam's Apple bobbed.

"Christ, Georgie," he groaned.

I took a deep breath, closing the distance between our mouths. The cold sweetness of the ice cream on his tongue sent shockwaves of desire shooting through every nerve ending, converging between my legs as his free hand came up to clasp the back of my neck, tangling in my hair and pressing my face closer to his.

His tongue flicked into my mouth, teasing, his teeth grazing my lip. I gasped into his mouth when one hand slid down my back, cupping my butt and lifting me one-handed like I was a feather, until I was straddling his lap.

"This dress," he growled against my lips, nibbling and sucking at them, "I need your tits out of it."

Lowering myself so his erection pressed against my clit through panties that were already soaked, I pulled back enough to take another slurp of my semi-melted ice cream.

"Well, what are you waiting for?" I asked, arching my back so my breasts strained against the fabric. "You like ripping my clothes off, don't you?"

His cock pulsed beneath me, his eyes black as he watched me licking my Bubble-O. "Are you trying to get me to lose control?"

I leaned so my mouth was at his ear. "Rip it off me, Xander," I breathed, my words punctuated with a gasp as he fisted the fabric at my chest and tore it, one-handed, until it split from the neckline to my waist.

"You have no idea what I'm going to do to these beautiful tits," he murmured, flicking one skinny strap, then the other off my shoulders, leaving me completely topless.

"Braless is my new favourite lingerie," he murmured, one hand caressing my hip, the other holding his ice cream as he stared at my chest with undisguised longing.

"They're not big enough to need one—oh!" I hissed as cold hit my nipple. I stared down, my pussy throbbing as he circled his ice cream around the quickly pebbling peak, staring hungrily as chocolate and caramel and strawberry dripped over my skin. I shivered at the sensation.

"They're perfect," he said, his free hand pressing me closer to him again.

Warm lips, hot tongue. The sudden change of sensation ripped a moan from my throat as he sucked hard on the nipple he'd just covered in ice cream, pulling it deep into his mouth, flicking it with his tongue, running his teeth around it until I was undulating against his hardness. Then he pulled back, licking up all the drips he could reach, sucking and nibbling my skin while he switched hands. My other nipple received the same attention.

Back and forth he repeated this, until all his ice cream was gone, and mine had been abandoned over the side of the tray. Both my nipples were pointy, needy peaks, jutting towards him, my breasts were peppered with red love bites, and I was in panting, soggy disarray. He pulled away, and we both stared down at how my breasts and belly glistened with melted ice cream and his saliva.

"Georgie," he rasped, throwing the now empty stick away. "Look at you, sticky and messy and …" His fingers trailed up under the hiked-up remains of my dress, his thumb brushing against my soaked underwear. "Yes, so wet for me."

Another rip, and the rest of my dress was gone, and his fingers were bruising on my hips, moving me, rubbing my wet core back and forth over his bulge. My head fell back and I gasped, rocking my hips in earnest against him.

"I'm not finishing like this, and neither are you, Blondie," he grated, nipping at my collarbone, sucking skin into his mouth. Branding me. Just like he'd said he wanted to.

Then he was lifting me away from his erection, smirking darkly at me as he fisted my panties and tugged until the flimsy fabric gave way, leaving me completely naked against his fully clothed body.

"Plant that sweet pussy up here on my face," he commanded, gripping my arse and moving me up his body as he lay back on the blanket. "I want to lick you into next week."

I crawled up his body, gripping the side of the truck to steady myself as I lowered my core down towards his mouth. His tongue parted me, laving one long lick up from my entrance to my clit, and I shook over him, my thighs quivering.

"Fuck, Blondie, I want to eat, not just taste." With a growl, he gripped my hips, pulling me down, burying his face so deep in me I was shocked he could still breathe.

And then his tongue was pushing inside of me, his groans vibrating through my core as he devoured my pussy.

"Oh, God!" I moaned, wanting to writhe, to lift myself to escape the intense ache that was already building deep in my abdomen, but he held me firm, locked against his mouth, the flat of his tongue rubbing against my clit, his lips latching around it, sucking hard, his tongue flicking against the swollen flesh he'd caught in his mouth.

"It's too much, Xan!" I hissed, my hands slipping from the side of the truck, fisting in his hair, staring down into his burning eyes as he fucked me with his tongue. He chuckled against my clit, grazing it with his teeth as he thrust his tongue deep into me.

Pleasure so intense it verged on pain raced from my core, burning along my arms and legs and up into my chest. My cry was incoherent as my orgasm crashed all around me, pounding, throbbing tsunami waves of it.

He didn't stop, his lips and tongue riding out my climax, rubbing against my swollen, tender skin as the waves subsided, leaving me wrung out, shaking and whimpering, my clit pulsing, almost painfully sensitive against his lips.

"Please, Xander, I … I can't …" I breathed, all my muscles tremoring against the assault.

"Hmmm," he mumbled against my clit, making me flinch at the sparks of painful pleasure that zinged through me. With a sigh, he lifted me off his face, sitting me on his chest as he smirked up at me. He licked my orgasm off his lips—not that it made a scrap of difference; my arousal glistened all over his cheeks and chin. It had even dripped onto his neck a little.

"I could bottle that up and drink it for breakfast," he said, waggling his eyebrows at me. I grinned the sated grin of someone who had just come harder than ever, slipping down his body until my still dripping pussy was planted over his cock, straining against his shorts.

"You could just drink your breakfast straight from the source," I murmured, gripping the hem of his t-shirt and dragging it up his body. He sat up, his ab muscles working deliciously before my eyes, and he helped me pull it off over his head. My nails raked down his chest, combing through the sparse, golden hair there and down his six-pack.

"Could I, now?" he asked hoarsely, running fingertips over my stomach, making it contract. "My girl wants me to wake her up with my tongue inside her?"

"*This* girl might want to enjoy you in the morning, too." It was the most truth I could manage. But it seemed to be enough for him. His palms reached up to cup my breasts again, thumbs flitting over my nipples and making me roll my hips on him. I hissed at how over-sensitised my nerve endings were there … and how it had that ache building between my legs again.

"You promised me I could do this with my pants off this time around," he growled. With a tiny, sly smile, I rolled myself against him one more time, biting my lip at the way his cock, through the fabric of his shorts, rubbed my clit. Then I got up on my knees and lifted the waistband of his shorts and underwear up and over the bulge, letting his impressive cock spring free, bobbing against his stomach.

"Pants off this time round," I agreed, shimmying them past my body until he could kick them off. Would you like me to untie your shoes, too?" I asked coyly, turning so I faced his feet, the cleft of my arse grazing his cock.

"Fuck, yes, untie them … let me enjoy that view for a moment." I loved how on-edge his voice sounded, so I rocked against him, rubbing the length of his dick between my butt cheeks as I unlaced his shoes and tugged them and his socks off.

"Turn around, Blondie," he demanded once I was done. "As much as that arse is making my mouth water, I want you facing me, want to see those sweet tits bouncing for me while you ride my cock."

"Condom?" I asked sweetly as I turned back to face him, suppressing a giggle when he cursed under his breath.

"I didn't … I wasn't expecting to be fucking you in the back of this bloody Ute tonight."

I leaned down on him, my pussy wet against his length, my nipples brushing his chest as I reached for the ruins of my sundress, rummaging until I found the foil packet I'd put in the pocket.

"It's lucky I *was* expecting to fuck you in the back of this bloody Ute, then, isn't it?" I purred against his jaw, nipping him and moaning when his cock pulsed against my pussy.

He wrenched the packet from my hand, eyes intent on where my pussy was slicking his length. Tearing it open, he gripped my hips, slipping me away from him enough to cover himself.

"Get that pussy where it belongs," he growled, one hand fisting his cock, the other coming back to my hip, guiding me until his head was pressing against my entrance. His palms slid around to cup my arse, spreading me so I could slide down his length.

"God, so thick," I gasped, feeling him stretching me.

"Because you make me so damn hard," he replied with a grunt, angling my butt so he could slip in a little deeper. "Watching you come apart on my face … Christ."

I rolled my hips, taking more of him, slowly sinking down with each movement until he bottomed out inside me, and a low groan burst from me. "So full."

"So bloody tight," he hissed, holding me still on him. "Just … give me a moment." He closed his eyes, taking deep breaths, and I was halfway to another orgasm just from the feel of his cock pulsing inside me as he fought to get control of his arousal.

"I need to move, Xander," I whined. "I need to fuck you."

His eyes snapped open, his jaw tight, his stomach braced under me. "Fuck me then, Blondie. Fuck me just how you want it."

With a little, relieved sob I raised myself up and sank back onto him, rolling my hips when he was fully seated. Digging my nails into those hard abs, I moved again, finding my rhythm.

"That's so damn perfect," he rasped, his fingers kneading the flesh of my butt, controlling my movements just enough that I was angled so his cock rubbed against my G-spot with each downward motion of my pussy.

I knew what was going to happen. I wanted it to happen, even as nerves battled with desire deep in my belly.

"Xander, if we keep going like this, I'm going to …" I broke off with a whimper as he gripped my arse tighter, changing the angle again, and … oh … if I'd thought he was hitting my G-spot before, I'd been wrong.

"Going to what?" he asked between panting breaths. "Come so hard you see stars? That's the plan, Blondie." His hips were thrusting up to meet me as I sank down now. In no world was I the one fucking him anymore. He owned me, and all I could do was let him bounce me up and down on his hot dick and ride out the over-whelming pleasure that was building.

I bit my lip, heat growing deep inside me with each stroke against my G-spot. "I'm going to … oh God!" I whimpered, scrabbling for purchase against his stomach, his chest, his shoulders. The heat swelled, my insides started to clench, and I knew it was too late. I wanted it to be too late.

"I'm so sorry, Xander!" I cried, my pussy slapping wetly against his groin as I approached the edge. "But … oh my God, I'm coming!"

Heat and delicious aching, and pulsing, soaking wetness, and an explosion behind my eyelids as I ground myself down on him, drenching him with my orgasm, rocking on his dick as I clenched over, and over, and over around his thick length.

"Holy … Christ Georgie, that … fuck, yes, I'm coming too!" Xander shouted, his fingers digging bruises into my flesh as he rocked my drenched, fluttering pussy on him, his hips thrusting upwards powerfully as he groaned out something incoherent and his cock swelled impossibly huge inside me, and his body shuddered with his release.

I collapsed against his chest, still dripping from my orgasm. Fluid was running down my legs, and no doubt down his too. I buried my face against his chest, not wanting to look at him. Not wanting to see how he reacted to the realisation of what had just happened.

For a long moment we both just panted, too exhausted to speak. But then, "Georgie," he murmured against my hair, reaching down to cup my chin until I had to look up at him. I met his eyes with what I hoped was an apologetic expression. But my face morphed into confusion at the dimple popping, self-satisfied smirk on his face.

"Did I just make you squirt?"

XANDER

The blush spread across Georgie's nose, flooding her cheeks. I reached up, stroking the heat there.

"Did I?" I repeated. Something hot and aching and … possessive … expanded in my chest as she sucked on her top lip, her eyes uncertain.

"I'm sorry, it's … not pleasant," she mumbled, and then she was climbing off my softening dick, scrabbling for her ruined dress.

I wrapped my fingers around her wrist, stilling her. She glanced at me, then away again. She looked absolutely bloody divine, her hair sweaty and dishevelled, completely naked except for the pair of battered old boots she still wore.I wanted to laugh with unrestrained joy, thinking that she'd been so into what we'd just done she hadn't even cared she still had her shoes on.

But I had a feeling that laughing right now might shatter whatever bubble we were currently in. The bubble where Georgie seduced me, where we fucked without the need for anger-fuelled lust.

"Not pleasant?" I repeated, mystified. "What the … that was the fucking hottest, sexiest thing I've ever …"

Georgie's eyebrows shot up under her fringe. "You don't have to lie to me to make me feel better, you know," she muttered, tugging her wrist from my grip and attempting to work out how to cover herself with her ripped clothing.

With a sigh, I handed her my t-shirt. "Put this on, but then we're talking."

Her mouth curled into a tiny sneer that was so adorable I wanted to kiss it as she tugged the shirt on over her head, tucking her knees up and stretching it over her legs so she was fully covered. She leaned against the side of the tray, staring up at the night sky.

"Talk, then, if you have to," she huffed, and I couldn't help but chuckle. The comment was so Georgie that my chest ached.

"Why are you apologising to me for getting off?" I asked, shuffling towards her until my knees met her toes peeking out from under the shirt. "I mean, it's kind of the goal of fucking, you know."

Georgie snorted. "Because when that happens, it's so … messy, and … I've been told before it feels like I'm … like I'm peeing …"

Jesus, what dickhead was shaming her for coming like that? I looked down, my dick already starting to swell again inside the condom. Shit, I needed to get rid of that. But I didn't want to climb out of the tray to sort it, not when she was feeling so vulnerable.

"You want to see messy?" I asked her instead, rolling the condom off my semi, knotting it and gesturing to it. "Sex is messy, Blondie. Christ, tonight was extra messy, and I'm getting hard again just thinking about it. You're sticky from ice cream all over your tits, I can still taste your pussy in my mouth, and it could not have been hotter. You squirting on my cock is icing on the cake."

She rolled her eyes, but I noticed her gaze flick down to my dick. I grinned cheekily back at her as it swelled more.

"What sort of moron told you that you were peeing on him?" I asked, then clenched my jaw shut when I realised that I didn't really want to know. James the poncy ex had already been more than enough information about her past for me.

"Was it him? James I mean." Clearly I was a sucker for punishment.

Georgie huffed a little breath out of her nose, nodding. "After that we went back to missionary … so we didn't have to change the sheets before we went to sleep."

I couldn't help myself. I reached out, found her waist, and pulled her into my lap. She squeaked, but she didn't protest. Her forehead pressed against my shoulder.

"Well, he's a prudish fuckwit," I mumbled into her hair, and her back shook beneath my hands. I stilled. "I hope that's a laugh, and not a cry, Blondie."

She leaned back, and there it was, that little, secret smile that once upon a time I'd thought would only ever be mine. And maybe it would be mine again. Maybe we didn't need to have a big conversation. Maybe we could just fall back into … us.

"He was a fuckwit," she agreed. "And he was a prude. In hindsight it's ridiculous I stayed with him as long as I did. Before him, I'd never really felt self-conscious about enjoying sex."

I winced. I wasn't sure I could cope with where this conversation was headed. I didn't want to know the details of all the men who had come before me. All the men who'd had a chance with her because I was a complete idiot.

"Why did you? Stay with him, I mean?" I asked, trying to turn the topic back to James the prudish fuckwit, and not all the hot sex she'd had before him.

Georgie shrugged, her fingers running through my chest hair, sending electricity shooting to my dick. Which, I was unable to forget, was naked, and rubbing against her bare arse.

"It was … easy. Safe, I guess. We never really argued because I never cared enough about his opinion to bother. I never felt strongly enough about him for him to be able to …" she trailed off.

"To hurt you?" I asked, finishing her sentence.

For a moment she did nothing except stroke her nails over my abs. I shuddered, my dick pulsing, but I ground my teeth against my arousal. She was opening up to me, and I couldn't squander the opportunity. Also, she probably hadn't brought another condom.

Note to self. Always pack multiple condoms when going anywhere with Georgina Menzies.

Then she shrugged again, which I took as a yes. Guilt bubbled up in my stomach.

"When I first … when you told Lachy about James that night …" I began, before pressing a kiss to her shoulder. "I was so bloody angry. I couldn't believe that you'd been able to have a long-term relationship, that you'd been able to move on from what happened, to have something normal."

Her hands went to my hair, gripping me and tugging my head back until she could look me in the eyes. Hers glinted with that silver fire I bloody loved.

"I have been emotionally unavailable for every single man in my life for the last twelve years, Xander," she said, her voice furious. "Tell me that's normal!"

I met her gaze. "It's not. Does it make you feel any better that I've been the same?"

"What about Montana, or whatever the hell her stupid name is?" she scoffed. I reached up, gripping the back of her neck, wrapping my free arm around her waist and flipping us until she was under me. I leant over her, watching her struggle to stay angry as my dick grazed between her legs.

"Dakota," I corrected automatically, silently cursing myself when her expression darkened.

"I slept with her twice, maybe three times. I've never spent the night with a woman … until a certain bossy blonde drunkenly demanded I spoon her to sleep." I tried for a grin, but I couldn't quite make myself in the face of her angry scrutiny.

"I've never wanted to let anyone in, Georgie," I said, propping myself on my elbows and stroking her cheeks, her lips. "I'd just resigned myself to never feeling … anything, for anyone, after you. All the women before now are just a blur for me."

Her lips parted, her eyes lost some of that burning intensity.

"This is … I think we need a subject change," she mumbled. I swallowed back the disappointment that I'd said something honest, and vulnerable, and she dismissed me like that. I pasted on a smirk instead.

"So …" I began, rocking my hips, my cock slipping in her

wetness. She let out a shuddering breath. "Have you ever squirted from any other positions?"

A shocked laugh burst out of her, her cheeks reddening again. "I … not that I can remember. And before you act all cocky, there's just something about me being on top that just … hits the right spot. It's got nothing to do with your sexual prowess."

I growled, nipping at her jaw until she squirmed under me, coating my cock with more of her arousal. "Challenge accepted," I whispered against her ear before slipping my t-shirt off her body and kissing my way down it.

"Xander …" she said, and there was a warning and a pleading in her tone that made my dick ache so badly to sink into her. But I wasn't going to fuck her again tonight. No, I had other plans for her.

"Just one thing, Georgie," I said as I gazed up her body before meeting her eyes. "You never, ever apologise to me for your pleasure. But I'll take your enthusiastic thanks every day of the week."

She snorted, then moaned as I knelt between her legs, pressing her knees wide. Her pussy, spread out before me, soaking wet and glistening, her clit still swollen from my mouth, was the most beautiful thing I'd ever seen. I reached down and palmed her, rocking my hand against her, coating myself in her wetness.

"Still so turned on, Blondie. I'm not even sure this is going to be a challenge at all," I said, circling two fingers around her clit. She let out a little panting moan, but her legs stayed wide, and she watched me with a dare in her eyes.

"There's my girl," I murmured, turning my hand, slipping my middle and ring finger inside her pussy. My eyes fell closed at how she was already clenching around my fingers.

"Do you want me to make you come so hard you squirt all over my hand?" I asked.

"God, you're such a cocky bastard, Xan—oh!" she broke off with a moan as I found her ridged G-spot, tickling it.

"Better get that name calling out of your system now, Blondie, because when you're drenching my hand, your voice is going to be so hoarse from screaming, you won't be able to speak again tonight."

"Oh, Jesus … God!" she panted as I started moving my fingers inside her in earnest, curling against her G-spot, flicking the thumb of my other hand over her clit, groaning myself as it swelled.

"I'd suck this swollen little clit again, if I didn't want to watch you gush so badly I think I'm going to blow all over your stomach the second it happens," I muttered.

"You're excellent at making me come," she panted, "but I really don't think you can get me to … oooooh!" Her pussy tightened around my fingers as I pinched her clit the way she'd begged me to in the clinic bathroom.

"Touch your tits, Blondie," I growled. "Play with them for me."

Her hands flew to her perky breasts, squeezing and kneading, rolling her nipples between her fingers. Christ, my cock was so hard that just the view of her, spread so wide for me, touching herself while I finger fucked her, was likely to send me over the edge. But I gritted my teeth against the ache in my balls, curling my fingers a little more as I moved my hand faster.

The wet, filthy sound of my fingers inside her slick pussy, her panting, gasping moans as she clenched around them, my own harsh breaths as I stared intently at where they disappeared inside her.

Her stomach muscles started contracting, her thighs quivering. "Oh God, please … I think you're going to …"

"That's my perfect girl," I praised, her G-spot swelling under my fingers, her pussy tightening in a way that pulled a ragged groan from my throat. "Come hard for me, let it go, soak me with it."

"Xander—oh God, oh Goooood!"

Her eyes slammed shut, her body arched, and liquid gushed over my hand as her pussy pulsed violently, squeezing my fingers so tight my eyes rolled back in my head.

"Fuck, it's not over," she panted, rocking herself on my hand and moaning, pinching at her nipples as she rode my fingers to another climax, her legs shaking violently as her pussy continued to throb.

"Christ, Georgie, you're incredible … oh God I wish I could fuck you right now," I hissed as I stroked her down from two back-to-back orgasms. Her skin shimmered with sweat, her tits bouncing as she panted raggedly.

"I've got a better idea," she said, propping herself up on her elbows and cocking her head to the side to grin slyly at me. "Come on my tits."

"Jesus … fuck," I snarled, but I was already fisting my cock, coating it with the wetness that covered my hand. "This is going to be fast."

"Please," she pleaded, arching her back so her tits were closer to me. I gripped myself, thrusting my hips, fucking my own fist as she watched, mouth parting, tongue darting out to lick her bottom lip.

"Christ, you're … everything," I muttered as heat pooled at the base of my spine, pleasure shooting through my groin.

"That's my perfect boy," she murmured, reaching one hand out to cup my balls. "Come hard for me, let it go … soak me with it."

"You're incredible," I gasped, back bowing as my orgasm raced through me, and we both moaned together as I painted her perfect little tits with my cum.

"So, safe to say we're both really good at making each other squirt?" Georgie said as I stared down at the mess on her tits. I laughed, leaning down to press a kiss to her beautiful mouth.

"Safe to say that sex with you is the best sex of my life," I mumbled against her lips. "And I want more. I want weeks, and months, and years more."

She didn't reply, but her tongue caressing mine was enough for me. For now.

Now: The Remnants Of Him

GEORGIE

It was around three when I crept back into the house. Mim, thankfully, wasn't waiting up this time. She'd probably assumed I was planning to spend the night with Xander.

I was sure he'd been assuming the same. Confusion and disappointment had shadowed his face when we'd returned to his place, and I'd told him I wanted to shower and sleep alone.

But after his last comment, while I lay stunned in his arms, his orgasm cooling on my chest, I couldn't. I just couldn't stay the night. I didn't want him getting ideas about this being more than just a country fling for the duration of the show.

I hated how much my heart hurt as I walked away, dressed only in his t-shirt and my battered old cowboy boots. I hated feeling his eyes following me all the way across the lawn.

I hated that I wanted to turn, to run to him, to cling on and tell him that weeks, and months, and years, was exactly what I'd started secretly fantasising about.

I couldn't.

I couldn't disappoint him with a future he could never be satisfied with. With a secret from the past that would always lurk between us. So instead, I had to disappoint him now and pull back.

It had to just be about sex.

And holy hell, the sex!

I ducked into the bathroom, dragging his shirt off over my head and staring at the sticky spots on my breasts where he'd coated me. I hadn't had sex this hot since uni. And even then, it had been with younger men, who almost felt like boys compared to how Xander treated me.

He'd taken something that I'd been told I should be disgusted by and had made it into something beautiful, and sexy, and oh God, the way he'd coaxed me to it with his fingers … I'd be replaying that during future masturbation sessions.

'My perfect girl'.

I shivered at the memory, turning away from the mirror and running the shower cold. I might have teased him about those words, repeating them back to him in reverse, but I could happily hear him call me that every night for the rest of my life.

But I could never tell him that.

I rinsed the remnants of him off me, wincing at how tender I felt between my legs. I hadn't come that hard or that many times in a row for … well I couldn't really remember the last time. It was inevitable I'd be tender.

But when I stepped out of the shower, towelling myself, my heart shuddered when a reddish pink smear appeared as I wiped between my legs.

I glanced up at myself in the mirror. Eyes wide, frightened. Face pale.

Your period's due soon, I reminded myself, trying not to hyperventilate. *It could be coming a bit early. It's probably just premenstrual spotting. That's a thing that happens sometimes.*

It had never been a thing that happened to me before. But I could convince myself that was all it was … as long as my period did show up in the next day or two, I could write it off as that.

It was a silly, dangerous thing to do. I should be calling Dr Hartley and reporting it as unusual. But then he'd want me to go back to Sydney to have scans and swabs and he'd want to lecture me about the fact that cervical cancer has a recurrence rate of about thirty percent in women who choose not to have a full hysterectomy, and that wasn't a figure to be sneezed at.

I just didn't want to think about it.

So, when that night I started feeling pain in my lower abdomen, I told myself it was just premenstrual cramping. But I might also have had a momentary brain snap and gone scrounging through my drawer to find the little pouch of crystals the guy with the stone dildos had sold me. And I might have fallen asleep with them laid out in an odd configuration on my lower abdomen.

When I woke up the next morning to find my period had started, I breathed a sigh of relief, telling myself I must have gotten my days mixed up, or my cycle was out of whack, or something. Totally possible. All the tension with Xander had been really stressful. Stress screwed with menstrual cycles.

It had nothing to do with my cancer. That was what I told myself as I dressed that morning, deciding to forego my morning run in favour of a coffee and a dose of ibuprofen.

I drank the coffee as the sun rose, watching out my window as Jord and Alex walked hand in hand over from the caravan, Jase following, his equipment still in its case. Xander opened the door for them, and Jase set up from his sneaky spot to 'catch' Alex doing the walk of shame to her car. Jord seemed to be engaged in a heated discussion with Xander as they secured a mic to him—always difficult when we insisted on him being shirtless.

I turned away from the spectacle, not wanting to watch him kiss her goodbye on the porch, as per Jord's production notes. The ones I'd scowled over last night just before I snapped and started a chain of events that ended with multiple orgasms in the back of Xander's Ute.

When I heard the car drive off, I peeked out the window, watching as Xander took off his mic and started his morning routine of working out on the deck.

His body was really something else.

That body had shuddered over me just last night, his ab muscles contracting with his orgasm.

That body had held me, had reassured me that I never needed to feel sorry for or ashamed of my pleasure.

That body had grounded me, had slept twined around mine when I had drunk more than was sensible and the room was spinning so much it felt like my whole life was spinning out of control.

I sipped my coffee as Jumbo galloped around the side of the house, looking for Molly.

What would happen to him when Molly returned with her dad to Sydney? When Mim sold this beautiful old place and moved into town with Liz? I had no doubt that Liz and her Corgis would welcome Mim and Jumbo with open arms. But this house, this farm, was his home.

It was Mim's home.

It was my home, really.

I fell onto my bed, dragging my laptop over, intending to send a gentle reminder email to Kenneth about making a call on future seasons of *Beach Vet Goes Bush*.

Clearly, Kenneth had pre-empted me. The first email in my inbox was from him.

As I scanned the words, my heart dropped into the pit of my stomach

… Sceptical that the format will work over multiple seasons … Xander is a rare talent, finding another vet of his calibre willing to do a three-month stint in the middle of nowhere is essentially impossible … The premise will get old fast for viewers … Your input is appreciated, but Beach Vet Goes Bush is a one season documentary … The town being without a vet after filming wraps isn't Reelflix's problem …

I snapped my laptop shut, pushing my fingers into the corners of my eyes in an attempt to stop the tears that threatened to overflow. I was only on the verge of blubbering because of stupid period hormones anyway, I was sure.

It had nothing to do with the fact that I felt personally responsible for simultaneously raising the town's hopes of a permanent vet … and dashing them.

Now: Marginally More Productive Blathering

GEORGIE

The week before Christmas flew by. The clinic was booked out, and there were a couple of livestock emergency call outs, which Alex was able to talk Xander through on the phone, given her own practice in Millstone was just as busy, and she couldn't spare time to be there for him in person.

"I'm not sure how much footage worth airing we're getting right now," Jord grumbled the day before Christmas Eve. "I mean, there was that one constipated cat that got really upset about having an enema, that was fucking hilarious …" they scratched at the back of their head. "But we need more Alex and Xander."

I raised an eyebrow at Jord. "We need more Alex and Xander? Or you're missing having Alex around this week?"

Jord scuffed a toe on the floor, nose and cheeks tinged pink. "Hey, don't you get on your high horse with me, Ms 'I did my best cowgirl impersonation in the back of the Ute down the paddock with Dr Fox'."

I took a step back. "How did … what are you talking about?" I stammered. Jord smirked back at me.

"You know, my caravan has a great view—all the way down to the river."

I silently cursed my stupidity, heat flashing up my neck. Jord's face softened.

"G, I'm not attacking you, okay? Sorry if it came out that way. Something about him … it softens you." My heart pounded sickeningly against my ribs as they continued. "It's like he's found all those sharp edges and filed them away." My fists clenched, unclenched, clenched again.

"I think he's good for you. I think—"

"I don't care what the fuck you think," I hissed, not being able to hold in my anxious outburst any longer. "There is no future for us! It's just scratching an itch, and only because there's nothing much else to do around here. It's a bit of fun, but it can never be more than just fun for me."

My mouth tasted disgusting with the lie.

"Have you told him that?" Jord asked, biting their lip.

My shoulders slumped. "Not explicitly, no."

"Well, he's explicitly aware of it now," they said, nodding behind me. I spun, to find Xander, mere feet away, staring dark-eyed and tight-lipped through the office door at the pair of us.

"I …" I began, but my throat caught.

"I'm going on lunch," he muttered, disappearing from the doorway, his footsteps heavy, angry. The clinic door slammed shut a moment later.

"Shit," I muttered, dropping my face into my hands. Jord nudged me.

"Go and talk to him, explain that you didn't mean it!" they insisted. I peered at them between splayed fingers, my skin clammy.

Jord's face went cold. "Unless you *did* mean it."

I shook my head. "No! I … there's a lot you don't know. There's a lot *he* doesn't know. I don't want to … but what I just said isn't even close to …"

Jord turned me and pushed me out the door. "Don't blather to me! Go blather to him, it's marginally more productive!"

I managed a weak laugh tinged with hysteria, wiping my sweaty palms on my shorts. I stopped on the verandah when I spotted him on the footpath outside, scrubbing a hand over his face and glaring at Bird Turd Tree. Jase had followed him out and was filming every excruciating second of Xander's misery.

I sucked in a breath, having no idea what I could say that would not be more lies. Maybe I should let him think it was just fun, that he meant nothing more to me.

It would be easier when this ended if he thought that.

He glanced up, mouth twisting bitterly as he spotted me standing next to Jase. He reached under his shirt, ripped off his mic and tossed it back over the fence.

"I'm off the clock. Piss off with that camera," he snarled, striding off towards the shops.

"Back inside, Jase," I mumbled, watching Xander retreat. "Ask Jord to organise Calli for a bit of one on one, see if we can drag more about Lachy out of her." At least one love story on this damn show could be real.

Jase paused, then nodded, heading back into the clinic. On shaky legs, I followed Xander down the street.

Now: Just One Of Your Weird Stone Dicks, Thanks

XANDER

I knew she was following me, but I didn't turn.

I had no idea why I felt so blindsided by what I'd just overheard. It wasn't exactly shocking that she wasn't interested in anything deeper than a bit of fun in a town where there wasn't a whole lot else to do except bone.

But I'd thought we were reaching some sort of breakthrough. Her drunken confessions to me … the way she'd let me hold her when whatever she and Dom talked about had freaked her out.

The night in my Ute, and her honesty about her past. And the way she'd trusted me with her pleasure. It had felt so bloody incredible … and so right.

And then she'd shut down the second I'd opened my stupid mouth and said words like 'more' and 'years'.

I should have seen this coming a mile off. I shouldn't have let myself start to hope.

"Xander!" she called out breathlessly. My footsteps stuttered, but I didn't stop. Glancing up, I grinned fiercely at the shop sign. Emporium of Intuition. What a stupid bloody name.

After what Levi had told me about the weirdo who owned this

shop, and the conversation he'd had with Amanda and Georgie, chances were good she wouldn't follow me inside.

And I might have a second or two to breathe and work out how to play this.

I took the steps two at a time, pushing through the door with a jangle of wind chimes. Because of course.

It was dim, verging on shadowy, inside, and the blistering December heat didn't follow me in. A strong, smoky, herbal smell invaded my nostrils and a table in front of me was covered with carved wooden bowls full of tumbled stones.

Now, if I were a loopy new-age crystal seller, where would I keep rose-quartz dildos? May as well sort out Levi's request while I was in here.

I wandered past stacks of affirmation cards, Tarot decks, and a bunch of books on meditation and chakra healing. I felt like I was getting close when I came across a poster showing graphic photographs of tantric sex positions, and I scanned the shelves more closely.

"I think this is the one you're after," a deep male voice said behind me.

"Holy shit!" I leapt about a foot into the air, spinning to find myself face to face with a tall man with dirty blond hair in a top-knot, and piercing eyes. "Uh, I'm sorry, what am I after?"

The guy's smile was creepily serene, and I glanced down to see he was holding a curved, pink, stone dick. I stifled a horrified guffaw.

"What … um, yeah, actually … how the hell did you know?" I asked, rubbing at the back of my neck, unable to take my eyes off the toy my brother wanted me to buy for him and his girlfriend.

"Just a hunch," the man replied, leaning closer. I instinctively leaned back until I was pressed against the shelf, but he reached behind me, plucking up a box and packing the dildo into it.

"It's not for me. My brother asked me to grab it for him—for his girlfriend, I mean," I stammered, face melting.

"Did you want one, or two?" the guy asked, as if I hadn't spoken.

"Uh, why would I want …?"

The guy stared intently at me for what felt like forever, then nodded his head towards the door. "It was possible your girl had come back to buy it. And maybe she was too embarrassed to come in again … after last time."

I turned to look out the door, seeing Georgie leaning against the timber siding, her head in her hands. My heart lurched. I could never read her, not fully. I hadn't been able to in high school, and I still couldn't. She may as well have been written in invisible ink for all the sense I could make of her.

Her words said one thing, but her body said another. I just didn't know which was real.

Maybe they were both lies.

"I don't … she's not my …"

The guy pinned me with a sharp stare. "She's yours. That doesn't necessarily mean there's a happy ending in the cards for the pair of you, though."

I gaped at the sheer bloody audacity of this guy. "Just one of your weird stone dicks, thanks. I don't need a toy to get her … get anyone off."

He shrugged, turning towards the counter. "It's a Yoni Wand. And of your abilities, I have no doubt. But what happens when you're not around anymore?"

That stopped me in my tracks. I stared between the strange guy and the shelf, littered with a range of crystal penises, and something snapped in my brain. Picking up another one, I stormed up to the counter and slapped it down next to the first.

"You're a very good salesman," I grumbled. The man laughed under his breath, boxing up the second dildo and ringing up my sale.

The tinkle of the chimes as I exited the shop had Georgie's head snapping out of her hands, and when she saw the bag I carried, her eyes sparked, her arms folding over her chest as she glared at me.

"What the hell were you doing in there?" she demanded. A bitter smile tugged at my lips. A feisty Georgie was one I could handle.

Maybe.

"Souvenirs," I replied, reaching into the bag and tugging out one of the boxes. "I heard that you and Amanda were very … intrigued by these."

Her eyes widened as she recognised the picture on the box. "You … how did you know about …?" her gaze flitted up to meet mine, then away, the colour draining from her skin. My heart dropped into my abdomen.

"What's wrong?" I asked her, shoving the box back into the bag, reaching for her.

She shook her head. "Did you … what do you know?"

"Only that you and Amanda had a bloody weird conversation with the guy in there about stone sex toys. He saw you outside and thought you'd sent me in to get it for you."

"Oh my God," she muttered, her head falling against her palm. "That was all? Nothing else?"

I pinched her chin, forcing her to look up at me. "That was all. Why is this freaking you out so much?"

She shrugged, staring off into the distance, her expression flat. "No reason. I hope you didn't get sucked into buying one for me."

I took it out of the bag and thrust it at her. Did I want to get a rise out of her? Possibly. I just needed to see something from her other than that cold, empty stare.

"I did. I guess, when you've ghosted again, this should be a 'fun' replacement for me. I mean, that's all I'm good for, isn't it? Getting you off when you're bored?"

Her face flushed crimson, and she shoved the thing right back at me. "Keep your voice down!" she hissed, glancing around and groaning. The only person possibly in hearing distance was across the road, but it was Liz, and she was staring at us with unabashed glee.

"Shit," I muttered.

"Shit is exactly right," Georgie agreed, and rage boiled under my skin at her accusatory tone.

"This really is just a bit of fun for you, isn't it?" I asked, looming over her, putting my body between her and Liz. "This was never going to go anywhere. Just another way to punish me for something dumb I did as a kid, that you're never going to get past!"

"You have no idea what you're talking about!" She poked me in the chest. I snatched her hand, weaving my fingers through hers and holding on just tight enough for it to be uncomfortable.

"I know exactly what I'm talking about! You'll never forgive me for hurting you. You want me, but not enough to let me in. Not enough to talk about what happened back then. Not enough to let it go!"

Georgie tried to tug her hand away, but I refused to relinquish my hold on her.

"You won't even give me a chance to get some bloody closure on the last twelve years!" I snarled. "And everything that's happened since we started filming this stupid bloody show—" I gestured wildly between the pair of us with my free hand "—all it's done is ensure that I'll feel even more fucked up over it all for the next bloody decade!"

Georgie's lips trembled, and my heart leapt into my throat.

"Hey." I stepped closer, bringing my free hand towards her face, but she pursed her lips and jerked her head away from me.

"It takes two to tango, Dr Fox," she muttered, her eyes piercing and cold. "Don't you dare try to blame me when you've been just as active a participant."

"I thought we were getting somewhere!" I argued. "I thought we were making progress, that maybe things were moving towards …" I rubbed at my forehead. "Forget it. I was obviously bloody delusional."

Georgie snorted. "I'll say it again, because apparently you are too stupid to have understood me the first time. You have no idea what you're talking about. Our past has nothing to do with … with my feelings right now."

"Bullshit!" I scoffed. "Our past has haunted both of us for over a decade."

"Let me go." Her words were emotionless. Her eyes clouded over, and something cold and hard and heavy settled in the pit of my stomach.

"Georgie, please just let me …"

"Let me go," she repeated. My hand slipped out of hers, and before I could even swallow around the lump in my throat, she'd catapulted herself down the stairs and was gone.

"Well, you screwed that up royally, Dimples."

I sighed, turning to find Lachy crossing the road towards me, Liz hot on his heels.

"I don't need a lecture from either of you right now," I argued.

"Seems like a solid kick up that squeezable backside of yours is what you really need," Liz interjected. "What the hell do you think you're doing?"

"Apparently we're just having fun."

"Which loosely interprets to 'fucking like rabbits, but not talking about your feelings'," Lachy explained.

I scowled at him. "Who asked you, Chippy?"

"As someone who has experience with getting their girl back, maybe I have some wisdom to impart."

I shook my head. "I don't want any wisdom right now. I just want a double shot of something brown and foul-tasting to help me forget that this won't be anything more than … than whatever the hell it is."

Lachy shrugged. "Well, the brown, foul-tasting part I can get on board with."

"Oh, me too!" Liz added with a delighted cackle.

"So, what's brought on this bout of self-sabotage?"

I groaned into my empty tumbler, squinting through the haze of alcohol at two Jordyns, both glaring at me.

"What can I do for you pair?" I asked, guffawing at how funny I was.

"Get him an iced water. And cut him off, for Christ's sake, Freddie. Responsible Service of Alcohol laws are a real thing, you know."

A cold schooner glass was shoved into my hand, and a straw was brought to my lips.

"Drink," Jord muttered. "I don't trust you not to spill it." I complied, the icy water giving me brain freeze. I pulled back with a splutter.

"Why are you such a buzz kill, Jord?" Lachy chuckled beside me. He was nursing a beer, maybe his second? Third? I hadn't really been counting. Calli had appeared on his lap and was glaring at me.

"Yes, Jordyn," Liz grouched. "We've almost got him lubricated enough to get the whole story out of him."

"Nope!" I blurted merrily. "There isn't enough alcohol in the world to get me to tell you bunch of creepers anything about me and Blondie."

"Do you think getting wasted is how you fix this?" Jordyn hissed in my ear. I rolled my eyes, swaying away from them.

"Nope," I repeated, not quite so bloody merrily this time. "There's nothing to fix. She's made that pretty damn clear."

I was jostled as Jord shook me. "You're such a dickhead."

I laughed sloppily. "You sound like my brother. According to him, I've been a dickhead for Georgie since I was thirteen."

"Oooh, hear that, Lach? Thirteen! That's quite some history!" Liz chortled somewhere to my right. I rolled my eyes, immediately regretting it when the room spun.

"Well, clearly your brother's the smart one in the family," Jord muttered, flicking a hand in Freddie's direction. "I'll need a Vodka, rocks, please Fred."

"You think it's easy, to get her to forgive me?" I muttered, taking another long sip of my water. "You think if I was just a little smarter about it, I'd have her in the bag? I fucked up. It was stupid, but what I did … it wasn't worth her disappearing for twelve years. And I … Jesus, bloody … I need to know why! Why it was so easy for her to cut me out of her life."

I slammed a fist against my chest. "If I'd tried to cut her out of me, I would've bled out."

"And he gets melodramatic when he drinks!" Liz commentated.

"He's adorable," Lachy added. "Like, seriously, 'she's such a part of me I'd die without her'. I might have to start taking notes, Calli'd be naked in seconds if I said that to her."

Calli punched him on the arm, but snuggled against his body, whispering something in his ear that had his eyes sliding closed.

"You shut up," I growled, pointing a wavering finger in Lachy's direction. "Don't steal my lines."

"She never cut you out," Jord said quietly. "I've known her for almost three years now. I've never seen her drop the ice queen façade the way she does with you."

"Doesn't mean anything."

"Well, just give up then."

I squinted, bringing Jordyn into focus. Zany blue hair, septum piercing, black nail polish on fingers that drummed impatiently at the bar. A frown furrowing black brows, framing eyes that glared at me with disgust.

"Give up?" I asked, numb.

Jord nodded. "Give up on getting under her skin. Let her do her job here, without you muddying the waters, and we can all walk away from this relatively unscathed."

I snorted. "Too late for that. I'm very, very scathed."

"What do you want out of this scenario?" Jord asked, those eyes boring into me.

Georgie, mine. Late night kisses and midnight orgasms. Waking up next to her every day for the next … forever.

I laughed bitterly. "What I want doesn't matter. But I deserve a chance to explain what happened back then. And I want some goddamned honesty from her about it all. I feel like there's something I'm missing, some piece that would make sense of why she ghosted me back then. And why she's pulling away from me now."

"Jesus, the way you pair are carrying on about this, you'd think you killed her favourite pet or something!" Lachy muttered.

A sharp bark of laughter ripped from my throat.

"That's close to home," I rasped. "Very bloody close."

Lachy sucked in a scandalised breath. "You … you killed her pet?"

I shook my head. "But I didn't do the right thing when they died. I did the complete bloody opposite."

Then: Tonight Is A Big Night

GEORGIE, 18 YEARS OLD

"Elena! Can I use the ironing board?" I called out, tugging the dress I planned on wearing out of my suitcase and tossing it on the bed.

"It's in the hall cupboard, set it up wherever you want!" she called back from downstairs.

"That's a pretty dress," Dom said, and I looked up, finding him leaning against the door frame, arms folded. I grimaced.

"It's the only decent one I packed. I was kinda in a hurry," I explained, flustered, rummaging until I found the one pair of heels I'd brought. I nudged past him, returning with the iron and the board. My hands were shaking.

"Any reason you're so worked up about tonight?" he asked.

I shrugged, focusing on de-creasing my little black dress. "First time out as an adult, I guess."

"First time out with Xander now you're both eighteen, and your mum's stupid no-dating rule no longer applies to you," he pressed.

I scoffed. "Mum's rule stopped applying the second she walked out on Seth."

Mum, worried that I would rat her out to Seth, decided to beat me to it, confessing that she'd cheated. That had started World War

Three. Seth was totally blindsided. Mum accused him of cheating on her first, he vehemently denied it. Mum insisted he was lying. Seth told her he was moving out, that he was sick and tired of her bullshit.

Mum lost it then, said he didn't get to leave her, she was leaving him. Within an hour, she had a bag packed and was waiting out the front, having the gall to get her side piece to come and pick her up.

Apparently in all the drama, she'd forgotten that she had a daughter who was halfway through her HSC.

Half an hour later, I'd stood at the front door, a suitcase packed, Molly on her lead and the keys to the car they'd gifted me for my eighteenth in my hand. Seth was still standing at the window, staring out as if he expected her to come back any minute. He didn't even turn to look at me when Molly and I walked out the door …

Which was why I was living out of a suitcase at Dom's place.

"So, is tonight the night you and Xander finally get together?" Dom asked. I sucked in a shaky breath.

"Something happened," I started, then paused to turn the dress over on the board. "When you were in France."

"You kissed?" He straightened, his eyes intense as he moved into the room, sitting on the bed.

"Mmhmm," I mumbled, fiddling with the dress on the hanger, so grateful to have an excuse to leave the room, to put the ironing board away, just so I could get my expression under control. No way was I telling Dom that the something was much more than just a kiss.

When I returned, Dom's eyes immediately found mine. "So, you kissed, and you haven't seen one another since?"

"That's about it, yeah."

"Tonight *is* a big night, then."

I shrugged, wishing I could feel as nonchalant as I was acting.

It was Xander's eighteenth birthday. The HSC was over, and we were all drinking age.

Tonight, I was going to tell Xander that I was in love with him.

Then: More Alcohol Required

XANDER, 18 YEARS OLD

I'd been old enough to buy alcohol for a matter of hours, and I was making the most of it. I'd needed to be lubricated for the family birthday dinner Dad insisted on having at his favourite yacht club.

Levi was pissed that I refused to sneak him a bourbon and Coke, but there was no way I was tempting fate with Dad tonight. Not with him already furious that I'd applied for veterinary science degrees, and not medicine ones.

By the time I'd gotten through that debacle and had caught a taxi into the bar in North Sydney I'd agreed to meet Dom and Georgie at, I was well and truly ready to let loose.

Draining my beer, I sat back at the table that I'd reserved for us. No big birthday bash for me. The only people I wanted to hang out with tonight were the two I'd invited.

Well, if I was being selfish as fuck, I'd have uninvited Dom, too.

My leg jiggled, and I squeezed my knee to try and stop the nerves that were jittering through me.

Tonight, I was going to tell Georgie that I was in love with her.

And that required more alcohol.

Then: Might Be A Bit Late

GEORGIE, 18 YEARS OLD

"Oh, you look absolutely stunning!" Elena crooned as I walked downstairs, hoping my shaking wasn't too obvious. "Your legs! They go on for miles! Such an Amazon!"

I blushed, waving a dismissive hand at her, feeling the heat of Dom behind me.

"I've just ordered a taxi, should be here in about ten," he said. I nodded, taking out my phone.

> Georgie: Leaving Dom's in 10. We still meeting at Sprints?

> Hot Xander: Yep, I'm here now! See you soon xxx

"Well, have a lovely night, kiddos!" Louis said, wrapping an arm around Elena. "We're heading out now, too. Old person clubbing."

I laughed, stifling a wince at the nervous edge to it. "What does that mean?"

"It's like young person clubbing, but with less doof doof music, and more actual conversation," Louis explained with a laugh as he ushered Elena towards the garage. Moments later the sound of their car purred away.

"I think we should wait out front," I said to Dom, fumbling with my purse and heading for the door.

Dom chuckled as if he knew why I was so antsy, grabbing my hand and planting a quick kiss on my cheek.

"Tonight is going to be great," he whispered against my hair. I smiled, squeezing his hand before letting go to open the door.

Molly scuttled out from nowhere, her claws scratching against the timber floor as she raced towards us, almost bowling me over in my too-high heels, darting around Dom's legs and out the door.

"Molly! Not again!" I moaned as Dom took off after her. But the ratbag was fast, and she was out the open front gate and down the darkening street before he could catch her.

"Why does she keep doing that?" Dom asked, panting in the driveway as I scowled, kicked off my shoes and dropped my clutch, taking my phone and turning on the flashlight, jogging down the path and onto the road after Dom.

"No idea. She likes to hide in bushes and jump out at me. Molly!" I called as Dom fiddled with his phone.

"I'm cancelling the taxi. We'll be able to get another one easy."

"Hopefully," I muttered, scanning the road and calling out again. No bushes rustled. I flicked off a text to Xander.

Georgie: Molly just escaped. Might be a bit late

Then: Stood Up?

XANDER, 18 YEARS OLD

I hated the taste of bourbon, but with Coke it was bearable. I tried not to check my phone. There hadn't been another message since she told me they were running late.

That had been almost an hour ago. And two glasses of bourbon and Coke.

"Happy birthday," a female voice purred. My heart slammed against my chest, and I jumped to my feet.

But it wasn't a leggy blonde looking back at me. It was a petite brunette with enormous knockers and a dirty smirk. My shoulders slumped.

"Rhiannon, what the hell are you doing here?" I asked, falling back onto the lounge and picking up my drink.

"A little birdy told me you were having birthday drinks here tonight. Thought I'd crash the party." She looked around, her lips curling. "Not much of a party though, is it?"

I took a too-big gulp of my drink. "My friends are running late. Pet emergency," I muttered. "Really thought they'd have been here by now, though."

"Maybe they stood you up?" she suggested, sliding onto the

lounge next to me. "I mean, it's almost nine, there's only a few hours left of your birthday. Doesn't seem very friendly to me."

I grunted, but I kind of agreed. No way I'd admit it, but knowing that Georgie had moved in with Dom two weeks ago when everything went to shit at her place filled me with possessiveness.

She was my girl. Not his. And while rational me knew she saw his mum and dad like a second set of parents, so the move made sense, three-beers-and-two-bourbons me felt suspicious … and jealous as hell.

"Well, at least I'm here to buy you a birthday drink," she said, standing up and strutting over to the bar. Her dress was tiny and tight, her arse round.

I looked for just a moment too long, before blinking and turning away.

Then: I'm Just So Sorry ...

GEORGIE, 18 YEARS OLD

The screech of tyres and Dom's panicked shout made me drop my phone. And then I was running.

"No!" I screamed, my knees giving way, scraping on the asphalt. Molly tried to stand. Her legs wouldn't work.

The car, the bloody arsehole in the car, sped off. Dom tried to chase them, but the car was around the corner, and there was no point anyway.

"Molly!" I cried as she struggled again and fell to the side, panting. I frantically looked around but couldn't see my phone.

"Call someone!" I screamed. "Dom, please!"

"Who? Is there an emergency vet?"

"I don't know! Google it!" I shrieked, trying to put my arms around my dog. Her panting was so fast. I stroked her face. My hand came away sticky and wet.

"Oh, God, she's bleeding!" I moaned.

"Okay, I'm going to run home, get some towels. I'll call a vet on the way. Then I'll drive your car back here and get you both."

"My phone! I don't have it!" I said, panicked.

Dom disappeared for a moment, returning with it. I tucked it into my bra, stroking my panting dog with shaking hands.

"I'm going now, okay, Georgie?" he said. I nodded. I couldn't speak. My throat was filled with rocks.

And then it was just Molly and me. Her breathing was too rapid. I turned the flashlight on the phone again and gasped, turning it off again immediately.

There was blood everywhere.

"It's okay, Molly," I whispered, putting my arms around her as gently as I could. "We'll get you fixed."

She felt cold. Too cold for such a warm night. My arms shook. My eyes burned. My throat ached.

"I love you," I said. "I love you. I'm here."

And when the panting stopped, her body going still, the burning behind my eyes turned into a river of tears.

Dom returned, and through the haze of grief, we wrapped her body in the towels he'd brought. We placed her in the boot of my car. Dom helped me into the passenger seat to drive the five minutes back to his house.

"We'll need to let Xander know we can't make it," he said softly.

I pulled my phone from my bra, but when I tried to text, my hands shook, my fingers slipping over the screen.

I squeezed my eyes shut and then navigated to the phone app, hitting his name in my favourites. It rang three times, then went to voicemail. I pressed my lips together, my eyes overflowing again when I heard his voice asking me to leave a message.

"Xander … I'm so sorry. Molly was hit by a car … she just died in my arms. I … we won't make it out tonight. I'm so sorry … I wish … I'm just so sorry."

Then: Without You

XANDER, 18 YEARS OLD

The noise in the bar was deafening. I tipped back another glass of whatever Rhiannon was buying. The looser my body felt from the alcohol, the angrier my brain got.

Where were they? Molly escaped all the bloody time—it took them about five minutes to get her back.

The more I thought about it, the more it felt like an excuse. But I refused to text her, to find out what was going on. I didn't want to be the one chasing them … chasing her.

I was starting to feel like a bloody idiot.

"Lucky I'm here, isn't it?" Rhiannon said, curling up against my side. "You'd be so bored and lonely without me."

I grunted. But she was right.

"Listen," she said, tugging on my arm. "Why don't you send them a pic, show them what they're missing out on. I mean, this bar is absolutely banging, the drinks are amazing, and you … you look fucking hot."

I smirked at her. "Fucking hot, huh?"

She leaned closer, and I could smell the sickly-sweet cocktail on her breath. "Hot enough to fuck, that is."

Something in the back of my mind started buzzing a warning,

but I ignored it. I wasn't going to fuck Rhiannon. I had no desire to, even if her arse was pretty much hanging out of her dress.

But I could maybe make Georgie wish she was here already.

I tugged Rhiannon into my lap, snatching my phone up from where I'd put it face down on the table to stop me checking the time so often. There was a voicemail notification on the screen.

Weird. Probably my dad checking in on me. No one except my parents ever called me. I ignored it, tapping the camera icon.

"Smile for my friends who are missing all the fun!" I said, holding it out and fumbling it into selfie mode. Rhiannon shifted in my lap until she was straddling me, and … yep … her arse was poking out the bottom of her dress as she stuck her tongue out at the camera. On a whim, I reached around her hip, gripping a fistful of her round butt.

Just as I clicked, she licked right up the side of my face, from chin to eyebrow. The shock of it made me drop my phone.

Then she grabbed my chin, and her tongue was in my mouth.

For a handful of stupid seconds, I let her kiss me, let my tongue play with hers. Research, I told myself fuzzily. I hadn't kissed anyone but Georgie, had nothing to compare it to.

The thought of her name was like ice water dousing me. I shuddered, pushing Rhiannon off me.

"No," I muttered. "Get off me!"

With a pout, she slid off my lap. "That's a shame. I could do so much more to you with my tongue."

I turned away from her, my anger at being abandoned by Georgie warring with a sick, churning sensation clawing at my gut.

I tapped through to my messages app. Nothing new from Georgie. Just the last one she'd sent about Molly getting out.

I added the selfie to a new message, squinting at it for long moments. Something in the back of my brain was screaming at me to stop, but the thought of her and Dom blowing me off to hang out without me had me typing with shaky fingers and pressing send.

> Xander: Having so much fucking fun without you.

Now: I Won't Let You Down

XANDER

"Merry Christmas Eve to me," I muttered, sipping at my depressingly non-alcoholic drink and watching the sun sink over the plains.

I was never drinking whiskey again. Thank God Christmas Eve fell on a Sunday. Sundays meant no clinic, and no filming. Just me, wallowing in my hungover misery. It had only been an hour or so since I'd felt like myself again.

What was worse, I couldn't even remember much of the previous evening after Jord arrived. I remembered being lectured about Georgie by Jord and Liz and Lachy ... I vaguely recalled Calli berating me that she'd had to cancel four afternoon appointments because I'd taken myself to the pub instead of coming back to work.

Things got ... hazy after that. And my stupid eighteen-year-old-boy mistake had been at the front of my drunken mind.

I'd spent the morning in bed, the afternoon aimlessly wandering the yard, Molly and Jumbo trying to trip me over.

I'd been hoping she'd come out. I needed to talk. I didn't need her to respond. Just listen.

But apart from Miriam heading in and out a couple of times,

there had been no movement. The curtains in her bedroom were drawn.

The sun dipped below the horizon, bathing the grass in the silver of twilight. I called out for Molly, who'd been racing laps around the homestead with Jumbo last time I saw her.

The evening was still. No panting, galloping dog. No clumsy, weird little sheep.

"Jumbo!"

I stepped off the porch, heading towards Georgie's voice.

"Molly!" I called again. Nothing. I rounded the corner of the homestead, colliding with Georgie.

"Oh!" she grunted, stumbling back a step. Instinctively I reached out and grabbed her elbow to steady her. Her fingers came up to grasp my wrist.

"Are you looking for Molly?" she asked, her eyes wary, worried.

I nodded. "She was playing with Jumbo last time I saw them."

Her fingers tightened on me. "Maybe they've gone into the paddocks. The gate's been open all day."

"Well, let's go check," I said, turning towards the gate. Her hand stayed on my arm, gripping me tight.

"What if something's happened to them? What if one of them is hurt?" she asked, and the breathless, broken sound of her voice echoed across the years, hitting me deep in my chest.

I hadn't been there for her last time. But I sure as hell could be now.

"Let's not get ahead of ourselves, okay?"

"Jumbo!" Georgie cried, her voice shrill with panic, her nails digging into my wrist. I extricated myself from her grip, wrapping my arm around her shoulders instead, giving her a reassuring squeeze.

"Molly!" I called, peering into the dark. I pulled my phone out, turning on the torch.

"Oh, God," Georgie muttered shakily, tugging her own out and doing the same. "Jumbo!"

We neared the fence into the next paddock when I heard barking. "That's Molly," I said, and we both raced towards the sound, flashlights cutting a jagged path of light across the dusty grass.

Molly stood on the other side of the fence, her eyes glowing eerily in the torchlight. Her barking became more frantic when she saw us.

"Where's Jumbo?" Georgie asked. I reached the fence, swinging my torch left and right as Molly barked and barked.

There, in some scraggly, overgrown grass around a fencepost, a flash of off-white wool. A feeble bleat punctured the night.

"He's here!" I called, crouching down, tugging some of the grass away. Jumbo's bleating intensified, and he struggled.

"What's … oh God!" Georgie breathed, dropping to her knees beside me just as I realised what was wrong.

"He's tangled in some barbed wire," I told her, using the calm voice I'd perfected over years as a vet, as Georgie hyperventilated beside me. "It looks like it's wrapped around his hind leg." I held him as still as I could, stroking his side gently to calm him.

"Get him out!" she cried, reaching towards him. I grabbed her hands and turned her to me.

"Georgie, listen to me. It's buried in his skin. I'd risk injuring him further if I try to detangle it down here in the dark."

"Don't you dare leave him here to die!" Georgie rasped. I squeezed her hands again.

"That's not what we're going to do. I'll stay here and keep him calm. You need to run back, bring the Ute down—my vet kit is in the back seat. Get towels, and a pair of wire cutters."

"I can't … he can't …" Georgie gasped. Instinctively I leaned forwards and kissed her forehead.

"I'll help him. I promise. I won't let you down."

Georgie's eyes searched mine, and finally, she shakily nodded, getting to her feet and sprinting back towards the gate. I put one warm hand back on Jumbo.

"It's okay, you funny little sheep," I mumbled. "I'm going to fix this."

Now: Merry Christmas, Georgie

GEORGIE

Déjà vu. This was all too horrible. Seeing my pet, lying there, bleeding. Scared.

It's not the same, I told myself. *You have a vet right here with you. And it's just his leg. He hasn't been run over by a car.*

I sob-coughed as I reached the Ute, flinging myself into the driver's seat, throwing the towels and wire cutters I'd grabbed from the shed onto the passenger seat. The keys were already sitting in it, so I started it, gunning it towards the paddock gate.

He's going to be fine. He's going to be fine.

Xander's face came into view in the headlights. He looked so calm, so in control. The way he had with every patient I'd watched him with over the last few weeks. Just knowing he was here with me sent cooling waves washing through the heat of my panic.

He could fix this.

Oh God, I hoped he could fix this.

With the towels and cutters in my hands, I leapt out of the truck. Xander reached out, taking the cutters from me.

"I'm going to cut the wire away from the fence. Then we'll wrap him up and take him to the clinic. I can sedate and untangle him, and treat the wounds there."

I nodded, feeling useless as I held the towels, watching Xander get to work. Worry jangled in the back of my mind, but in my chest, a warm feeling of trust bloomed.

Xander would fix this, because he was capable, and smart. And he cared.

He cared about animals. He cared about Jumbo.

He cared about me.

That feeling continued to grow as we travelled into town, me sitting in the back seat, Molly on one side of me, Jumbo wrapped in towels and bleating pitifully on the other. Every bleat reminded me that he was alive, that he was getting help.

Inside the clinic, Xander strode through, switching on lights as we made our way into the surgery out the back. I followed, cradling my tiny sheep.

"Well, I did ask Santa to bring me a big, strapping veterinarian," Liz said sleepily from the doorway that separated her living space from the clinic. "But I didn't …"

Her eyes widened when she saw me carrying Jumbo.

"What happened?" she asked, her expression suddenly sharp.

"A bit of a run-in with some barbed wire," Xander explained.

Liz nodded. "Well, we'd better give you space to work your magic. Molly can sleep with Empress and Kingston. And Georgie girl, you can come with me for a cup of tea."

I started to shake my head as I placed the bundle containing Jumbo down on the operating table. "I'd rather—"

Xander's big, warm hand reached for me, his pinkie hooking around mine. I met his earnest gaze.

"He'll be safe with me, I promise," he said softly. "Go and rest. I'll find you when I'm done in here."

I nodded, and he leaned close again, his lips brushing my forehead. And I let Liz draw me through the door and into her home.

"Georgie."

I sat up with a grunt, looking around. I was lying on a sofa,

Xander's big, hazel eyes gazing down at me. For a second, I was completely disoriented, but then I remembered where I was. And why.

"How's Jumbo?" I asked, sitting bolt upright, swinging my legs to the floor. Xander pressed a hand to my shoulder, holding me there, taking the seat beside me.

"The wire was deep," Xander explained gently. Too gently. My heart kicked against my ribs as his hand reached for mine, our pinkies entwining through muscle memory more than anything else.

"It had embedded itself in the bone. I could have removed it, cleaned the area thoroughly, given him antibiotics, and hoped an infection didn't develop."

"But," I whispered, closing my eyes against the sting there. Waiting for the blow I was sure he was about to deal me.

"But it was a messy wound. I was worried that nothing I could do would prevent infection. I'm so sorry Georgie, I wasn't able to save his leg."

"Oh God," I moaned, my free hand coming up to cover my mouth. "He's …" I stopped, turning to look Xander right in the eyes.

"His leg?" I asked, my hands trembling. Xander nodded, stroking the back of my hand with warm, strong, capable fingers.

"I had to amputate. It was the best way to ensure we completely prevented infection. And I think he'll cope just fine with three legs. He's sleeping off the anaesthetic now." He sighed, wiping his free hand over his face, and I realised how truly exhausted he looked. "I've never done a surgery entirely on my own before. It was … intense."

"What time is it?" I asked, glancing towards the curtained window.

"It's three. Merry Christmas, Georgie."

I threw myself into his arms.

Now: I Let You Assume

XANDER

My back thumped against the lounge, and I let out an "oof!" as Georgie launched herself at me. My arms came up around her, clutching her to me. She nuzzled her face into the side of my neck.

"Thank you," she breathed, her mouth warm and soft as her lips moved against my skin. I wrapped my arms tighter around her. "Thank you," she repeated.

"Anytime," I rasped, my throat suddenly thick. My eyes stung, but probably just from exhaustion. Not from the way she felt in my arms like this. Not from the little voice in the back of my head telling me that for her, this was just relief and gratitude.

"Can I see him?" she asked, and I nodded against the top of her head, sitting up with her cradled in my arms, not wanting to let her go. But knowing I had to.

I took her through to the clinic, gesturing towards the holding cage with its blanket and the tiny, three-legged miniature sheep in the middle of it. Georgie approached, her fingers weaving between the bars to gently stroke his fleece.

"They brought him in to have him euthanised … the family that owned him before me," she murmured, her forehead pressing

369

against the bars. "They'd bought him on a whim for their daughter, but then they had to move to the city, and they couldn't keep him. They couldn't even be bothered trying to find another home. They just dumped him on Liz's husband, said 'get rid of him,' and left town."

I stepped closer, pressing my palm against the flat of her back, stroking up and down the ridges of her spine.

"Well, it was lucky you were around to love him, then, wasn't it?" I said roughly, stifling a yawn. Amputation after midnight without any assistance. This was the life of a rural vet. Always on the clock, mostly on your own. It would be so bloody lonely.

But the warmth of Georgie's back seeped through my hand, and for just a moment, my exhaustion-addled brain conjured up a fantasy where this was *our* life. This little town, with its colourful bunch of weirdos. Her, in the office, using her incredible organisational skills to run the back end of the clinic while I ran the front.

Pub dinners with Mim and Liz … and Chippy and Calli, too, I supposed. Nights twined around each other, staring up at stars that just weren't visible in the city.

I shook myself. I was overtired, and delusional.

"The spare room is just through here," Liz said behind us. "You both need some sleep. I remember what it was like for my Frank when he had a patient late at night."

She stumped away, her floral nightie swaying.

"You take the bed. I'll stay on the lounge," Georgie murmured, still stroking Jumbo. I shook my head, my forehead rubbing against her hair. Without a word, I drew her back through the surgery, through the door separating the clinic from Liz's house, and down the hallway to the spare bedroom.

"We can share."

Georgie paused for a moment in the doorway, but exhaustion swayed her, and she nodded, stripping out of her shorts and climbing onto the bed in her tank top and underpants.

"You know," I chuckled, tugging off my running shorts and t-shirt and sliding onto the bed in my boxer briefs. "The first time I saw you asleep in your underwear, you were wearing Slytherin green. And I thought how that was absolutely your Hogwarts house, while at the same time laughing like the thirteen-year-old I was at the word Slytherin—Slither In—written on your undies."

Georgie's laughter shook the bed. But it didn't take long for that laughter to turn to quiet sobs.

I rolled towards her, pressing her back up against my front and wrapping a tentative arm around her waist. "This okay?" I asked gently. She sniffed, tucking her body closer to mine.

"It's very okay," she murmured.

She fell asleep with me stroking the tears from her cheeks. And I drifted off not long after.

Early morning sun was peeking through the blinds when I woke. Georgie had rolled over in her sleep, her nose tucked against my chest, our bodies fitting together like two puzzle pieces.

I swallowed down the misery. *This isn't real*, I told myself, even as I brushed her hair off her face. She stirred, and I moved back, putting a bit of space between our bodies.

"Hey," she mumbled groggily, rubbing at her eyes. My heart lurched.

"I want this," I blurted. She blinked at me, sleepiness and confusion wrinkling her adorable little nose. I pressed a kiss to her there. "I want you, waking up in my arms. I want to be the one who holds you when you cry. The one who you snuggle up to at night."

"Xander—"

"I want to be the one who you come to when you need help, or when you have important news, or when you're angry and need to vent. I want you to argue with *me*, be mad at *me* … and then make up with me." I ran my hands down her back, grazing the top of her arse before sliding them back up to her shoulders.

She stared, wide-eyed, at me, all traces of sleep gone from her face. Her mouth was tight, a small frown pulling the corners down.

"I know you don't want to talk about what happened back then … and I can respect that. But I need to know—can you move past it? I want to be with you, Georgie, but we either open up about the past … or we agree to *leave it* in the past."

I cleared my throat, shocked at how much had just come out of my mouth. "That … I mean … shit. I didn't mean to say all of that. I just … I do want you—this. All of it. But if you're not …"

Her lips crashed into mine, her leg hooking over my hip. I gasped against her mouth, and her tongue darted in, flicking against mine and ripping a groan from my chest.

"I can't give you forever," she murmured against my mouth, her hands sliding on my bare chest, making me shiver, her words not quite sinking in. "But for now … I want this too."

"Uungh," I grunted as she nipped at my jaw, running her teeth over my stubble. "I can be down with that … for now."

"Good," she mumbled into my ear as I kissed along her cheek-bone, my hands sliding under her tank, stroking her taut belly. She shuddered against me. "Because I … I need you so badly."

"I need you, too," I grated, knowing that in my brain, the words 'need' and 'love' were interchangeable. For me at least.

There would be time to convince her. If she was willing to give me now, that could become more. But one thing needed to be said first.

"I just need you to know that it was just a kiss—with Rhiannon that night. I took that stupid photo, she kissed me, and I—"

Georgie gripped my head, pressing her tongue into my mouth, silencing me. When she pulled back, she mumbled, "The past stays in the past."

Before I could fully register what she was saying, her hand tucked under the waistband of my boxer briefs, wrapping around my cock and stroking. I stilled.

"Are we really doing this here? In Liz's spare bedroom?" I grated.

Georgie's breathy laugh fanned over my collarbone. "It's not as if she doesn't know what we've been up to anyway. She knows everything that goes on in Budgerigar."

"Can you be quiet?" I asked against the shell of her ear.

"Can you?" she countered. I dragged her tank off over her head, kissing down her neck.

"I can do anything for you," I said against her breast, running my lips towards her nipple, rolling us until she was under me.

"Then so can I," she whispered, her fingers tangling in my hair, her legs parting further, allowing me into the cradle of them. I rocked my hips once, grazing her core with my erection.

"Please," she begged breathlessly, and I lifted my hips, chuckling at her moan of protest as I tugged off her underwear, then mine, tossing them to the floor.

I paused. "I don't have a condom," I muttered with a silent curse. Georgie's hands gripped my hair harder, a huff falling from her lips.

"I don't care," she said, bringing her mouth to mine. "I want you bare."

With a groan, I kissed her. And it didn't feel angry, or lustful … it didn't feel dirty, or erotic, or forbidden.

It felt perfect. Like home.

Her lips moved against mine, our tongues danced, and her hands moved on my body, grazing down my back, gripping my butt. She wrapped her legs around me and rocked her wetness against my straining cock.

"You're mine," I murmured against the damp skin of her shoulder, reaching between us to stroke her.

"Yours … for now," she mumbled into my hair.

I growled into the crook of her neck, slipping the head of my cock against her entrance. "Let me convince you it can be more than that."

"Please," she begged again, her nails clawing into the muscles of my back. My heart leapt as I lined myself up and slid inside. Her lips parted in pleasure, and I licked into her mouth, cupping the back of her neck as I moved, slowly, inside of her, pressing deeper with each rock of my hips.

"I'll do bloody anything to convince you, Blondie," I promised, our foreheads pressed together as I moved in her, as she tilted her hips to take me deeper. She said nothing, but I tried not to read too much into it—we'd just agreed to be quiet, after all.

I stroked inside her, reaching between us to circle my thumb around her clit. She moaned softly against my shoulder, her heels pressing into my butt, forcing me deep.

"You were made for me," I rasped against her mouth. "Everything about you is perfect."

We found our rhythm, me thrusting, her rocking, my thumb circling, pressing against her swollen clit. She panted, sweat clung to us, and our bodies moved together in a way they never had in our other encounters. In a way that felt like making love.

Georgie made a little sobbing sound, her body tensing, pulsing as she came around me. And it felt so good, so right, skin against skin, everything amplified by the lack of a condom. My movements sped, became erratic. I lifted her legs until they rested on my shoulders, pushing deeper and deeper into her.

"More," she muttered, her words muffled as she pressed her lips to my forearm.

So I gave her more. I snapped my hips faster, harder, watching as she squeezed her eyes shut, her nose wrinkling as her body started to tense again. Just as my own orgasm rocketed down my spine, pooling in my balls, I watched a single tear slip from the corner of her closed eyes. Too late for me to stop myself. I shuddered inside her, spilling even as I reached up to thumb away that tear.

"You okay?" I asked gently, lowering my body onto hers, wrapping her up in my arms.

"Just … happy," she mumbled into my hair. I let her tell that lie, ignoring the way my stomach flipped with apprehension. I brushed a soft kiss against her mouth, stroking my thumbs over her cheeks.

"Do you think we can make a run for the clinic bathroom?" I asked.

Georgie chuckled. "Liz is probably right outside the door, ready to ambush us."

I smiled against her face. "Let her. I'm game if you are." I pulled out of her with a sigh, glancing down between our bodies at the slick slide of my semi-hard dick.

"Hey," I muttered, squinting, touching two fingers to myself and bringing the wetness up to look. "Are you due for your period?"

Georgie sat up so fast our heads cracked together. I flinched backwards, rubbing at my forehead, watching her do the same.

"No, it finished a couple of days ago, why … oh, God." Georgie looked down in horror at the red smears on me and on her thighs, the colour draining from her face. She leapt out of bed, grabbing her underwear and shorts and trying to dress with hands that shook. I stood, holding her still.

"Hey, is everything okay? What can I do?" I asked, running my palms up and down her arms. She shook her head, shrugging out of my grip and tugging her clothes on as she hopped towards the door.

Confused and worried, I grabbed my own clothes, dressing hurriedly.

"I have to go. I have to … I just have to go," she muttered, opening the door and storming out. Liz materialised out of nowhere, her knowing smirk quickly morphing into concern.

"What happened?" she asked, reaching for Georgie.

"I have to get back to Sydney."

Liz nodded as if she understood completely.

"Why?" I asked, following her into the clinic. Jumbo looked up, bleating plaintively. Georgie ignored him, which was more terrifying than anything else she'd done in the last couple of minutes. Shit. His fluid IV was empty, he was due for another dose of IV antibiotics, and I needed to check on his surgery site. But I needed to help Georgie more.

"Liz, can you give him some water, please?" I asked, not stopping as Georgie raced through reception and out the front door.

"Of course," Liz said, her voice subdued. More alarm bells. "I'll give Alex a call, she can talk me through what needs to be done. You take care of our girl."

"I plan to," I breathed, and then I was out the door.

Georgie was racing down the street, past my car.

"Are you going to walk back to Sydney?" I called out. Her footsteps faltered, but she didn't stop.

"I'll walk to Mim's and borrow her car," she called back to me, her voice strained.

"Let me drive you to Sydney!" I said. "I told you, there's nothing I won't do to convince you to give this a proper chance."

"No." She turned to face me, skin bleached ghostly white. "You can't drive me to Sydney. But you can drive me back to Mim's. Please."

I swallowed, feeling like a rock was sitting in the pit of my stomach. "Okay, just get in the car."

She walked past me silently, climbing into the passenger seat.

"Are you going to tell me why you need to get to Sydney so badly?" I asked. My sweaty hands slipped on the steering wheel. "I'm worried about you, Blondie!"

Georgie choked on a bitter laugh. "I don't think …"

"Do you not trust me?" I pressed, the heavy feeling in my stomach growing. "Is it something bad? I mean, you were bleeding, and then you freaked out."

"Please, don't," was all she would say to me. "Don't ask me again."

I sighed, but it came out as more of a growl, frustration growing in me.

"Every time I think I'm getting closer to you, you pull away. Every time I show you I want to be here for you, you shut down!" I grated, turning into Mim's driveway. "Tell me what I can do to make you understand that *I'm here*!"

Silence. And as soon as I pulled up beside my tiny home, she was out of the car, racing across the lawn. I followed, knowing it was a terrible idea, but not being able to help myself.

Mim looked up as we burst into the kitchen, but didn't seem shocked at all to see the state Georgie was in. Liz must have called her. What did they all know that I was in the dark about?

"I'm bleeding," Georgie said simply to her grandmother. Something sickening flickered in Miriam's eyes, but she nodded.

"You can take the Ute."

"Don't do this!" I begged, following Georgie down the hallway.

"Don't do what?" she asked, voice stark, not looking at me as she turned into her bedroom, rummaging through drawers for clothes, underwear, a sanitary pad.

"Don't do this again!" I insisted, panic filling my chest, making breathing difficult. "You can't … last time you disappeared without an explanation I didn't see you for twelve fucking years! I can't lose you again."

She tried to push past me out the door, her bundle of clothes in her hands, but I blocked the doorway.

"It's not the same," she muttered. "Please, let me go, I need to go."

"It feels the same to me!" I insisted, reaching for her, wanting to pull her against me, hold her, reassure myself that I wasn't going to lose her again. She stepped back, out of my reach.

"You're pulling away, you're keeping something from me. Just fucking *talk* to me! Tell me what's wrong! I want to help you!"

Georgie's expression was so devastated that I felt my own face crumpling, eyes burning, throat aching.

"Let her out," Mim grated behind me. I flinched, but I didn't move.

"I just want to know what's wrong!" I insisted.

Mim huffed. "You don't get to come in here demanding answers from her! Not after you knocked her up and then broke her heart all those years ago!"

"Mim!" Georgie gasped. I looked up at her horrified expression, then spun to find Mim glaring at me in the hallway, hands on hips.

I shook my head, perplexed. "What are you … knocked her up? But we never …" I turned back to Georgie, who was frozen to the spot, eyes wide, lips pressed so tightly together, wringing the bundle of clothes in her hands with white knuckles.

"Back then, we didn't …" I sucked in a deep breath, my nerves jangling, shivers racing over my arms. I turned back to Mim. "I never slept with Georgie back then." Some awful inkling filtered into the back of my mind, clawing at me.

Mim stared intently, her eyes judging. Then they slid shut, and when they opened, she was staring past me, at Georgie.

"You said it was him."

"I didn't." Georgie's voice was barely more than a whisper. "I just let you assume it was."

Mim sighed. "But why? I didn't know Xander from a bar of soap. I wouldn't have cared *who* it was or *how* it happened! You know I just wanted to help you!"

"What happened?" I asked, but I had an awful feeling I knew. And it was probably all my fault. "Who got you pregnant?"

She tried to push past me, but I gripped her shoulders. "What happened, Georgie?"

She blinked, two tears rolling down her face. "After you sent me that photo, I slept with Dom."

Then: Help Me Forget

GEORGIE, 18 YEARS OLD

I scrubbed and scrubbed at my skin, letting the scalding water cascade over my body. But I still felt like it was on me. Molly's blood.

Only when my skin started to sting did I turn the shower icy cold, hoping it could numb me. It didn't work.

Eventually I gave up, stepping out, staring at the stark face in the mirror, my hair wet and lank and nothing like the loose curls I'd styled it in for my night out. The big night where I was supposed to tell Xander I loved him.

I shook, a fresh wave of silent sobs wracking me. Could anything else shitty happen to me this year? Finding out my mum was cheating on Seth, them breaking up, and in the process, essentially abandoning me.

Molly …

And now Xander, being left high and dry on his birthday through no fault of his own.

I loved him. And I needed him. And it wasn't fair to want him to be here comforting me when he should be enjoying what was left of his birthday.

Tugging on a t-shirt over my underpants, I crept across the

hallway to Dom's room. The door was open, and I slipped inside, sitting down on the bed beside him.

"Sorry the night was ruined," I mumbled, my voice hoarse from the screaming, the crying.

Dom wound an arm around my shoulders. "Don't you dare apologise for what happened tonight. I'm sorry. I should have been watching closer when I opened the door."

I shook, biting my lip hard because I was sick to death of crying.

"What are you going to do … with Molly?" he asked quietly. We'd wrapped her in towels and put her in the garage. I didn't want to think about what we had to do next. But I needed to.

"Do you think your parents will let me bury her in the backyard here? This place has been more like a home to me than anywhere else. I'd like to think of her here."

Dom was silent for a moment. "I think they'll be fine with it. We can do it tomorrow."

I nodded, reaching for my phone, needing a distraction. Maybe Xander had texted.

There was a message from him. I clicked through.

The phone fell from my hands. Dom leaned down to pick it up as I hyperventilated. Giving me a strange look, he turned it over, saw what was on the screen.

"What the fuck?" Dom muttered. I sucked in a breath and ran for the spare bedroom. I climbed onto the bed, grabbing a pillow and hugging it tight. As if that might stop my insides from exploding all over the place the way it felt like they might.

Dom followed, standing in the doorway.

"Why would he …?" I whispered, my eyes aching.

Dom sighed, crossing the room and climbing onto the bed with me, wrapping an arm around my shoulders.

"I don't know. I thought he loved you." There was a tightness to Dom's voice that made my stomach bottom out. I shook my head wildly.

"What a way to show it!" I couldn't get enough breath into my lungs. "Did you know she was going out with him tonight?" I peered up at Dom through blurry, tear-filled eyes. He shook his head, face bleak.

"Has he been seeing her?"

"Georgie … of course not!"

But I didn't believe him. After the things she'd said two years ago, how could he even want to be in the same room as her … but there he was, with her all over him. And his hand was on her butt. And he was having a 'fucking great time' without me.

"While you were in France, we … fooled around. More than kissing … not everything, but … I thought he enjoyed it!" I stopped, sucking in air that felt too thin. "I thought that he wanted … with me …"

"He's obviously drunk."

I laughed in mirthless hysteria. "And that makes it okay? He's probably fucking her in the bathroom of the club as we speak!"

"I'm going to text him." Dom pulled out his phone, but I snatched it and shoved it under my pillow.

"Don't." I wiped at my streaming eyes, but it made no difference. "I don't want to know anything more about it. I … she told me this would happen."

I leapt from the bed, full of anxious energy, pacing the room. Dom watched me with heartbreaking sympathy, which only made everything a thousand times worse.

"She said that all she had to do was wait for him to get bored of me." I fell back onto the bed, burying my face in my pillow. "It didn't even take much for that to happen. Apparently fingering me once was enough for him—" I broke off into wretched, wracking sobs.

"Georgie, I'm so sorry." Dom's warm body was beside me, his arms coming around my waist, pulling me against him. I couldn't stop shaking. "I'm sorry that he's done this to you. I'm sorry for everything that's happened tonight."

He turned me until my face was pressed against his chest and rubbed soothing hands up and down my back. He was warm, and he smelled familiar, like earthy aftershave and the fabric softener Elena used.

"I'm so sorry, Georgie," he murmured, his lips in my hair, his fingers tickling my shoulder as they moved in little circles. "I wish I could make it better … all of this."

More tears built behind my eyes, but I blinked them away. I didn't want to cry. I didn't want to think. Dom brushed my hair away from my forehead, pressing a light kiss there. The way he always had when I was sad.

Something snapped inside my addled, heartbroken mind.

I tilted my head, gripping his neck, pulling his mouth to mine.

He froze. "What are you …"

I licked the crease of his mouth, frantic to do something … anything … that would distract me. He smelled familiar, comforting. And nothing like Xander.

"I'm kissing you," I mumbled into his mouth, sucking on his bottom lip. A strangled groan erupted from him.

"This isn't—" he began, but I silenced him, running my hand down to cup him between his legs. He sucked in a breath, and his head fell back. I nuzzled into his neck, kissing and licking.

"Please …" I begged, stroking him through his shorts. "I just need you to help me forget." I grabbed his hand, pulling it up to press it against my breast. Dom made a strangled sound, his fingers trembling against my nipple. Under the determined stroking of my hand, he was getting hard.

"Georgie," he hissed as I grabbed the bottom of my t-shirt and tore it off over my head, suddenly frantic, needing to block out everything else. To wipe the image of her all over him from my soul.

"Help me forget," I pleaded, lying down on my bed, wearing nothing but my underpants, and dragging Dom on top of me.

"Georgie … you know I'll do anything to help you. But this is a mistake," he muttered, but he was hard against my thigh.

I shut him up with my tongue in his mouth, my hand slipping into his underwear, pulling him out and stroking him.

"Oh, God," he grunted. And then he was kissing me back, hard and fast, and his hand was between my legs, and my underpants disappeared, and it was frantic, and desperate, and my nails were clawing at his back as he pushed himself inside me.

And the pain of it was exactly what I needed to make me forget
…

<hr>

Afterwards, he sat up, his head in his hands as I padded across the hallway to wash away the evidence of what we'd done, the evidence that was trickling out between my legs.

What had I done? What had *we* done?

I dried off for the second time that night, feeling no better than I had before. When I returned to Dom, he hadn't moved.

"We can never tell Xander about this," he muttered into his hands. Cold spread through my body. Xander, with Rhiannon all over him. Xander, who had sent a photo of it to me, like the worst possible break-up text known to man. Xander, who I thought cared about me. Xander, who I thought had maybe loved me. Xander, who had betrayed me.

But I'd just betrayed him, right back.

"He won't even care," I mumbled. "He's got her now."

"I wish you hadn't … we shouldn't have—" Dom cut himself off with a heavy sigh. "I'm going to take a shower. I'll see you in the morning."

I nodded as he brushed past me, not looking me in the eyes. Shit. With one stupid, reckless choice, I'd screwed up my oldest friendship. And it hadn't even worked. I hadn't forgotten anything. My heart was still broken over Xander. And now it was smothered with the awful ache of guilt on top of it all.

I fell onto the bed, suddenly wishing I had more tears to cry. But my eyes were dry. I was sore between my legs, but my heart felt numb.

How would I face Dom in the morning, after what I'd just made him do? And Xander when … or if … he wanted to try to explain himself. What if it had just been a drunken mistake? I felt sick, imagining him trying to apologise for a drunken night with Rhiannon, while I stood there, knowing deep down that I'd done something a thousand times worse. I'd tried to forget his betrayal by sleeping with my best friend—with *his* best friend.

I couldn't face it. Couldn't face either of them.

I suddenly felt claustrophobic in this large, airy guest bedroom in a house that had been just as much a home to me as the one I'd lived in.

Before I could think about it too much, I stood, dragging my suitcase out of the cupboard, packing it for the second time in as many weeks.

While the shower was still running in the bathroom, I crept downstairs and loaded my suitcase into the back seat of my hatchback. In the garage, I gingerly collected the cold bundle of towels that was poor Molly, placing her gently in the boot.

I reversed out of the driveway, driving several blocks away before pulling over. With shaking hands, I opened my phone. I had to tell someone where I was going. I didn't want anyone to worry. But I couldn't tell either of the boys I normally shared everything with.

Elena. It had to be Elena. She'd been like a second mother to me most of my life. I could trust her to respect my wishes.

I typed out a message that was probably far too long and rambling, that I was going to stay with family, promising that I would let her know when I arrived safe, that things were difficult between me and Xander and Dom, and I needed to have space, that I didn't want them trying to contact me.

I pressed send and dropped my head to the steering wheel, taking a few deep, shuddering breaths. When I felt calm enough, I grabbed my phone again and blocked the two most used numbers in my phone. I blocked two people on socials.

And then I typed an address into the maps app. An address that I'd handwritten many times over the last few years. An address in a town called Budgerigar.

Then: The Biggest Arsehole On The Planet

XANDER, 18 YEARS OLD

My head throbbed like a bitch.

I sat up, reaching for some water but finding none. I'd forgotten to get myself a glass before bed. I'd barely managed to piss without falling down before bed.

I was never touching bourbon again.

"Looks like you had a fucking blast last night!"

I winced, squinting over at Levi, lounging in my desk chair looking smug.

"Piss off," I mumbled. "Or at least get me a glass of water, make yourself useful."

"Did you and Georgie bang last night?" Levi asked. "Got drunk enough to not be such dickheads around each other?"

I shook my head, climbing gingerly out of bed and heading into the bathroom, drinking water straight from the faucet and splashing some over my face. I looked like shit.

"Georgie and Dom never showed," I muttered, climbing back into bed, propping myself up on a pillow. "Last thing I heard, Molly got out and they were running late. Then radio silence."

Levi pinched his top lip. "That's fucking weird. Have you checked your phone this morning?"

With a groan, I sat up, unplugging it from the charger and squinting at the screen. The voicemail notification was still there, as were a bunch of messages from Dom.

> Dom: You callous man-whore, you broke her fucking heart!

> Dom: How could you send a picture like that, and with Rhiannon? Are you an idiot?

> Dom: You do know while you were out grinding on some other girl, having the 'fucking best time' without Georgie, she was dealing with her dead dog?!?

> Dom: She thought this was your fucked up way of breaking up with her!

> Dom: I hope I never have to see that look on Georgie's face ever again

> Dom: You really fucked up

> Dom: Have you heard from Georgie?

> Dom: She left last night, her car's gone. My messages aren't delivering

"Shit!" I muttered, pinching the bridge of my nose as I remembered sending the stupid bloody photo.

"What have you fucked up now?" Levi asked, as with shaking hands I clicked through to my message thread with Georgie. And there it was. Rhiannon, on my lap, basically dry humping me, her arse hanging out of a too-tight dress. You could see her G-string, and my hand gripping a fistful of her butt-cheek. I groaned. She was licking my face; I was grinning like a dickhead.

I showed him the message.

"Fucking Christ, Xan," Levi hissed. "What the fuck were you thinking?"

I typed out a message to Georgie.

Xander: That photo isn't what it looks like. I was pissed that you and Dom bailed on me. It was just a stupid selfie. Nothing else happened, I swear. I went home about five minutes later

Xander: She kissed me too. But I pushed her off me

Xander: What happened to Molly? You should have texted me and told me! I feel like such a piece of shit right now

Xander: Can we meet and talk? I just need to explain

Xander: I'm so fucking sorry

Xander: Where are you? Dom said you left last night

I waited, but none of my messages showed as delivered.

"Shit." I exited out of the messages app, planning to swallow my hatred of talking on the phone to call her, when the voicemail message caught my eye again. I tapped on it, holding it to my ear.

"Oh, shit," I mumbled when it finished.

"What the fuck is going on?" Levi asked, looking concerned. The fact that he wasn't smirking at me told me that whatever expression was on my face, it was freaking him out.

"I am the biggest arsehole on the planet," I muttered.

Now: I Never Un-Fell

XANDER

"You look like you could use a cuppa," Mim said, taking my elbow and dragging me down the hallway to the kitchen.

I would have preferred to stand outside the bathroom door, listening to the shower and wishing I could turn back time to twelve years ago and undo everything about that night.

Did she sleep with him because I'd hurt her, and she wanted to hurt me back? But she wouldn't do that to Dom. She wouldn't have used Dom that way.

And she wouldn't have run off without another word if she wanted to hurt me. She would have made sure I knew that she'd moved on from me as easily as she'd assumed I'd moved on from her.

I'd pushed her to this. My stupid actions had pushed her into his arms. That night had been a complete trainwreck for her, and that was before I sent that stupid bloody photo. God, I could remember the text-bombing from Dom I'd gotten the morning after. He'd told me, straight out, how badly my actions had affected her.

I'd been a selfish, stupid, arsehole kid. When I sent that photo I hadn't even thought twice about what might have been going on for her to have not shown up at the bar. It had been all about me, and my wounded pride.

No wonder Georgie had never wanted to talk about that night.

No wonder things between her and Dom had seemed so uncomfortable. I supposed I knew now why Dom got ghosted as thoroughly as I did.

What a clusterfuck. We'd all been broken that night.

I blinked when a steaming mug was placed in front of me. I hadn't even realised I was seated at the kitchen table. And the present came flooding back into my brain. Georgie, bleeding and freaking out, and not talking to me.

"What's going on with her?" I asked Mim, running a finger around the rim of the mug, hissing when I scalded myself. She didn't answer.

I grunted bitterly. "Well, I'll just resign myself to never bloody knowing, seeing as Georgie clearly loves a big secret or two."

Mim laughed humourlessly. "I'm just as shocked as you are. Until today I could have sworn that you'd slept with her, and then gone and shacked up with some other girl."

My jaw twitched. "I never shacked up with anyone. She's the only one I've ever wanted. If I hadn't screwed things up with her back then …" My voice cracked, and I cleared my throat. Mim reached out and patted my hand.

And engine roared outside, and I jumped to my feet. Out the kitchen window, I saw Mim's old Ute zooming off down the drive, a cloud of dust in its wake.

"You knew she'd sneak out!" I snarled, narrowing my eyes at Georgie's grandmother. "You distracted me so she could leave without speaking to me."

Mim glared defiantly at me. "My loyalty will always be to my granddaughter. Even if you aren't the arsehole I'd originally thought you to be, she will always come first for me."

I strode to the window, watching the dust settle. "She'll always come first for me, too." I rubbed my forehead, taking a couple of breaths to get my temper under control before turning back to Mim.

"Will you please tell me why she was in such a rush to get back to Sydney?" I pinched the bridge of my nose. "I just need to know how bad it is … whatever it is."

"Georgie had cervical cancer last year," Mim sighed, shifting in her chair. "They did an operation, removed her cervix. But the chance of it returning is … well it's not low. They told her she had a window of a few years at most before she might have to have more invasive surgery."

I staggered back a step. "She was bleeding this morning after we … and she said it wasn't her period …" I met Mim's tight eyes. She already knew what I'd just put together.

"She thinks the cancer is back."

"Where d'you think you're going?" Jordyn asked, leaning against the Ute as I slung a bag into the back seat. "You're having Alex over for an intimate Christmas dinner tonight, remember?"

I scowled. I'd forgotten I'd agreed to that bloody farce in my whiskey-haze the other evening.

"Sydney," I snapped.

Jordyn raised an eyebrow. "You know, contractually you can't leave Budgerigar for the duration of filming, with the exception of extenuating circumstances."

"Pretty sure Georgie having bloody cancer is an extenuating circumstance!" I snarled.

Jordyn paled. "What?"

I rounded on her. "She has cervical cancer!"

"No. She *had* cervical cancer. She had it removed over a year ago." Jord's expression was stricken, and for a second, I felt bad. They were friends, even if their friendship seemed a bit combative at times.

"She thinks it's come back. She left earlier. I need to find her."

Jord looked sick, leaning against the Ute. "How? How are you going to find her? Do you even know where she's going?"

"Sydney," I repeated. Jord rallied, eyeing me darkly.

"Maybe you've forgotten in the few weeks you've been out here, but Sydney is a pretty big place."

I met Jord's stare. "Are you going to help me? Or are you going to snark at me?"

Jord pursed their lips. "Well … her oncologist—Dr Hartley—works out of Frankwright Hospital."

I nodded my thanks, heading for the driver's door.

"How bad is it?" Jord asked.

I frowned. "If I knew, I wouldn't feel so bloody terrified right now."

Jord's face softened. "You've fallen for her again."

"I never un-fell for her."

Now: I Couldn't Forgive Myself

GEORGIE

I could barely remember anything about the last eight hours. I knew I'd stopped for petrol, and to use the bathroom. The bleeding had stopped, but that didn't mean anything.

I knew I'd called Dr Hartley, and he'd promised to meet me at Frankwright first thing in the morning, even though he was on Christmas leave.

I knew I'd spoken to Mim, but aside from assuring her that I would be in touch as soon as I had news, I didn't really have much to say. I certainly wasn't going to be asking her about Xander.

I knew I'd sung very loudly and very off-key to every Taylor Swift album at least once, with the volume cranked so high it managed to drown out some of my thoughts.

Most of those thoughts were about Xander. Which was ridiculous, considering my cancer was very likely back, and I was staring down the barrel of a hysterectomy.

I walked into my apartment, and as I switched on the lights, I was shocked at how cold and sterile it felt. Like a hotel suite, not a home. How had I lived here for years? I'd never felt like this when I returned from time away from Sydney in the past. So why now?

I knew why, and I hated the reason so much. Because there he was in my head again. And he'd wormed his way into other places too. One in particular that was beating a tattoo against my ribs.

He knew the truth now. Well. He knew my secret. But he didn't really know the truth. Only I could tell him that.

He wouldn't forgive me.

I'd forgiven him. If I was honest, I'd forgiven him years ago. But I couldn't forgive myself for that one stupid decision made when I was overwhelmed with too much emotion.

And if I couldn't forgive myself for ruining my friendship with Dom … for betraying my feelings for Xander … then how could he forgive me for it?

I checked the time. It was after seven. Xander and Alex would be having their romantic Christmas dinner right about now. I tried not to think about it as I rummaged through my cupboards, coming up with a protein bar and a bag of dry roasted almonds.

I crunched on the almonds as I wandered my apartment. It felt wrong to be here. Maybe because I knew I was back here for the worst possible reason.

Or maybe I was realising just how much I hated my life in Sydney. But that was another thing I couldn't think about too deeply right now.

I flicked off a quick email to Kenneth, advising him that I had a medical emergency requiring a trip back to Sydney, reassuring him that Jord was more than capable of running the show in my absence, and that I'd be in touch once I knew more.

Work sorted, I stared at my phone, my fingers twitching. Aching to click through and send a message to Xander. To explain. To apologise. To tell him that his past mistakes were never the reason I left.

Mine were.

To tell him that, if I didn't have stupid cancer, and wasn't about to become unable to give him children, then my 'for now' would have been something very different.

I typed out a text, which really contained nowhere near what my head … my heart … wanted to say to him.

And then I showered the day's travel from my body, curled up in my cold, foreign-feeling bed, and cried myself to sleep.

Now: More Than Anything Else

XANDER

"You won't find her by lurking in the fucking hospital foyer!"

"Got a better idea?" I asked Levi, holding the phone to my ear with my shoulder as I tapped my credit card on the vending machine, plugging in the number for sludge that barely passed for coffee.

"Oh, I dunno. You could get off the fucking phone with me, and actually call *her*!" Levi grumbled. "Dickhead," he muttered under his breath. I had to laugh. He was so bloody right.

I was acting like a dickhead.

I'd arrived in Sydney just after nine last night, and I hadn't bothered to go home and change. I'd driven straight to the hospital, parked, and stormed into the foyer, demanding that the poor night nurse running the desk check if Georgina Menzies was currently admitted.

It was ridiculous and melodramatic. And ultimately, it hadn't helped me at all, because the nurse refused to give out any information to me since I couldn't prove I was a relative.

When I'd taken a seat, resigning myself to wait and hope she showed up, my phone pinged. I frantically fumbled it out of my pocket.

Georgie: I'm sorry I kept so much from you.
I'm sorry that I fucked up. I understand if you
can't move past this

I'd squeezed my eyes shut, pinching the bridge of my nose until the sting of tears subsided.

Xander: We both fucked up. Please tell me
where you are, I need to see you

Twelve hours later, trying not to fall asleep in a hard plastic chair in the waiting area, I still had no idea where she was. She hadn't replied to my message.

"She was what, an hour or two ahead of you?" Levi continued. I could hear Amanda speaking quickly in the background. "Amanda says her oncologist wouldn't have admitted her for a bit of bleeding. He'd probably see her today for a consult, get some tests done." A pause while Amanda nattered away. "If you head to H wing, level four, that's Oncology. That's where Dr Hartley has his rooms. There's a waiting area there."

I sipped at the coffee and hissed when it scalded my lip, grimacing because it tasted like shit. "See? This plan will work. Tell Amanda thank you."

"You're welcome. Just … don't be a dickhead, okay?" Amanda said, and I realised I'd been on speaker the entire time.

I groaned. "Not you too."

"Bye Xander," Levi said. "Good fucking luck."

I hung up, heading for the bank of elevators that would take me up to level four, cursing when I saw the crowd of people waiting around them. Why were hospitals always so busy?

I turned, deciding I'd find my way to H wing on the ground floor first, and use a less busy elevator to get up to the fourth floor.

Why were hospital layouts so bloody labyrinthine? By the time I finally found H wing, I'd wandered around the ground floor for forty-five minutes. Half the people I'd asked for directions had no idea themselves—even some of the staff had no clue where I needed to go.

By the time I stumbled into the oncology clinic, it was after ten, and the waiting area was packed. Only a few chairs were free in the big, ugly space.

Why did they have to make hospital waiting rooms so boring? People were already on edge enough, waiting in a cancer clinic, without having nothing but beige walls and a few informational posters to distract themselves with.

I scanned the area, but there was no sign of Blondie. I headed for a free chair, but the woman sitting beside it with a toddler in her lap quickly put the toddler down on the chair, watching me warily. What must I look like to give people that reaction?

Well, since the last time you showered or slept a full night, you've rescued a sheep from a dusty paddock, performed an amputation solo in the middle of the night, had sex with the woman you love, driven eight hours, and sat in a hospital waiting room for twelve. In the middle of an Australian summer.

I sniffed myself. Yeah, I stunk. I should have gone home and showered.

"Can I help you, sir?" a woman behind the reception desk asked.

"Uh, yeah. I, uh, my girlfriend has an appointment today with Dr, uh … Hartley, but I forgot what time I was supposed to meet her here," I lied through my teeth, approaching the desk.

"What's your girlfriend's name?" she asked, looking at me with sympathy. She probably saw loads of wild-eyed, panicked-looking partners in here.

"Georgina Menzies."

"And your name, sir?" she prompted.

Shit. *My* name was getting me nowhere—just like downstairs, Xander Fox would not be on her list of people the hospital was authorised to provide information to. I wracked my brain for some way to sweet-talk my way into at least some information about what was going on. Nothing came to mind.

"Sir?"

I blinked. "Sorry, it's been a long couple of days," I muttered, rubbing a hand over my matted hair. No wonder people were looking at me funny.

"I understand," she said, and she sounded like she really did. "I just need your name, when you're ready."

"James," I blurted. "Sorry … I'm James."

Please don't ask me what that fucker's last name was. Please let her not have updated her details since they broke up.

But the woman seemed to take pity on the overtired, over-wrought man in front of her, giving me a warm smile.

"Ms Menzies is in with Dr Hartley at the moment. You must have driven a long way to get here."

I nodded, a relieved smile parting my lips. "Yeah, it's been a very long journey," I replied. *Twelve years,* I thought to myself, an exhausted chuckle bursting out of me.

"If you take a seat, I'll call through to Dr Hartley and let Ms Menzies know you're here."

"Oh, uh, I'll just wait until she gets out," I said, my palms sweating. "I'm sure she wants a private discussion with … him?" I hedged, wincing.

The woman's smile faltered for just a second, and there was a distrustful edge to it now. "It's no trouble, if she wants you to wait out here, she can let me know."

I scrubbed a palm over my face as she picked up her phone and dialled. I turned away, not wanting to see her expression the moment she realised that 'James' was very much not welcome here.

Probably as unwelcome as 'Xander' was. What was I doing? This was borderline stalker behaviour.

The door next to the reception area slammed open, and I (along with seventy percent of the waiting room) turned.

Georgie stood there, her furious expression dropping into horror the second her eyes found mine.

"Xander!" she squawked. "What the hell are you doing here?"

"Wait, isn't his name James?" someone behind me muttered.

Face flushing, I took a step towards her. She took a step back. I stopped, shoving my hands into my pockets.

"I don't want you to have to do this stuff alone anymore," I said simply. Georgie's brow furrowed as murmuring started up behind me. Apparently I'd drawn a lot of attention to myself.

"Oh, that's adorable!"

"Hang on, I was sure he said his name was James!"

"Why does he look like a hobo?"

"A freaking gorgeous hobo!"

I winced as Georgie glared around the room at all the muttering people. She stormed forwards and grabbed my arm, dragging me out into the corridor.

"What were you thinking, busting in here and pretending to be my ex?" she hissed, her cheeks pink. Clearly *she'd* been home and showered. She was dressed in a navy wrap dress, the exact same style as the grey one that she'd taunted me with on that first drive to Budgerigar.

"What did you expect me to do?" I grated, frustration rising with every rapid beat of my heart. "You were bleeding, and your reaction scared the crap out of me, and then you left—again—without telling me anything! Your grandmother had to explain what the hell was going on!"

"Bloody hell, Mim," Georgie muttered.

"Thank Christ for Mim!" I argued, taking a step towards her. This time she didn't step back. "I'm here, Georgie! I want to be here for you!" Reaching out, I hooked my pinkie around hers, squeezing gently. Her gaze darted down to our joined hands.

"You were never supposed to—"

"Georgina, we need to finish our consult."

I glanced up to find an older man in a blue shirt watching us with unmasked amusement.

"Of course, Dr Hartley," Georgie mumbled, face beetroot, her pinkie slipping from mine. "Sorry for keeping you waiting."

"Will James be joining us?" he asked, giving me a pointed look.

"No …" Georgie said quickly. "'James' will—"

"I'm Xander," I interrupted, reaching out a hand for Dr Hartley to shake. He took it with a wry smile as I turned to Georgie. "And I'll be waiting right here for you when you're finished."

Georgie's eyes flashed up to mine, her lips pursed. I could tell she wanted to argue, which only made me more determined.

"Our discussion isn't even close to over," I said. "Go. I'll be here."

With a sigh of resignation, Georgie followed Dr Hartley back into the clinic.

"What did he say?" I demanded the second Georgie stepped back out of the clinic forty minutes later.

"God! You really weren't lying when you said you'd be waiting right here!" Georgie grumbled, rubbing at her sternum, her eyes wary. She started walking, but I fell easily into step beside her.

"Well?" I pressed.

"I have no news. Test results don't come back immediately."

I blew out a breath. "So it's just a waiting game now? Did he have anything to say?" Georgie peered at me from the corner of her eye.

"He … Xander, this is … I don't think you really want to know about my messed up reproductive system," she mumbled. I stopped, grabbing her wrist and tugging her to a stop.

"Please, don't tell me what I want," I said, drawing her towards the wall, where there was a small alcove. "I followed you here because I want to know what's going on. If I know, I can help you, I can support you. I want you to let me support you."

I leaned against the wall, exhaustion from the last two days starting to creep in. "I thought I'd been making that pretty damned obvious lately."

Georgie huffed, shaking her head. "You have … but I never wanted you to know about it."

"Why not? Why wouldn't you just tell me you had cancer? Did you think I'd walk away if I knew?" I asked, the words coming out harsher than I intended. Georgie flinched, and I reached out, palming her shoulders and pulling her towards me. She hesitated for just a second, then she rested her body against mine, her forehead on my chest.

"I ... I know you want kids. You said you wanted a whole soccer team of them. And I saw the way you were with your niece. I watched your face light up when she smiled at you, and I felt sick, knowing that if I was selfish enough to let this happen ..." She dug her nails into my waist, her back trembling as she sucked in a breath.

"I'm a ticking time bomb to infertility, and I was scared that right now, with how ... intense things are between us, you wouldn't care about it. But later, when you realise you need the whole family thing, I would disappoint you, and you'd ... and it would break you. And that would break me, too."

My heart ached at her words, and I slid a hand up her arm, under her chin, to tilt her head back until she was looking up into my eyes. The silver of hers was dulled to a matte grey.

A soft smile pulled at my mouth. "Blondie, are you telling me that while you were pretending to hate me, you were secretly picturing us together long enough for us to be planning our future kids?"

Georgie rolled her eyes, and my stomach fluttered to see a spark of the silver reappearing in them. "Of course you'd assume I was only pretending to hate you, you cocky—"

I kissed her. Her lips froze against mine for a split second before she was kissing me back, her hands tangling in my hair, her mouth parting for mine.

"Us not being able to have kids ... that's not a good enough reason not to be with you," I whispered against her lips. "I can't even think of a good enough reason not to be with you."

She gasped, and I used that moment to suck her bottom lip into my mouth, then press my tongue to hers. She groaned, then pulled back again so just our lips were touching.

"But you *do* want kids," she told me. I shook my head, brushing my lips against hers.

"Not more than I want you," I replied, dusting kisses across her cheek, her jaw, around her ear.

"You won't feel that way forever," she told me, even as she tilted her head back so I could suck at the skin on her neck. I slid my hands down her back and slapped her lightly on the arse, bringing my lips back to hers, swallowing her outraged squeak.

"Don't tell me how I'll feel, Georgie," I growled, breaking away from her mouth to rest my forehead against hers.

"I don't want to be the reason you give up something you want!" she argued, her body stiff.

"Do you want me to spank you again?" I asked, cupping her face in my hands. "If you don't want this because it's not what *you* want, that's one thing. But if you pull away from me because you imagine some future where I won't want you, you're already making me give up the thing I want most."

"More than kids?" she whispered, but I could feel her softening against me once more.

"More than anything else." My thumbs found her cheeks, feeling wetness there. I brushed it away, nuzzling my nose against hers. "Besides, there's more than one way to skin a cat."

She giggled wetly, her breath warm on my face. "I could take that literally, Dr Fox. What are you doing to your patients?"

I spanked her again and she yelped. I smothered the sound with my lips.

We broke apart again sooner than I would have liked, but I was all too aware that we were making out like teenagers in a hospital hallway. Georgie's eyes gleamed as I stepped back, stroking my knuckles along her jaw.

"I don't think this conversation is over," she grouched. "You're very good at distracting me from … everything."

I chuckled, taking her hand and drawing her out into the corridor. "So … now we wait. Your place or mine?" I asked.

Georgie blinked up at me, then glanced away. I squeezed her hand as we reached the elevators, pressing the button with my free hand.

"Let me put it this way, Blondie. I'm not letting you out of my sight. I still consider you a flight risk."

Georgie snorted. "Your place. But I'll have to follow you there. I can't leave Mim's car here—I'll owe a fortune in parking fees. So I suppose you'll just have to trust me out of your sight for a little while."

The elevator doors opened. I pulled her inside, squeezing in beside a mother with a surly-looking teen on crutches, and a nurse pushing a sleeping man in a wheelchair.

"I missed out on twelve years with you. I'm not missing another one," I murmured into her hair. "I drove across the state and sat for twelve hours in a hospital waiting room just in case you walked in." I pressed a kiss to her head. "I think we've established that the lengths I will take to be with you now don't really have a limit."

Georgie sighed, tilting her head up to mine, her expression adorably frustrated. "Text me your address. I'll be there."

Now: All The Ways To Skin That Cat

GEORGIE

The cherry red monster truck was already parked in the driveway of the adorable Bondi cottage when I pulled Mim's Hilux up to the kerb. I slid the gearstick into park, pressing my hands between my thighs and sucking in shaky breaths.

Everything, from the moment I saw his name on the production brief, had been leading up to this. And it still felt like things were flying and my head was spinning, trying to catch up with my heart.

Cancer. Children … and all the ways to skin that cat. Change. Was I ready for all of this? Was he ready for it? Would he change his mind about everything once the thrill of us wore off?

And where would that leave us? More hurt, more damaged than we had been at eighteen? I had no control over him.

I wanted him so much, but if I wanted this, I would have to trust. Which was something I was pretty useless at.

And then there was the giant elephant stomping around the room. Xander needed to know the truth about what happened with Dom. There was no way I was starting anything with him with that hanging over our heads, unsaid but always lurking in the backs of our minds. Driving a wedge between us…between him and Dom.

The thought of telling him made my chest ache. The thought of bringing it up, of watching his face change, almost had me hyper-ventilating.

"You know, it's not just dogs who shouldn't be left in hot cars," Xander said, opening the passenger door and picking up my purse. He was in fresh clothes, his hair still wet from a shower. I swallowed back my feelings of terror and climbed out of the car, following him up a stone path and through his front door.

His house was lovely. Unlike my sterile apartment, even unlived in for weeks, it felt homely. The small entry opened into an open-plan kitchen and living, with a hall to the left that I assumed led to the rest of the house.

"This is …" I murmured, my eyes raking over the leather lounge and two mismatched fabric chairs that somehow looked like they belonged together.

"It's home," Xander said quietly, and my eyes met his. Heat surged through me, nerves bubbling up in their wake.

"We need to talk about Dom," I blurted.

Xander's eyes flicked between mine, his body suddenly still.

"*What* about Dom?" he asked, his voice strained.

Jesus. I had no idea how to continue. I chewed on my lip until Xander leaned on the back of the lounge, crossing one foot over the other ankle. "We don't have to talk about it if you—"

"We do have to talk about it!" I insisted. "Because it's always going to be there, hanging over us, if we don't …" I dropped my head into my hands as words started bubbling up my throat.

"It's why I've never wanted to talk about what happened back then. Why I didn't want you to explain yourself. Because if you didn't, then *I* never had to explain *myself*! I knew you'd want to apologise for the stupid picture with Rhiannon, and whatever else happened with you both, and I knew I'd never be able to look you in the eyes, knowing that I was lying to you, that on that same night, I'd done something so much worse … It was easier to run away, to convince myself I hated you, to blame you for my actions that night, than recognise that it was all my fault."

"I'm going to stop you right there," Xander said, uncrossing his ankles and stepping towards me. I let him put his hands on my arms, running them down to my hands until our fingers were inter-locked. I stared at the way our hands fit together.

"Firstly, I want you to have the truth … after that bloody selfie, she kissed me. I let her, for a stupid, drunken moment, but then I shut it down, because I knew deep down that I didn't want her. I only wanted you.

"I only put her on my lap in the first place to try and make you jealous. It was a shitty thing to do, I know that. I knew it the next morning when I realised what I'd done. I left about five minutes after I took that photo, because I was so lonely and miserable without you … and Dom."

An involuntary sound tore from my throat at the mention of his name, and Xander stepped closer again. "But the selfie wasn't the only shitty thing I did that night. You told me Molly had escaped, told me you were running late. And instead of being concerned when you took longer than I expected, I got angry, and jealous … and bloody resentful."

My head tilted up to look at him, shocked. He looked haunted.

"I was already envious of Dom, because when everything went to shit with your mum and Seth, you moved in with him. It was a stupid, childish way to feel. But I wanted you to be mine … all mine … and he was there.

"In my head, I convinced myself that Molly was just an excuse, and something else was going on. You were having too much fun together without me … I don't know, it made sense to me back then. It sounds bloody ridiculous now.

"And while I was being a jealous shit, you were watching your beautiful Molly die … violently."

My cheekbones ached and my eyes filled with tears. "But I did exactly what you thought I was doing anyway. And I ruined my friendship with Dom, and I … I lost you too."

I tried to pull my hands away from his, to cover my face, but he wouldn't let me. He pressed my hands to my cheeks, caging me there, his hazel eyes too intense, glistening with his own unshed tears.

"We were both kids. I can't even imagine how you must've …"

Xander's voice was thick, his thumbs catching my tears. "I have no right to be angry with you. We all did stupid things that night. The only thing that upsets me about what happened back then is that it kept you away from me for twelve years."

"Don't say things like that," I whispered. "Please ... because that's my fault too. I left. I blocked you. I disappeared without any warning."

"But we found each other again, Blondie," he murmured against my forehead. "And I am more in love with you now than I ever was at eighteen."

My throat closed over at those words, and I pressed my face into his shirt, sobbing against his chest.

"Hey," he whispered, enveloping me in his arms, stroking up and down my back. "That wasn't supposed to be the thing that made you ugly cry."

I snorted wetly. "Are you ... telling me I'm ... ugly when I cry?" I gasped through the tears. Xander wrapped his arms around my waist and lifted me until my face was level with his.

"You're beautiful all the time."

I wriggled until he put me down, but he didn't let go of me as I wiped my face and sniffed pitifully.

"I was going to tell you I loved you that night. I was so excited ... and terrified," I confessed. Xander rubbed the tip of his nose back and forth against the top of my head.

"Well, you could just tell me now," he said quietly, and I realised that he was terrified too. Here he was, pouring his heart out, and all I had talked about was how much I regretted the past ... how much I regretted not being able to give him the future he wanted.

"I think I realised I still love you when you walked into that boardroom, and you frantically scanned the room, until you found me."

"Jesus, Georgie. All the way back then?" he teased, relief flooding his tone. "And yet you acted like you hated the sight of me."

A wobbly smile started growing on my lips. "It was easier to pretend to hate you than to acknowledge how scary my real feelings were," I admitted. I tilted my head back, brushing my lips against his. "Besides, if I hadn't hated you, we'd have missed out on fucking on the dining table …"

Xander groaned into my mouth. "And that blowjob in the bathroom … and you squirting in the back of my Ute … twice."

I pinched his arm. "You knew I didn't hate you by then. That wasn't hate—"

"No, it was love. It was all love, Blondie."

His lips parted mine, his tongue tasting me, and I arched myself into him, revelling in the feel of his strong arms cradling me, supporting my body even as he plundered my mouth.

In my purse, my phone started ringing.

"Leave it," Xander growled, gripping my butt and nipping my lip. But I pulled away.

"It could be Dr Hartley," I said, disentangling myself and rummaging through my bag just as it stopped ringing. Aside from the missed call notification, there were a bunch of text messages from Jord. I swiped to read them just as my phone started ringing again.

"It's Kenneth," I said to Xander. "I should probably get it."

Xander leaned back against the lounge, pulling my back to his front and wrapping his arms around me as I answered.

"Hi Kenneth."

"Georgie, sorry to hear about your medical emergency. I hope everything is alright?"

"I'm not sure yet. I'm waiting on test results."

"Is it serious?"

"I … I won't know until the results come back," I said. I hadn't disclosed my cancer diagnosis with Reelflix, and I didn't want to unless … or until I had no other choice.

"Fair enough. Sounds like you've had an eventful Christmas."

I laughed weakly. "It was a bit boring, actually. I spent the whole day driving back to Sydney."

"Hmmm," he mumbled. My heart thrummed, but I had no idea why. "Well, *my* last twenty-four hours have been quite the opposite of boring. You see, first I found out that my showrunner had abandoned her post, without any warning, to drive back to Sydney, claiming a medical emergency."

Xander's fingers tightened on my waist. "Put him on speaker," he breathed into my ear. I nodded, fumbling my phone and holding it in front of me. Kenneth's voice sounded tinny over the phone speaker, but his words were spreading ice through my body.

"And then Jordyn informed me that my star veterinarian had mysteriously also decided to make an urgent visit to Sydney."

My breath caught in my lungs, and I twisted to see Xander's face. His lips were tight, jaw clenched, which didn't make me feel any better.

"I ... uh ... I don't know anything about ..."

"Please don't insult my intelligence, Georgie." Kenneth's voice was suddenly cold. "Jordyn added some very ... interesting footage to the drive last night. I must say, our vet is a very good actor. I was fully convinced he was falling for Alex ... until I saw all the outtakes of you and him together—the ones you were hiding from me."

I thought I was going to be sick. My hand shook. Xander took the phone before I dropped it, holding it steady for me.

"Those were outtakes for a reason, Kenneth," I said, managing a little firmness in my tone. Xander's free hand pressed against my stomach as if he could sense the swirling mess it was in. "Xander and I ... there's history there. But it's superfluous to the documentary we're making."

"Really," Kenneth deadpanned. "I would argue the exact opposite. You've spent so much time manufacturing a romantic plot, when you had the real thing sitting in a folder on your desktop. The real story that you were keeping from me."

My eyes flashed to Xander's. He looked ready to reach through the phone and strangle Kenneth. I wanted to strangle someone else entirely.

How could Jordyn do this to me? How could they throw me under the bus like this? I thought of all the sly comments they'd made, about Xander and me. The plan to make me jealous. I should have seen this coming a mile away. My fury with Jord burned away some of the anxiety gnawing at my gut, and I cleared my throat.

"My contract states very clearly that I have final say on footage on any show I produce," I reminded Kenneth. "And that footage falls outside of the story I'm telling."

I felt Xander's cheek move as he smiled against my face. But I was too keyed up, too absolutely furious to smile.

My phone screen flashed, asking me if I'd like to place Kenneth on hold to answer an incoming call from Jordyn. I tapped ignore. I could only deal with one shit fight at a time.

"The fine print in your contract also states that final say is at the ongoing discretion of the CEO, and is subject to performance criteria," Kenneth countered, his voice oozing smugness. "As CEO, I'm officially exercising my discretion."

Xander punched the back of the lounge so hard the sound echoed around the room. Meanwhile, I could feel bile rising in my throat.

"Now, having a hissy fit and throwing things isn't going to help you." Kenneth's tone implied that he thought I was nothing more than a toddler throwing a tantrum. "You've got two choices. You leave, I retain ownership of the footage, and the rights under your contract to air any footage of you taken during your employment with Reelflix, with whatever spin I choose to put on it."

Xander growled as Kenneth continued, "Or, you can stay on, agree that this is the story we should be telling our viewers, and have input into the narrative we build around your relationship."

"Narrative!" Xander exploded behind me. I turned in his arms, trying to put my hand over his mouth, but he held my wrist, the soft way his thumb caressed my veins at total odds with the furious expression on his face. "This isn't a fucking narrative, it's her life! Our life!"

"Well, hello Xander," Kenneth said. "Why am I completely unsurprised to discover that the two of you are together?"

I managed to shove my hand over Xander's mouth before he made this even worse. He glared at me, but when I pressed a finger to my lips, my eyes deadly serious, he deflated a bit, nodding, and I removed my hand.

"Why are you doing this?" I asked Kenneth.

"It's business, Georgie. It's just business. Now that I've been made aware of all of this, it's clear that the story this documentary needs to tell is yours and Xander's. There is no other story. Oh, and no matter what you decide, Xander is obligated to continue filming for the duration of his contract. In fact, he's in breach of it right now, by being out of town."

I pinched the bridge of my nose. "Give me a day to think. I'll be back to you tomorrow evening."

"Xander will be back in Budgerigar tomorrow, no matter what *you* decide," Kenneth said, and I recognised the venom in his tone.

"I understand."

I tapped to end the call, taking my phone back from Xander. He snatched me to him, his arms tight around my waist.

"I'm so bloody sorry, Blondie," he muttered against my forehead. I shook my head.

"It's not your fault. I was stupid keeping that footage. I should have dumped it."

"Why didn't you?" Xander asked, his palms rubbing up and down my arms.

I laughed sheepishly. "I liked watching it back. I liked the way your eyes looked when the camera caught you watching me."

Xander took my mouth, his tongue tracing the seam of my lips. I sighed, letting him taste me, losing myself for just a moment in the warmth of his mouth, in the gentle, caring way he kissed me.

I broke away with a sigh. "What the hell am I going to do?" I muttered. Xander's grip tightened on my shoulders.

"What are *we* going to do. No more going it alone, okay? I'm here," Xander said earnestly, his fingers trailing down my arms, his pinkies linking with mine. "We're in this together now."

"I hate how much I like the sound of that," I admitted, and Xander's relieved laugh vibrated through both our bodies.

"Why the hell are you home, Xan? I thought you were—"

Xander and I looked up to find Dom standing in the entry, staring at both of us with undisguised shock on his face.

411

Now: Front-Row Seats To That Showdown

XANDER

"You need to tell him. No secrets anymore," I said gently through the bathroom door.

"How are you handling this so well?" Georgie mumbled from the other side. "How are you not furious with me … with both of us?"

I pressed my head against the door, all too aware that Dom was sitting out in the living room, sipping a scotch and probably wondering what the hell we were doing.

"What would be the point of that, Georgie?" I asked. "What do I achieve being angry about something that happened over a decade ago, something that was as much my fault as anyone else's?"

There was a long pause, then Georgie opened the door. Her fringe was wet, her face damp. I tucked my hand into hers. Her face was determined, and it set my heart racing.

"Let's do it together."

"I bloody love you," I said, leaning in for a quick kiss. She grabbed the back of my neck, clinging on for just a second longer than me, before turning us, leading the way down the hall.

Dom looked up, his lips a thin line, his eyes worried.

"You told him," Dom said, his voice tight, his eyes fixed on Georgie.

"He knows," Georgie agreed. I looked between the two of them, watching them have a silent conversation with their eyes. That they could still do that, years later, pricked me with the remnants of old jealousy. As if Georgie could tell where my thoughts were going, she leaned closer, wrapping an arm around my waist.

"No more secrets. I want us all to be able to move forward." She glanced up at me, a small smile tickling her mouth. "Together."

Dom stood, stuffing his hands in his pockets, then taking them out again. I'd never seen him so nervous.

"It wasn't premeditated," he said softly. "She was … I've never seen her like that before. It was like she was hanging by a thread, and …" His piercing black eyes met mine. "You know I would do anything for her. And the look on her face … she asked me to help her forget … and it all just happened so fast, I barely knew what was …"

I held a hand up to Dom. "Mate. You don't have to explain. It's in the past."

Dom nodded once. "I just want you to know that it was never about … that … with Georgie and me." He turned to Georgie. "I thought I was doing what you needed. Hindsight being twenty-twenty, it just made things worse. I probably should have stopped it before it …" he rubbed at his short black beard. "But you're right. It's in the past."

"We all made mistakes that night," Georgie added softly, her gaze falling to the floor. "But … there's more."

She looked up at him, eyes wary. "I had an abortion."

Dom's face went white, and he fell back into the chair. Georgie rocked on her feet, and I tugged her tighter against me.

"I … I need to get this out, okay?" she said, her voice husky but her eyes dry. "I wasn't entirely shocked when I missed my period—I mean, we didn't use a condom." Georgie glanced up at me, a sad smile on her face.

"Mim—my grandmother—she was so supportive. She told me that whatever I wanted to do, she'd be there for me. I couldn't … I know it sounds selfish, but I couldn't do what my mum did and have a baby as a teen."

"Not at all," Dom rasped as I squeezed her arm reassuringly.

"So, we booked an appointment in Dubbo. They gave me some pills. I took them that night, and then, well, that was that."

"My brave girl," I whispered into her hair, ignoring the churning of my stomach. I'd guessed there were three possibilities when the truth had been thrown in my face back in Budgerigar. She miscarried, she put the baby up for adoption … or she had a termination. But hearing her talk about it, seeing the look on Dom's face …

"I'm sorry, Dom!" Georgie said, her voice cracking. "I should have told you, back then. But I was frightened, and stubborn, and ashamed … and I'd burned our bridge."

Dom stared at his scotch for a long moment, his head propped in his hands. Then he shot to his feet, strode across the room, and pulled her into his body.

"I'd never have let you go through it alone if I'd known. It was my mistake too," he whispered. I stood to the side, knowing I needed to give them this moment. But then Georgie tugged me closer, dragging me into their embrace.

"I have you both again, now. That's all that matters," Georgie mumbled, her cheek resting against Dom's chest, her fingers gripping my waist. Holding onto us both.

When we finally broke apart, Dom was wiping at his eyes, Georgie was laughing and crying at the same time, and my chest felt so full.

"So … what else is going on with you two?" Dom asked huskily, staring at our joined hands.

"Well, what isn't?" I said.

***

"I can't leave Mim's car behind!" Georgie protested. I folded my hands over my chest.

After a long discussion the previous afternoon with Dom, who was genuinely happy for us, but simultaneously furious about Kenneth, we'd gotten no closer to a solution to what to do about the Reelflix debacle.

In the end, we'd realised that no matter what, we couldn't drive back to Budgerigar in our exhausted state, and both Georgie and I had collapsed into bed. By that point I'd been awake for almost forty-eight hours. I'd been out cold the second my head hit the pillow.

Upon waking, we started getting ready for the drive. The means of getting there … that was under discussion.

"We'll leave the bloody sparkly beast here then, I don't care. You're not driving eight hours on your own. Not with how distracted you are."

Georgie's eyes flashed, and my dick twitched. I was almost certain at this point that riling her up was an aphrodisiac for me. I ignored my arousal, though, because now was not the time.

"That car's part and parcel with the show. If you're driving on camera, you're in that car," she snarled. "I am perfectly capable of driving on my own, even distracted! I did it on Christmas Day while freaking out about my cancer!"

"What about your test results? Maybe you should stay here until they come in. No matter what we decide to do about Kenneth, there's no way he could begrudge you a few days, given it's cancer-related," I said.

Georgie's jaw flexed, and I was suddenly sure she hadn't told Reelflix about her cancer. "I'm not traveling to another planet! Besides, it's all the more reason to get back there tonight, so I can fix this before the results come back in."

She had a point. I didn't have to like it, though.

"Look," Georgie said, using her bossy voice, glaring icily at me. "We need to get back to Budgerigar, ASAP. You need to be filming. I need to deal with Jordyn. I need to know exactly what Kenneth got his hands on before I give him an answer. We can't leave either vehicle here. We drive separately. We leave *now*. Sorted."

"You've got an answer for everything, don't you, Blondie?" I stepped into her, scooping her into my arms. "I love that about you." Jesus, I loved telling her I loved her. Especially when it softened her face, parted her lips, and let me kiss her. Which I did. Enthusiastically.

"You got an answer for how to deal with Kenneth yet?" I asked against her mouth.

Georgie pulled back. "I need to talk to Jord."

I growled under my breath. "You need to rip Jordyn a new arsehole," I muttered.

Georgie threw me a withering glare as she collected her purse, rummaging in it for her car keys. "I can get my point across with a bit more finesse than that."

"How much for front-row seats to that showdown?" I asked, kissing her again. She indulged me for just a moment.

"If we want to get back there tonight, you need to stop kissing me," she protested. So I did it again, nipping at her bottom lip until she gasped, and I had to break away because I was grinning so hard.

She didn't smile back, and I tried not to dwell on that as we climbed into our respective cars.

Now: Crossing A Major Line

GEORGIE

"What the fuck did you do?" I hissed the second I slammed into the caravan. So much for finesse. Eight hours in a car on my own, stewing over Jordyn's betrayal had left my temper shredded.

"Shit! You scared me!" Jord gasped, clutching a hand to their chest. "How are you … is your cancer back?"

I flinched at the anxious look on their face, swallowing back the cancer worry. I had to put that out of my head. Deal with one shitty thing at a time.

"We aren't talking about me right now," I said, leaning against the tiny kitchen bench and glaring her down. "What. The fuck. Did you do?"

"Did you read my messages?" they asked.

I shook my head. "I wanted to see your face when you told me how you fucked me over. My private folders? Really? What was the point? What do you get out of throwing me under the bus to Kenneth?"

Jord's eyes fell closed. They looked exhausted, like they hadn't slept in days. I didn't want to feel anything about that, so I clenched my jaw and waited.

"It was a fucking accident, G. I fucked up."

I raised an incredulous eyebrow. "Are you telling me you 'accidentally' copied folders on my desktop into the cloud, and 'accidentally' told Kenneth that Xander followed me to Sydney?" I puffed out a breath. "Seriously, do I look that gullible?"

"It didn't happen like that!"

I snorted, sliding into the little booth beside the kitchen. "Well, please, take a seat. I'd love to hear just how it *did* happen."

With a look of trepidation, Jordyn plonked down. "Xander's in love with you!" they said.

I sucked in a breath. "So, because he's in love with me, you thought it would be totally fine for Reelflix to air our interactions?"

Jord shook their head, face pale. "No … I didn't think that at all. I … G, you know that I care about you, right?"

I snorted, pressing my lips tightly together. "I'm not sure anymore."

The way Jord's face fell almost made me feel bad for them. Almost.

"Well, I do. And I've watched you change over the last month. I've watched that sparkle in your eyes happen more often, and for things other than work."

I glanced out the window through the stand of eucalypts that separated the crew caravans from Mim's homestead and Xander's tiny home, in which he was waiting, obediently for once.

"Again, I don't see how any of this relates to your decision to make my personal life public."

"I think you should give him another chance," Jord blurted. My eyebrows flew up under my fringe. "I think that whatever happened when you were kids, you can get past it. I think you know that, deep down, you two have a real connection.

"And I think you need someone who will care about you—*for you*—if the cancer is back." Jord swallowed, eyes glistening, and I blinked away, not wanting to feel the bond of our friendship when I was so angry, so betrayed.

Jord cleared their throat. "So when Xander told me why you'd left, I sat down and went through all the footage, looking for proof that you two belonged together, trying to find something I could show you to help you get past whatever it is that's stopping you from taking the leap with him. But in all the footage on the shared drive, there was only one scene with you and Xander—the one where you helped him with that dog with the anal glands, remember?"

I nodded, trying not to let a hint of a smile slip through at the memory.

"But I knew we had so much more footage than that. So I used my remote access to get into your computer, and I found *the* folder." Jord's lips twisted. "And I should have left it at that. I fucking know I should have. But I realised when I saw that folder, that maybe your feelings were more than you were letting on, and I thought a little push …" Jord's head fell into their hands.

"A 'little push'? That's what we're calling Kenneth deciding that the entire documentary is going to be centred around a budding romance between Xander and me?" I slapped a palm down on the laminate tabletop.

"He was never supposed to see it!" Jord groaned, looking up at me with a pleading expression. "I was trying to copy the files over to my computer. I was going to edit them together myself to make a montage of the two of you, to try and show you what you have is really special. But in the copying process, I must have somehow uploaded it to the cloud as well."

"So, while trying to insert yourself into my private life, you made an IT fuck up, and what, you ran to Kenneth and told him everything?" I sighed. "Please don't lie to me, Jord."

"I never went to Kenneth! I didn't even realise that I'd fucked up with the file transfer until he called me, ranting about the footage, demanding to know how much I knew about it all! And all I said was that you two had known each other years ago, that filming had been a bit tense, but you were both making it work. He wanted to know what your medical emergency was—I didn't tell him—and then he wanted me to find Xander, put him on the phone."

I pinched the bridge of my nose. "And you told him that Xander had followed me back to Sydney."

"No," Jord insisted. "I just said that Xander had a family obligation. I guess Kenneth made the connection himself."

I sat back, staring at the ceiling, running through everything Jord had just said. It sounded insane, but knowing what I did about Jord, it was less crazy than them going behind my back to win points with Kenneth. But it hardly mattered—either way, the result was the same.

"This was crossing a major line, Jordyn," I muttered. "And in the process, it has royally fucked me over." I turned to them. "Whether it was intentional or not," I held up a hand when Jord's mouth opened in protest, "doesn't matter at this point. Kenneth has issued an ultimatum—leave the show, and he can use the existing footage as he likes … or stay and agree to air my private relationship in public, and at least have some control over how that all comes across on-screen."

Jord looked sick. "What are you going to do?"

I sighed. "I don't know. I mean, the footage wasn't terribly incriminating. Kenneth could be bluffing, because I don't think he has enough to build a story out of a few fleeting looks, and a couple of angry altercations." I winced at the thought of me slapping Xander and then storming off being used out of context to gain viewers. "I could call his bluff, convince him he doesn't have enough to tell a story, promise him more Alex and Xander content, and hope that he accepts it." Even if asking Xander to PDA with Alex was about as enticing as removing my own toenails.

I glanced at Jord, who somehow looked even sicker than before. "G … the footage on your desktop … that wasn't all that I accidentally copied over."

<hr>

"Why?" I breathed, after Jord showed me everything they'd mistakenly copied over to the cloud.

"It seemed like a good idea at the time," Jord muttered, swiping a hand over their face. "Jesus, G, there was so much chemistry between you two, and there were times when Jase was around, and we just … I don't know, we just decided to hit record. We kept it all on a separate memory card. I guess, maybe, I had planned on showing it to you at the end of the show … but it was *never* meant for Kenneth, I swear to God."

Xander, coming up behind me at the reception desk the day Lachy finished up, murmuring into my ear—and his mic—about how he wasn't a fan of appropriate when it came to me. His hips thrusting. My mention of foreplay …

Xander and me, dancing drunkenly on his porch. The way I nuzzled into his chest. Again Xander had been wearing his mic, so every drunken confession I made was clear as day.

Then there was footage of him all but carrying me into his house while I giggled and pressed my face into his neck.

And then, me showing up at his door the night we'd driven down to the river. I hadn't even bothered to check if Jase was still lurking in his hiding spot after filming Xander's fake sleepover with Alex. In itself, not too incriminating. Except the next clip was taken from a distance, looking down over the paddock, and there was Xander and me climbing into the back of his Ute.

"I'm shocked you had the decency to shut the camera off when we started getting naked," I quipped, my stomach churning. Jord looked horrified.

"Jase was mortified! He packed up immediately and locked himself in the caravan with Karl. He hasn't been able to look you in the eyes since. And he refused to film you on the sly after that."

"Well, at least Jase seems to have a conscience."

Jord blanched, but I was too furious to care. "There goes my calling Kenneth's bluff plan."

"Would it be so bad to let your relationship play out for the show? No one's asking you to stay with him afterwards," Jord muttered. "And since Kenneth does have this footage, you really need to control how it goes out."

I fixed Jord with a cold stare. "Xander and I … we're together. It's new, and there are still a lot of things that we need to work through. But I want to make it work. And trying to do that on camera is a sure-fire way to sabotage us."

Jord's sudden smile felt like a slap in the face. "You're together?"

I raised one eyebrow. "So everything you've done, and the shit-show it's created … unnecessary."

"How can I make this better?" Jord asked.

I shrugged. "Got a time machine?"

Jord slumped down in the booth, staring out the window as I wracked my brain for a solution. And came up with nothing.

"When we first started this … when you first came up with the idea of bringing the show out here, what did you want to achieve?" Jord asked.

I chuckled humourlessly. "Aside from putting Xander right out of his comfort zone?" I leaned my head against the back of the booth. "I wanted to show the reality of vet life in a remote town, show why it's so hard to tempt vets out here. I wanted to show that real people live here, and they deserve to have access to services just the same as city dwellers."

I scraped my fingers through my bob. "And all I've succeeded in doing is giving the town a taste of it again, and then we'll all go away, and they'll have a brand spanking new, state-of-the-art vet clinic, with no vet." I turned to Jord. "Even before this debacle, Kenneth sent me an email saying no to future seasons. Without a show, trying to tempt a vet out here will be next to impossible. Rural vet life is too tough, and they can pick up positions in places where it's much easier to work, and live."

Jord straightened. "What if you could have more, though. What if you could leverage the extra hype the show will get because of your story with Xander into future seasons starring the pair of you? Into something more permanent for the town? Into something fulfilling for you, here in Budgerigar?"

I huffed. "Two problems. One, I can't continue to work with Kenneth. Not after this. So even if I stay on to produce this season, once it's over I'm handing in my resignation. And two, Xander's going back to Sydney in March."

"Says who?" Jord asked. I glanced sharply at them.

"Says his contract. Do you really think he'd sign on for more with Kenneth after the shit he's pulled?"

"He would if you were there by his side."

"Refer back to problem number one."

Jord's scheming smirk didn't fill me with confidence.

"There's more than one way to skin a cat, G."

I groaned. "Why do people keep saying that to me?"

Jord ignored my complaining. "What if you could have it all, AND stick it to Kenneth?"

I sat up warily. "I don't think that's possible, but … I'm listening."

Now: It's Bringing Me To You

Georgie made her way through the trees, picking her way over scraggly fallen branches in the dark. She'd been gone far longer than I expected. What had Jordyn said? What was going through Georgie's mind right now?

If she decided she was leaving, that she wanted nothing to do with this shit show, where did that leave me? I was stuck in a contract, but I'd hate every single second of the next two months.

I just had to hope that Georgie would stay on, stick this out with me, and then we could both head back to Sydney, put this behind us, and start making a future together. Seeing her in my house had felt so bloody right. I was already picturing her making coffee in one of my t-shirts, her hair all rumpled from sleep and morning sex. Walks on Bondi Beach, date nights, sharing our favourite restaurants with each other.

Babysitting Lily together. Maybe our own kids, one day. If we couldn't have them naturally, we'd adopt. Use a surrogate. Or just be cool Aunty Georgie and Uncle Xan. Whatever she wanted.

The knock startled me, which was stupid, considering I'd been waiting on tenterhooks for her to return. I strode over, hauling the door open and tugging her inside, over to the sofa, depositing her on my lap, my arms coming around her, fingers caressing her warm skin.

"Jord been successfully chastised?" I asked, massaging the nape of her neck.

"It's all just a complete mess, Xan," she mumbled, nestling against me. "Jord was trying to make a video of you and me—for my eyes only—to convince me to give you another chance. But the footage copied over to the shared cloud as well. It was an accident. A fucking big one, but I'm pretty sure there was no malice in it."

I leaned back until I could see her face properly. "You believe that?" I asked.

Georgie bit her lip, nodding. "Jord's been my best friend for almost three years now. Plus, they're a shit liar."

A laugh burst out of me, and I buried my head against her shoulder, shaking with manic mirth that was born from not enough sleep over the last few days, too much emotion, and a shitload of relief that I had my girl in my arms. No matter what the next few weeks did to us, I could hold onto this. I could. I would.

"So, have you made a decision about Kenneth?"

Georgie spun her legs, standing up and moving over to the kitchen. As she filled a glass with water, she stared out the window at Miriam's house.

"My grandmother is planning to sell the property once the show is over. She needs the money now she's officially retired."

I stood, coming up behind her, leaning my hands against the sink as I looked over her shoulder at the stately, if rundown, old home. "Well, that must be bloody tough for her."

Georgie nodded, sipping at her water. Her body felt tense.

"It's been in the family for generations, so, yeah, it's a bitter pill." She sighed, her fingers gripping the counter. I put my hand over hers, feeling the tightness of her knuckles.

Why did I feel like she was pulling away from me? My heart dropped into my stomach.

"Has this got something to do with your decision about the show?" I asked. Georgie was quiet for a long moment, her breaths hissing and whooshing.

"I've decided to stay. I'm going to tell Kenneth that I'll stay on and finish the project. There's no way in hell I'm letting him have control over our story."

"All good with me." I pressed my lips to her neck. She didn't soften against me the way she had before we left Sydney. Worry churned in my stomach.

"But," Georgie said.

"But?"

"When March rolls around, and edits are complete, I'm done with Kenneth and Reelflix."

I nodded, my chin resting on her shoulder. "Absolutely. That arsehole doesn't deserve your talent."

I felt her cheek lift in a fleeting smile against the side of my face, but it disappeared all too quickly.

"And … I'm not going back to Sydney once we're done with the show."

My stomach bottomed out. "Come again?"

Georgie sighed, her shoulders drooping. "I'm staying here. I'll sell my unit in the city, give the money to Mim. She can stay here, the house can stay in the family. When the drought is over, I might even look at building up the flock again."

I opened my mouth and closed it, over and over, trying to find words as the future I'd been picturing came crashing down around me.

"Jord just gave me an idea. I'm going to start creating social media content about life, about community, in a remote township. I'm going to tell the story that Kenneth wants to push aside in favour of us. I want people to know Budgerigar, the people here, how funny and unique and kind this little community is."

She reached up and brushed at her face, and I realised that tears were dripping down her nose.

"Blondie," I rasped. "I—"

"This has been in the back of my mind for weeks now. It doesn't sit right with me, waltzing into town, throwing wads of cash around, giving the community their own vet again, and then waltzing out again, nothing but dust and an empty clinic in our wake."

That was a sentiment I could agree with. "You're right," I managed, my voice husky. I was holding back my own tears.

"The social media thing, it'll give me something to do, something to focus on. And Jord reckons I could even make money out of it … if I can gain enough followers. And maybe with the exposure, I'll be able to find a permanent vet for Budgerigar in the process."

I cleared my throat. "So, you don't want to go back to Sydney." It wasn't a question. It wasn't an accusation. It was just a raw statement of the reality staring us down.

Did she really think I was going to let her go that easily?

Georgie shook her head.

"Well, shit—"

"But I was thinking," Georgie interrupted me, her words hurried, tension radiating from her body. "I mean, it's a huge ask, and this is still so new, but it would mean I wouldn't have to try and find a new vet, and—"

"Blondie, are you asking me to move to Budgerigar with you?" A grin started forming on my face.

She froze, then turned around, her body caged between mine and the kitchen sink. Her expression was hope and fear combined. "If I was, would you say yes? I mean, it's taking you away from everything—"

"It's bringing me to you," I argued, leaning down, my mouth seeking hers, but she pressed a hand to my chest, holding me back.

"But you have your brother, your niece … your beautiful home in Bondi!" she protested. I chuckled, bringing my hand up to cover hers on my chest, hooking my pinkie around hers.

"My home is *you*," I murmured, my eyes meeting hers, holding her gaze. "Wherever you are, that's home. But what about your cancer? Won't you need to be close to Dr Hartley?"

Georgie grabbed her phone out of her pocket. "That's a good question. I guess I won't know until the results come in, but I'll send him an email to sound him out."

She tapped her email app and her mouth fell open. "I've got an email from him." She tapped again with a shaking finger. "It's

probably not my results, they couldn't have processed them that fast
…"

Her eyes darted back and forth, scanning the text, her brows furrowing. I couldn't breathe.

"Don't leave me hanging!" I groaned. "What does it say?"

Georgie's face flushed, and she let out a shocked little exhale. "All the tests came back clear."

"What?" I couldn't believe what I just heard. "But—"

"He said the bleeding was most likely just my period. He said it's probably due to my … well the stitch they used to replicate a cervix when they removed mine. Sometimes … this is very graphic, Xan, are you sure you want to hear it?"

I tilted her chin up to mine. "Nothing about your body is embarrassing, or uncomfortable for me, Blondie."

She sighed, her eyes softening. "Well, sometimes some … menstrual tissue can block the opening, making it seem like the period has stopped, but then when it passes, things get heavier again. I suppose I saw that much blood, two days after everything had eased off, and I jumped to the worst-case scenario."

"So … no cancer?" I asked again, needing to be sure.

"For now. No cancer for now. It could still return at any time, and I'll need to have regular screens for years … but there's an imaging and pathology lab in Millstone, and Dubbo isn't very far, if I need more specialised tests, and Dr Hartley can do telehealth consults …"

I swept her into my arms, lips crashing into hers, silencing her. "For now is all I need, Blondie," I pulled back to murmur against her cheek. She wrapped her legs around my waist.

"And if it does come back?" she asked, her voice nervous. I pressed a soft kiss to the tip of her nose.

"Then we will deal with it together," I said. "Now, can we finally christen the loft bed? I need to make love to my perfect girl."

March: The Queen Of Humping

GEORGIE

"Jesus … fuck, look at how wet you are," Xander groaned, kneeling over me and palming his straining cock, pumping it in his fist, thumbing the tip. "Deeper, Blondie. I want to see it disappear inside you."

My eyes went hooded as I took in his twitching abs, the way the muscles in his arm worked as he stroked himself. One blond curl was falling into his eyes, fixed on my dripping pussy.

"Oh, come on, Dr Fox, let's make this last, please," I murmured coyly as I teased my entrance with the rose quartz dildo, dipping it just inside, then bringing it out, using it to spread wetness up to my clit. I gasped at the feel of the cool stone against my sensitive nerves, my legs falling wider on the loft bed.

"You damn tease," Xander growled, but his pupils were so dilated the hazel was almost completely overtaken with black. He eased off his own pace, his free hand stroking up my inner thigh. I shuddered under his touch, biting my lip as I gave in, sliding the dildo inside, two fingers finding my clit, circling the swollen flesh, my stomach muscles tensing at the delicious intrusion from the hard stone.

"My dirty girl, watching you fuck yourself is my favourite thing in the world," Xander muttered, his words clipped as he picked up his own pace, stroking himself in time to the thrust of the dildo inside me.

I laughed breathlessly. "Better than fucking me yourself?" I turned the dildo so it curved up, rubbing against my G-spot as I picked up the pace, my fingers working my clit faster. I pinched it between two fingers, and my pussy twitched, tightening around the dildo.

"You're close, aren't you?" Xander panted, his fist tight around his cock. He leaned down on one arm, thrusting his hips into his fist. "Tell me you're close, Blondie, because I'm … Jesus," he groaned.

"So close," I hissed, lifting my hips just slightly, finding the angle I needed—the one I knew he was waiting for.

"Oh, God, I'm going to …" I squeaked, rocking my pelvis, taking the dildo deeper into me as heat flashed through my limbs, my abdomen clenched, and Xander got exactly what he wanted as my orgasm exploded, liquid gushing over my hand, running down between my butt cheeks, trickling onto the towel he'd had the foresight to put down.

"You're perfect," he rumbled, moving my hand as I gasped, panted, twitched on the bed. He gently removed the Yoni Wand from my pulsing pussy. "I hope you're okay with hard and fast this morning."

I nodded with a satisfied smirk as he crawled up my body, his cock leaving damp spots of precum on my thigh as he positioned himself between my legs, sinking into me.

"Christ, I love it when you're so wet, and still quivering," he rasped, reaching under me, lifting my butt to angle himself deep, finding his rhythm. I wrapped my legs around his hips, my fingers scratching red lines into his pecs as he pounded into me, filling me, stretching me until I ached in the most incredible way.

I clutched at the nape of his neck, pulling him down until his lips were on mine, licking into his mouth, stroking his tongue with mine.

"Just for the record," I breathed into his mouth, nipping his lip. "You fucking me is my favourite thing."

His movements became jerky, his hips snapping against mine, his ragged breathing, my panting, and the wet slide and slap of our bodies joining the only sounds until he groaned into my mouth, tongue swirling mine as he came, his cock throbbing, spilling heat into me.

"I lied," he whispered, his hands sliding up from my butt to wrap around my back, rolling me until we were side by side, his cock still pulsing gently inside me, his face nuzzling into my shoulder, sucking and licking at my sweaty skin. "Making love to you is my favourite."

"I love you," I whispered, combing my nails through his hair. It was getting a bit long—he was definitely overdue for a haircut. But I wasn't going to say anything. I loved it a bit messy and floppy.

"I love you more," he argued with a chuckle against my throat. I grinned. We'd had this teasing argument many times over the last two months. So far, neither of us was conceding defeat.

Eventually he sighed, pulling his still semi-hard cock out of me. "God, I wish we didn't have such a busy day today. I want to be inside you again … and again … and again."

I smirked, sliding off the bed and grabbing the Yoni Wand. "Well, just think about how good it will feel tonight, knowing you'll finally be free of filming."

He swatted at my butt, the sting from his slap making me squeal and race for the ladder. "I'm not bloody free. You and your YouTube channel have made sure of that!"

"Don't pretend you aren't enjoying every second of it," I argued, heading for the bathroom and running the shower. "Besides, the camera loves you."

"The woman behind the camera loves me. That makes all the difference," he murmured against my hair, his arms wrapping around my waist, enveloping me in his warmth.

"Oh, is that why every comment on posts featuring you is women swooning over how they feel like you're eye-fucking them?" I asked, stepping into the warm water. He followed me, grabbing the soap before I could and massaging it into my breasts.

"It's all for you, Blondie." He pinched at my nipples, twirling them into tight, achy peaks, grinding himself against my backside. I hissed at the feel of him getting hard for me again. "Now, do we have time for one more round?"

"Always," I whispered.

Towelling my hair after a longer-than-anticipated shower, I stopped dead at the bathroom door. Glaring up at me, silently judging, sat a glossy black Labrador and a three-legged miniature sheep.

"Don't look at me that way, you two!" I hissed, edging my way around them. Their eyes followed me. "Molly, you can't talk, you're the queen of humping!"

"I think it's been a good month since you claimed that title from her," Xander commented, squeezing my butt as he slid past me. I watched him head for the loft ladder, naked. The play of morning light over his quads, his glutes …

"Well, what do you expect, walking around looking like that?" I asked, pursing my lips as he smirked over his shoulder at me. "It should be illegal, your naked body in the morning sun!"

"You can arrest me any time you like, Blondie," Xander chuckled. "I'll even buy you the handcuffs."

I shook my head, because if I let myself think too long about that statement, we'd definitely be late.

Usually, a wrap party was an off-the-clock occasion for the cast and crew, but given this was supposed to be Xander's last day in Budgerigar, Kenneth had wanted it filmed in front of as many locals as possible. He wasn't aware that Xander and I had a big announcement to make today.

I'd never worked harder or longer hours than in the last couple of months. In addition to producing the remaining weeks of *Beach Vet Goes Bush*, I was on-camera, too: working around the clinic, PDA-ing with Xander, doing sit-down interviews to fill in some of the gaps in Xander's and my story. I was reviewing all the previous footage, reshuffling to include anything I could of Xander and me, recording voiceovers from Xander, directing Jase and Karl to increase the stock footage of the town, the countryside for segues.

And on top of all of that, I was building my own YouTube channel. *Out Back in Budgerigar* was gaining traction; I'd only last week joined TikTok and Instagram to promote the channel, now that we had a back catalogue of short episodes.

I'd steered clear of focusing too heavily on Xander, instead showing life in a remote farming town. Featuring many of the locals talking about their lives, why they loved the town, what the community meant to them, documenting events in the town. Of course, Xander had featured in several of the posts, and once we were free of Kenneth, his presence would increase dramatically. One thing Kenneth and I agreed on—Xander was made for on-camera work. He was a natural. Being hot as sin didn't hurt either.

If Kenneth, the old bastard, got cranky with me over my social media presence, I planned to remind him that it would throw people in the direction of the documentary when it dropped on Reelflix in May. He couldn't deny that me building a social media following would increase interest in the show.

Xander and I made the documentary bingeworthy, even I had to admit that. And the documentary would play well into us shifting the focus of *Out Back in Budgerigar* from the community in general, to Xander and me living our lives out here.

That was my big fuck you to Kenneth. He relinquished any control over us past one season. I'd show him everything he missed out on as a result.

"You okay?" Xander asked as we pulled into town, and he searched the street for a park. It looked like every man and his dog was on Main Street today. No surprise, seeing as Xander had really endeared himself to the community, and they were all devastated to see him go.

They didn't know yet that they wouldn't have to say goodbye. Xander and I were just beginning our outback adventure.

"I'm just really happy," I said, turning so he could see my smile.

He beamed back at me, reaching over and tucking his pinkie around mine. "Me too, Blondie."

We climbed out of the car and walked hand-in-hand down the street, past the little Milk Bar where I bought our Bubble-O-Bills. Past the sports field where Xander had played soccer with the local boys.

"I'm going to volunteer to coach the soccer team," Xander said, giving my hand a squeeze. "I mean, I'm at least as good as Messi these days."

I tilted my head back and laughed. "You keep telling yourself that. But yes, absolutely coach the team, that's amazing."

I glanced up at the Emporium of Intuition, my cheeks heating just a tiny bit, remembering our morning.

"I need to go in and thank that guy profusely," Xander growled in my ear. I poked him in the side.

"Don't you dare," I hissed. "He'll probably try to upsell you an aromatherapy butt-plug or something!" I dragged a guffawing Xander past, towards The Budgie. Jase and Jord were already out front, stopping locals for a quick chat on-camera.

"Ready to do this?" I asked. He turned me until I was facing him, his hands so big and solid and warm on my shoulders.

"I am so bloody ready," he said, scooping me into him and kissing me deeply, right there in the middle of the street, his hands wandering to the hem of my mini dress.

"Get a room, Dr Dimples!"

We broke away, laughing, to see Lachy and Calli heading into the pub, grinning at us. Lachy cheekily saluted Xander, who flipped him the bird, but the smiles on both their faces spoke volumes about the growing friendship between the two of them.

"Feeling a bit sentimental today?" Alex appeared, pushing her way between us and slinging arms around us both. I gave her hand a squeeze, sharing a secret smile with her. She knew what we were planning. It was impossible to keep anything from her, not if Jord knew about it. Those two had no secrets between them.

"How are you feeling?" I asked, nudging her with my shoulder. "With Jord heading back to Sydney tomorrow?"

Alex sighed. "Well, one of you has to oversee post-production to make sure Kenneth doesn't screw up this entire project. It's only temporary, so we'll cope. As soon as the show drops, they're coming back."

I was entirely unsurprised about that. "Well, I'll put them to work behind the camera for *Out Back in Budgerigar*. I need to free my hands up to be on-camera more. Lachy and I are doing a full restoration of Mim's place, with a big focus on the history of farming and homesteads in the area."

Alex chuckled. "Of course you are. You can't possibly not be busy, can you?"

I glanced up at Xander, who beamed down at me. "Well, I've got to keep up with him. He's doing professional development to upskill for livestock care, he wants to coach the soccer team … and then he'll be featuring so much more on YouTube, plus the clinic of course."

Xander smirked. "And I have an insatiable woman I need to please. It's bloody exhausting!"

I blushed, play punching him as Alex guffawed.

March: A Taylor Swift Song For Every Moment

XANDER

The beer was warm, the eighties pub-rock blasting from the jukebox was truly awful, and the company was … eclectic. But I'd grown to love all of it.

We'd lost no time once the festivities began to take the stage, making our announcement that Budgerigar wouldn't need to look for a new vet, because this one was sticking around. The result was screaming hysterics from some of the school mums who still hung around the clinic fence, eyeing me thirstily if I had time to pop out for a chat. Georgie narrowed her eyes at them, and I smirked at how adorable jealousy looked on her.

The tears from Liz were the most shocking thing of all.

"How could you not tell me?" she sniffled, slapping Georgie on the arm.

Georgie's jaw dropped. "How did you not know? You know everything that goes on around here before anyone so much as breathes a word of it!"

Liz winked, her head tilting slightly in the direction of Jase, camera trained on the wily old bat. Georgie snorted but wrapped the woman in a hug.

"Oh, get in here too, you gorgeous hunk of man-meat!" Liz said, dragging me into their embrace. When we pulled apart, Jase moved off to film elsewhere, and we headed for Mim, over by the bar chatting with Freddie and Diedre.

Mim had known our plans from the start. We'd told her we'd be buying the homestead from her once the sales of our Sydney properties went through, but that it was her home for as long as she wanted it to be, on the proviso that we could restore it to its original glory. A proviso she'd tearily accepted, with gruff thanks that I knew meant she was too emotional to do more.

Mim turned to Georgie, letting her granddaughter wrap her up in a hug. Mim grumbled something, and Georgie laughed.

I smiled at the sound, leaning against the bar and ordering a merlot for Georgie, a schooner of beer for myself.

"Does your mum know you're moving out here?" Mim asked Georgie. She didn't answer right away, instead taking a sip of her wine.

"You know we don't really talk, haven't for years … but I sent her a text message," she eventually admitted. "I haven't heard anything back." Georgie didn't seem upset by her mother's behaviour, just resigned, as she turned towards Mim.

"Will you ever tell me why you and Mum stopped speaking to one another?" she asked frankly.

Mim's mouth twisted, and her eyes flicked from Georgie to me, but then she shrugged. "No more secrets, isn't that your new motto?"

I palmed Georgie's shoulders, letting the warmth of my hands seep into her skin as she waited. Mim took a long pull from her schooner.

"I learned my lesson with your mother. I did better by you, I think, Georgie. I promised myself that I'd support you no matter what decision you made, about your pregnancy."

Georgie's brow furrowed. "Did you … did you make Mum keep me?" she asked.

Mim shook her head, her expression stricken. "Quite the opposite. I booked her an appointment to … to do what you did. She was only sixteen, it seemed like the only sensible option. But she was furious with me, told me I was controlling her. I … didn't handle it well."

Mim gripped Georgie's suddenly shaking hands, as I squeezed her shoulders in support. "You must know how sorry I was that I didn't support her to make her own mind up, and how thankful I am that she was stubborn. I lost her, but I got *you*. I tried to reach out, so many times, to apologise, but I guess that stubborn streak never faded. I never meant to hurt her. I just didn't want her to …"

Georgie squeezed Mim up in a big hug. "If I'd been in your shoes, I would have done the same. And while I'm grateful that Mum made the decision she did, I understand why you wouldn't have wanted that for her. I didn't want it for myself, at eighteen. And I'm so thankful that I had you there to support me through that time."

I swallowed back the lump in my throat as I watched these two strong, brave women hug, and cry, and heal. I leaned down and pressed a kiss to Georgie's cheek.

"I'm going to go chat with Calli and Chippy," I murmured. Georgie nodded, nuzzling her cheek against my stubble for a brief second, then chuckling wetly, swiping at her face and gripping her grandmother tightly.

Mim's eyes met mine, over the top of Georgie's head and she gave me a nod, her mouth forming the words, "Thank you."

I nodded back, then turned away, letting them have their moment together.

"Better late than never, hey Xan?"

I spun, gaping, to find Levi and Amanda grinning back at me.

"What are you doing here? You've only got a couple of months until Paris!"

Levi beamed at me. "Well, I could hardly let my big brother make a giant life decision and not be here to drink too much fucking beer to celebrate."

"No Lily?" I asked, wondering if she was in a stroller somewhere, but Levi shook his head.

"She's with her mum and Mat. We're having a *grownup* getaway." The way he looked at Amanda as he said that, and the way she blushed, made me glad I wouldn't be anywhere in the vicinity of the hotel rooms upstairs at The Budgie tonight.

"Dom's around here somewhere, too," Amanda added, looking around.

"Yeah, another fun day of driving with Dom and his fucking woman troubles," Levi grumbled.

"What?" I asked. "He wasn't rambling about Georgie again, was he?" I hadn't said anything to Levi about Georgie and Dom's past. I figured it was not my story to tell. Had Dom told him?

"Nah, some student he's lusting after. Who he can't touch, of course, which is just making things a thousand times fucking worse."

"You make it sound so sordid," Dom said behind me. I turned to him, one eyebrow raised.

"A student? Really?" I asked.

Dom shook his head. "Levi is misrepresenting it entirely," he grumbled.

"So, she's not a student?" I pressed.

Dom's jaw tensed. "She *is* a student, but—"

"No buts—she's your student!" I said sharply.

"She wasn't when she climbed into my lap in a bar last month."

I gaped at him. "You're not serious!"

"I'm deadly serious. When she showed up for her first coaching session, I almost swallowed my tongue. But she doesn't seem to remember me. So, the issue is that every time she has a lesson with me, all I can picture is … well, I'm sure you can imagine. And it's killing me."

"Is she a decent singer?" I asked, knowing that a lot of the less talented ones didn't last long at the National Institute of Musical Theatre Arts, where Dom worked as a vocal coach.

"She's fucking phenomenal," he moaned. "And beautiful. And sensual …"

"Okay, you need something stronger than beer," I said, heading for the bar and hailing Freddie, ordering two glasses of scotch on the rocks.

"What are you going to do?" I asked once Dom had taken a good slug of his drink.

"Fantasise furiously, but not act on any of them," Dom muttered, staring down at the amber liquid in his glass.

"Sounds like a slippery slope," I said. Dom sighed into his palm, as Georgie joined us.

"Hey! I didn't know you were coming!" she said, delight in her voice as she wrapped an arm around Dom's waist. He kissed her head, and all I felt was happiness that we could all have this friendship again.

"How are you?" Georgie asked, taking a sip from her wine glass and reaching out for my hand. Dom glanced between us, his smile warm and genuine.

"I'm so happy that you're both happy," he said, meeting my eyes and shaking his head minutely—a silent plea not to share his woman problem with her.

A rumble of thunder outside had heads turning. The verandah was so deep that I hadn't noticed storm clouds rolling in.

"Looks like rain," Dom said. A hum of muttering took over the space. There had been bugger-all rainfall in Budgerigar for eighteen months—a fact I'd heard bemoaned by every farmer I visited.

"It does," Georgie added as people started moving out onto the verandah, watching the black clouds towering over the town. The sky erupted with chattering budgerigars swooping down to land in Bird Turd Tree.

"We'll probably just have a lightning show," Mim said beside Georgie. "Don't get your hopes up."

But the smell of petrichor was strong, and as we watched, drops began to fall.

"It's raining!" a child squawked, racing down onto the bitumen. "Mum, it's raining!"

"He told me just this morning he'd forgotten what rain was like," his mother said beside us, flashing a watery smile at Georgie.

"Well, let's hope he gets a good show of it today," Georgie replied. The mother followed her son as more people filtered down into the rain, grinning and talking excitedly.

"Want to get wet with me, Blondie?" I murmured into her ear, my palm sliding around her hip, fisting the silky fabric of her pink dress and grazing the curve of her arse.

"Dirty, Dr Fox," she purred. "But yes, that sounds incredible."

With a laugh, she took my hand and tugged me down the stairs and into the street, as the clouds opened up in earnest, drenching us all. Steam rose off the road, and I watched the rain turn the thin fabric of her dress translucent.

"You look indecent right now," I groaned. Georgie's fingers dug into my abs.

"You can't talk, Mr Walking Wet T-shirt Competition," she countered. Rain dripped off her eyelashes, her hair was plastered to her head, and she grinned up at me, her hands finding mine, our pinkies interlocking.

"You're the most beautiful thing I've ever seen," I told her as water slid down her nose. I closed the distance between us, kissing away the droplet. "I'm never going to stop falling in love with you."

"I'm not falling," she said, blinking water out of her eyes. "Every moment with you is like flying."

I reached up, tangling my fingers in her sodden hair, grinning down at her. "There's got to be a Taylor Swift song for this moment, hasn't there?" I asked, swiping my thumbs over her cheekbones.

She smirked. "There's a Taylor Swift song for *every* moment." Reaching up and taking my mouth, her kiss slow and sensual, her lips soft and full and opening for me to slip my tongue between them as she melted against me.

When we came up for air, she slid one palm up to my shoulder, taking my hand in her other. "Dance with me. I mean, we're in a storm … and I'm in one of my best dresses …"

"Are you feeling fearless, though?" I asked.

She raised an eyebrow at me, slowly shuffling her feet from side to side until we were slow dancing. In the middle of the street, in the rain, with half the population of Budgerigar around us.

"I'm oddly proud that you got the reference," she said with a little chuckle.

"Well, are you?" I persisted, my hand splayed on the small of her back, her skin warm through the wet fabric of her dress. Georgie leaned her head against my chest, her ear against my heart.

"With you? Always."

442

Acknowledgments

My husband always gets first dibs on this page. He's endlessly supportive of this expensive hobby of mine. Also, he came up with one of my favourite lines in this whole book.

Lani, who brainstorms, critiques, and always offers unfiltered and honest opinions. Looking forward to the ride that Dom's book will be for us next!!!

Sacha, beta reader and unhinged late-night instagram message sender. Thank you for loving these characters, and for reassuring me that the medical research I did for Georgie's cancer all made sense. I'm so honoured to call you a friend!

Calli, my fabulous veterinarian friend, who answered loads of often ridiculous questions about the technical side of treating pets.

Elena, my editor, who was so enamoured with Xander that I had to make changes to two particular scenes that have really improved the character growth throughout the book.

Leisha, who as always brings my cover visions to life.

About the Author

Layla has been writing stories ever since she could pick up a pencil and shape words. The most memorable works of her tween and teen years included a rap version of 'Little Red Riding Hood' and an embarrassingly pornographic high school camp/murder mystery (which was possibly a sign of things to come).

Layla lives on an acreage in regional NSW with her husband, two rambunctious children, five mostly feral cats, and two wilful Corgi puppies named Kingston and Empress (you can meet them in her novel Hating Dr Fox). Oh, and some angry Plovers that swoop her every spring without fail.

When she's not writing, or reading, she's bellowing Taylor Swift at the top of her lungs.

Join Layla's Facebook Reader's Group, Layla's Pining Woodies, for early access to WIP's, character art, and the unhinged life of Layla.

www.laylapine.com

facebook.com/laylapine.author

instagram.com/laylapine_author

tiktok.com/@laylapine_author

Also by Layla Pine

Aussie Cravings (Contemporary Romance)

Ace My Heart—a slow burn, antagonism to lovers, forced proximity, reverse grumpy sunshine tennis romance (with a splash of murder)

Strokes at Midnight—an insta-lust, one night stand, opposites attract, right person wrong time sports romance (with a splash of surprise pregnancy WITH A TWIST)

Singing My Tune—a taboo, forbidden, teacher student, musical theatre college romance (with a splash of emotional damage)

Renegade Strangers (Paranormal Romance)

Greenrock (book 1)

A human girl … A mysterious stranger … A forbidden attraction … A deadly craving …

Taiga (book 2)

A female dying for revenge … A male who hates what he is becoming … locked within the confines of a shady government facility, their blood calls to one another …

Standalone Titles

My Soul For A Donut (Coming 2025)

He owns her soul … but she's stealing his heart … What happens when you get a bit drunk and accidentally sell your soul to the son of Satan … for a gluten free donut?

Jemma Bliss is about to find out …

9 780645 577082